"I WANT TO HAVE SOMEBODY KILLED."

If the world had suddenly turned upside down, Rook Rydell couldn't have been more thrown. It wasn't that he'd never heard of such things. Hell, it wasn't even the first time he'd been asked for such a thing. He just hadn't expected it from this woman. Hadn't expected those words to come out of her soft pink lips. Hadn't thought eyes so sad could have such a hard purpose.

What secrets lay behind her sorrowful eyes? Who had hurt her so deeply that she wanted him dead? A husband? A lover? But he didn't care. Not really. Caring only caused pain. He'd learned years ago not to give a damn about anything.

Especially a hauntingly beautiful woman with a death wish....

Watch for RACHEL LEE'S
newest MIRA title

November 1997

RACHEL LEE

A FATEFUL CHOICE

MIRA BOOKS

ISBN 1-55166-173-X

A FATEFUL CHOICE

Printed in U.S.A.

To my darling husband, Cris.
Thanks for pushing me to the edge of the envelope,
and for believing I can do it.

Prologue

He had lain all night in the snow on the side of the ridge, watching and waiting for the sky to lighten.

Winter covered the mountain valley below him, burying it in an icy blanket. Only the lifeless, bony fingers of the leafless aspens rose above drifts so deep they almost swallowed the A-frame cabin in the valley's heart. Above all, a leaden sky hung low and threatening.

Along one side of the valley's shallow bowl ran a stand of blue spruce trees. Their tops poked bravely up through the enshrouding snow, looking small and youthful instead of like the huge grandfathers they actually were.

The hunter lay among the spruces, his skis and backpack beside him. Camouflaged in white, from a small distance he appeared to be nothing but wind-drifted snow. Only his eyes showed. In his hands he held a long, dark rifle, its barrel steadied on a spruce branch. With one eye, he peered through the high-powered scope toward the cabin in the valley below. Even wearing insulated survival gear, he was beginning to feel chilled, and the tips of his fingers, poking out of his gloves to hold icy metal, were beginning to feel frostbitten. He ignored it; he had a job to do. Nothing else existed.

Through the cross hairs of his scope he was looking into a kitchen. Since it was early morning, it was not surprising that the room was brightly lit. Sooner or later his target would step in front of that window. When she did, he would squeeze the trigger and finish the job.

He loved the sense of power these moments gave him, the knowledge that someone's life was utterly at his mercy. He lived for the job. He lived for the thrill of the kill.

The target came into view at last, a youngish woman with long dark hair. His cold eyes caressed her features through the scope, mentally comparing them to the features in the photographs that had been given to him. A pleasant excitement settled in the pit of his stomach as he made the positive identification. This was it.

He picked his target, the delicate shell of her ear, behind which she had tucked her hair. She was doing something at the counter, and, even if she turned, her head would still be properly placed for his shot.

Perfect.

An utter inner silence gripped him. It seemed as if his heart even stopped beating. He filled his lungs with air, then gently began to squeeze the trigger.

It was the first time he had been hired to kill a woman. The first time he had been hired by a woman. He wondered briefly if he was killing some man's mistress, or some man's wife. Not that he really cared about such things. All that mattered to him were these exquisite moments when everything stilled and fell silent as he slowly... slowly... squeezed the trigger.

1

Damn, he wanted a cigarette. The craving was crawling along his nerve endings like a steady irritation, but he'd vowed to quit. Refusing to let himself brood about it, he instead focused his attention on the small hubbub near the door.

Through narrowed eyes Rook Rydell watched a woman enter the tavern and glance uncertainly around. She didn't belong here. He wondered if she had any idea at all of the kind of risk she was running. Not that he cared.

The barroom was dimly lit, smelling like stale beer and cigarettes. Ceiling fans turned lazily, slowly stirring the smoke-filled air. The bartender and three bouncers all looked capable of handling a small war. An old black man with shoulders like a linebacker played bluesy piano as if he and his music were alone and all that mattered in the universe.

This was the union hall of the damned. The men who came here lived illicit existences, and this was their pied-à-terre in a hostile world. Here they could rest, drown their sorrows, or get tapped for a another job.

The woman in the navy blue suit no more belonged here than a saint belonged in hell.

He watched her turn hesitantly toward the bar, then walk with a surprisingly determined step across the room. The bartender, Pepe, saw her coming and didn't look pleased. Two of the bouncers, anticipating trouble, closed in.

Rook looked around and saw that everyone else in the bar was watching, too. This woman looked as if she came from another world. Not only was she young and pretty, but he was willing to bet she even smelled good, something most of the men in this room hadn't enjoyed in a long time.

Something, however, was preventing the men around him from reacting raucously as they usually did when a strange woman turned up here. Maybe it was her professional appearance. Maybe it was just that she had taken them all by surprise. Or maybe it was the unutterably sad, haunted look around her eyes. Her eyes made her one of them.

She reached Pepe, spoke to him briefly. The bartender looked in Rook's direction, cocking a brow.

What the hell, Rook thought. What else did he have to do except finish the tequila in front of him, listen to whatever this woman wanted and try to forget how much he wanted a frigging cigarette? He gave a slight nod in response.

But he couldn't escape the feeling that serious trouble was heading his way. As she wound her way between tables, looking to neither the left nor the right, a chill prickled the back of his neck. As soon as he felt it, he knew he was going to send her on her way just as fast as he could. He never ignored a premonition.

Every eye in the bar followed her progress, but when she reached Rook's table, they all looked away. She was now off-limits.

When she stopped before him, he glanced up reluctantly, not really wanting to look into her haunted eyes. In the dim light it was impossible to tell what color they were, but there was no mistaking their expression. This woman had stared into the jaws of hell.

She spoke without preliminaries. "A friend said you could help me."

"I doubt it." What he really wanted to say was that he doubted anyone could help her. "Which friend?"

"Alan DeVries."

Rook felt the hairs on the back of his neck stand up with even more determination. It had been a long time since he had called DeVries a friend. "He's in prison."

"I know. I spoke to him there yesterday. He sent me to you."

"What'd you do? Use thumbscrews?" He was ready to get up and leave, just walk out of the bar and disappear into the night. It smelled too much like a setup.

"Actually, I just asked him."

"DeVries knows better."

"Maybe he's forgotten. He said you could help me. He said to remind you that you owed him one for La Palma."

Rook froze. Only DeVries could have said that. "Are you a cop?"

She shook her head. "If I were a cop I'd have had the sense to dress down before I came here."

Either she was telling the truth or she was a damn good liar. "So what are you?"

"I'm a lawyer. Mr. DeVries is a client of my firm."

He was beginning to believe her. "Just what is it you need?" He expected a request for information or the offer of some minor job of surveillance. Something that would fall within his more ordinary capabilities. Her next words came like a punch in the gut.

"I want to have somebody killed."

If the world had suddenly turned upside down, he couldn't have been more thrown. It wasn't that he'd never heard of such things. Hell, it wasn't even the first time he'd been asked for such a thing. He just hadn't expected it from this woman. Hadn't expected those words to come out of those soft pink lips. Hadn't thought eyes so sad could have such a hard purpose.

What secrets lay behind her sorrowful eyes? Who had hurt her so deeply that she wanted him dead? A husband? A lover? But he didn't care. Not really. Caring only caused pain. He'd learned years ago not to give a damn about anything. "You've come to the wrong man," he said flatly.

For an instant she looked stunned, as if she had been so intensely focused on her purpose and the anticipated outcome that she had absolutely no idea how to handle this unexpected development. If he had allowed himself the luxury of such things, he might almost have felt sorry for her.

"I—" She broke off, her eyes wandering almost wildly. Then, desperately, they came back to his face. "Please . . . Mr. DeVries said you would know what I should do."

"What is this? Some kind of setup?" But he didn't believe it for an instant. This woman wasn't acting. What he wanted was to rattle her bars until she came to her senses. Not that he cared. He never cared.

"No! Oh, no! I just need . . . information. I need to know who to talk to. . . ."

"Why?" As soon as he asked, he wanted to snatch the word back. He didn't care, damn it!

A shutter seemed to close over her face, leaving it expressionless, and in some subtle way she appeared to close up on herself. "I don't think that's any of your business. I'll just ask one of these other gentlemen."

I'll just ask one of these other *gentlemen?* Either this woman was nuts or she was blind. Probably both. If she started wandering from table to table, she was going to get into worse trouble than she could possibly imagine. Not that it was his problem, but if she set off a wildfire, he would have to leave and look for some other place to spend the evening. Given that it was cold and wet outside, and given that he'd already had too much tequila, he preferred to stay right where he was.

Giving in, he pulled a small notebook from his pocket and tore a blank sheet from it. With a pen pulled from another of his capacious pockets, he scrawled a phone number on it. He shoved the paper toward her. "Call this number. He might be able to tell you what to do."

She snatched the paper as if she were afraid he might take it back. "Thank you," she said with surprising dignity, and tucked it in her skirt pocket.

"Just don't tell him too much about yourself. You don't want to be traceable."

She nodded as if she'd already considered the possibility—or didn't care. "May I buy you a drink?"

He leaned across the table, his tawny eyes narrowing, his face hardening even more. "Just get out of here before I tell you what I think about people who can't do their own dirty work."

Every last drop of color drained from her face, leaving her looking as lifeless as a three-day-old corpse. Without another word, she rose stiffly and hurried out of the bar.

He thought briefly about following her to make sure she got safely to her car, then cast aside the idea. He damn well didn't care. Jesus. She wanted to hire a hit man!

Jennifer Fox made it safely to her car. She made it safely home, in fact, probably because she didn't care if she did. Once inside her house, however, she leaned back against the closed front door and began to shudder from head to foot.

Even in her present state, even as low as she had sunk, she could still be horrified by what she had just done. Could still tremble with reaction to the terrible tension of the past couple of hours. Her hand, thrust deeply into her skirt pocket, clutched the scrap of paper the mercenary had given her. She had been successful.

Gradually the shuddering stopped. On legs that still felt a bit weak, she went to the kitchen and poured herself a shot of Jack Daniel's. She didn't like the taste of the stuff, but it had the desired effect, warming her and relaxing her. Up until a few months ago, she had rarely touched alcohol. These days she was drinking it often.

Don't do this to yourself, Jennifer. She could hear Mark's voice almost as if he were standing there with her. A fist seemed to grip her heart and squeeze until a tear leaked from her eye. She stopped breathing, fighting to hold it in. Crying didn't help. Nothing helped. Mark would never scold her or hold her or laugh with her again.

She drained the glass and left it sitting on the counter next to the sink. Beside it were the glasses from yesterday, and the day before, and maybe the day before that. She couldn't remember the last time she had eaten, and even now, considering the question, she felt no stirring of hunger.

For an instant her mind lifted out of the morass of her gloomy preoccupation, and she looked at herself with a detached eye. How strange, she thought, to be thinking of such mundane things as if they truly mattered.

The only thing in the world that she wanted to do was die.

But she had to be careful about how. There were her parents to consider, and her sister's family. Her death would wound them enough without making them feel as if they might have prevented it. An obvious suicide was out of the question. Hence the crackling slip of paper in her skirt pocket.

With another glass of bourbon, she climbed the stairs on her daily pilgrimage to the tomb of dreams lost. She hadn't moved a thing in the months since the crash, and dust layered every square inch. She saw past it, though. As if she had X-ray vision, she saw through the dust to the way it had been before it had become a mausoleum.

Bethany's room, decorated in all the colors of a bowl of pastel mints, the side of the crib still down as she had left it that last morning when she had lifted her daughter out of bed. Closing her eyes, Jennifer could still feel that warm little body in her arms, the way Bethany had wriggled playfully and laughed.

Another tear rolled down her cheek, and Jennifer blinked hard to clear her vision, to take another long look at a room that was full of furniture and stuffed animals but would forever be empty.

Down the hall was Eli's room. His stuffed animals looked a little ragged from years of being dragged around and kicked into corners. His Lego table still held the construction project that had been in progress that last morning, something that looked like a cross between a castle and a space ship. On the floor were scattered the small metal cars he liked so much, and a plastic snake. Lifting his pillow to her face, Jennifer thought she could still detect the sweet, warm smell of her little boy.

And finally there was the master bedroom. She still slept here, when she slept. Still rolled over in the middle of the night and reached for Mark, only to embrace empty air.

Empty space. Her life had become empty space. Everything that mattered was gone.

Huge tears were rolling down her cheeks now, and she felt the crinkle of the paper in her pocket as she moved. That, at least, was a reassurance.

There was a way out.

Back downstairs, she removed the paper carefully and spread it out next to the phone in the library, wondering if she should call now or wait. Somehow the dark hours seemed best for this kind of thing.

She couldn't bring herself to reach for the receiver, though. She had thought that sitting at Mark's desk would make it easier. Make it right somehow. But all sitting at his desk did was drag her down into the whirlpool of anguish that had been tearing her apart ever since the private plane crash had taken Mark and the children from her.

Huge tears poured from her eyes and rolled down her cheeks as great, gasping sobs racked her. She'd cried this way nearly every day since the accident, and she would cry this way every day until she died. She cried so hard that it hurt, but it was nothing compared to the hurt in her heart.

The phone rang, but she ignored it. It was probably her mother, calling to check up on her, and hand her a new batch of lame aphorisms about how it would all get better. It was never going to get better. Initially she, too, had clung to the belief that eventually she would learn to live with her losses, but her anguish was bottomless, growing deeper with time instead of easing. Each successive day grew more painful than the last.

By the time her sobs eased, her blouse was soaked, her throat was raw, and her eyes were swollen nearly shut. The discomfort was only a small atonement for her biggest sin: that she hadn't been on the plane with them.

When the phone rang again, she reached for it, hoping for even a few moments of distraction, and feeling guilty for the hope.

"Hi, Jennifer." The warm, deep voice of Scott Paxton greeted her. "Maureen and I have been thinking about you and just wanted to see how you're doing."

How was she supposed to answer that? This man was one of the partners in the firm that had recently fired her. Once she had believed he was a friend, but wouldn't a friend have stood up for her? Why hadn't he insisted she simply take a leave of absence until she felt better? Not that she was ever going to feel better.

"Jennifer? Are you there?"

"I'm here." She ought to just hang up. Instead she clung to the receiver and listened to his voice. He had been blessed with an incredible voice—warm, soothing and hypnotic. Any distraction would do. Any at all, including Scott Paxton. She had to get herself together enough to call the number on that scrap of paper.

"I'm sorry. Did I call at a bad time? Maureen and I have both been worrying about you, and we were wondering if you'd like to come to dinner this weekend. It'll just be a small gathering, a few of your old friends from the firm. Felix and Rochelle, Dowd and Sally, Karl and Gretchen, perhaps a couple of the others."

Some spark of her old self surfaced, a spark that hadn't been completely drowned in this valley of tears. "Why would I want to spend any time with people from the firm, Scott? All of you were eager enough to see the last of me."

"Now, Jennifer, that's not fair, and you know it. We've been all over this ground. You didn't leave us any choice."

"*I* didn't leave *you* any choice? Why didn't you suggest I take a leave of absence instead?"

"We had no option. Allied Technologies threatened to move to another firm if we didn't get rid of you after your screwup over the royalty clause."

"I managed to correct that."

"Yes, you did, but Allied gets nervous when its lawyer makes that kind of mistake. They come to us to get the best, and they didn't feel they got it. You know they're one of our biggest clients."

"So you've thrown me to the wolves, and now you want me to have dinner with you?"

"Just to show there are no hard feelings. And there really aren't, Jennifer. Believe me, we understand how difficult these last months have been for you."

"Do you? Do you really, Scott? Somehow, I doubt it."

This time he didn't respond immediately. When at last he spoke, his voice had taken on a strained note. "Perhaps not, Jennifer. How *could* we really understand what you've been through? But we care. If Allied had left us any other option, you'd still be with the firm. But they didn't, and I have to consider more than a hundred other employees of Paxton, Wilcox and Moore. Without the Allied account, quite a few of them would have lost their jobs."

She hadn't looked at it quite that way before, and even in the midst of her anguish, she was able to feel a pang of self-disgust. Grief, she was discovering, made her incredibly shortsighted. People would have lost their jobs along with the Allied account—and she probably would have been one of the ones to be fired, anyway. Maybe if she went to this dinner and saw these people again, she could put away at least part of her hurt. "When is dinner, Scott?"

"Saturday. Come at six-thirty. Dinner is at eight, but we'll have cocktails beforehand."

"Have you ever wondered why they're called cocktails?" she asked him.

He was laughing when he hung up. She wasn't.

On Mark's desk there was a photograph of the four of them. She had been keeping it facedown so it wouldn't ambush her unexpectedly, but now she turned it over and looked at it. Soon she would be with them.

With a hammering heart, she lifted the receiver and punched in the number. On the third ring, a grating male voice answered.

"Yeah?"

"I—I want to have someone killed." The words would barely emerge from her throat, and she didn't sound at all like herself. Only a glance at the photograph in front of her stiffened her resolve.

"Ya got the wrong number, lady."

"I—" She hesitated, wondering wildly if Rook had made up a number just to get rid of her. Then the lawyer in her rose to the fore. "Rook told me to call."

This time there was a long silence from the other end. "I don't do that kind of shit."

"Rook thought you might be able to send me to someone who does. Or who knows someone who does."

Another long pause. "Maybe. You want top-notch?"

"The best."

"Well, if I happen to run into somebody, I'll give him your number. What is it?"

She told him.

He coughed, a smoker's hack. "Maybe somebody will call you. Get rid of my number. *Capisce?*"

"Yes."

But he had already disconnected.

Not wanting to leave any trail behind her that might reveal that her death was actually a suicide, she took the scrap of paper to the sink and burned it.

She didn't want to leave the house for fear she might miss the call, but she had told Scott she would come to dinner. A dozen times she reached for the phone to call

Maureen Paxton and make her excuses, and a dozen times she stopped herself. The hit man couldn't possibly expect her to be sitting beside the phone every minute.

Besides, going to this dinner would give her a chance to explore the suspicion that Allied hadn't been the only reason for her firing. Allied could just as easily have demanded only that she be removed from their account. Scott and his partners must have had other reasons for their intractable position—and she wanted to know what they were. At the bottom of her heart she believed some other lawyer in the firm had sandbagged her.

Each of the partners had his own style of entertaining, but with Scott it was fairly formal. Jennifer wore a black cocktail dress with a high neck and long sleeves and wasn't surprised to discover her hostess in a floor-length gown.

Scott greeted her even more warmly than was his custom, going so far as to give her a hug. Maureen always hugged her and pecked her cheek, but tonight the hug was tighter. Jennifer tried to ignore the way her throat tightened. God, had she been so isolated lately that a simple hug could undo her?

She had arrived late on purpose, because it was easier to greet a roomful of people than to have to greet them one by one as they arrived.

"What's your poison?" Scott asked. His hand was already reaching for the bottle of club soda, which was her usual request.

"Bourbon with a splash."

His eyebrows rose, but he gave her the bourbon. "You don't drink, Jennifer."

"I do now."

"That's not a good thing. Don't do this to yourself."

She gave him a brittle smile. "There isn't a whole lot else to do anymore." Then she turned away, hoping they would all just let her hide in a corner until she got past this urge to flee from all these people whose very existence reminded her of her losses.

Sally Carstairs, however, came straight toward her. Sally was another associate of the firm, and she and Jennifer had been involved in a friendly rivalry over who would make partner first. Sally had always seemed good-natured about it, and the two women had often taken lunch together. Sally's husband, Dowd, was another matter. Dowd Carstairs had seemed to believe that Jennifer Fox was a serious threat to his ambitions for his wife. Though he'd never said anything outright, or taken any overt action, Jennifer never felt comfortable around him—not even tonight, when she was no longer any kind of threat to Sally's future.

"Honey, I've been so worried about you!" Sally told her, giving her a big hug. Sally called everyone except clients and bosses "honey." Jennifer sometimes wondered if it was an affectation, but regardless, from Sally it seemed somehow so natural that it was impossible to take offense.

"I'm fine, Sally. Really."

"No, you're not," the younger woman said bluntly. "There's no way on earth you could be fine, and you *never* drink."

"I do now."

Sally shrugged one shoulder. Her cocktail dress was as flamboyant as the woman herself, off-the-shoulder red sequins and net. Sally had a lot of red in her wardrobe. Dowd, she had confided, believed it was a color that exuded confidence and power. Jennifer thought it was overdone.

"Well, I can't say anything," Sally continued, waving her own martini glass. "It's just that you were about the only one of us who never had a drink. It's so strange to see you with whiskey."

"It could be ginger ale."

Sally laughed. "No bubbles. You can do better than that, honey. Next time call it apple juice."

Jennifer turned, wondering how she was going to get through this miserable evening of light chitchat. Now that she was no longer a member of the firm, no one was going to discuss a case in front of her. She was on the outside looking in, and her presence was going to affect the entire evening.

Dowd Carstairs was standing in the corner by himself, watching everything. When Jennifer's gaze scraped over him, he nodded and lifted his glass in salute. It was the friendliest acknowledgment he'd ever given her. Well, of course, she was out of the loop now, no longer any kind of threat.

Karl and Gretchen Gruber were the next to come talk to her. Karl headed up the firm's tax law division. The son of German immigrants, he had gone back to Germany to find a wife and had come up with Gretchen, a blond, blue-eyed Teuton with a quiet smile and effervescent personality. When Gretchen hugged her, Jennifer felt warmed.

Even Karl greeted her warmly, though he seldom had in the past. They had worked together often during mergers and other contract negotiations, because everything a corporation did had tax ramifications. But while their working relationship had been good, they had never really established a personal one of any kind.

Karl was a very reserved man—and also in line for the same partnership Jennifer had wanted, though he had freely acknowledged that Jennifer would get it if for no other reason than that she was a woman and the firm as yet had no women partners.

That she *would have* gotten it, Jennifer amended, feeling a pang at what she had lost. Feeling an even older pang because she damn well didn't want to get anything simply because she was a woman.

He held her hand a few moments longer than usual when they shook, and told her, "I'm sorry, Jennifer. I am *truly* sorry."

For some reason she couldn't believe him.

And then, at last, there was Felix Abernathy. Dear, dear Felix, who had been her closest friend at the firm, even though they were in different divisions and had never worked together. Felix handled criminal cases—in fact, he'd handled the case of Alan DeVries, the man she had gotten Rook Rydell's name from. Felix didn't know about that, and for his sake, she wanted him never to know.

Felix was already a junior partner, so they didn't even share the usual rivalry. What was more, he had helped Jennifer through her first difficult year with the firm, when the work had seemed overwhelming and the hours had been killing. She had never forgotten his generosity.

When he urged her to a quieter corner to talk, she went gladly, eager to escape any more difficult meetings with people she wasn't sure she liked any longer.

The Paxton house was a large one, designed for entertaining, and it was easy to find a small conversational nook off one of the larger rooms. They settled on a small sofa that was covered in royal blue moiré.

Felix took her hand. "I'm sorry, Jennifer. I know I said that at the funeral, and I know I said that when you were...let go, but I want to say it again. Rochelle and I can barely imagine the hell you must be going through."

She felt tears prickling in her eyes and had to blink them back. "I won't pretend it's been easy."

"Nor should you." He squeezed her hand, then released it. "I think it's a crying shame that the firm didn't stand beside you, but who listens to junior partners? Nothing I've ever said has made the least bit of difference."

"It's okay, Felix. Really. I know you did what you could, and I also know there wasn't a whole lot you *could* do." Felix was the one person she felt she could honestly say that about.

"Just so you know." He shook his head. "I can't imagine why Scott invited you tonight. This has to be terribly uncomfortable for you."

"He wants to keep things friendly." She gave him a wry smile. "I could sue the firm, and he knows it."

"Will you?"

"I doubt it." What was the point, when she was going to end it all?

Felix searched her face, as if he suspected that something lay behind that decision, but to her vast relief, he didn't pursue it. Instead he chose an entirely different direction. "I've been worried that you might think I don't remember the favor I owe you."

"What favor?" She honestly couldn't remember having done anything for Felix that would have made him feel in her debt.

"Well, the...you know. Remember last winter, when that friend of mine—that no-longer-friend of mine, by the way—bought that stock and you heard about it on the grapevine?"

She remembered. The stock he'd referred to had been in a company she had just assisted through a merger. The appearance of impropriety was strong, and even though she knew Felix couldn't have been involved in such a thing, for the protection of the firm it was necessary to report it. But first she had gone to Felix with the information, so that he wouldn't think she was going behind his back. Felix had been as disturbed by it as she'd been, and when she said she had to take it to the firm's head counsel, he'd picked up the phone, called the man and told him they were both coming up to see him on an issue of extreme urgency.

When they'd gotten up to Ted Wilcox's office, however, Jennifer had decided not to go in with Felix. "I don't want him to even suspect that you came to him just because I confronted you with this," she had told Felix. "You tell him yourself."

"I'm grateful to you for that," he said now. "I always have been. The SEC cleared both me and the firm, of course, but that's not why I'm grateful. I'm grateful that you let me report it. I'm grateful that you gave me the opportunity to deal with it. And I cut that friend of mine off. You know, Jennifer, I'm sure I never gave him insider information—hell, none of us ever discusses a case outside the firm—but even though we were all cleared, I could never escape the niggling feeling that he had used our connection somehow."

She nodded. "But coincidences happen, Felix. And that's probably all it was."

"Probably, but I don't care to run the risk. Even a breath of that kind of thing could have ruined my career and severely damaged the firm." He shook his head. "What I'm trying to say is, if there's anything at all I can ever do for you—*anything*—just let me know. I owe you. In fact, I think I could probably get you a senior position at Cleary, Barnes. I play golf with Frank Cleary all the time."

"Thank you." She touched his arm. "Let me think about it, okay? I'm not sure I'm ready to go back to work."

Not while she was waiting for a hit man to call.

Another week passed, and no one called except her mother. Claiming to be job hunting and waiting for phone calls, she turned down every one of her mother's attempts to drag her out of the house. But the call never came, and finally Jennifer took a look at herself in the mirror and was disgusted.

Moments later she was in the shower, scrubbing as if she could wash away the grime of a lifetime, rather than the dirt of a few days. After she emerged squeaky clean, before she was even fully dry, she called her mother and suggested lunch.

Lenore Compton met her daughter at a small café that served wonderful soups and sinful desserts. After a lifetime of denying herself, Lenore had decided that she deserved to indulge herself once in a while. "After all," she explained to her daughters, "I never ate a fattening thing in fifty years, and I still got plump! I may as well eat cake." Now sixty-five, she was a lovely woman with steel gray hair and bright blue eyes—and an extra fifteen pounds around her middle.

She wasn't thinking about the dastardly, unwanted fifteen pounds this afternoon, however. Every cell in her was focused on her daughter, and what she saw appalled her. Jennifer had always been a very pretty woman, and she still was, but now, instead of merely being slender, she looked anorexic. There were smudges beneath her eyes that didn't look at all healthy, and her cheekbones were far too prominent. Lenore was willing to bet that the younger woman had needed a safety pin to tighten the waistband of her skirt so that it wouldn't fall down.

This could not be allowed to continue.

"I have been so worried about you!" Lenore said. "Jennifer, honey, you've got to get past this."

Jennifer picked up the menu and snapped it open, her mouth tightening. "*This,* as you call it, is the loss of my husband and two children, Mother. It's not something to be gotten past like an obstacle in the road."

Lenore ached. She knew that stubbornly angry expression from way back and found herself remembering Jennifer at two years of age, giving her that same mutinous look. "I know, dear. But it's been six months, and you're not getting any better. You don't take care of yourself the way you should. When was the last time you had a haircut? Your hair used to be so pretty, falling just to your chin. The way you have it pulled back isn't at all flattering. And you've lost more weight. I know the boyish look is in, but the good Lord intended you to have more curves than that. You just don't look well."

Jennifer put the menu down. "Mother—"

"Really," Lenore interrupted. "You apparently need some help with this. I know a good doctor—"

"Mother." This time the interruption was firm, the tone unmistakable. The older woman fell silent. "Really, I'm fine."

Lenore was not so easily cowed. "No, you're not. Now, pick up that menu and order something, or I'll order for you. We are not leaving until you've eaten a decent meal."

If she had been capable of laughter anymore, Jennifer would have laughed. Her mother hadn't talked to her that way since childhood. But even as the thought flitted across her mind, it was displaced by another wave of melancholy, this one entirely different. In the blink of an eye she connected with the child she had once been, sitting up so tall and trying to remember all the manners her mother had taught her, becoming almost too self-conscious to eat. How innocent that child had been! How innocent she had remained until just six months ago.

Lenore saw the wistful, yearning look appear on her daughter's face and felt a vise grip her own heart. The most painful part of motherhood began when a kiss would no longer make it all better. When nothing a mother could do would make it any better at all.

"Jenny, think of something else," she said gently. "Mark and the children will forgive you for allowing other thoughts to enter your head. In fact, Mark would probably be the first one to tell you to find peace and make a new life for yourself."

"Yes, he would have been." Jennifer blinked back tears. "But you see, Mother, Mark laughed for both of us."

Those simple words slashed at Lenore's heart. That couldn't be true. It simply couldn't! But remembering how serious Jenny had been as a child, and how she had brightened after meeting Mark, she felt cold fingers of fear grip her. "Honey, I'm so sorry. If anything I could do would bring them back... But that's useless wishing. As my grandma always said, 'Shit in one hand, wish in the other, and see which one is full.'"

In spite of her tears, the corners of Jennifer's mouth twitched upward. It had always struck her as so funny that her straitlaced great-grandmother had said such a thing, and her mother was relieved to see that she could still manage that much of a smile.

"That's better." She reached across the table and patted Jenny's hand. "Now, find the most fattening thing on that menu and order it."

Under her coaxing, Jenny finally ordered bratwurst and split pea soup. "I'll never eat all of that."

"You might be surprised how hungry you are once you start eating something that tastes good." Lenore couldn't believe that her daughter's body wasn't absolutely crying out for nutritious food and calories. "I would willingly bet that half the reason you've lost so much weight is that you haven't bothered to get any good food into the house. What does your refrigerator look like? Is everything in there green with mold?"

"How did you know?"

"Somehow I just guessed. We'll go shopping together after lunch. And I don't want to hear any arguments."

Jennifer sighed, but for once she didn't disagree.

"I still think," the older woman said when their soup was before them, along with a basket of crusty dark bread, "that you might consider getting some professional help. Counseling, perhaps, to work through your grief. Or maybe even some psychiatric care. They have pills for depression that do wonders, I hear."

"What I'm going through is perfectly natural. I just have to get through it. No pill will change that. And as far as I know, there isn't a specific timetable for grieving."

"Oh, no, but I'd certainly feel a whole lot better if you had started to get angry." Lenore put her spoon down and regarded her daughter with loving concern. "Honey, it's been six months. I'd feel a lot better about you if you'd begun to show interest in something. Anything. Hell, a TV soap would be enough."

"I hate TV."

"Well, what *do* you like? Tennis? Golf? You always loved to play golf. Why don't we get out to the course together a couple of times a week? The sun and fresh air will do you good."

"It's going to start snowing any day now. I don't think golf would be too enjoyable."

Lenore reined in her growing sense of exasperation. "Well, then, let's take an aerobics class together. You always said you'd take one with me some time."

"I'll think about it. I promise."

"Don't think too long. My blood pressure has gone up lately, and the doctor's been nagging me about exercising. If you'd come with me, I might actually do it on a regular basis." Extortion. A classic mother-induced guilt trip. Another small smile escaped Jennifer as she recognized her mother's ploy, and Lenore felt good for having extracted it.

"How bad is your blood pressure?"

Lenore shrugged. "Borderline, he said, but they don't ignore borderline anymore."

It suddenly struck Jennifer that her mother had gotten older while she hadn't been looking. Somewhere along the way while she had been absorbed in her career and her marriage, Lenore's fifty had turned into sixty and sixty had become sixty-five.

Death was the constant companion of life, it seemed. Knowing that an end would eventually arrive was the only thing that made sorrow tolerable. "This, too, shall pass," was another of her mother's favorite sayings, and it was true. Everything passed, good or bad, right into the grave.

"How's your health otherwise?" she asked her mother, concerned.

"Oh, I'm fine! You can't keep a good horse down. No, I'm just getting up there in years, and I'm carrying fifteen pounds too many. Your dad seems to like me plumper—or at least he claims to, the sweetheart—but my doctor is forever reading me the riot act about it. I just ignore him. But I *do* think some aerobics would do me good, honey. It's just that I won't stick to it on my own. I need someone to motivate me."

"And you think *I'm* the one to do that?" The thought amused Jennifer. She could hardly motivate herself to get out of bed these days.

"Of course you can! You have enough drive and determination for ten people. How else did you get to the top of your career field?"

Jennifer looked quickly away, trying to hold back a sudden and unexpected burst of anger. She had indeed gotten near the very top of her career field. The plum had been right there, ripe for the picking. Now it was forever out of reach. She would never find work again when she had been fired at a client's demand. Not that it mattered anymore. Very soon nothing at all was going to matter.

Lenore must have been reading her mind. "You'll find work soon, honey. Someone will understand that making a few mistakes was natural, given all that you were going through. And I'm sure it will be an even better job than the one before."

Her mother was an inveterate Pollyanna. Ordinarily that didn't bother Jennifer at all, but today it grated on her nerves like fingernails scraping over a chalkboard. She didn't want to be optimistic, and she didn't want people to insist that she be.

Damn it, she *hurt.* She hurt so much that sometimes just drawing another breath was almost too painful to bear. In the dead of the night, when she reached out for Mark, all of it came slamming down on her as the roof of her life caved in all over again. Better jobs, more friends, more activities...none of those things would prevent reality from crashing down on her again and again.

"I'm sorry," Lenore said abruptly, her tone gentle. "Let's just get away from this entire subject. Did I tell you that Massie is pregnant again?"

Jennifer turned her head jerkily back to her mother. Massie was her parents' mastiff, two hundred pounds of furry adoration. "Again?"

"Again. I would dearly love to know which dog in the neighborhood manages to get past our fence!"

"You could have Massie spayed."

"Dear, I wouldn't put any female of any species through instant menopause. I've been there."

"I don't think it's quite the same for dogs."

"How would we know? Has anyone ever interviewed a dog to find out? Massie isn't just a baby, she's three years old. It would throw her entire system out of whack, I'm sure, and I can't bear the thought of the poor thing having hot flashes. Heavens, she couldn't even ask for an ice pack!"

Jennifer felt herself relaxing again, able to eat more of her soup, even managing small smiles. This was Lenore at her best. "What will you do with the pups?"

"That would be a lot easier to answer if we knew something about their sire. As it stands, I imagine I'll saddle you with one, and probably Melanie, as well." Melanie was her other daughter, Jennifer's older sister.

"I don't know that I want that much dog, Mother. Or any dog at all, for that matter."

"Of course you do! There's nothing more lovable than an English mastiff."

Jennifer couldn't deny that. Well, she thought, it wouldn't hurt to agree. The pups wouldn't be born for a while yet, then couldn't be weaned for another six weeks...by then all her problems should be over with. "Just be sure I don't get the biggest pup in the litter."

"Well, I certainly won't give you the runt! You want a strong, healthy pup."

"Maybe Massie mated with a Chihuahua and size won't be a problem."

The thought made both of them laugh, and the laughter made lunch go much more smoothly. Jennifer even managed to finish her soup and most of the sausage.

Later she felt guilty, but that was the price of forgetting Mark and the children for even a brief time. She always felt guilty if they slipped from her mind.

Maybe, she found herself thinking, maybe a little counseling would be wise. Maybe she *did* need some help in dealing with things. Intellectually she knew she shouldn't feel guilty for laughing with her mother any more than she would have felt guilty when Mark and the kids were alive. Life went on, but somehow her heart couldn't accept that. She was burying herself alive in guilt.

The phone rang that evening as she was getting ready for bed, jarring her, because she wasn't expecting any calls this late. She reached for the receiver, automatically anticipating bad news. Her father...her mother...one of her sister's children...

"Hello?"

The voice that answered sounded as if it came from the depths of a very deep pit. "I hear you want to hire someone to do a delicate job."

2

Rook Rydell watched the eddies in the smoke-filled atmosphere of the bar, drinking a Corona and thinking that there was nothing more miserable than being between jobs. It gave a man too damn much time to think. As for hanging out in this bar—it was great to hit a bar on a Friday night after a long spell of hard work, but sitting here every night just wasn't his style. It was, however, marginally better than sitting around that lousy room he'd taken, watching reruns on a twelve-inch black-and-white TV and trying to talk himself out of buying a pack of cigarettes.

What he needed was to get wind of another job. Every day he checked his post office box, but so far, nothing. Sooner or later something would turn up; it always did, for a man of his talents.

In the meantime, boredom tried his patience, but he had plenty of patience. A man in his line of work often needed it.

He lifted the beer bottle to his lips again, surveying the room through narrowed eyes. Vaguely, he could remember a time when he really knew how to unwind, how to let go of it all when life gave him a night off.

Not anymore. Not since he'd become a mercenary. During the past five years he'd spent far too much time in places where he couldn't even trust the man who was supposed to be guarding his back. Sometimes he wondered if he would ever truly relax again. Tipping his head back, he downed half the bottle of Corona.

"That'll kill you," said a voice from behind him.

Rook didn't even turn his head. "I'm not going to live long enough to pickle my liver. Pull up a chair, Jay."

The younger man rounded the table and straddled a chair, facing him. Jay had once been Rook's protégé, but the years had taught him enough of his own hard lessons that he didn't need to rely on anyone else anymore. These days the two men were equals, and sometimes friends.

"If you're not going to live long enough to pickle your liver, why the hell did you quit smoking? You're not likely to live long enough to get cancer, either. And what's with the Coronas? No serious stuff?" Jay's voice was deep, rough, ruined by some soldiers who had tried to hang him.

"I quit smoking because I like to breathe. And I'm not aiming to get drunk because I don't like the way I feel in the morning."

Jay flashed a half smile. "Ya don't care for the excitement of a pounding head and a heaving stomach? Whatsamatter? Gettin' old?"

"Ancient." Some days he felt as old as Methuselah, as if the last bit of life and joy had been wrung from him and he was a used-up husk. Too much experience of the wrong kind. He took another swig of beer.

Jay signaled the waitress and gestured that he wanted a couple of Coronas. When she waved acknowledgment, he turned back to Rook. "Hear anything about another job?"

"Not a damn thing."

"Something will turn up."

"Yeah." One thing you could say about this sorry little planet was that there was always another war to go to. Sooner or later someone would need Rook Rydell's particular services. If he let himself think about it too hard, he could make a good case for terminal depression, so he didn't let himself think about it. Much.

The waitress, a woman who might have been anywhere from forty to seventy, put a couple of fresh beers on the table and picked up the bills Jay had laid out.

The old black man at the piano started a new tune, and a group of men nearby began to stomp their feet in time. Almost in spite of himself, Rook felt his feet twitching in response. A long time ago he had liked to dance. A very long time ago.

Jay spoke. "Remember that night in La Palma when you and Alan DeVries were drinking straight tequila?"

"I try to forget."

Jay laughed. "Nobody else ever will."

"How the hell was anyone supposed to know that *puta* was the police chief's wife?"

"It probably occurred to the thirty or forty guys who were sober enough to see her walk in with him."

In spite of himself, Rook smiled faintly. It *was* funny, in retrospect, but at the time he'd wanted to kill the woman, her husband and Alan DeVries. Mostly Alan, because he'd almost gotten them both caught. That had kind of put an end to *that* job. Neither he nor Alan had ever gotten a dime of what they'd been owed . . . not that either of them had been in any hurry to head back to La Palma to collect it.

Jay started his second beer before he spoke again. "That woman called me."

"What woman?"

He turned to Rook, looking surprised "The one you gave my number to. Who else?"

For an instant Rook didn't remember. "Oh. Yeah. The one looking for a contract hit. Sorry about that, but she was getting ready to buttonhole everybody in this bar, and I figured that wouldn't be good for her health."

"Probably not. Kinda threw me, though."

"I was so drunk at the time that it was the only way I could get her out of here."

"That's okay. I gave her number to somebody who can help her."

Until that very moment, Rook had believed there was nothing left on the face of this planet that could seriously throw him. As Jay's meaning penetrated, however, he discovered he was wrong. He could still be thrown. Badly. "What do you mean?"

"I gave her number to somebody who does that kind of work."

"You don't *know* anybody who does that kind of work. That's why I gave her your number! So you could tell her to get lost."

Jay looked confused. "How was I supposed to know that? She said you told her I could help her. So I did."

Horror began to sink into Rook's very bones. Jesus. In his entire life he'd never been party to anything like this. And he never wanted to be party to anything like this. "Who'd you give her number to?"

"I can't tell you that. You know that, Rook. These guys work in secrecy. If I told you, *I'd* be dead."

"Jesus." He felt as if he were suddenly caught in a nightmare. He *couldn't* be party to this. "Do you still have the woman's number?"

Jay shook his head. "I gave it to somebody. What's wrong?"

Other than that he might have just helped get someone killed? Other than that Jay knew a hit man? Rook couldn't answer that question. He'd thought he'd known Jay, but apparently he hadn't known everything. The younger man obviously had more to him than being a decent soldier and a hell of a marksman. Maybe he even had a darker side. How would Rook know? He'd made a stupid assumption, and now he was discovering that as much as the two of them were alike, they weren't *exactly* alike.

Besides, it was all his own doing, anyway. He should never have drunk all that tequila. He'd tried to take the easy way out of a difficult situation, and he had no one but himself to blame for the ultimate outcome. He should have thought to tell Jay to brush the woman off. He should have dealt with her himself. "When did you give the guy the woman's number?"

"Right after she called."

It was too late, then. By now someone had been hooked into the job. Whoever it was wasn't going to back off that kind of money just because Rook Rydell didn't want any involvement, however indirect. No, even assuming he could discover who had eventually taken the job, he wouldn't be able to stop him. Hiring a hit man was like firing a heat-seeking missile—the only way to stop it was to blow it up.

He was screwed. And so was some other poor bastard who'd probably done nothing except run afoul of a vindictive bitch with too much money. Nor did it help to remind himself that the woman would have found someone eventually anyway, with or without Jay's assistance. It was wrong, and he was a part of it.

If he ever met that bitch again, he was going to make her sorry she'd ever been born.

"I hear you want to hire someone to do a delicate job."

Jennifer's breath locked in her throat. Every muscle in her body became rigid as stone, and even her heart seemed to stop beating. This was the call she had given up on. She had even concluded that she was going to have to find a different way of ending her life. Now, all of a sudden, she wasn't prepared.

"Look, I guess I got the wrong number."

"No!" The word escaped her on a sudden gust of breath, emphatic, sharp. "I mean...you have the right number."

"What is it you need?"

"I want..." The words came out jerkily, as if she had to force them through concrete. "I want...someone killed."

There was a pause from the other end of the line. "Does the target have any kind of protection? Bodyguard?"

"No." Everything inside her felt frozen into ice.

"Prominent public figure?"

"No."

"How soon do you need this?"

"Not...not too soon. I mean...it's flexible."

"How do you want it done?"

"Swiftly. Painlessly. It can't look like suicide." She was beginning to feel as if she were handling a case. Detachment was starting to set in, distancing her from what she was doing, allowing her brain to function.

Another pause. "Fifty thousand."

Jennifer, who had dealt with numbers in the millions and even billions as an attorney, found this amount incomprehensible. It wasn't that she didn't have the money, it was that she hadn't expected the price to be so high. "So much? I've heard ten thousand—"

He interrupted ruthlessly. "The ones you've heard about have all been caught. You haven't heard about me."

He had a point. "All right."

"I need a description of the target and a couple of photographs. Good ones, for identification. Name, address, occupation. Anything you can tell me that will help identify and locate the target."

"All right." Suddenly it was difficult again. Her knuckles turned white as she clenched the receiver to her ear.

"Put it all in a suitcase along with twenty-five thousand in cash. I'll give you until Friday to deliver it." He proceeded to give her directions to a trash bin behind a convenience store, telling her to throw the suitcase into it at midnight on Friday. "After the job is done, I'll call you and arrange to get the rest. Okay?"

"Yes."

"Anything else?"

"No. Except . . . you *will* make it painless?"

"Lady, I ain't sadistic unless I get paid to be. It'll be clean and quick." With a click he was gone.

She was suddenly shaking so hard that she barely managed to get the receiver in the cradle. It was done. She had taken the step at last.

Sinking into a deep armchair before her legs gave way, she thought, *Fifty thousand!* Far more than she had anticipated. Not that she didn't have it. Her bank account was bulging with insurance money as a result of the plane crash. Money she would *never* touch, even if by some awful chance of fate she lived to be a hundred. But for this she would touch it. For this it seemed appropriate.

Finally she went into the kitchen and poured herself a finger of bourbon. It was done, and a strange kind of peace began to come over her now that she had taken the step. Only a few more details to deal with, and then it would be out of her hands.

Out of the clear blue, as she was staring into her bourbon, she found herself remembering the mercenary she had met in the seedy bar nearly a week ago. What made a man become like that? So hardened, and cold.

She could see him vividly, an unusual-looking man with a face etched deeply by the elements and tawny eyes that almost appeared lit from within. Such strange eyes. Remembering them made her shiver for some reason. With eyes like that, she was surprised he wasn't called Wolf instead of Rook. And where had a name like Rook come from?

A little while later, exhausted from emotional tension, and strangely eased by having taken the big step, she tumbled into bed and into deep sleep. In her dreams she was pursued by a wolf with tawny eyes and huge fangs that dripped blood.

* * *

On Wednesday, she called her bank and told them the size of the withdrawal she planned to make late Friday. There was some consternation on the other end, but as she firmly reminded the bank officer, it was *her* money, to do with as she pleased, and she didn't need to answer to the bank for her decision.

Of course, they were just being concerned. Fifty thousand dollars in cash, if stolen, couldn't be replaced.

That was the one thing that concerned her; if she got robbed on the way to the drop, she might lose her chance to hire this guy, and she would have to start all over again. It never occurred to her to worry about her own safety. Somehow, plotting her own death made ordinary risks seem trivial.

Indeed, as Friday drew close, a kind of peace seemed to steal over her. Soon it would be set, and there would be no way to change her mind. She liked that part for some reason. For once in her life, instead of trying to leave options open and escape clauses available, she was taking a totally irrevocable step. In that she found a kind of freedom.

When she arrived at the bank on Friday afternoon, she was escorted directly into a windowless room. Mr. Chaney, one of the bank officers, was there with two tellers whose job it was to count the money in her presence. He tried once again to dissuade her.

"Really, Mrs. Fox, if this money gets stolen—well, no one can afford to lose so much, and you won't have any recourse. If you take a cashier's check, on the other hand, that can be replaced if it's stolen. It's just a matter of caution we're talking about."

"I appreciate your concern, Mr. Chaney, but my mind is made up."

"You *do* understand that we'll have to report this to the IRS?"

"That doesn't concern me. They already know I have the money." She shook her head. "Really, it's of no consequence."

"Dear lady, I realize you've been through a terrible trauma—"

Jennifer leaned forward in her seat, her anger blazing suddenly, and cut him off with a voice as sharp as the blade of a knife. "Don't you *dare* imply that I am not thinking clearly."

"I didn't mean—"

"Of course you didn't. Now let's just get on with this."

Her driver's license was photocopied, her Social Security card was examined, and her signature was required on a stack of forms, some for the bank, one for the government. The latter irritated her; a person ought to be able to do whatever she wanted with her own money without having to notify the government.

The tellers counted the money for her while she watched. It didn't amount to very much, actually, in terms of size. The stack of hundred-dollar bills, banded into groups of twenty, was less than five inches tall, and it was hard to believe that it was so much money. She was able to tuck it all in the oversize purse she had brought, with plenty of room to spare.

Out on the street, she had that strangely dislocated feeling that she usually had when coming out of a movie theater, as if she had been far, far away and time was somehow out of sync. The bright, clear sky seemed out of place, as out of place as it had the afternoon her husband and children had died.

It was cruel how the world went on when terrible things were happening.

"Honey, why don't you come spend the weekend with us?"

"Mother..." Jennifer couldn't believe this. She was putting the money in a small brown suitcase, along with photographs of herself and other useful information, getting ready to depart in a half hour, and now her mother called.

"I know, I know, it's late, and I probably woke you up, but I just had this bad feeling and... Oh, Jenny, honey, I'd feel ever so much better if you were staying with us this weekend."

Jennifer felt the hairs on the back of her neck prickle, and she sat slowly in the ladder-back chair beside the telephone table. God, how she hated it when her mother got psychic. "Really, Mother, everything's fine."

"I'm sure it is! It's just that...oh, honey, I've got this horrible feeling that something awful is about to happen to you. I've been trying to shake it for days, and it just won't go away. Finally, tonight, I got this feeling that if I could just get you to come here tonight, everything would be fine."

Jennifer almost glanced over her shoulder, feeling as if someone must be watching her and reporting to her mother. "I don't see what coming over there would do," she said, but her lips were stiff around her lie. If she didn't drop this money in the Dumpster tonight, she would fail to arrange the hit. She would have to start looking all over again for someone to do this.

Lenore gave an uncomfortable laugh. "You're right, it probably wouldn't do anything at all. But it *would* make me feel better."

Jennifer glanced at the clock, feeling a growing sense of urgency. *Midnight,* the voice on the phone had said. She had to leave the money at midnight, not at eleven-thirty, not at one-thirty. That meant she couldn't go to her parents' house at all, unless she went to the drop first, and how was she going to explain to her mother why it had taken her so long to get there? "Mother, I really can't come tonight. I'm tired, I was about to take a bath. I'll see you tomorrow, okay?"

"Jenny, please, I won't be able to sleep a wink!"

She was thinking fast, considering and discarding possibilities with rapid-fire speed. Finally, giving in to guilt, she said, "All right, I'll come over. But I'm going to be late, Mother. I want to take my bath and do my hair first, so don't look for me before...one, I guess. I should be able to get there by then."

Lenore wanted to argue some more, but time was running out, so Jennifer gently ended the conversation. Then, staring blankly at the wall, she blinked back tears and wondered why life had become such agony.

The convenience store was open around the clock, so her car wouldn't look out of place in the parking lot. She had been worried about that, knowing that if the business were closed, a policeman might well stop to investigate what she was doing there. She just wanted to get this over as quickly as possible.

She pulled in to a parking slot on the side of the building, away from the front door, at exactly three minutes before midnight. There were some youths hanging around out front, but they couldn't see her where she parked, nor could anyone else, except passing traffic on the street.

Clutching a can of pepper spray and the brown suitcase, she headed around to the back of the building cautiously, more than a little afraid that someone would be waiting there. No one was.

Her neck, however, crawled with the certainty that she was being watched. Wouldn't the gunman be watching right now, to be sure that someone threw a suitcase into the Dumpster? He wouldn't want to have to go pawing through that thing looking if nothing was there. Yes, he must be watching her. Her scalp prickled.

What would he think when he saw the photograph was of her? Would he think anything at all? Probably not. Why should he care, as long as the money was good? One target was the same as another, wasn't it?

It would certainly explain to him why she'd put the entire fifty thousand in the suitcase, instead of just half, as he had requested. She had to hope he wouldn't run off with it, but she couldn't ask anyone she knew to get involved by asking them to deliver the rest of the money for her.

Why would a man get into this line of work? What about that guy at the bar? Rook. What about him? What made a man become a mercenary? What made him become friends with people who did things like this? Rook had said he didn't have any part of this kind of work, yet he had been able to direct her to someone who was able to make the connection for her. What happened to conscience?

At precisely midnight, she hurled the suitcase into the Dumpster. It thudded as it hit the bottom. Apparently there was nothing else in there except maggots.

The night wind kicked up, carrying a bite down from the mountains, and she shivered. Turning, she hurried back to her car, no longer caring if anyone saw her. What did it matter? What did anything matter anymore?

As she rounded the corner, she nearly bumped into a policeman. He was holding a soft drink in his left hand, but his right hand rested conspicuously on the butt of his gun. "Are you okay, lady?"

Just what she needed. "I'm, uh, fine. I just felt a little sick, but I'm okay now."

"You been drinking?"

The question nearly froze her. She hadn't had a drink since that afternoon, right after she came home from the bank. Since she'd eaten, bathed and changed clothes since then, there was no way he smelled alcohol on her. Unfortunately, contrary to what most people thought, a drink in the afternoon could still show up as elevated blood alcohol late that night. If this policeman decided she was drunk, a blood test could conceivably bear him out.

She managed to shake her head and said with desperation, "I'm pregnant."

It worked. "Oh!" At once he removed his hand from his gun. "Are you all right now? Do you need any help?"

"I'm fine. Really." She gave him a wan smile. "I just want to go inside and get some mineral water."

He insisted on accompanying her, telling her how dangerous it was for a woman to be out alone at night, especially in neighborhoods like this one. Inside the store, the clerk agreed vociferously with him, and she found herself sandwiched between two men who were apparently feeling very male and very protective, while she sipped the bottled water she didn't really want.

"There was a woman raped right across the street just last week," the clerk told her. "Terrible thing it was. She was really preggers. Y'know, I can't figure why a guy would want to rape a pregnant woman, can you?"

The cop shook his head. His nameplate identified him as Coons. "It's a thing about violence and power, Del. They don't care. I mean, who would think anybody would rape a ninety-year-old woman? But it happens."

Jennifer clutched the bottle of mineral water desperately and suppressed a shiver. Would the man come to get the suitcase out of the Dumpster when she was still here? Or would he get concerned because of the appearance of the cop and suspect this was some kind of trap?

She had to get out of here and over to her parents' house before too much longer or her mother would call out a search party, especially if Jennifer wasn't answering her phone at home. But she didn't want to make the cop suspicious.

"It's really late," she said finally to the officer. "I need to get home and get to bed. Thanks so much for looking after me."

"No problem." His brown eyes were surprisingly kind. "Let me walk you to your car."

He also followed her in his cruiser for several blocks, as if making sure she was indeed able to drive. Finally he flashed his lights once and turned away to go back to his patrol.

Jennifer was shaking so hard by that time that she hesitated to get onto the highway. God, she hadn't thought it would be so difficult! Not just dumping the money, but everything that had followed. That policeman had really put her nerves on edge, and she was damn near convinced he hadn't believed her story. Thank heavens he hadn't decided to make her take a field sobriety test. Nervous as she was, she wasn't sure she could have passed it.

And what if the man hadn't picked up the money because he saw her with a cop? What then?

Damn it, why couldn't she just have been on the plane with Mark and the children?

But the night didn't offer any answers.

"You need to start rebuilding your life, Jennifer." Glenn Compton spoke as he turned the pages of his newspaper and snapped them flat. "You're spending too much time alone, brooding."

The morning air was crisp, but her mother nonetheless had chosen to serve breakfast on the deck, complete with a linen tablecloth and fine china. The house was up in the foothills west of Denver, and from the deck Jennifer had a splendid view of rocky ravines and tall pines. "I'm looking for work, Dad."

"I don't mean work. I mean a *life*. You need to find some new friends, people who don't have any old associations for you. You need to get out and do things for the fun of it. You can't spend the rest of your life grieving. It would be a sinful waste."

"I don't intend to."

Lenore stepped out through the glass door with a bowl of fresh melon balls. "I know you love these, honey. Dig in. I'll have your toast in a moment."

"Thank you, Mother."

Glenn looked at his daughter over the tops of his reading glasses. "Why did you start calling her 'Mother' instead of 'Mom'? I've always wondered."

Jennifer felt a smile tug the corners of her mouth upward. "I thought it sounded more grown-up. After all these years it's a habit I'll never break."

Glenn laughed, apparently tickled by that piece of information. "But you never called me 'Father.'"

Jennifer shrugged. "It just never felt right."

"I'm glad. I always liked being your dad. Which brings me back to the original subject of conversation."

Jennifer averted her gaze, looking up the ravine toward a waterfall. There were other houses around here, but all were cunningly placed so that each one seemed to be alone in the wilderness. "Dad, don't. Healing takes time, and right now I don't need any lectures."

"Maybe you don't think you do, but the simple fact is, if you don't make an effort yourself, you'll spend the rest of your life grieving. I've known people who've devoted their lives to nursing a grief or a sorrow, and I don't want to see my daughter turn into one of them. It's been more than six months, and it's high time you stuck your head out of your shell."

Flames of fury were beginning to lick at her stomach, fueled by her anger at the deaths of her loved ones. "Everybody knows what I should do," she said tautly. "It's amazing how much well-intentioned advice I keep getting. You know what's really astonishing? The people who are full of all this good advice have never been in my position. It's real easy to be glib when you don't know what you're talking about."

Without another word she pushed back from the table and walked into the house, passing her mother without even looking at her. Upstairs in the guest room, she closed and locked the door and curled up on the window seat in one of the dormers. Tears blurred her vision and tightened her throat, while anger simmered in the pit of her stomach.

God, what a joke! Her entire life had turned to ashes, but everyone seemed to think she ought to take up tennis or golf, and start going to the movies again. Good God, she hadn't been able to sit through a movie since the accident. Her mind wouldn't focus on something so unimportant. Read a book? Five or six sentences into it, her mind would wander off to Mark, or Bethany, or Eli. Every time she walked into a room at home or here at her parents', she expected to see one of her absent loved ones. She couldn't even enter this damn guest room without remembering the first time she and Mark had shared it, just after their law school graduation, just before their wedding. They'd always wondered if her parents had known about it.

When she looked out over the mountains, she could still hear Mark talking about their changing moods as clouds accumulated overhead, or as rain swept over the slopes. Driving down any street in Denver there was a memory waiting to pounce. In every one of her friends' voices she heard the echo of Mark's voice. In the laughter of children she heard her own kids.

Forget about it? Never. Put it behind her? Not very likely. Not when a million little things reminded her a million times a day.

Briefly, after she'd lost her job, she'd toyed with the idea of packing up and moving to some place where she and Mark had never gone together, a place where there would be no memories to torment her. That meant a whole new set of losses in that she would have to leave her family and friends. Why, she wondered, should the only way be by giving up more? And if she was going to give up so much, why not give it all up?

A knock on the door disturbed her. "I'll be out in a while," she called. Miserable as she was, she could understand that her parents were concerned.

"I just want to talk to you for a minute," Lenore replied. "Open the door, honey."

Dashing the tears from her eyes, Jenny went to let her mother in. Lenore's expression surprised her. Her mother wasn't worried, she was angry. Closing the door behind herself, she wagged a stern finger at Jenny.

"How dare you talk to your father that way, young lady? He's worried sick about you. So am I, for that matter, but we're not giving you glib advice! How dare you insinuate that we don't understand your loss! We've lost friends and family before, you know. And in case you've forgotten, we also lost Mark and Eli and Bethany." Tears suddenly sparkled on her lashes. "How dare you tell us we don't know what we're talking about? Right now we're watching our daughter draw further and further away, and we're scared sick that we're losing her, too...."

Jenny felt a crack in the stone wall of her grief as her mother's words pierced her. The image she suddenly had of herself was horrifying, and she shuddered to think she had become so selfish and self-absorbed that she was causing terrible pain to those she loved. "Mom... Mom, I'm sorry... I'm so sorry...."

Lenore gathered her daughter close and hugged her tightly. "It's okay... it's all right, honey. We love you so much...."

A little while later, when they both had stopped crying, they went downstairs to resume breakfast. Massie, the family's huge fawn-colored mastiff, joined them, planting her head firmly on Jennifer's thigh and watching her with soulful eyes.

"See, she's worried about you, too," Lenore said.

Glenn laughed. "More likely she wants a piece of that toast. She's shameless."

Jennifer was only too happy to oblige, and she noticed that her parents didn't scold her for it, although they normally disapproved of feeding dogs from the table. Massie's head was far bigger than her own, but the mastiff was as gentle as could be, even delicate, in the way she licked crumbs from Jennifer's hand.

"Are you *sure* you don't want a pup?" Lenore asked again. "Massie's a wonderful companion and a great guard dog."

"That depends on what you're guarding," Jenny reminded her. "Mastiffs let intruders into the house, they just don't let them out. It'd be great against a burglar but wouldn't be much protection against a rapist."

"Actually," Lenore said dryly, "one look at Massie is enough to send most people into flight."

"Which reminds me," Glenn said. "Your mother and I are thinking about getting away for a few days next week. If we decide to go, can you baby-sit the dog for us?"

Jennifer wanted desperately to refuse. She loved Massie as much as they did, and the thought of having the dog with her when the hit man found her made her cringe. Even if he didn't kill the dog, too, her death would undoubtedly leave the animal scarred. But how could she refuse without cuing her parents to the fact that something was going on? "I'll be glad to take her." Bending, she dropped a kiss on the dog's big head. Maybe she would be dead before then, anyway.

The sun was warm and bright, causing Jennifer's skin to tingle pleasantly, but the breeze that blew down the mountain was as cold as death.

Wrapped in a sweater, she made an effort to smile and talk casually with her parents, all the while wondering when the hit man would find her.

Monday morning she headed home, exhausted by the effort she'd expended all weekend to conceal her depression from her folks. Equally difficult had been trying to make her farewells appear normal, when every cell in her body shrieked with the awareness that this might be the last time she saw them.

At any moment a bullet might burrow through her brain, ending all of this. The thought obsessed her as she headed back down to Denver. How would it come? And where? She was only assuming he would shoot her, but there were probably other ways to do the job, ways she couldn't even imagine.

And for the first time she honestly considered the impact her death would have on people she cared about, like her sister and her parents. She had been so absorbed in her pain that she hadn't really considered the cost of her actions to other people. Guilt began to prick at her, making her even unhappier.

What the hell, she told herself. Before long, none of it was going to matter.

Feeling defiant, she pulled in to her driveway and switched off the ignition. In the bright morning sunlight, the house looked every bit as beautiful as it had the day she and Mark had fallen in love with it. Instead of the glass-and-wood structures that were so popular now, they had fallen for an older home, with white clapboard and black shutters and a wide, columned porch.

The gardens and lawns didn't show the least sign of neglect, owing to the company that came once a week and took care of it all. No one would ever guess the barrenness that existed within those walls.

Enough! She was getting sick of her own company, sick of her whining and mewling all the time. God! It was one thing to hurt because she had lost so much, it was entirely another to wallow in it.

What she ought to do today was look up some of her closest friends and say her secret farewells. There had to be something she could say to each of them that would make her death easier for them to handle. All she had to do was figure out what it was.

The light on the answering machine was blinking furiously when she stepped through the door. Automatically, she reached out and pressed the button.

"Mrs. Fox, this is Avery Wilson. I'm an investigator with the FAA. You may remember we spoke last May about the accident involving your family. Would you please give me a call at 555-3121? I have some information for you."

Kicking off her shoes and dropping her purse onto the floor, she punched in the number on the phone. Her heart had speeded up, because some instinct told her that something had happened that was going to change everything. At some level it had seemed to her that the investigation of the crash was taking too long, but what did she know about such things? Now the FAA was calling, and it must be because they had reached a conclusion.

Her knees suddenly felt shaky, so she perched on the edge of the chair. The receptionist transferred her call.

"Avery Wilson."

"Mr. Wilson, this is Jennifer Fox. I had a message to call you."

"Yes, Mrs. Fox. We've concluded our investigation, and I wanted to inform you of the results before we release our report."

"Thank you." The response came automatically, although she couldn't imagine what she was thanking this man for. For the courtesy of not letting her discover this from the newspapers? Probably.

"The results show that the plane crashed because of a failure of the elevators. We found metal filings embedded in the rear of the fuselage that are consistent with the condition of the elevator cables."

Something icy trickled down her spine. "Metal filings in the fuselage? What does that mean?"

"It means, Mrs. Fox, that the plane was sabotaged. The elevator cables had apparently been sawed nearly through some time before they snapped. Your family was murdered."

3

There was a rushing sound in her ears, and the world seemed to recede down a dark tunnel. Dimly she heard Wilson's concerned voice.

"Mrs. Fox? Mrs. Fox, are you there?"

"I'm here." Her lips felt stiff, as if they were carved from ice, and her voice seemed to belong to someone else.

"I hated to dump this on you like this, but there was no good way to tell you. And I certainly didn't want you to read it in the newspapers."

"Are you—are you sure about this?"

Wilson hesitated. "Yes, ma'am, we're sure. Sure enough that we're going to turn it over to the police. Maybe they can find out who was behind it. I expect they'll want to talk to you."

"Talk to me?" For an instant it didn't connect. Her mouth felt as dry as cotton, and her head seemed to be swimming in molasses. Murdered. Her family had been *murdered.*

Wilson sounded distinctly uncomfortable. "Well, to see if you know who might have been angry enough with your husband to do something like this. That kind of thing."

And she herself would be their primary suspect. Spouses always were. Understanding ripped through her in alternating waves of heat and cold. Her family had been murdered, and the police were going to look first at her. People were actually going to wonder if she had done that horrible thing.

She had thought it couldn't get any worse. How wrong she had been!

The next couple of days passed in a despair even blacker than before. She kept waiting for it all to end, for the bullet she had paid for to take her away from all this, but it didn't come. Of course not. She hadn't put a time frame on it. He might have other things to do, or just not be in a killing mood this week.

Somebody had killed her family. The thought drummed on her brain like the steady drip of water in a rainstorm. She could scarcely encompass the notion. Why? Why would anyone in the world want to hurt Mark or her children? Especially her children. It was inconceivable to her.

Initially she refused to believe the FAA could be right. They had to be mistaken. The cables had snapped because of age, and they were misinterpreting the evidence.

But then she remembered just how careful Mark had been about that plane. Good grief, he'd just had it in for whatever they called that checkup where an FAA-certified mechanic had to go over the thing from stem to stern. If the cables had been wearing, the mechanic surely would have noticed it.

Finally she believed, but then she couldn't comprehend why. *Why* was too big a question to have any answers.

And at some point it dawned on her that she was supposed to have been on that plane, too. Which meant she, and not Mark or the children, might well have been the intended target of the sabotage.

Once she had thought she would never feel warm again, but finally, through despair and disbelief, the flames of anger began to burn. Somebody had deliberately killed her husband and children. Somebody deserved to die.

When her doorbell rang on Wednesday afternoon, she wasn't surprised to find two policemen on her porch.

"Mrs. Fox, I'm Detective Lewis and this is Detective Murray." He flashed a badge. "We wondered if you could spare us a few minutes to talk about the plane crash that killed your family."

Part of her wanted to tell them to go away, that nothing they or anyone else could do was ever going to remedy what had happened. Another part of her wanted vengeance, and the police might well be the means for getting it. She stepped back and invited them in.

She didn't offer them anything, because it didn't occur to her. The black dress she was wearing hung loosely on her, testimony to her lack of interest in eating. She already had a glass of bourbon in her hand, though, and the policemen noticed it. They also noticed the dust that layered everything.

They sat side by side on the couch facing her. Lewis was the shorter and thinner of the two, most memorable for the thin strands of hair he had carefully combed over his bald pate. Detective Murray had a face and eyes that reminded her of a basset hound.

Lewis spoke. "Mrs. Fox, you've probably heard from the FAA that there's reason to believe your husband's plane was sabotaged."

Jennifer nodded, feeling again the lick of flame in her stomach, a flame that was stubbornly trying to burn away the black despair of her depression. "Mr. Wilson called Monday."

"Do you have any idea who might have wished your husband dead?"

She shook her head slowly. "Everyone loved Mark."

"He was an attorney." The question implied that being an attorney meant a person had enemies.

"Yes, but he worked for the school system. I'm not aware that anyone was particularly angry with him."

"There must have been someone."

She looked at him with hollow eyes. "I was supposed to have been on that plane, too, and I've made a lot of people very angry."

The detectives exchanged looks. "Why *weren't* you aboard?"

"There was a last-minute hitch on a merger I was working on. I needed to iron it out before I could leave."

She rose from her chair and walked to the window, taking a sip of her bourbon as she stared out at the brilliant, chilly day. "You don't know how often I wish I'd been on that plane."

An uncomfortable silence answered her, but not for long. Detective Lewis broke it. "Who might have hated *you* that much, Mrs. Fox?"

She shrugged a shoulder. "Anyone involved in the merger I was working on. Toes invariably get stepped on in those deals. Any number of people from past negotiations. Some of my co-workers. A few attorneys that I've made look like fools in front of their clients. I'm the one in a cutthroat business, Detective. Not Mark."

"You got fired just recently, didn't you?"

She turned to look at him. "Yes."

"Why?"

"The client wanted it. They didn't think I was performing well enough because of...because of my grief."

"Is that true?"

"Probably." She turned back to the window.

"How was your relationship with your husband just before he died?"

So they *did* suspect her. She had anticipated this, but anticipation had hardly prepared her for the stark reality. It horrified her to realize that anyone could think her capable of such an act. Sickened her. Stunned her. Couldn't they see how much this had hurt her? Her grief was such a consuming beast that it seemed impossible that everyone around her couldn't see it. How was it possible that she could hurt so much and the whole world not feel her pain?

She faced Lewis again, and this time the flames of anger licking at her stomach grew into a bonfire. "Let's not pussyfoot around here, Detective. You want to know whether I killed my husband and my children."

"You have to understand—"

"No, I *don't* have to understand!" She was shaking so hard that bourbon sloshed over the lip of her glass onto her hand. "I don't have to stand here calmly and take it like a good little lamb while you insinuate, however indirectly, that I killed...that I would ever have...that I could have..." She couldn't continue. Fury so strong that she could hardly breathe had risen in her. Moving quickly, she set the glass down before she spilled it. "My life ended when they died! There's nothing left! *Nothing!*"

An uncomfortable silence answered her, but she didn't care. Shivering, she wrapped her arms tightly around herself and closed her eyes. The nightmare just kept getting worse. If that bullet didn't find her soon, she was going to explode into a thousand pieces.

"I wasn't insinuating anything, Mrs. Fox," Detective Lewis said.

"No?" Her voice cracked with bitterness and grief. "What else do you call it when you ask how my relationship with him was? You want to know how it was? Ask people who know me. They'll tell you I've hardly been out of this house since he died." Her voice was rising, but she didn't have enough energy to try to modulate it. "Hardly the merry widow, Detective! I haven't run to Cozumel with my young boyfriend, or thrown a single wild party, or even spent a dime of the insurance money!"

Her heart caught in her throat suddenly, as she recalled the fifty thousand dollars she had just withdrawn from the bank, and realized how that could be interpreted by someone with malice. But, damn it, it didn't matter! She'd be dead soon. Oh, God, please let it be soon!

"You told us your husband didn't have any enemies. I was just trying to find out if your husband had been acting strangely right before the accident. Whether he was preoccupied, or distant, or very much on edge. Whether there might have been something going on that he didn't tell you about."

Swallowing her anger for now, she forced herself to resume her seat. More than a minute passed before she felt calm enough to speak. "I didn't notice anything out of the ordinary. Mark seemed glad to be going on a vacation, glad that I was going to be able to get away—we spent most of our vacations at home because our schedules rarely meshed. This was one of the few times we were both able to arrange time off. I just—" She had to swallow hard before she could continue. "I just remember that he was so happy about how it was all working out."

"And when he heard you had to stay behind?"

"He was disappointed. But it was only for a day. I booked a flight for the following morning."

"Did many people know your husband owned his own plane?"

"I guess. I mean, it wasn't a secret. A couple of times we took friends on trips with us."

"The people who worked with you knew about it?"

"Certainly. A couple of my former co-workers also have their own planes. They ran into Mark all the time out at the airport."

"And you heard about those meetings from them?"

"Of course, and from Mark. What are you trying to get at?"

"A general idea of how many people knew about that plane and knew that you and your husband were supposed to be on it that morning. Do you want to take a guess?"

Once Jennifer started to think about it, it seemed as if a surprising number of people had probably known.

"The partners at the firm...that's how I was contacted just before we took off—"

"Wait, wait, wait," Lewis interrupted. "You were contacted by the firm just before you took off? How much just before?"

"Just a few minutes. We were all in the plane. Mark was getting ready to start the engine...." Her voice faltered as she began to relive those last precious few moments with her husband and children. "My...my pager went off." She swallowed hard and closed her eyes, remembering how she had felt when she heard that beeping and realized she hadn't left her beeper at home, but instead, out of long habit, had hooked it to the waistband of her jeans. How different it all would have been if she had just left the damn thing at home!

"You didn't ignore it?"

"It was the firm. I never ignored their calls, because they never bothered me unless it was really important." That was true, too, but God, how tempted she had been to pretend that she had never gotten the page.

"So you got out of the plane right there?"

"Yes. I went into the airport, called the office, made the decision to stay and went out to tell Mark I wouldn't be able to come until the following day. He wasn't thrilled, but he was understanding." *I love you, Jen, but I wish to God you'd get a different job.*

"What about your baggage?"

"I left it." She frowned, puzzled. "Why would I do anything else? I was going to join them the next day."

"Okay. Now, what about the flight you booked for the next morning? When did you do that?"

"When I called the office. I told my secretary to make the reservation."

"Why didn't you do it right then? You were at the airport."

She was beginning to feel as if she were being cross-examined. These cops were never going to catch the culprit if they focused their investigation on her, but she didn't know how to deflect them. "Because it would have taken a lot of time, and I needed to get back to the office to take care of the problem that had arisen."

"What problem was that?"

"I told you, a problem with a merger. I can't tell you any more than that because it would violate confidentiality."

"Do you know much about planes?"

"Me?" The change of subject took her by surprise but confirmed that they still thought she might have done it. "No, not really. Mark was the pilot."

"Well, you must have hung around with him when he was working on the plane, picked up a lot of shop talk, that kind of thing."

Jennifer shook her head. "I'm sorry, Detective Lewis, but I've never been particularly interested in mechanical things. I didn't even know a plane had an elevator until Mr. Wilson mentioned it."

They had a few more questions for her, but nothing that seemed terribly important. She didn't think they were really satisfied, nor did she care anymore. She had ceased to care at all about what anyone else thought of her. All she cared about, all she would ever care about again, was that someone had killed her family.

And somehow she had to live so that she could make him pay.

* * *

The old black man was playing "Basin Street Blues" when Jennifer stepped into the tavern. She was wearing jeans, a baggy old flannel shirt and a man's leather jacket. This time she didn't stand out.

She'd half feared that she wouldn't find Rook there, but he was the first one she saw, sitting at the same table, nursing a bottle of beer. He looked even more careworn than she remembered, and more formidable. But perhaps she had been too intensely focused on her task last time to have really noticed him.

He looked up as she approached the table, and recognized her immediately. Some part of him had expected this since the moment he had first set eyes on her. He didn't feel that prickle of premonition over fleeting things. But maybe, if he tried real hard, he could sever this connection now, before it went any further. The last thing on earth that he needed was to get tangled up in this woman's machinations.

"May I join you?" she asked.

"No." The single syllable was flat, uncompromising.

Her hands clenched until her knuckles were white. The back of her neck prickled with awareness that a bullet might find her at any instant. Time was running out, and she had to stop her executioner now. "I just need that number you gave me last time."

"Why? Did you find someone else you want knocked off?"

Fury filled her, causing her to lean over the table and glare into his tawny eyes. "Just give me the number, Rook."

"Whatever you're up to, I don't want any part of it."

"You're already part of it! You gave me the damn phone number. I need to stop the guy before he does anything."

The worst of it was knowing that she was right—he *was* already a part of it. But he was damned if he was going to get in any deeper. Nor did he believe her. "No."

"Damn it, I'll go to the cops. What'll they think when they hear you put me in touch with a hit man?"

"Probably not nearly as much as they'll think when they hear you *hired* one."

In that moment she came as close as she ever had to wanting to kill someone. This man was being deliberately obstructive, and she couldn't imagine why. Hadn't she just told him that she wanted to stop the killing? "Please." How she hated to say that word to him. "I've got to stop him!"

"Sorry, darlin'. Once you put that juggernaut in gear, there's no calling it back."

"He can keep the money! I don't care. I just don't want him to carry out the job."

"He won't see it that way." He jabbed a finger at her. "Get it through your head. You don't stop these guys once you start 'em. He's got a contract, and he's going to fulfill it or he'll never work again."

"I refuse to believe that."

"Believe whatever you want, babe. You're shit out of luck."

"At least give me the number so I can try."

He made an exasperated sound. "You think he's going to stop just because some voice on a telephone says she's changed her mind?"

"It's worth a try!"

He shook his head slowly, never taking his eyes from her. "Scram."

She would have liked to grab that bottle of Corona and knock him on the head with it, but it wouldn't do a damn bit of good. After giving him one last long look, she pivoted sharply and stalked out of the bar. No one followed her.

Jesus, Rook thought. What the hell was the woman up to? Did she really think she could pay for someone to be killed and then blithely change her mind? Did she really think she could put events into motion and then stop them midstream? What planet did she come from?

If he had thought she had a snowball's chance in hell of stopping the execution she had ordered merely by contacting the killer, he would have moved heaven and earth. But there wasn't a chance. No contract hit man could be called off by anyone claiming to be the person who had hired him. That was the disadvantage of handling everything so anonymously. The guy that bitch had hired would have no way of being sure she was the same woman. Consequently, nothing would call him off now. His reputation depended on doing the job come hell or high water.

Signaling the waitress for another beer, he shook his head and wondered why he was even wasting a moment's thought on her. She was just like all the rest of her sex: gift wrapped on the outside with soft smiles and delicious bodies, but when you opened 'em, all you found was writhing maggots and rottenness. Like Cheryl. Oh, yes, Cheryl. Lovely ex-Mrs. Galen Rydell, soldier's wife par excellence—until the going got a little tough. Then she hightailed it out of town with the first man who was young enough and rich enough. Christ. All of 'em were lying, cheating, conniving bitches, bent on taking a man for everything he had. Life was better without 'em.

And he was getting drunk and a little too maudlin even for his own taste.

"Mr. Rydell?"

Rook looked up and found a balding guy in jeans and a sweater standing beside his table. He didn't look like the usual regular here. What now? "Yeah?"

The guy flashed a badge. "Detective Lewis, Denver PD. Mind if I ask you a few questions?"

Rook spread his hands, indicating he didn't care. He didn't especially like the idea of being questioned by the police, but there was no particular reason to tell them so.

Lewis pulled up a chair and sat, facing him. "We're doing a little checking up on that woman who was just here talking to you. Have you known Jennifer Fox long?"

"I don't know her at all." He should have listened to that prickling unease he'd gotten the very first time he saw her and should have stayed out of her way no matter what it took.

"She seemed to know *you.*"

"She doesn't."

"That's not the impression I got."

Rook stifled a sigh and wished like hell he had a cigarette. He could just tell them the truth, but somehow he didn't want to do that. He had a constitutional dislike of siccing the cops on anybody. Besides, he didn't know what was *really* going on, anyway. "I didn't even know her name until you told me. How's that? We ran into each other once before and shared a few words. She had some cockamamie idea that I might be interested in sleeping with her." That was at least within the realm of possibility. Women occasionally did want to get into his bed.

Lewis's smile wasn't pleasant. "A high-class dame like her?"

Rook leaned forward, keeping his voice level and his eyes narrow. "Some high-class dames get a thrill out of slumming."

Lewis backed off. "You wouldn't know anything about a lot of cash, would you?"

"If I did, would I be sitting in this dive?"

"The lady made a big cash withdrawal last week. Did she give any to you?"

"I've never slept with anybody for money in my life." He leaned back and smiled. "Might be fun to try sometime."

"What do you do for a living, Mr. Rydell? Apart from drinking beer."

Rook was awfully tempted to tip the bottle of Corona in the idiot's direction, but he refrained. Cops could always come up with a reason to put somebody in the pokey overnight. "I'm a consultant."

Lewis's brow arched disbelievingly. "Who do you consult for?"

"Foreign governments."

"When did carrying a gun become a form of consulting?"

Rydell kept right on smiling, though he was getting a strong urge to wipe the floor with this cop. "I don't carry a gun. I consult. I advise. I help train troops."

"Right." The detective couldn't have poured any more sarcasm into the word.

"You know, Lewis, you'd get a lot further with your questions if you were nice about it."

"I don't have to be nice to slime."

Rydell could have killed him. It would have been simple, really, for a man with his training. But he refrained, simply because Lewis wasn't worth it. "Get out of here. I've said all I'm going to. I don't know the woman, and I don't want to know her."

Ten minutes later, when he was sure that Lewis must have moved on, Rook left the bar by the back exit. Jennifer Fox. At the first phone booth he found with a phone book, he looked her up, but she wasn't listed.

That was when he remembered Alan DeVries. Alan knew who she was, and by God, Alan was going to tell him.

Waiting for a bullet in the brain was nerve-racking. Jennifer found herself staying at home even more over the next couple of days, avoiding sitting or walking near windows. A week ago she had been impatient to die. Now she wanted to live so she could find the bastards who had killed her family.

There was not a doubt in her mind that someone had been out to get her and not Mark. Mark was impossible to hate, and in his job with the school district he did nothing that could have made him this kind of enemy.

But *she* had done plenty of things that made enemies. Every merger she had assisted might make someone mad enough to kill. Sometimes her negotiations cost people their jobs. Often enough, if she served her client well, the opposition lost a great deal of money. Never had she done a dishonest or unethical thing, but other people might not see it that way.

There were also things besides mergers, mainly contract disputes that engendered messy lawsuits between corporations. Those, too, could have made her many enemies.

And, of course, there were some lawyers who had good reason to want her out of the way simply because they didn't like being shown up by a woman. If she had to make a list of the people she thought might wish her dead, she wouldn't have much trouble filling a few pages of paper.

It was a surprisingly sobering thought. All this time she had been living in the rarefied atmosphere of intellectual gamesmanship, loving the wheeling and dealing and the art of negotiation, and she had never really given much thought to the *impact* of what she'd been doing. Nor was it any solace to remind herself that she had *always* been ethical in her dealings. The fact that her hands were clean would be scant comfort to someone who had been hurt by her behavior.

Mark had commented on it a couple of times, in his teasing, gentle way. Oh, nothing overt or hurtful, but she'd been aware that he would have liked her to find some other kind of work. That he had felt her job was changing her.

It *had* changed her, she supposed. She had become decisive, aggressive and impatient with lies. Worse, she had become accustomed to going over every statement with a fine-tooth comb, looking for the hidden meanings that could later cause trouble. That was a particularly difficult trait to turn off, and she was sure that sometimes it had annoyed Mark no end.

But Mark had been a lawyer, too, and he had loved her, and while he might have teased her a tiny bit, he had never held her foibles against her. The love he had given her had been rare.

But all of this was pointless. The one thing she didn't want to think about was that her children and her husband might have died because of *her*. That fear pierced her heart as deeply as their deaths had. An accident, however senseless, was somehow easier to live with than murder. But that they might have been accidental victims of a murderer who had meant to kill *her*... She couldn't bear to contemplate it.

So she had to find a way of stopping the assassin she had put on her own trail, at least long enough for her to find out who the culprit was and see that he, or they, were punished. It was the least she owed her lost family.

But how to stop the hit man? She had no trouble believing Rook was correct when he said that nothing would stop him. Still, it frustrated her that she couldn't at least try to get in touch and put it off. Maybe she ought to try Rook again. Maybe this time, instead of getting angry and demanding, she ought to just simply beg. She had never been the type to get on her knees to anyone, but this time, if that was what it took, that was precisely what she would do.

Because there was no other possible way to track down the man who was going to kill her.

The night had turned stormy, heralding the winter that had already arrived in the mountains to the west of Denver. Jennifer listened to the rattle of sleet on the window glass. It would be dangerous to drive out there tonight, and life had suddenly become very important to her again. She had to survive long enough to avenge her family.

Maybe she wasn't being quite rational. The thought drifted across her mind as she sat at Mark's desk and looked at the photo of them all together. Just last year they had gone to a photographer to have this picture taken. Just last year they had all been so happy and so sure of a bright, beautiful future. It had never crossed her mind that it could all end so abruptly and so terribly.

Whatever her sins, those children hadn't deserved to die.

Her throat tightened until it hurt, and tears burned in her eyes. This time she didn't give in to her grief, however. This time she used it to stoke her rage.

A gust of wind blew sleet against the window with a shotgun rattle. All the curtains in the house were drawn to prevent anyone from seeing in—in order to give her some protection from the assassin she had hired—but she suddenly wished she could draw them back and look out at the wild night. In the past, on such nights, her home had always seemed so cozy, a bastion against the ravening elements. Tonight she felt no such thing. Tonight the elements seemed more inviting than the empty interior of this house.

Suddenly she froze. Unmistakably, from the kitchen, came a hammering sound, as if someone were banging on the back door. Why would anyone come to the back door?

Unless it was the killer come to get her. But wouldn't he break in somehow, rather than announce his presence? Or if he simply wanted to blow her away when she answered his knock, why not come to the front door—which she was more likely to answer? There sure wouldn't be anyone out there to observe him on a night like this.

The hammering came again. She considered not answering it, but some deep-seated instinct to face the threat brought her to her feet. Better the known than the unknown. She had always believed that.

The back door was heavy, a solid-core wood door that she and Mark had installed for security and heat conservation purposes. Just like the front door, it had a peephole. She approached cautiously, glad she had drawn all the curtains in here, too. The kitchen was full of windows, and only the insulating curtains protected her.

She put her eye to the peephole and peered out. The outdoor security lights were on, and she was clearly able to see that a man stood there. She didn't recognize him.

Her heart was already beating fast, but now it slammed into high gear, thundering in her ears. What now? What should she do?

Ignore it. Maybe he would think no one was home. But what if he was a burglar and took that as an opportunity to break in? What would she do then?

He hammered again, no louder, but loud enough. Still hesitating, she looked out again and this time recognized the man called Rook.

Her internal alarms should have sounded wildly at his totally unexpected appearance, but somehow she simply felt relieved that what lay beyond the door was a familiar face.

Opening the door a crack, she peered around it. "What do you want?"

Instead of answering, he put his hand flat against the door and shoved it open, pushing her back into the kitchen. Frightened, she backed up until she was pressed against the counter and could go no farther.

"What do you want?" she demanded again, hating the way her voice cracked.

He didn't answer immediately. Turning, he slammed the door and locked it. Just as she was about to turn and run in the instinctive hope that she could somehow escape him, he crossed the room in two long strides and trapped her against the counter. His hands settled on the tile to either side of her, locking her between his arms.

"I want answers," he said. His tawny eyes were fierce, tigerlike, and his mouth was set in a grim line. He was a big man, and towering over her like this, he made her feel unbearably small.

"Answers?" She was visibly shaking, and her knees felt as if they were going to give way. Oh, God, why had she opened that door?

"Answers," he repeated harshly. "Why did you hire a hit man? Why the hell did the police follow you into the tavern the other night and question me about you?"

She gasped, shocked.

"What is this money they're talking about?"

"Money?"

"And most of all, lady, why the hell is your house under surveillance by cops?"

"I—I didn't know..."

She was stunned, as much by what he had said as by the way he had entered her kitchen. He glowered down at her for another few seconds, then stepped back and released her.

He was so big, she thought yet again, filling her kitchen even as he backed off and allowed her room to breathe. Dressed in jeans and a black ski jacket, he was a dark presence in the softly lit room.

"It's damn cold out there," he told her bluntly. "I stood out there for more than an hour waiting for those cops to be distracted long enough for me to get around back. I nearly froze my damn ass off, and I'm not leaving until I get some answers. Are we clear?"

Jennifer managed a jerky nod. It was as if he had brought the night's iciness inside with him, for she felt cold to the very bone. Shivering, she wrapped her arms around herself and waited the way a mouse waits for the snake to strike.

"Good." He leaned toward her and touched her cheek. It was a soft touch, but it conveyed an unmistakable threat. "Now that we understand each other, why don't you sit down right there—" he indicated the breakfast nook "—and tell me why the cops are watching you?"

She didn't move. She couldn't have moved to save her life. Shaking so hard her teeth nearly chattered, she managed to say, "They think—they think that I—that I killed my husband and children."

Rook settled his hands on his hips and stared at her, his eyes hard. "And the hit man? Who's he supposed to take out?"

Her chin lifted, and she looked straight at him as huge, heavy tears spilled over her lashes. When it emerged, her voice was small and weary. "Me. He's supposed to kill *me*."

"Yeah, and I wasn't born yesterday. What do I have to do to get you to tell me the truth?"

The question hung unpleasantly between them. Looking at him through a blur of tears, Jennifer discovered that her mind was capable of conjuring up quite a few terrifying methods of persuasion, and this man looked capable of resorting to even the most cruel of them. But she had already reached the absolute nadir of her existence, and she had only one goal left in life. This man who was threatening her was the only one who could help her achieve it.

The realization that she had nothing left to lose, nothing at all in the whole wide world, banished her fear and left her once again in the grip of the rage that had driven her since the FAA had called her.

"I *am* telling you the truth," she heard herself say as anger swept through her, squaring her shoulders and strengthening her. "Somebody killed my husband and children, and I want to find them. I want to find them and kill them. I want *revenge.* Will you help me?"

"You expect me to believe—"

She interrupted him. "Six months ago they left on my husband's plane for a vacation. I was supposed to be with them, but something came up at work, so I had to stay behind. They crashed. All I've wanted to do for six months was die. Do you hear me? I just wanted to die. But I had to think of my parents, so it couldn't look like suicide. So finally I came to you, and you gave me the phone number."

He was watching her with narrowed eyes, but he didn't interrupt.

"Only—only just three days after I paid the hit man to kill me, the FAA called and said that someone had—someone had—" She had to stop and draw a couple of deep, ragged breaths. "Someone had sabotaged the plane. The cops think maybe I did it. I *know* I didn't do it, but I want the blood of the person who did. So I came to you again about getting in touch with the hit man. I don't want to die now, Rook. I don't want to die until later. Because first I have to find the person who killed my children and my husband. I have to! Will you help me?"

He stared at her for long moments, saying nothing. He didn't even blink. Then he pivoted on his heel, unlocked the kitchen door and strode out into the frigid night.

Jennifer stared after him, alone with the rattle of sleet on the windows.

Never had she felt so desolate.

4

Rook slipped out of the house into the blustery night, feeling the sting of sleet against his cheeks. The soft ice had begun to accumulate on the grass, making the ground treacherous. Winter was descending from the mountains.

The cops were still parked out front in their unmarked car. Streetlights kept the street bright and puddled light on Jennifer Fox's front yard. From where the policemen were parked, they would be able to see anything that twitched in front of the house, and privacy fences in the rear made that direction of escape undesirable. Oh, he could clamber over an eight-foot fence without any trouble, but he had no way of knowing what lay on the other side. A vicious dog or an alert homeowner could bring the cops right down on his head.

He swore under his breath, blaming all his frustration and anger on the cold night, reluctant to think about the woman he had just left. He didn't want to think about her feelings or her problems, because if he did, he might start to give a damn about them.

Christ, what were these cops doing? If they honestly believed she had killed her husband and kids, they couldn't really think she was going to do something to prove it. Unless that big withdrawal they had mentioned had convinced them that someone else was involved, too. The money she had most likely gotten to pay for her own execution could very well look like serious hush money to the police. Anyone she had contact with now would be under suspicion.

Well, he sure as hell didn't want to be on that list—although he probably already was. He didn't want to freeze his fingers and toes off, either, but he didn't want to give the cops any more reason to suspect him of complicity.

Sooner or later one of those guys would have to get an urge to pee. He would just have to wait.

Hunkered down against the side of the house so that he could just see around the corner and keep tabs on the cops, he shivered and tried not to think about what Jennifer Fox had told him. Tried not to think about the anguish in those green eyes of hers. If that woman had killed her kids, he would eat his hat.

The cops didn't move, and neither did he. The night grew colder, the stinging needles of sleet giving way to softer flakes of snow. At this rate he would be stuck here all night and they would find his frozen corpse in the morning. He'd always figured he would buy it from a bullet in some tropical hell—there wasn't much call for mercenaries in cold climates. Somebody ought to do a nice piece of academic research on that fact. It would all be bullshit, of course, but it would sound good....

The attempt to distract himself didn't work. He couldn't stop thinking about Jennifer Fox and the anguish in her wet green eyes. Christ, the woman was in trouble so deep that an accusation of murder looked like tun by comparison. Nobody could stop a hit man. Why was he even thinking of it?

But finally, disgusted with himself, with the cops, with Jennifer Fox and the whole world in general—not to mention Jay Miller, who wasn't supposed to know any hit men—Rook rose to his feet and strode around to the back door once again.

He was sure as hell going to regret this.

When Jennifer heard the knock on the door, she was huddled at the table, feeling colder and more alone than she would have believed possible. She felt as if an icy wind were blowing through her soul, emptying her of everything except the deepest despair. Even her anger drowned in the tidal wave of hopelessness.

She was past railing at fate or feeling sorry for herself. Past feeling anything at all except a bleakness so pervasive she was empty even of herself. She sat, staring blankly, waiting like a dumb animal for the next blow. Nothing was within her control. Not even the one thing she had believed she was at last able to control: her own death. Her puny efforts made no difference at all before the inexorability of fate.

Why bother?

The knock sounded again, and she stirred, no longer caring who might be on the other side of the door. There wasn't a thing she could do about what was destined to be. She didn't even bother to look through the peephole before flinging the door wide open.

Rook Rydell stepped out of the freezing night into the warmth of her kitchen and locked the door behind him. For long moments he stood and stared into her eyes, saying nothing, seeking something.

And that was when Rook realized that, cold as he was, this woman was colder, and in a far worse way. Something in her had snapped.

"Sit down," he told her roughly.

She obeyed, watching with dull eyes as he rummaged around the kitchen and eventually found the coffee. He used her drip coffeemaker as confidently as if it were his own. Only when the coffee was brewing did he at last look at her.

"Why do they think you killed your family?"

Her head jerked a little, as if his words hurt. Good, he thought. Good. She was thawing out a little. So was he, for that matter. He yanked down the zipper on his jacket.

"There has to be a reason," he said harshly.

"I...don't know." Slowly her gaze lifted to his, and there was something stirring in the depths of her green eyes. "I mean, they didn't give me a reason. They didn't exactly come right out and say it. It's just that the spouse is always the first suspect...."

"Because it's *usually* the spouse who commits the murder."

Her chin jerked again. "You don't think I..." Her voice trailed off as her throat closed. She couldn't say the words. Even from the abyss of despair, she couldn't say those words again.

"I didn't say that. I just want to know what happened. Can *you* think of any reason they would suspect you?"

She closed her eyes tightly, reaching for some of the backbone and steel that had made her a formidable lawyer. For some of the resilience that had always been there for her—until the death of her family. Surely there had to be something left inside her. She couldn't just be an empty husk awaiting execution.

"Can you?" he demanded again. He watched her struggle to connect thoughts, to find speech, and something deep inside him stirred. *Shut up,* he told it. The Don Quixotes of the world tended to get badly bashed up. He'd left those stupid impulses behind a long time ago.

"I...I guess because I wasn't on the plane. I was supposed to be, but I got a call and couldn't go...." Her voice trailed off again as she found herself reliving horrible events. She should have been there. *She should have been on that plane!*

"Cut it out!" Rook's harsh command jabbed into the mire that was sucking her down, and yanked her out. "Jesus, lady, some people live and some people die and the stupidest damn thing you can do is ruin your life feeling guilty because you didn't buy it, too."

She looked up, ready to argue, tired of advice from people who didn't know. But he *did* know. Looking into his tawny eyes, she saw the certain light of knowledge. The words stayed locked in her throat.

He yanked a chair out from the table and straddled it, facing her. "When are you going to get over this self-pity gig?"

Shock locked her breath in her throat. How dare he?

"Get off the pity pot, lady. People die. People lose their loved ones. Fathers die, mothers die, kids die, and the rest of us just have to pick up and go on. Grieve, but don't drown in it."

Anger sparked deep within her, burning away the dark, suffocating cloud of despair. "Fuck you," she said tautly.

"That's better." Rising, he hunted through her cupboards until he found two mugs. He filled them both with black coffee and set one in front of her. "If you don't like it straight, find your own sugar and cream."

God, what a boor, she thought, glaring at him. How could she have, even for one insane moment, been intrigued by him? "Why don't you get the hell out of my house?"

"Because the cops are out front and it's cold outside. Because you need somebody to get a hit man out of your hair."

Everything inside her stilled, hushing like the depths of a snow-filled night. Her voice was little more than a whisper. "You'll help me?"

"If I had half a brain, I'd say no, but . . . I'm thinking about it."

The return of hope, however slender, was nearly as painful as the complete loss of it. Resignation and emptiness had a strange, cold comfort. Hope brought with it the possibility of more hurt and disappointment. She almost wanted to reject it.

"How do they know your family was murdered?" he asked her.

"I don't really understand the mechanics of it. The FAA investigator said they found metal filings in the fuselage, which indicate that the elevator cables were nearly cut before they took off. I don't even know what an elevator is!"

"The tail of a plane has movable airfoils that are called elevators because they control the up and down movement of the plane. If the cables controlling them snapped, the plane would nosedive."

She struggled not to see it in her mind's eye, not to hear how her children must have screamed as their father struggled to save them. Those screams had been haunting her dreams for months. How many seconds—or, worse, minutes—had they suffered through that dive? "That's pretty much what happened."

"And they're sure it wasn't an accident?" Although he already knew the answer to that, since they had found metal filings.

"Sure enough that the FAA informed the police."

"And sicced them on you."

"I... don't think so. The man from the FAA called me to warn me of the findings before they hit the papers, and he kind of... hinted that I would be the first person the police would look at. I don't think he suspected me at all."

"Who do *you* suspect?"

"God, I don't know. There are so many people who..." She allowed her voice to trail away as she stared off into space, battering down unwanted memories. She had to stay in control of herself, even if she could control nothing else. It wasn't easy. For months she had been like a weather vane, turning helplessly in the winds of her heart and soul. If she was ever to get revenge, she had to stop letting her emotions control her that way.

Rook sipped his coffee, grateful for the bitter warmth of it, and watched her struggle with herself. He wondered how she could be any good as a lawyer when everything she thought was written so plainly on her face. It was almost like mind reading.

Finally, apparently reaching some inner compromise with whatever was tearing her apart, she reached for her own coffee and sipped it. No cream and sugar. Somehow that seemed appropriate for her. "I want to get whoever did it."

"The police should do that." Not that he was brimming over with confidence in the cops. Generally they looked for the easiest suspect and then built a case to fit—at least, from what he'd seen.

"They aren't doing that if they're investigating me and staking out my house." She shook her head as if to emphasize her words. "I want to get my hands on the person who did this. The only thing I want to do in my life is kill him."

"Revenge is a bitter pill, Lady Fox." The nickname slipped out before he realized he had created it, and he wanted to kick himself. What was he doing? Putting this woman above him on some kind of social ladder? Falling into the pit of quixotism? Yeah, she was some Dulcinea.

"It's all I've got left."

"I hate to repeat myself, but get off the pity pot. You've got forty or fifty years left, plenty of time to bury the dead, make peace with your ghosts and build a new life." Christ, listen to him! What a joke! He couldn't even get past his *own* stupid past.

"I don't want a new life. I want to make a murderer suffer the way he made my children suffer. Do you have any idea what it must have been like for them when they were...crashing?"

"Thinking like that isn't going to fix anything. How old were your kids?"

"Eli was six. Bethany was almost two."

He hadn't imagined them to be so young. Somehow that tore at him. He knew the kind of scum that could hurt kids that young, and it was the kind of scum that ought to be crushed under a man's boot heel. "I'm sorry."

Looking at him, she believed he really was. A trace of the ice inside her thawed. "Thank you."

"Well, I won't buy into the revenge thing," he said after a moment. "That's something that tends to backfire, and I don't want any part of it. I'll help you find the scum, but you ought to turn him over to the cops."

"If you want to help me, you'll have to accept that that's going to be *my* decision."

He felt a flicker of admiration for her. Down as she was, depressed as she was, she could still dicker about terms. Maybe she *was* a hell of a lawyer. "We'll leave that for now. The main thing I'm concerned with is saving your neck. What the hell possessed you to put out a contract on yourself? Jesus, woman, you must be nuts!"

She shrugged. "Probably."

"If you're so determined to die, why didn't you just kill yourself?"

"Because of my family. I just decided that it would be easier on them if they thought I was the victim of a random murder."

Simultaneously he felt a deep spear of anger and another faint flicker of admiration for her. She thought further than most suicides, but that didn't excuse her. "You don't make sense."

"That's not my problem."

"No, but it could be mine if you start acting crazy."

"I won't."

Apparently he was supposed to rely on that. Rising, he went to get another cup of coffee. "Want a refill?"

"No. Thank you."

He ought to get out of this right now, he told himself. There was no telling what this woman might do in her search for revenge. As a suicide she had proved unpredictable. How could he trust that she wouldn't be erratic in every other way?

But he kept sticking at the thought of those two little kids. Nobody capable of killing kids ought to get away with it. Not little kids who looked at the world with big eyes full of trust. Once there had been a pair of eyes that had looked at him that way.... He brushed the memory aside, refusing to give it a foothold. Living in the past was a waste of time, even when there wasn't a future worth looking forward to.

"You know," he said finally, "I'm willing to get involved to stop the hit because I feel I'm responsible for it."

"You're not. If you hadn't given me that number, I'd have found someone who would."

"Well, it doesn't feel that way to me. So figure I'm going to save your hide so I can sleep at night. The rest of it—I'll get involved because of your kids. Because a scumbag who would do that needs to be caught. But don't ever get the idea I'm doing any of this for *you.*"

She wondered why he felt a need to tell her that, then shrugged it aside. His motives didn't matter, only that he would help her. "Whatever. I just need to put this hit man off until I can find the killer."

"No, you don't understand." He leaned forward, his tawny eyes boring into her. "Your money's gone, Lady Fox. Because if I find the man, I'm going to have to kill him to stop him. Because nothing short of death will do it."

"But—couldn't you just... disable him?"

"You don't get it, do you?" He shook his head, wondering how someone who was so obviously bright could be so damn obtuse. "I'm going to *stop* him, for *me*. And there's only one way to do it."

She looked at him steadily, weighing her only two options. "All right." Revenge was more important to her. Catching the murderer was something she *had* to do. She would worry about her own death later. "Where do we begin?"

"You start by telling me how the hit man contacted you and what you remember about the conversation."

"I don't see what good that'll do. We talked for only a couple of minutes. Neither of us said very much."

"How did he tell you to contact him?"

"Just to dump the money and information in a trash bin behind a convenience store. There's no other way for me to contact him."

"Was there anything memorable about his voice?"

She sighed, closing her eyes and trying to remember. She'd been so stunned by the call, stunned by the amount of money he wanted, that she didn't retain a very clear memory. "It was rough, low. I hardly remember what we said."

"What did you tell him about yourself?"

"Just my name and address, the make and model of my car and its tag number. I figured that was enough. And I gave him a couple of photographs."

Shit. He didn't know why, but he'd been hoping she hadn't given him enough to go on. "We've got to get you the hell out of here."

She nodded slowly. "I guess so. But where would I go?"

"Let me think about this. Getting you out of here isn't exactly going to be a piece of cake. Not unless we can get rid of those cops. We also have to consider the possibility that the hired gun is watching this place, too."

"Which means he might know *you're* here."

The back of his scalp crawled, even though he'd already considered that possibility. "Could be. This is going to require some tactical genius, I guess. Maybe you ought to just head on up to bed and let me stew about it for a while."

Her stomach fluttered uneasily. "You're staying here?"

His golden eyes dared her to argue. "Damn straight. It's cold out, and there's no frigging way I'm going to sit outside and figure out how to get past those cops. Get used to it, lady. I'm here until I figure out how to get us both out of here. Now get your butt to bed. I'll make sure nobody cuts your throat in your sleep."

She hadn't even considered that possibility. Never had she fully imagined anything except a bullet slapping into her unexpectedly and ending it all before she knew what had happened. But having her throat cut... Her stomach turned over. "He said it would be quick and painless."

Rook shook his head in disgust. "Jeez, you're naive. He's going to take you out in the way that's quickest and easiest for *him*. He might do it from a distance with a sniper rifle, but that's not as certain as moving in close and taking you out some other way. He doesn't care if it's painless. What are you going to do? File a complaint with his boss?"

The feeling of being trapped in a nightmare was washing over her again, and she struggled to batter it down. "He promised, and he took my money."

Rook released an exasperated breath. "Forget it. All that matters is that he's going to kill you unless we stop him first. Just trust me—he'll be ready to take advantage of *any* opportunity. So we have to stash you someplace where he can't find you."

Jennifer's head snapped up. "I don't want to be *stashed.* I've got to find the murderer, and I can't do that if I'm hiding somewhere."

"You're going to have to hide away until we get this damn assassin off your back!" His voice was getting louder, and he wondered if he had *ever* dealt with a woman this frustrating. "Come on, Counselor, use your brain!"

She glared at him as if he had just slapped her. A moment later, however, her anger faded into weary agreement. "You're right. Sorry. It's just that I'm feeling like a rat trapped in a very small maze with no alternate paths and no solution. I've been running around and around about this until my brain is fried."

"I imagine so. Just go get some sleep. Your brain'll work better in the morning. In the meantime, I'll make sure you're safe."

She looked at him, taken unawares by the first real emotion other than grief and anger she had felt since the crash. What she felt made tears well in her eyes and her heart ache with yearning. *I'll make sure you're safe.* God, she couldn't remember the last time she had felt safe.

Rook looked away, unnerved by the emotion he saw in her eyes. "All the lights are on upstairs." He had noticed that when he approached the house. Every window was ablaze with light.

"Yes." Tonight she had needed to hold back all the shadows.

"Well, either leave them all on, or turn off the light in some other room last. If the gunman's watching, he'll assume that's the one you're going to sleep in."

"Oh!"

"And turn off all these down here on your way up. Who knows? If the cops think you've gone to bed, they might get lazy."

"Okay."

He watched her switch off the kitchen light and walk away, and thought that maybe he was losing his marbles at last.

Rook moved from window to window in the darkened house, checking latches while taking care not to catch the attention of a watcher outside. Being cautious made it a long, tedious process, but it also made him very familiar with the ground floor of this house. If someone should happen to break in, he would have the advantage in the dark.

The cops remained outside, but he was willing to bet that their vigilance would taper off in an hour or so when they truly believed that Jennifer had turned in for the night. They might even leave until dawn.

If they did, he had to get her out of here while they were away. But what about the gunman?

Hell. The thought processes of a hit man were as alien to him as a Martian's. He could only guess how the guy might be weighing this situation . . . if he was even stalking Jennifer yet. It was entirely possible that he was on another job right now, or was just postponing this one. After all, the guy must know his target was the woman who had hired him. It was entirely possible that even though he had the money he suspected a trap of some kind and was going to hold off until he was sure about the setup.

The more Rook thought about it, the more he considered it a distinct possibility. After all, if he were in the gunman's shoes, he would sure as hell wonder why someone was willing to pay him a huge chunk of money to do something they could do themselves for the price of a gun or a bottle of pills. It would make him even more suspicious when Jennifer, instead of making an easy target of herself, started to hide.

That might buy them some time, but it was nothing he could count on.

It was, to put it mildly, a rotten situation. The cops, not knowing what the real threat was, would provide no useful protection at all. Hell, if he himself had gotten around to the back and into the house, the hit man certainly could. And her being tailed everywhere by the police would only make it easier for the gunman to tail *her.* So he had to cut her free of the whole kit and caboodle and stash her someplace where no one would ever think to look for her.

There was his mountain cabin. He didn't really want to take her there, but that was because he didn't want to take *anyone* there. A couple of his friends knew of its existence, but none of them had ever been there, and he intended to keep it that way.

He had learned the hard way that buildings, particularly the ones a person lived in, collected memories. He'd once had to sell a house because there wasn't a room in it that he could walk into without remembering his ex-wife. He didn't want his cabin to become like that, filled with memories of other people. He had intended that it would never have any memories at all except those that he made all by himself. To make his solitude complete, there had to be nothing and no one there except himself. Memories were definitely unwelcome.

What the hell did he have to remember, anyway? The wife who'd deserted him? The army that had betrayed him? The ash heaps of all the broken dreams? No, there was nothing in the past worth recalling.

Taking care not to stir the curtains, he peered between them out the living room window. The cop car was still there. It was snowing for real now—big, wet flakes that had begun to cover the world. The guys in the car were evidently getting weary, because it had been a few minutes since they had turned on their windshield wipers. Their tracks were still visible, but soon they wouldn't be able to see out the window any longer. The snow was even beginning to cake the side windows.

Excitement began to spread its tendrils through him, a sparkling sort of alertness. He might be able to get Jennifer out of here tonight. Those guys might well have dozed off, which would explain the accumulating snow. He doubted they would sleep long, because the car wasn't running and they were going to get cold, but this could be a window of opportunity.

Turning from the window, he hurried up the stairs, wondering which room she had taken. Somehow he suspected she'd gotten the hint not to sleep in the master bedroom.

She had. He found her curled up fully clothed on the twin bed in a little boy's room. Her arms were wrapped around a teddy bear.

He didn't want to be affected by it. The last thing on earth he wanted was to feel anything for this woman other than disgust at the mess she'd gotten herself into with this crazy notion to hire an executioner.

There was little light to see by, just the faint glow of the streetlights that reflected off the falling snow and sifted through cheerful curtains over the bed. He'd been in the dark for the past two hours, though, and his eyes had adapted enough that he could see the soft curves of the woman's cheek, could tell how tightly her hands clutched that teddy bear, could even see the faint glimmer of a tear trail from the corner of her eye. She was crying in her sleep.

Christ.

How could life be so goddamn brutal? Nobody deserved to lose a family, not an earthquake survivor, not someone caught in a battle zone, not some poor woman lawyer whose worst crime in her entire life had probably been to reduce some jackass's profit margin.

Not that he cared much for lawyers. The one that had represented him at the court-martial had been about as useful as teats on a bull. But it remained that no one deserved a loss of such magnitude. No one ought to be left with nothing to hold but memories and a teddy bear.

A pressure started to grow in his chest, but he battered it down. He didn't have any sympathy left to waste, and he sure as hell didn't want to feel anything at all for this woman. Caring just got in the way of reality, fogged the brain and clouded the impulses. He would be no use to her if he gave a damn whether she lived or died.

Steeling himself against the poignant sight of the teddy bear, he crossed the room and touched her shoulder. She jerked awake in instant terror, but other than a gasp, she didn't make a sound.

"It's okay," he said roughly. "It's just me."

"What's wrong?"

"Nothing. Just get some stuff together, warm clothes that you can wear in the snow. I'm getting you out of here tonight, and we're going up to the mountains. Dress for it."

Then, as if he feared the shadows of her grief might somehow reach out and snare him, he turned and left the room, plunging Jennifer once again into the shadow-filled emptiness.

5

Through the crack between the curtains, Rook peered out at the unmarked car. The snow was thicker on its windows now, impossible to see through, even out the side. The cops were definitely asleep.

"Hurry up," he called up the stairs, keeping his voice down. The potential danger had shot up the minute it became apparent that the cops were no longer paying attention to the house. If the hit man *was* watching the place, he would choose right now to move in.

He could hear Jennifer moving around upstairs, but she was being hampered by lack of light. He knew she was hurrying, but fast might not be fast enough right now.

Moving silently, he went to the kitchen and peered around curtains, looking for any sign of movement. The snow magnified what little light there was outside, making the night unexpectedly bright. If anything moved in the backyard, he would see it.

Nothing stirred. He heard Jennifer come down the stairs, her steps light and nearly silent despite the heavy boots she must be wearing. The woman had potential, he thought automatically, then realized he wasn't going to be training her for covert operations. At least, he didn't think he would have to.

When she entered the room behind him, it was the merest whisper of sound, nylon against nylon. Wool was better for operations like this, more silent, but he couldn't exactly run out and get her a proper jacket right now. She was stuck with her ski parka.

"Come here," he said quietly. When she stood beside him, he stepped back. "Watch the backyard. If you even *think* you see anything move, even if it's just a small shadow, you tell me when I get back, hear?"

She nodded.

Leaving her behind, he slipped through the dark house to the front once again, to make sure the windows of the unmarked car were still covered with snow. They were, and thicker than before. Boy, weren't those guys going to be embarrassed when they realized their quarry had given them the slip while they snoozed? Rook grinned into the darkness, enjoying the thought.

In the kitchen, he opened the back door and stood listening. Jennifer waited patiently, a heavy suit bag hanging from her shoulder. Smart move, he thought as he looked at her and listened to the night outside. The bag was bulky but could be easily carried.

No unusual sounds from without. The snow had muffled the world, deadening even the most usual noises. Occasionally he could hear the distant sound of a car on wet pavement, but nothing else indicated they weren't the only people alive.

"We're going around the side of the house," he whispered to her, pointing. "Move as quietly as you can, and stay close to the building. When we get to the front we have to move *fast*. Stay right on my heels. If I tell you to do something, do it immediately without questioning me, okay?"

She nodded, her eyes two huge, glistening pools in the dark.

He waited a few more moments, making sure once again that nothing moved in the backyard. There was a soft *plop-plop* as water dripped from the eaves, but nothing else. He stepped out, hearing the *swish* as she moved right behind him.

The snow was only a couple of inches deep, but it was wet snow, and the ground was slippery. He wished he was wearing a decent pair of boots instead of these smooth-soled cowboy boots he wore in town. Jennifer was keeping her feet better than he was.

He moved cautiously, not wanting to make unnecessary noise until there was no longer any choice. They would be going around the side of the house that the cops couldn't see from their car, so there was no need to hurry until they got out front.

But as he approached the rear corner of the house, something made him freeze. He wasn't sure what it was, but he'd been in situations like this too damn often to ignore the intuition. Quickly he signaled Jennifer to be quiet and stay where she was. When she nodded, he moved forward to peer around the corner of the house.

At first glance he saw nothing at all, but then his gaze zeroed in on disturbed snow alongside the house. It led up to the trunk of the tall blue spruce tree. Could that have been where he had walked earlier? But no, it looked too recent.

Christ! Hyperalert now, he started breathing through his mouth as he scanned the area. Someone had been there not too long ago. They hadn't come all the way around the house, to judge by the disturbed snow. Hiding in the bushes, maybe? But why, when no one was out here . . . ?

Slowly his gaze moved upward, following the trunk of the towering blue spruce. Just then a branch stirred, and a clump of wet snow fell with a plop.

Someone was in that tree.

He yanked his head back around the corner of the house and grabbed Jennifer's arm. "Someone's out there," he whispered quietly. "We're going the other way." As long as the cops hadn't wakened. But when he came right down to it, he would prefer to be stopped by the cops right now than by whoever was climbing that tree to the second story of the house.

Jennifer chose that moment to balk. "Why?" she whispered. "What's wrong?"

"Keep moving," he told her sharply. "Somebody's out there. Now hurry."

She stared at him for just an instant, then turned to obey. Both of them, he guessed, had a pretty good idea who was hanging around her house at this hour of the morning.

He had to get Jennifer out of here and to his car before the guy discovered no one was home. It would be too damn easy to follow his and Jennifer's tracks through the snow, and the guy would do precisely that. Rook wanted Jennifer safely in his car so she could get away if anything happened to him when he came back to face the hit man.

The windshield and side windows of the patrol car were still layered thickly in snow. The humor of it no longer struck him, however. He was just grateful they didn't have to contend with that.

He turned to Jennifer. "See the cops? Now we move fast, but as quiet as we can. My car's around the corner and we have to get to it before anybody notices us, okay?"

She nodded her understanding. "But why don't you go back in the house and face the guy?"

"Because you're with me. It's too damn dangerous. When I take him out, I want you to be as far away as possible. Just as soon as I get you out of the way up the street, I'll come back."

"But I could just go over and wake the police officers up...."

"He'll take them both out rather than get caught. And even if he gets away without killing them, you'll still have your police tail—which is so damn obvious you might as well wear an orange sign with flashing neon lights. Now let's get going before he discovers you aren't in there."

She followed him without further argument. Thank God for that. Of all the damn fool times to start asking questions!

He led the way around the front of the neighbor's house, keeping close to the shrubbery and avoiding the open space of the sidewalk. Their trail was still easy to follow, but they weren't as obvious.

The air was cold, clear, as fresh as it ever was in Denver, smelling like snow. Flakes still fell steadily, getting smaller as the temperature dropped. Rook heard the sound of a car approaching. He tugged Jennifer into the shadows beneath a tall tree and waited as the vehicle drew nearer. When it reached the corner, it skidded through the stop sign and turned dangerously, coming down Jennifer's street far too fast. A drunk.

Tensely, holding Jennifer close to his side, Rook watched the car. It was going to wake the cops. He hoped they would give up their stakeout and go after the jerk.

But the car skidded again, and this time it slammed into the unmarked police car with a deafening bang and a shriek of steel.

Rook stiffened, battling an impulse to go to the aid of the people in the cars. Jennifer. He had to protect her first.... He turned to her.

"Keep heading up the street. Stay close to the shrubs and in the shadows as much as possible. Around the corner, on the far side of the street, there's a white Explorer. Get in and start it. If you see anybody but me come around that corner, get the hell out of there. Understand?" He pressed the keys into her hand.

"Where are you going?"

"I've got to see if anyone's hurt. I want you out of the way in case the gunman comes out of your house. Now, damn it, get going!"

She gave him one last look, then turned and began moving swiftly away. Rook waited until she seemed to melt away under the trees that filled the front yards of these old homes. Only then did he trot toward the smashed cars.

The driver of the vehicle that had skidded was climbing out of his car by the time Rook got over there. The man was dazed, reeking of alcohol, totally confused about what was going on. He didn't appear to be injured at all.

No one had even tried to get out of the police car yet. When Rook bent down to the passenger door, getting ready to open it, a chill suddenly snaked along his spine. *Someone was watching him.*

Quickly he glanced over his shoulder. The other driver was leaning against the back of his car, holding his head as if he was about to vomit. Nothing else on the street moved.

Forcing himself to ignore the chill of warning, he yanked open the car door, wondering if the cops were even inside. They were. His gut twisted at what he found.

They had both been shot to death.

The chill prickle at the base of his skull intensified, and he whirled around, looking up and down the street. Nothing moved except the moaning driver of the other car. Nothing disturbed the peace of the night except his own uneasiness. Someone was looking at him. Someone had identified him.

Christ. He looked at the cops one last time. Nothing he could do for them now. Leaving them, he grabbed the shoulder of the other driver. "Go knock on one of the doors and ask them to call for help."

The drunk looked at him, barely focusing his eyes.

"Go on," Rook said, shoving him a little. "Over there. The lights are coming on. Go ask them for help."

The man nodded finally and began to shamble in that direction. Glancing one last time up at the second floor of Jennifer's house, Rook thought he saw a curtain twitch. He thought about going in there after the man, then discarded the idea. He'd been spotted, and the gunman knew the cops had been found. He wouldn't hang around now, not when a whole army of policemen was probably going to arrive within minutes. No, he would be out the back way and over the fence before Rook could get across the street. He might even go after Jennifer.

They had to get out of here *now*.

Rook took off toward his car, his boots skidding wildly on the snow, giving him about as much control as that drunk had had over his car, but he managed to stay on his feet anyway. Wheeling around the corner, he grabbed a lamppost for balance, then slid to a halt by the driver's door of the Explorer.

Jennifer had followed his directions and was huddled behind the steering wheel, trying to be inconspicuous while she kept the engine running. When she saw Rook approaching, she unlocked the driver's door and climbed over into the passenger seat.

"What happened?" she asked.

"Later. We've got to get out of here." He wasted no time doing exactly that. His studded snow tires gave them good traction on the wet snow and sometimes icy pavement. He turned them around in the middle of the street, not wanting to cross over Jennifer's street again, and headed for the highway, knowing his only hope of losing a tail in the snow was to get to a place where his tire tracks would disappear.

Jennifer snapped on her seat belt out of habit, then twisted in the seat, watching Rook and wondering if she had lost her mind. What was she doing running off into the night with a man she didn't even know?

As she had huddled in the car, trying to ignore the chill that was creeping into her fingers and toes, she'd wondered if she was totally mistaken in this man. What if he was the hit man? He could be. The whole thing with the phone number might have been a ruse so she wouldn't guess he was the one she was hiring. Alan DeVries had sent her to him, after all.

But then she realized that it didn't make sense. If he wanted to kill her, he had had ample opportunity. Why not when she had opened the door to him? Why not when she was sleeping? Besides, the way he had gone back to help the people in the accident didn't fit with her notion of a hired killer.

But she still didn't know what kind of a man he was. He apparently intended to kill the man she had hired. What kind of man did that make Rook? He was a mercenary, she knew that much from DeVries, and mercenaries were willing to fight and kill for money. Maybe it was stupid, but somehow it sounded better to her when people were willing to be soldiers for ideological reasons rather than pecuniary ones.

What did it matter, anyway? He had said he would help her find her family's murderer. Nothing else was of any consequence now.

"Hang on," he warned her.

She braced her hands on the dash as they cornered sharply. The Explorer skidded briefly, but the studs quickly caught pavement, and they sped forward again.

"Where are we going?" she asked him.

"Into the mountains."

"Why?"

"I'm going to hide you while I figure out how to make you safe."

"What did you see back there? Did you see who was in my house?"

"No."

"Then why are we in such a hurry? Were the cops hurt? Did they see you?"

"The cops were dead."

Trepidation trickled through her. "That collision wasn't that hard, was it?"

"No."

"Then..." Her voice trailed off. "Rook, you're not making any sense."

They were on the ramp to the interstate now. There weren't many other cars around, but there *were* cars. The pavement here was mostly just wet, with occasional patches of snow. He speeded up, taking care not to exceed the speed limit by more than five miles an hour. He didn't want to stop or be stopped for any reason.

"What happened?" she asked him again.

He turned to look at her. The dashboard lights didn't give a whole lot of illumination, but it was enough for her to see how hard his face had become.

"The cops were dead," he repeated.

"But... how?"

"Both of them had been shot."

For a second or two, it was as if he'd spoken Greek. She couldn't comprehend the words. When their meaning sank home, horror washed over her. "But... why?"

"They must have spotted him. Threatened him somehow."

Falling snow had always reminded her of Christmas. In the past the association had been joyous, causing her to think of baking cookies and shopping for toys. Now its beauty faded, leaving nothing but the frigid picture of winter she would hereafter associate with death.

"I'm sorry," she heard herself say pointlessly. Her mind was scrabbling wildly for purchase amidst a storm of emotions she couldn't begin to put names to. Or perhaps she didn't want to name them.

"What the hell for?"

"If I hadn't hired that man..." If she hadn't hired that man, those cops would be looking forward to

Christmas with their families. Oh, God, she couldn't bear this!

"It wasn't your fault," Rook said. "Look, you couldn't have known that you were going to have a police tail, or that something would happen to make him feel threatened by the cops."

That was supposed to relieve her of responsibility? "It's my fault."

"Right. It's your fault the world was made the way it was. It's your fault that this guy is bent in some strange way. Christ, woman, killing those cops was an act of supreme stupidity! Even if they saw him and questioned him about what he was doing, he shouldn't have killed them. Do you think the police are ever going to stop looking for him now? He put his ass in a real crack."

"But if I hadn't hired him..."

"If you hadn't hired him, he'd have found an excuse to kill somebody else." And what did he care whether she felt responsible for the deaths of those cops? She'd hired the guy. Maybe she *was* responsible. "Or try it another way. He didn't kill those cops because you hired him. He killed them because they threatened him—and you didn't have a damn thing to do with that."

She shivered and looked away. Icy needles of reality were beginning to prick through the layers of grief that had muffled her mind for so many months now. She had hired a hit man. It was as if she were suddenly faced with the *reality* of it, as if she had been seeing the whole thing through some kind of haze until this very moment. And all of a sudden it was in sharp—painfully sharp—focus.

My God, she had lost her mind. It was one thing to wish she was dead, another entirely to hire someone to commit an act of murder. She had induced someone to commit a serious crime. How could she even for a moment have considered it acceptable simply because she wanted to die?

And now, because of her, two other families would experience the same kind of grief that made her want to die. God, what had she been thinking of?

Nor was the worst of it over yet. What if the man killed others on his way to her?

She turned to Rook. "Take me back."

They were now on I-70, heading west toward the mountains. Without a word, he wheeled them down an exit ramp. Jennifer was astonished at his quick compliance. He struck her as a stubborn man, and she had expected to have to argue mightily with him.

But then he switched off his lights, turned into a deserted parking lot and stopped behind a building so that they were concealed from the highway by a huge trash bin.

"What—"

"Quiet." He slid out of the car and disappeared around the trash bin.

Fear began rising in her again. Had they been followed? The back of her neck prickled with the awareness that someone could come up behind her. Quickly she turned, but she saw nothing except the empty night.

He had turned the engine off, and its ticking as it cooled down was loud in the otherwise silent night. The snow had stopped falling, but the clouds hadn't cleared away. The sky reflected the dull pinkish glow of the city lights. It was bright enough to see if anyone approached, but that didn't ease her fear any.

"Okay." Rook was suddenly there, climbing into the car.

"We weren't followed?"

"Apparently not, but I wanted to be absolutely certain before we got any farther out of town. It only gets harder to hide."

Especially at this hour, when hardly anyone was on the road. "Take me back, please."

He ignored her, driving up the westbound ramp.

"Rook, please."

"Why?"

"Because that man may kill other people. There's only one way to put an end to this before someone else gets hurt. Before you have to do something awful yourself."

"So you're just going to offer yourself as a sacrificial lamb?"

"I'll go to the police. I'll tell them everything."

"In the first place, killing you isn't going to stop the hit man from killing someone else. Believe me, he intends to have a long line of victims. In the second place, at this point the police are more likely to believe *you* killed those cops. I'll bet the gunman even left the weapon at your place when he found you gone."

Jennifer hadn't even considered that possibility, but of course it made sense. It would be the surest way to get the cops off *his* trail. "But I can prove I didn't do it. You were with me."

"If they believe me. If they don't decide we did it together. You see, the problem is you have a motive."

"A motive! What possible motive could I have for killing two policemen?"

"How about that they believed you killed your family? That they were watching you and gathering evidence?"

"But it would be stupid for me to murder them! It would be so obvious."

"You're a lawyer. You ought to know just how often people do the stupid and obvious thing."

It was an unending nightmare, and it was getting worse and worse. It didn't seem possible, but it just kept compounding, and all because she had just wanted to die. Why had she ever thought that would be the best or easiest way out?

They left Denver behind, climbing up into the mountains on a highway that grew steadily more treacherous. The snow was deeper here, and while plows were working through the night, they hadn't reached all areas. Without the pole reflectors on the shoulder, in places it would have been impossible to tell where the road was.

"Where are we going?" she asked again, but she didn't expect an answer. For better or worse, she seemed to be committed to whatever this venture was. All she could cling to was his promise that he would help her find the person who had murdered her family.

Rook didn't answer immediately. He was still debating with himself whether to violate the sanctuary of his cabin by taking her there, but he couldn't imagine a better place to go. There was absolutely no reason why anyone on earth would look for her there. The few people who knew he had the cabin wouldn't connect him with her even if they should be questioned about her for some reason. If he took her somewhere else, they would leave some kind of a trail, either through credit card slips or people seeing them.

His cabin was the only place on earth where she could completely disappear.

But he hated to do it. She would leave her stamp there one way or another, and he would never be able to erase it.

He was strange. He knew it. People had told him so often enough. It was as if he had a sixth sense that made him aware of things most people never noticed. Like when he knew what someone was going to do before they did it. Like how he could see the traces other people left behind in buildings where they had lived for a while. He generally kept that kind of thing to himself, because it made other people feel uncomfortable, but anyone who hung around him for long usually discovered that he knew more than he should sometimes.

And maybe that was a stupid reason to be reluctant to take this woman to his cabin. Maybe she wouldn't leave any impression at all. Then again, maybe she would leave an indelible impression of sorrow....

He sighed and answered her. "I'm taking you to my cabin. Nobody knows about it. You'll be safe there until I can track this guy down."

"How will you track him down if nobody knows who he is?"

"He's got to look for you. He'll probably watch your house in hopes you'll go back there. Or maybe he'll check out other places you frequent."

An icy fist suddenly gripped Jennifer's heart. "My parents."

"What about them?"

"I visit them frequently, and a lot of people know where they live. He could track me there."

"Sure."

"Would he hurt them?"

As soon as she'd mentioned her parents, he'd started hoping she wouldn't ask him that question.

She turned in the seat. "Rook, I've got to do something. I can't let him hurt them!"

"I know." He *did* know. He sure as hell didn't need her to tell him that. "I'll take care of it. Can they go somewhere for a while?"

"They were planning to take a trip. The dog! They expect me to take care of the dog. They'll panic when they can't find me. And there's my sister. My God, what if he finds Melanie and her kids?"

Snow started falling again, and he turned on the wipers. They slapped back and forth lazily, while the headlights illuminated the whirling snowflakes and created the feeling that they were falling into space.

"I don't think he'd have any reason to hurt your family."

"But he hurt those cops."

"Look, they were shot from behind. That means he was in the car with them. There's only one way he could have gotten in there, and that's because they wanted to question him. They were a *threat*. Your family isn't. Yeah, it would be a good thing for your parents to take their trip, and I'll ask a friend to keep his eye on your sister and her family, but I honestly don't think they're at any real risk. If this guy wants to stay in business, he can't create a bloodbath. The more corpses he makes, the clearer a trail he leaves. If his profile gets too high, he either gets caught or gets dead. Besides, nobody's paying him to make any other hits."

"He said something about...oh, how did he put it? That he's only sadistic when he gets paid to be."

"Did he?" Rook turned that around in his mind. "It fits. It fits perfectly. And it means your family isn't in any danger, so relax. Like I said, the cops were something he had to do to protect himself. Anything else, he's not getting paid for."

It was four in the morning by now, and not even the blast from the heater could keep Jennifer warm. Shivering, she returned her attention to the swirling tunnel of snow ahead of them and wondered if she was ever going to be able to make all of this right.

Exhaustion caught up with her finally, and she fell asleep before they passed through the Eisenhower Tunnel.

Somewhere near Copper Mountain, Rook turned north on a little-traveled road. His cabin was in a valley near the Wyoming border, out of the way and discovered only by an occasional hunter in the autumn. Once there had been a ranch there, but the owners had grown old and died, and he had picked it up for outstanding taxes. The original house had fallen to ruin, so he had knocked it down and replaced it with a brand-new A-frame. He had been able to salvage the barn, though it still needed a lot of work, and for now it housed a snowmobile. Someday he thought he might have a few horses, too.

If he lived long enough.

In the summer the valley was verdant as only an alpine valley could be, full of lush grasses and carpeted in an unending profusion of wildflowers from the moment the snow was thin enough for them to poke their heads up through it. In the winter, more than two hundred inches of snow fell, making the valley virtually inaccessible.

That was why he liked it.

Apart from the Hollywood types who gravitated to Aspen and Telluride, the mountains drew an assortment of "rugged individualists," people who wanted to be left alone to live their own lives as they saw fit. They tended to congregate in tiny towns that were on the edge of extinction, or to find isolated spots where they could build their own shelter out of whatever materials they could afford. Some were sociable, and some were utterly antisocial, and you couldn't tell which you were dealing with merely by where they lived.

Ira Keller was one of those expatriates who generally preferred to be left alone, but he had made an exception in Rook's case. The two men had managed to become friends of sorts, recognizing in one another a basic trustworthiness that was hard to come by. Ira never spoke of his past, but then, neither did Rook. Both men were firmly focused in the present, and each respected the other's privacy.

Ira operated a garage in a haphazard fashion that suggested he wasn't interested in money but just liked to tinker with cars. Some days he didn't bother to open his shop at all, but this morning, even though the sky was just barely beginning to lighten, he was already hard at work under a car he had up on a lift. When Rook wheeled into the driveway, Ira raised a hand in greeting.

Rook parked around back, where his vehicle couldn't be seen. Jennifer woke as soon as he set the brake, coming upright with a start.

"Relax," Rook told her. "I need to talk to this guy. It's okay."

She looked at him, blinking owlishly as she tried to make connections. Finally she nodded.

Ira was waiting out front in the garage bay, his goggles hanging around his neck, wrench still in his hand. "Hey, man, I thought you weren't coming back this way for a while."

"So did I, but things change." He looked around, making sure no one else was in the garage.

"We're alone," Ira said, correctly interpreting Rook's concern. "What's wrong?"

Rook hesitated, then decided that he might as well lay it out truthfully. Ira had never let him down yet. "My lady friend has a bad guy on her tail. I want to stash her at my place until I can take care of him, but I don't want anyone to know she's out there."

Ira grinned. "Alfred Hitchcock time. Hey, I always like a little intrigue. What do you need me to do?"

"Lend me a snowmobile and groceries. And don't tell a soul you saw either of us. Can you hide my car until I get back?"

"Sure. Not a problem. And if you need me to pick up groceries for you on a regular basis, I'll be glad to do that, too."

"I hope I won't need to hide her that long." But he damn well might. Tracking a man was easier when you had a starting place. Right now, the only starting place he had was at Jennifer's house, and there wasn't going to be a whole lot there to get things going. Nor was it going to be easy to check out if the cops suspected her of murdering two of their own.

Ira scratched his chin, fingers rasping on beard stubble. "You need help?"

"Not unless you know how to locate a particular contract hit man."

Ira's eyes widened just a hair, the only sign that he was surprised. "I used to know some people. If they're still talking to me, I'll see what I can do. Give me what you have."

Now it was Rook's turn to be surprised. He'd known there was something dark in Ira's past, but he'd never guessed at anything like this. "I don't have much to go on. In fact, nothing except that the guy operates out of Denver and he's expensive."

"Well, there can't be a whole hell of a lot of hit men operating out of Denver," Ira remarked. "It's not exactly a hotbed of organized crime. Maybe my friends can get wind of something."

"I'd appreciate it."

Ira shrugged a shoulder. "No big deal. Now why don't you two come inside and have some hot coffee while I pack up some supplies for you?"

Jennifer was sitting nearly on the edge of the seat, poised for flight, when Rook came back around the corner of the garage.

"Everything's copacetic," he told her when she flung the door open. "Ira's gonna give us some breakfast while he packs up some supplies for us."

"Ira?"

"Ira Keller. He's a friend."

She hesitated only briefly before accepting that and following him into Ira's small cabin beside the garage. Ira was already pouring coffee and putting out a box of cinnamon rolls.

"You're in luck," Ira told Rook. "I laid in supplies just two days ago."

Jennifer accepted a roll with thanks and sipped the hot coffee gratefully. Despite the heater in the Explorer, she still felt cold to the bone this morning, probably from fatigue.

While they ate, Ira started loading a box with staples. "I've got a sled you can drag behind the snowmobile," he told Rook. "How long you going to be out there?"

"I'm not staying. I've got to get my hands on the bad guy, and I also promised Jennifer I'd look into some other things for her. She'll be out there alone for a day or two, then I'll come back up with food for her. Don't clean yourself out."

"You've got electricity out there, haven't you?" Ira asked.

"Yeah. Cost me damn near a fortune to get it put in, but yeah, I got it."

"Phone?"

"Nope. Never wanted one."

"Take my C-phone, then. If your lady gets into any kind of trouble, at least I can come charging to the rescue." He flashed Jennifer a shy but engaging smile. "I can be out there in about an hour."

"Thank you." *Your lady.* That seemed like a strange way for Ira to refer to her when speaking to Rook. She wondered what Rook had said about her, then decided it was irrelevant. Everything was irrelevant beside her need to find out who had murdered her family.

Her dreams while she had slept in the car had been disturbed by her children's tearstained faces. Both of them had been reaching for her, receding from her even as she fought her way toward them through air as thick as mud. This morning her legs felt like lead, aching as if she had indeed struggled for hours, and her grief was sharp and fresh.

"Let's go."

Startled, she looked up and realized that Rook was standing, breakfast was over and Ira was already carrying the box of supplies to the door. Rising, she grabbed her jacket from the back of the chair and put it on, zipping it to the chin. When Rook handed her a ski mask, she pulled it on without hesitation.

In a battered old pickup, Ira drove them and the snowmobile as close as he could to the valley where Rook's cabin was hidden. It took only a few minutes to get the snowmobile down from the truck and hitch the sled to it.

And in almost no time at all she was riding off into the silent, snow-filled forest behind a man she hardly knew.

She had utterly lost her mind.

6

When Rook and Jennifer set out, snow was falling infrequently, just an occasional flake as if the clouds didn't know exactly what they wanted to do. Once or twice it even seemed that the sun was about to burn through, but then the clouds thickened again, and snow began to fall more heavily.

That was good, Jennifer told herself. The snow would cover their tracks, making it even harder for anyone to follow them. It served, however, to make her feel even more cut off and isolated. Even more vulnerable. She was essentially a city person who was used to having a hospital or a doctor only minutes away and a grocery store right around the corner. Used to the idea that if she needed help all she had to do was pick up a phone and dial 911.

Out here, all that changed. The nearest source of help if she needed someone was Ira Keller. Or Rook Rydell.

Wrapped around him on the snowmobile, she felt an uncomfortable awareness of her vulnerability and his greater size and strength. Even with the layers of winter clothing between them, the position felt too intimate.

But what completely and utterly shocked her was her reaction. Not once since her husband's death had the thought of sex crossed her mind, but suddenly her body, deprived for so long, was alive and aware in a way that was purely sensual. The insides of her thighs all of a sudden became exquisitely sensitive to every movement of her slacks. And when they cornered and she had to tighten her thighs around Rook, it was as if her whole body responded with a throb of yearning. She hated herself for it, feeling as if she were betraying Mark's memory.

The snow grew heavier, as if they were driving deeper into the storm as well as deeper into the woods. Even through the ski mask, her ears and nose began to ache from the cold, and her fingers within her leather gloves were beginning to feel numb. If she had known they were going to be snowmobiling, she would have worn better protection on her head and hands.

At last they crested a rise, and before them a huge valley opened up below them, a snow-filled bowl punctuated by leafless aspens and the mysterious shadows of evergreens. At the very heart of the bowl rose a large A-frame, its shoulders white with snow.

Rook paused a moment on the brow of the ridge, studying the cabin and its environs for any sign of disturbance, but the valley looked even more undisturbed than usual beneath its cloak of fresh snow. Then he gunned the motor and took them down the slope at top speed.

Jennifer's arms tightened around him instinctively, and her thighs pressed against his hips. He tried not to think about how that made him feel, because he didn't want to get involved with this woman any more than he already was, not even in the most casual of ways. Hell, she was a walking disaster. The sooner he got her settled and the sooner he got out of here, the better.

He'd built the A-frame because it would shrug off the sixteen or seventeen feet of snow that could be expected in the course of a normal winter. Since he didn't expect to spend a lot of time up here for several years yet and wouldn't be able to shovel the roof, he didn't want to have to worry about snow load. This way he could forget all about it even when he retired here.

Windows were something else he'd given a lot of thought to. Even with double paning, there was considerable heat loss. On the other hand, he wouldn't have been able to stand living in a cave. He had compromised, finally, on sliding glass doors in the living room at the front of the house, a large window in the kitchen at the back, and no window in the loft bedroom. Now he was wishing he hadn't put in any windows at all. They might become a serious problem if someone located Jennifer.

But there was no reason on earth why anyone should find her, because there was no reason the gunman should link him with her. And even if someone should make the connection, only a handful of people knew about this place, and even fewer had any idea how to find it.

He pulled up in front of the house, beside the deck. Nearly a foot of snow already lay on everything, burying the short staircase that led up to the deck. The way it was drifted, it would probably be easier to go around back.

He dropped Jennifer off by the back door, then drove over to the barn and parked the vehicle inside.

Carrying the box of supplies, he tramped back to the house and let them both in.

The house was dark, cold, musty smelling. It had been months since he'd last lit a fire in here, and only the dryness of the mountain air kept the place healthy.

He needed to start the well pump, fill the hot water heater, start a fire.... He dropped the box of supplies on the table and turned to Jennifer. "Put this stuff away wherever you want. I'm going to bring in some wood."

She nodded, shifting from one foot to the other as if she were cold to the bone, looking exhausted enough to drop. He could sympathize; his own head was beginning to feel as if it were full of angry bees of fatigue. All he wanted to do was crash for an hour or two.

But first he had to build a fire and get the water on. He'd winterized the place before he left it six months ago so that he wouldn't come back to burst pipes and a flooded house. Now he had to pay the price for that caution.

Ira had been generous, Jennifer realized as she unpacked. He had thrown everything, from pancake mix and syrup to powdered milk, into the box. He'd given her more than enough for five or six days, and was probably going to have to go shopping for himself again almost immediately.

Jennifer found herself smiling faintly as she put the food away in the empty cupboards. Ira seemed like the kind of guy who would give you the shirt off his back if you needed it, and people like that were rare.

Of course, there was Rook. He hadn't wanted to get involved in her problems, but now he was involved right up to his neck in them. For some reason that made tears prickle in her eyes, not the tears of loss but a very different kind. It was hard to express in words how it affected her to feel as if she actually mattered.

Weird. She mattered to her family, but it somehow affected her more strongly that a total stranger could be so caring. Probably just an indicator of how low and alone she'd been feeling.

Rook came through the door with a double armload of wood, pausing to stomp the snow off his boots before he proceeded to the living room. Jennifer followed him, watching as he dropped the logs into a wood box next to a wood stove.

"I didn't put in electric or gas heat," he told her. "Too expensive. The stove makes all the heat you could ask for, though. Ever used one?"

"Yes." It gave her a sense of satisfaction to prove it, too, by adjusting the damper and laying the kindling on the grate. At least there was *something* she could do. Over the past twelve hours Rook had made her feel totally dependent, and she hated it. He was the kind of man who just took over, and she'd been aiding and abetting him by traipsing after him like a lost lamb. Well, enough of that!

Soon the stove was radiating heat. The two of them stood beside it, bundled in their winter clothes, holding their hands out to the warmth.

"I don't like this," Jennifer said.

"What don't you like? This place isn't that bad."

She felt embarrassed, realizing what her remark had sounded like. "I didn't mean your house. I'm sorry. This is really a very nice place. Much nicer than I expected when you called it your cabin."

And it was. The furnishings, though scanty, were perfectly adequate. From what she had seen so far, he kept it exceptionally clean, too. There certainly wasn't any clutter.

"Then what do you mean?"

He was as tired as she was, Jennifer realized, and getting a little truculent. Perhaps understandably, considering that he'd been up all night for no better reason than that some woman he didn't know had gotten herself into a serious mess. "Just that...I don't like not being in control. I don't like hiding out this way. I ought to be looking for my family's killer."

The look he gave her was straight and hard. "You gave up control when you hired a hit man. The next call is his—unless I can find him first."

Before last night she hadn't thought much about Rook one way or the other, but her initial impression of him hadn't been very favorable. He was, after all, a mercenary, and she'd located him in one of the seediest bars in Denver, a place he apparently frequented. He was also acquainted with Alan DeVries, a man who had made enough money in the international drug trade to be able to afford one of the priciest law firms in Colorado.

That initial impression was changing, though, and had begun to shift when Rook had told her he was helping not for her sake but because he didn't want any part of a contract hit. That had been a harsh statement, but an honest one, and certainly more believable than if he had suddenly claimed to be a white knight who felt honor bound to aid a damsel in distress. With those words he had established himself as a man of uncompromising principles.

"I need to let my parents know I'm alive and safe," she said, desperately wanting to change the subject. She felt as if she had glimpsed something within him that was uncomfortable for them both.

He continued to stare hard at her for a few more seconds, then nodded. "Use the C-phone. Just don't tell them where you are."

"I don't have any idea where I am. I slept through the last part of the trip."

Her unexpectedly dry tone brought the faintest of smiles to his lips and softened the harshness of his expression. "You're in the Rocky Mountains north of I-70 and west of I-25."

"That covers a whole lot of territory."

"That's the idea."

She laughed. It was just a bare ghost of sound, and so unusual for her since the crash that for a moment she didn't recognize the chuckle as her own.

When she started to dial the number on the cellular phone, however, she hesitated. "He won't be able to find me through this?"

"I don't see how. Don't get too paranoid, lady. There's no reason to assume he's checking phone calls to your parents, or even that he could. And even if by some weird chance he could do such a thing, the call is coming from a phone that isn't registered to you."

"That's true." She was a lawyer, though, and she knew how incredibly easy some information was to get. But Rook was right—the phone wasn't registered to her.

"Jenny!" Her mother sounded relieved and exasperated all at once. "I've been trying to get you all morning! You were going to watch Massie for us while we're away, remember?"

Clutching the phone tightly, Jennifer sat on the couch. What was she going to do about this?

"Um...could Melanie watch her? I've had something come up."

"Melanie's going with us. She and Dave decided to join us. Well, you know they haven't had a vacation since before Carrie was born, nearly four years. We thought a little time in the sun would be good for all of us. But we can't leave Massie with the vet. You know how she pines!"

"Umm...just a minute, okay?" Covering the mouthpiece, she looked at Rook. "Could you get the dog from my parents and bring her here? They have no one to leave her with, and she nearly dies when she has to stay at the vet. She won't eat...."

He was still standing by the stove, trying to thaw out. The look he gave her was disbelieving. "You're kidding, right?"

Jenny shook her head. "No. They're all going away, my sister and her family, too, and I was supposed to watch the dog...."

"What about a neighbor?"

"Massie has to stay with family. I'm serious, Rook. She'll starve herself to death, and she's pregnant."

"Pregnant." He repeated the word without inflection, as if he couldn't quite gauge the dimensions of a major catastrophe. "Oh, Christ, why not?" He was mostly thinking of Jennifer having to be here all by herself, and a dog would at least be good company. Maybe even some protection. "Tell 'em I'll get the dog. They *do* live in Denver, don't they?" He had a sudden vision of having to drive to Pueblo or Durango to get the animal.

"Actually, west of Denver. Near Golden."

"Yeah, I'll get the dog, but not until late this afternoon. I have to cadge a little sleep first."

"Jenny? Jenny, are you still there?"

Jennifer looked down at the handset, wondering how she was going to explain all this to her mother. When she lifted the receiver to her mouth, she still had no idea what she was going to say.

"Mother? Listen, I'm staying with a friend. He'll come by and get Massie late this afternoon, okay?"

There was a long silence from the other end. Then Lenore spoke cautiously. "Did I hear you correctly? You're staying with a friend? A *male* friend? Jenny, what's going on? Why can't you come get her yourself?"

Good question. Jennifer's tired brain scrambled wildly for an explanation that wouldn't include telling her parents that she had hired a hit man.

"Stay as close to the truth as you can," Rook advised her from across the room.

He was right, of course. She nodded and drew a deep breath. "Mother, I didn't tell you this because I didn't want to upset you, but the FAA says Mark and the children were murdered. Somebody tampered with the plane before they took off."

"Oh, my God..." Shock and disbelief laced the words.

"What's more, somebody tried to break into my house last night. I think...I think someone may be after me, too."

Lenore uttered a wordless sound of shock and horror. "Jenny..."

"Mother, just listen, please. Just to be safe, I'm staying with a friend in the mountains, until we can find out what's going on."

"Why don't you just go to the police?"

"Because the police think I..." Her chest suddenly tightened, making it almost impossible to breathe. She closed her eyes. "They think I may be the one who...murdered them."

"Oh, my God...oh, my God...Jenny..."

Suddenly a hand was gripping Jennifer's shoulder. Startled, she looked up and found Rook was standing beside her. He squeezed her shoulder gently, comfortingly. "Mother...Mom...Mom, just listen, please. Please? My friend will come get Massie. His name is Rook Rydell. He'll tell you as much as we can about all of this."

"Well, we're not going anywhere at all," Lenore said with sudden determination. "If you're in trouble, we're certainly not going to laze around in the sun and pretend nothing is going on! We'll be right here where we can be of some help!"

"Mother, no!" This was the worst possible outcome. How could she possibly persuade her parents to go anyway? "Mom, you *have* to go!"

"Absolutely not!"

"But...but if this man is the same one who killed Mark and the children, and he's really hunting me, then he might come after you and Dad to find out where I am. Or Melanie and her kids! Don't you see? The best thing you can do right now to help is to go on your vacation just the way you planned to."

Lenore started arguing, but Rook took the receiver from Jennifer. "Ma'am? Ma'am, this is Rook Rydell. Galen Rydell, actually. Jennifer's right. The best thing you can do is take your trip. It's dangerous for you and dangerous for Jennifer if you remain."

He listened for a few moments, and Jennifer watched him, not sure whether to be glad he had taken over or to resent it. She decided to be glad. Lenore could be unbelievably difficult sometimes.

"I'm a soldier," Rook said into the phone. "Until recently I was in the army. Believe me, I can look after your daughter, and I intend to. But it would be a really great help if you and your family were out of the way, because I can't protect you *all.*"

He made a few agreeable noises, then added, "I'll be there this afternoon. If I can answer any more of your questions then, I will." Then he passed the receiver back to Jennifer.

"I don't like this, Jennifer," Lenore said sternly. "And your father's not going to like it, either, when I tell him."

"Where is he?"

"He went out to get another suitcase for me. Mine started to fall apart. Jenny, I really can't believe that you can't go to the police and work this all out!"

For a moment Jennifer couldn't even bring herself to speak. *If you only knew, Mother. If you had any idea at all what I've done . . .* "I can't. If I for one moment believed it would do any good, that's exactly where I'd be, Mother. But it *won't* do any good. Not when they think I'm responsible for the crash." Not when two officers had been killed while staking out her house. Nobody in their right mind would believe she had hired a hit man to kill herself. Nobody. Oh, God, it was all such a mess!

After more fruitless argument, Lenore finally let her go. Jennifer switched off the phone and sagged back against the couch, emotionally exhausted.

Rook stood looking down at her. "You have a good mother," he said finally. "She cares."

"Too much, sometimes. And I'd better warn you—she's psychic."

"Psychic?"

"You'll see. Mark my words, that woman reads minds."

Rook laughed then, a genuine, warm, easy sound that tickled her somewhere inside in a pleasant way. "All mothers read minds. The good ones, at any rate. I'm not worried about it."

"Of course not. *You* didn't hire the hit man. I did."

He laughed again and shook his head. "Look, we both need to crash for a while. Do you want the loft or the couch?"

She craned her neck, looking upward. "What's the loft?"

"The bedroom. There's a thick comforter on the bed, and the sheets are clean, I swear. I changed 'em just before I closed the place up. Look, you go upstairs. That way I won't wake you when I leave."

It didn't feel right to take his bed, but she was too tired to argue. For the first time in days she actually felt safe, and her entire body seemed to be screaming for sleep. "Thank you."

Rook watched her climb the ladder staircase, her shoulders drooping with dejection and fatigue, and he wondered if he was going to see her on those stairs, just like that, every time he looked at them from now on.

Useless to think about it. It was too late now.

Jennifer's directions were excellent, and Rook found her parents' home with no trouble at all. The Comptons lived in an exclusive subdivision where upper-middle-class comfort expressed itself in the appearance of solitude. Driving along a recently graded winding dirt road, he could have believed himself in the middle of nowhere except for occasional glimpses through the trees of redwood-and-glass homes.

There were two cars in the driveway when he at last pulled up in front of the Compton place. A nine- or ten-year-old boy was building a snowman out front.

The boy regarded him solemnly from dark green eyes that reminded him of Jennifer.

"Hi," Rook said. "I'm here to see Mr. and Mrs. Compton."

"They're inside."

"Thanks."

He could feel the boy's eyes still on him as he walked up to the front door. His knock was answered so swiftly that he was sure they had been watching for his arrival. A tall, gray-haired man opened the door wide. Now Rook knew where Jennifer's green eyes came from.

"Mr. Compton? I'm Galen Rydell. Rook to most folks."

Rook couldn't remember the last time he had been scrutinized so carefully. Glenn Compton looked him over from head to toe, missing nothing, not even the scuffed and snow-stained state of his cowboy boots. Rook pulled his hands from the pockets of his black ski jacket and offered one. After a moment, Compton took it.

"Come in," said the older man. "We've got a lot of questions."

"I kind of figured you would." And he'd been rehearsing his answers all the way down out of the mountains.

The living room was large, with a sweeping cathedral ceiling and a glass wall that overlooked a deep ravine. There were several conversational groupings, but everyone had congregated at an octagonal table near the window. He picked out Lenore Compton without any difficulty, a beautiful woman with graying hair and brilliant blue eyes. Beside her was her other daughter, a woman of about forty who looked enough like her mother to have been a sister. The man, he presumed, was the daughter's husband. He was introduced as David Dobbs. A little girl with blond curls played on the floor with small toy cars and a big plastic horse.

There was an awkward moment or two when no one seemed quite sure how to treat his visit. He wasn't here on business, but it wasn't exactly a social call, either. Finally the daughter, Melanie, rose. "Would you like something to drink, Mr. Rydell?"

"A glass of water, a cup of coffee—whatever's convenient. Thanks."

She nodded, giving him a cool smile, then headed for the kitchen. The little girl followed her immediately.

Glenn Compton was in no mood to bother with social niceties. "What is going on with our daughter, Mr. Rydell? Where is she, and who are you?"

"I'm a security specialist," Rook told him. Close enough to the truth, since that was part of what he did for foreign governments: train security personnel. "I'm working with your daughter on the murder of her family."

Lenore's hand flew to her mouth, fingertips pressing tightly against her lips as if she had to forcibly repress a cry.

"My wife said the police suspect Jennifer."

Rook nodded. "They do. Your daughter naturally wants to find the real killer, but having suspicion focused on her makes it *imperative* that we find out who really did it. It wouldn't require much circumstantial evidence at all to put her in a very awkward position."

"I can't believe they suspect her," Lenore said. "I can't believe it!"

"Unfortunately, they do." And by now they probably believed she had murdered two police officers, as well. He hoped the Comptons and the Dobbses got out of there before the police came to question them about Jennifer's whereabouts. "Last night someone tried to break in to your daughter's house. It wasn't a routine burglary attempt."

"How can you know that?"

"Because the two police officers who were staking out the house, watching Jennifer, were shot."

Lenore gasped, stunned. Melanie, returning with a steaming cup of coffee, nearly dropped it, and cried out when some of the hot liquid splashed on her hand. David leapt to his feet at once and took the cup from her, putting it down in front of Rook. Then he hugged her tightly. Glenn Compton put his arm around Lenore.

"She's got to go to the police," Glenn said. "Hiding only makes it worse."

"The police can't protect her very well," Rook told him flatly. "They sure didn't do a good job of it last night. Besides, at this point they may well believe your daughter killed those two officers."

Lenore leapt up from the table and went to the window, where she stood staring out at the gray day, her arms wrapped tightly around her own waist. "Nobody could seriously believe Jennifer is capable of any of this," she said in a strained voice.

"I certainly don't," Rook agreed. "But the police don't know your daughter very well. For now it's really best to keep her hidden until we've got something concrete to give the cops. Until we find out who was trying to get into her house last night. And it's important that all of you go on your trip as if nothing has happened. Whoever is after Jennifer might try to find out from you where she is."

Lenore and Glenn exchanged looks as they tried to absorb everything he had told them. Melanie, still within the circle of her husband's arms, broke the strained silence.

"Jennifer called you, didn't she, Mom? This is what she wants us to do."

"Yes." But Lenore looked at her husband uncertainly.

Several minutes passed while Glenn frowned out the window. Rook sipped his coffee, grateful for its bitter warmth, and wondered how he had ever allowed himself to get tangled up in this. It would be just his luck to check his post office box tonight and discover he'd been offered some cushy job in some tropical paradise and he would have to turn it down.

Finally Glenn spoke. "I want to talk to Jennifer one more time. If she really wants to handle things this way, then we'll go on our trip as planned." He turned to look at Rook. "With the promise that you'll keep us informed of everything that happens."

Rook nodded. "No problem."

Glenn Compton put the call on the speaker phone. Jennifer sounded a little down when she answered, and even a trifle hesitant, a tone Rook already realized was not natural to her. She did, however, insist that she wanted her family to go on their trip, that she was perfectly safe in her mountain hideaway, and that there wasn't a thing any of them could do to help.

There was a tug on Rook's leg, and he looked down to find that the little girl had come back into the room to stand beside him. She lifted her arms, silently asking to be picked up.

The memories that washed over him were so sudden and so intense that he couldn't even respond. He simply stared down at the child and battled the waves of loss.

"Carrie." Melanie called to her daughter, saying apologetically, "I'm sorry, she doesn't understand about not approaching strangers yet."

Rook looked at her, relieved to be free of the little girl's demand and the pain it caused him. "It's okay. It's just . . . these days a man shouldn't pick little girls up." Easy lie to cover the stark truth. Easy to say, easy to believe.

"No, of course, you're right. It's terrible, isn't it? Children have to be taught to fear, and adults can't respond in the natural, caring way they should be able to." Melanie shook her head. "I don't know what the world's coming to."

"Actually," Rook said, clearing his throat, "it's probably a good thing. In the past I don't think we were suspicious enough."

Glenn Compton had fallen into quiet conversation with his wife after he disconnected from the call to Jennifer. Now he spoke. "It's settled. We're going on our trip. I can't see how we'll help anything by staying here, and Jennifer and Mr. Rydell both seem convinced we might actually make things worse."

He turned to Rook. "You don't know how it goes against my grain to trust you."

Rook nodded acknowledgment. There sure as hell wasn't anything he could say.

"Jennifer seems to believe she can trust you," Glenn continued, "and she's always been a fairly decent judge of character. Of course, that doesn't mean she can't be wrong."

Rook met his look steadily. "I don't personally care one way or the other about your daughter, Mr. Compton. But I *do* give a damn that an innocent person shouldn't pay for the crimes of others. She didn't kill her family. I intend to prove it."

"You believe in her, then."

"I wouldn't say I believe *in* her. But I *do* believe her."

Compton tightened his lips, then nodded. "That'll have to do, I guess." It clearly didn't sit well with him, but he wasn't being left with many choices.

"I'll go get Massie," Melanie said.

"You will take the dog right to Jenny?" Lenore asked. "Massie won't eat when she's with strangers, and with her being pregnant..."

"I'll get her there tonight." After he checked out a couple of things. Massie and her pups would survive if she got one of her meals a little late.

"I'll get her food and dishes," David said.

"Don't forget her table," Lenore called after him.

Her *table?* Rook was getting a mental image of a small, furry, tyrannical animal that had been doted on until it was spoiled to death...exactly the kind of dog he loathed.

"Here she is," Melanie said. "Massie, this is Mr. Rydell. He's going to take you to Jenny."

Rook didn't even want to look. It would be a vicious Pekingese and would probably bite him the instant he laid eyes on it.

He felt a blast of hot breath on his cheek and turned to find himself eyeball-to-eyeball with a dog whose head was bigger than his own.

"Good God," he heard himself say. "What is it? A mule?"

7

Twenty minutes later, Rook was driving away from the Compton house with a vehicle full of dog, dog food and associated accoutrements, including a rope tug toy that looked strong enough to serve as a towline for an ocean liner. Behind him in the back seat was a dog with jaws big enough to make him uneasily aware that Massie could probably bite his head off if she got annoyed with him.

Although, to be fair, Massie seemed friendly enough, and he'd been assured by the Comptons that she was a sweetheart. Mainly, she seemed to want to be petted and hugged.

Still, he figured he wasn't going to make her wait too long for her next meal. A wise man didn't argue with a dog that was as big as he was.

But first he had to go see Jay Miller, to find out if he could pry some kind of information out of the man. Jay justifiably did not want to share the name of the hit man, but he might be able to share other information that would put Rook on the right trail. After he questioned Jay, he would take the dog up into the mountains to Jennifer.

When he thought about it, he decided he was a sucker. He should never have allowed himself to get tangled up in Jennifer Fox's problems, but even allowing that he hadn't had any real choice in the matter, *why* had he then been sucker enough to agree to get the damn dog?

It wasn't that he didn't like dogs. Dogs were nice critters, friendly most of the time, and fun to have around. No, he didn't have a thing against dogs. But dealing with two hundred pounds of English mastiff in the midst of everything else that was going on was going to be one hell of a headache. Oh, the dog wouldn't be a problem out at the cabin with Jennifer, but what if he had to move her? He could disguise Jennifer easily with a wig and some padding, but how could he disguise this damn dog? In a horse suit?

Christ.

When he parked his Explorer in the parking lot behind the tavern, he intended to leave Massie in the car, but she started barking and grew agitated. Well, of course, he thought. She was alone with a stranger. Hell, she was probably afraid of being abandoned.

It was then that the whole situation struck his funny bone. This dog, bigger than most human beings, was afraid to be left alone. And he had a sneaking suspicion that nobody would dare to tell him that he couldn't bring her into the bar. Tickled suddenly by the whole idea, he hunted up the leash in the back and hooked it to Massie's collar.

Then, surprising him with her obedience and training, she jumped down and heeled on his left side.

"Good dog." He patted her head and scratched behind her ears, and got the feeling that he had just made a friend for life.

At the front door, the bouncer looked nervously at the dog. "You can't bring that animal in here."

"You want to tell her that?" Rook just kept walking, and Massie moved right beside him. The bouncer didn't say another word.

Pepe, the bartender and owner, did, though. "Rook, you can't have that animal in here. Health codes."

"We'll be gone in a minute, and she'd be allowed in here if she were a seeing-eye dog."

"But she's not. You'll have to take her out of here."

Rook grinned. "In a minute, Pepe."

The bartender didn't press the issue.

Jay saw him coming from across the room, and his eyes got a little bigger as he took in the dog. "What the hell is that?"

"I'm baby-sitting a friend's dog for a couple of days." He pulled out a chair and sat. Massie, he noticed, settled right beside him, as far from Jay as she could get. Shy, maybe? Or maybe she just didn't like something about Jay. There were things about him Rook wasn't all that sure about himself.

"That's not a dog," Jay said, pointing at her.

Massie curled her lip and made a low growl deep in her throat. Jay stopped pointing.

"Trust me, she's a dog."

Jay regarded the mastiff doubtfully, then shook his head. "Can I buy you a beer?"

"No, thanks. I'm driving. But Massie here would probably like a plate of scrambled eggs."

Jay looked at him. "You want me to buy a plate of eggs for a *dog?*"

"Guess not. I'll buy it myself." He signaled the waitress, who approached with considerable trepidation. "I'd like a cheese omelet, please, and a bowl of water."

She nodded and hurried away.

That was when Jay chuckled, then broke out into a laugh. "This is a joke, right? You rented the dog."

"Nope. She's staying with me. So, what's the word? Got a job yet?"

"Nothing." Jay took a swig of his beer and tipped his chair back. "You heard of anything?"

"Not a peep. I can't believe nobody's fighting anywhere in the world, though. Something'll turn up." Although, much to his own surprise, he was actually hoping nothing would. For some weird reason, he didn't want to be offered another job. He didn't even want to think about the possibility of flying off to some foreign land where he wouldn't understand the customs or the language in order to train young men how to fight and die. What was wrong with him? Had some kind of bug bitten him? Damn, he wished he had a cigarette.

Massie's eggs arrived, along with a stainless steel bowl full of water. "The kitchen don't believe it," the waitress said. "They thought I was kidding. It's a big dog, ain't it?"

Rook set the plate of eggs on a chair. Massie looked up at him uncertainly. "Go ahead, girl. It's okay. Eat it." When she continued to hesitate, he tore off a piece of the omelet and offered it to her. She licked it with surprising gentleness from his fingers.

"It's probably too hot yet," the waitress said. "Give it a sec. She'll eat it." She took the money Rook held out to her.

Aware of the dog's soulful eyes on him, Rook turned back to Jay, wondering how to broach the subject without giving away too much valuable information. Since Jay had helped arrange the hit on Jennifer, however indirectly, he was no longer sure how far he could trust the younger man. It wasn't that he thought Jay would go running to the hit man with information—Jay wasn't likely to do any such thing unless he was being paid for it—but if he ran into the guy, he might let information slip in casual conversation.

Massie sniffed at the eggs and began to eat. So much for pining away, Rook thought.

It was Jay, much to his surprise, who brought up the subject of Jennifer Fox. "You heard any more from the woman who wanted the hit?"

Rook pretended not to remember for an instant. "Oh, yeah. The one I had call you."

"That's her."

He figured Jay had probably heard that Jennifer had come looking for him that second time, and that was why he was asking. It gave him an easy entry to the topic he really wanted to discuss. "Yeah, she came in here one night looking for me. She wanted to stop the hit."

Jay's eyes narrowed. "She did? Why?"

"She changed her mind."

"Great timing." He shook his head and signaled for another beer. "You can't stop something like that once it's started."

"That's what I told her. You can't expect a hit man to quit a job just because some strange person calls and claims to be the one who hired him and says they want him to stop."

"Damn straight," Jay agreed. "I think your dog wants something."

Massie was looking up at Rook with yearning eyes. The plate of eggs had been licked clean.

"Water? Are you thirsty?" He set the bowl down on the plate, and Massie began to lap it eagerly—and messily.

"I never thought you were the doggie type, Rydell."

"I never thought you were the type to know a hit man, Miller."

Jay gave a short laugh. "Life's full of surprises, huh?"

"Guess so." Absently he reached out and scratched the dog behind the ears.

"When was it she came in here?" Jay asked.

"Just the other night. Maybe...Friday? Yeah, I think it was Friday. She wanted your number."

Jay stiffened. "*My* number? Why?"

"Because she figured if she called you, you'd be able to get in touch with the hit man again. Or that you could tell her how to get in touch herself."

"You didn't give it to her, did you?"

"No." He was disappointed that Jay didn't feel even the least obligation to try to stop the juggernaut he'd helped put into motion. "Don't you think you should at least try to pass the message along?"

"You think he'd listen to me any more than her?"

Rook hesitated. "What if I want to talk to him myself?"

"Oh, yeah, he'd listen to *you.* Christ, Rook, give it a rest. You know these guys. Their reputations ride on finishing every job they take."

"Is it someone I know, Jay?"

Jay looked startled. "What makes you think that?"

Rook shrugged. "Hell, I don't know." But he did. He had this niggling feeling at the base of his skull, and he never ignored those feelings—at least, not without regretting it.

"I thought you didn't know any hit men."

"I didn't think I did. But I *do* know a whole lot of people, and I suppose it could be one of them."

"Well, I sure as hell wouldn't know if you knew him."

"So it's not someone I hang out with?"

Jay opened his mouth, paused, then laughed. "I'm not that stupid, man. I'm not going to sit here playing Twenty Questions until you get something out of me. Hey, it's my life on the line here, too."

And, unfortunately, that was also true. Nor could he think of any other way to get Jay to talk. Hell, Jay hadn't talked even when the men questioning him had put a noose around his neck, and each and every time he'd refused to tell them what they wanted to know they'd lifted him off his feet, strangling him until he blacked out.

Feeling grim and not too hopeful, Rook looked around the room, not really seeing anything in particular, but seeing *everything*. It was a state of relaxed alertness he had learned long ago in the army, and it allowed his mind to wander over other things while never losing track of what was going on around him.

Right now, though, his mind was wandering like a hamster on a wheel, around and around and around and getting nowhere. What he *didn't* want was to have to guard Jennifer and hope to take out the hit man when he struck. That was coming far too close for comfort. Somehow he had to find the guy before he got that close.

It never paid to have only one option.

Jay was working on yet another beer, but the alcohol didn't seem to be affecting him at all.

Rook watched him take a long swallow. "I always wondered," he said, "what makes a man kill for money."

Jay looked at him over the bottle he held to his mouth. "It's no different from what *we* do."

"Oh, it's a lot different. War is a kill-or-be-killed situation. Stalking somebody who has never caused you any harm, somebody who will never cause you any harm, for the purpose of putting a bullet through their head is a little different."

"That's what soldiers do."

Rook smiled faintly. "Not quite. The motivation is a whole lot different."

Jay shrugged a shoulder. "It's the same thing, whatever the motive. The thrill of the hunt and the kill. The *power.*"

And that, thought Rook, is where we part ways, my friend. A nudge on his arm drew his attention downward, and he found Massie looking at him rather impatiently. "Need a walk, girl?"

Her tail thumped affirmatively. It was as good an excuse as any to end a conversation that was going nowhere.

Outside, Massie took care of her business in some snow beside the trash bins, then climbed docilely into the back seat of the car and stretched out, apparently ready to take a nap. Rook wished he could join her.

Instead he drove to his lodgings, an old, run-down hotel where nobody asked questions and the owner took only cash payments. It was a good place to be anonymous, and for some time now he'd been feeling a strong need to be unnoticed and unseen.

Not that he had any reason to hide, because he honestly didn't. It was just that ever since his wife had left him, ever since the court-martial and his dishonorable discharge, he'd wanted to be invisible somehow. As if he'd been beaten up and was ashamed of the bruises—which wasn't a bad analogy, now that he thought about it.

Nobody looked up when he entered the lobby, not even with Massie beside him. He'd kind of expected the dog to draw some attention, but the desk clerk and the guy over by the wall reading a girlie magazine didn't even glance his way. Of course, this was a place where paying too much attention to something could get you in serious trouble.

Upstairs in his room, he changed swiftly into clean clothes and a pair of boots better suited to traipsing through snow. He also dug out a survival parka and a pair of snow pants. Damned if he was going to ride that snowmobile again without proper clothing.

He packed a change of clothes and some necessities, looked around the room one last time, a habit born of changing domiciles frequently, then left with Massie. Again, no one in the lobby even looked at him.

He was approaching his car, chin tucked into his collar against a brisk, cold wind, when the back of his neck prickled in warning. Someone was watching him. He debated only an instant before pivoting abruptly and searching the area.

No one was to be seen anywhere. The street was deserted, a collage of wet, black pavement and patchy snow turned yellow by the streetlights. Several other vehicles were parked on the street, but none of them appeared to be occupied.

Massie whined as if she sensed something, too.

Hell, it could be anything or anyone. Just someone casually looking down from a window. There was certainly no good reason to assume he was being watched or followed—unless he had been identified at Jennifer's house last night.

"Come on, girl." He led Massie away from his car, as if he was just walking her. A good dog, she followed obediently, pausing to sniff at telephone poles and fire hydrants. He walked her up the street a block, then back down, glancing with pretended casualness into cars as he went. No one was inside any of them.

If someone was watching the street, they were doing it from above, he decided. That could mean a lot of things, but most likely it meant he wasn't being followed. Yet.

He paused and considered while Massie checked out the base of a street sign. The cops had already questioned him about Jennifer Fox, so they might well be checking up on him. Hell, given the murders last night, they might even have him under surveillance.

Finally he took Massie back to the car and drove away, heading not for I-70, but for Jennifer's house. Might as well find out exactly what the parameters of the situation were.

It was still early enough that there were a lot of cars on the streets, so he took a roundabout route, trying to discover a tail. There didn't seem to be one, but he wasn't counting on it.

When he at last turned down Jennifer's street, he drove slowly, scanning both sides of the road. The wrecked cars were gone. Tonight the pavement was black and wet in patches from snow melt. The sidewalks had been shoveled and were clear and dry except for the strip right in front of Jennifer's house. There, patchy snow was still in evidence.

And, as he had feared, a police tape surrounded her house, marking it off-limits. They thought she was involved in the murder of the two officers. He kept driving, hoping he looked like a casual passerby with a ghoulish interest in the scene. There didn't seem to be any surveillance, however.

When he reached the next block, he turned away from the house, heading south. No one followed him.

He didn't need to go inside to know what the police had found and what they suspected. Whoever had broken in to her house last night—most likely the hit man—had left his weapon behind. There would be no fingerprints on it, and it would have been discovered half under some piece of furniture, so that it looked as if it had fallen out of something unnoticed. They probably had a report from the drunk driver about the man who had been at the wreck and then disappeared. They most likely hadn't noticed that someone had broken in to the house, because the hit man would have been careful to leave little or no evidence of his entry, and the cops would already be looking for proof that the murderer had been Jennifer Fox.

Preconceived notions were the devil of criminal investigations. Cops all too often looked for the nearest and likeliest suspect, and then built a case accordingly. And once they started building the case, they became committed to it and didn't want to see any contrary evidence.

He debated going to the police station right now and telling them that he had been with Jennifer, and that she hadn't killed the cops. Telling them that someone had broken in to her house. The likely outcome of that, though, was that they would charge him as an accessory, or just hold him for questioning. Either way, he would be of no further use to Jennifer, and Massie would wind up in the pound.

Instead he pulled off at a convenience store and went inside to buy a bottle of water. The clerk was a garrulous guy who had the TV set tuned to a twenty-four-hour news channel. It was a great opening.

"Hey," said Rook, "did they find out any more about those two cops who were murdered last night?"

"Nah. They're still looking for the woman who did it. Jeez, she must be some kind of sicko. They say she murdered her whole family. What kind of woman murders her kids?"

Rook hoped Jennifer had a good lawyer, because she ought to sue the shit out of the Denver police when this was all resolved. If they had a lick of proof that she had murdered her family, he would be mightily surprised. No, they just couldn't think of anyone else who might have done it. Typical cop crap.

Christ, he would give his left arm for a cigarette. Nevertheless, he turned and walked out of the store.

Massie was waiting for him, looking as lost and forlorn as if she had been abandoned. "Didn't you see me through the window?" he asked her. She cocked her head attentively and thumped her tail twice. He guessed that meant everything was okay now.

He sat there for a few minutes, sipping his bottled water and trying to make up his mind about how to handle this. There were a few people he could call who would put their ears to the ground and see if they could get wind of this hit man for him. And for all he knew, Ira might already have some info for him.

He looked at Massie, thinking of Jennifer up there all alone at that cabin. As the hours crept by, it would get harder and harder for her. Having the dog nearby would certainly help her, but it wouldn't entirely ease the frustration of being able to do nothing. He needed to bring her at least a little information with which she could start to build some kind of theory.

Then there were the cops. With all that investigatory power at their fingertips, it was a damn shame they were wasting it chasing the wrong person. Well, he could sure as hell do something about that.

"Wait here, girl. I need to make a few phone calls."

Massie thumped her tail, but looked unhappy about it. Damn, he'd better stop reading too much into her behavior or he was going to get attached to her. He didn't want to get attached to anybody ever again, including a dog. It would be just his luck that even a dog would turn on him the way everyone else had.

There was a pay phone right in front of him. Grabbing some change from the little well in the console, he climbed out into the chilly, windy night and went to call a few people.

The first call was to a federal agency headquartered in Maryland. He'd done them a few favors during his years as a mercenary, and he figured they owed him one or two. The phone rang only once before it was answered.

"This is Tim."

Tim wasn't his real name, but these guys seemed to prefer nondescript, short, common nicknames. And they never used a last name. "This is Rook."

There was a pause. Then, cautiously, "What's up?"

"I need some info."

Another pause. "It's possible. Depending."

Well, thought Rook, at least Tim wasn't denying the possibility, or pretending he'd never heard of Rook. That was a favorable start. "A friend of mine has a hit man on her tail. I need to find him."

"That might be... impossible."

Rook understood that. If this agency owed the hit man any favors, they weren't going to turn him over. It was also possible that they might not know who he was. "I need a hint. Just a clue. Anything you can give me."

"Who is she?"

"Jennifer Fox. She's an attorney in Denver." He hesitated, then decided the information could be important to Tim in identifying which rumors on the underground he should pay attention to. "She hired the guy herself."

Tim was silent for a moment. Then, "I'll see what I can do."

"One more thing."

Another pause. "Maybe."

"Her husband and children were killed in a plane crash about six months ago. The FAA says it was no accident, and she's the prime suspect. I don't think she did it, but I can't prove it."

"I'll see if I can find out anything. But if I do, *you* owe *me*."

Rook chuckled. He couldn't help it. "Have I ever said no?"

"Just don't get all virginal on me. It's amazing what happens to a man's mind when he gets tangled up with a piece of tail."

"I'm not planning to get tangled up with anything."

"That's what they all say. Call me tomorrow, same time." Tim disconnected.

Rook hung up the receiver and turned to see that Massie had climbed into the front seat and was nearly pressed against the windshield as she watched him. When he looked at her she gave him a dog's grin and wiggled excitedly. He almost laughed.

"One more phone call," he told the dog. The others could wait, because he wanted to think a little longer about how many people he should call. Basically, he had to make up his mind as to how many folks he wanted to know that he was actively hunting the hit man. That might not be a good thing at all. Jay wouldn't mention it to anyone else, but some of the other people he knew weren't as trustworthy. And the last thing he wanted to do was tip off the guy that he was being hunted.

He picked up the phone again, and this time dialed the police. "I want to talk to whoever is handling the murder of those two cops last night."

He was transferred immediately and had to wait only about ten seconds before the phone was answered.

"Detective Fielding."

"Are you the guy investigating the murder of those two cops?"

"I'm one of them. Who are you?"

"You don't need to know that. I have information. Just listen. The woman did *not* kill those police officers. She was with me last night, and I'm prepared to testify to that in court. You need to check the upstairs window on the west side of her house. Someone broke in there last night by climbing up the tree."

"I need more than that," Fielding said. "I already got a million anonymous tips that aren't worth diddly."

"Then how's this for confirmation? I saw the cops after he shot them. They were each shot in the head once. It looked like the guy on the left got it first, and the other guy was just turning when he got it in the side of his head. The shooter must've been in the back seat."

"How do you know—"

Rook interrupted ruthlessly. "I saw them. I'm the guy who came running up after the drunk hit the side of their car. The shooter is a hit man who's been hired to kill the Fox woman. You're looking in the wrong place."

"But—"

Rook hung up without listening to the rest of it. If this detective was honest, he would at least check it out, and if he could find any evidence at all that someone had broken in to Jennifer's house last night, he would have to consider the possibility that she hadn't killed those cops.

He looked at the dog again and almost sighed. She had her nose pressed right to the windshield and had slobbered all over it. He was going to have to speak to her about that. But first, one more call, he decided.

This time he dialed the number of the C-phone that Ira had loaned Jennifer. It rang five times before she answered. Just as he was beginning to get a little antsy, she spoke.

"Hello?"

She sounded lost, he thought. A chill ran along his spine as he had a mental vision of her standing at the far end of a long, dark tunnel and slipping steadily farther away. If she had been there right then, he would have reached out and grabbed her and held her close so she couldn't slip farther away.

It was like that time a friend of his had been shot and had bled to death in his arms. He'd watched Ed drift away little by little, and nothing he had done, not all the tourniquets and compression and prayers, had stopped him.

"You okay, Lady Fox?"

"I'm fine. Really."

Yeah, he thought, and pigs fly. "I'm on my way back now with the dog. I had a couple of errands to run, though." He glanced at his watch. "There's a good moon tonight, so I should be back at the cabin by three." Actually, he fully anticipated being there an hour or so sooner than that, but he didn't want to give her anything to worry about if he was a little late.

"Why . . . don't you just come in the morning?"

It was hard for her to say that, he realized. She had been alone too long. "No. It's harder for somebody to tail me when there isn't any traffic."

"Oh."

"Don't wait up." He didn't know what made him say that, but the words sounded foolish to his own ears. "And if I'm a little late, don't panic. There are a lot of things that could slow me down."

"Like what?"

"Like losing a tail."

"Oh."

He thought he heard her sigh, and there was a little rustle in the background that made him wonder what she was wearing and whether she was sitting up in a chair or snuggled into his bed in the loft. Christ, this was no time for such thoughts! "The dog's doing fine," he told her, needing to change the subject. "I haven't seen any evidence of this pining you were all so worried about. She ate scrambled eggs and cheese for supper."

Jennifer surprised him with a sudden laugh, a deep, throaty sound that made something inside him tingle pleasurably. "Eggs and cheese? Oh, Rook, you're spoiling her! Didn't my parents give you any dog food?"

"About fifty pounds of it. And what's this stuff about raspberry leaves?"

"They help make a mastiff's labor easier. I don't know why."

"Well, you can give 'em to her when I get her up there, though God knows how I'm going to snowmobile her out to the cabin."

"I'm sure she'll ride on the sled. In fact, I'd be willing to bet that she loves it."

"We'll see." He was trying to sound vaguely put out by all this, but the truth was that he was enjoying Jennifer's suddenly improved mood. Hell, if what it took to get this woman to laugh was feeding a dog cheese omelets, he'd stuff Massie with the damn things. "Talk to you later."

He climbed back into his Explorer and had to argue with Massie about getting into the back seat again. She wasn't exactly difficult about it, but he could tell she was playing stupid. Thing was, how did you argue with a two-hundred-pound dog?

"Look, Massie," he finally said in his sternest voice, "if you don't get in the back seat, I can't take you to Jennifer." He didn't want the dog going through the windshield if he had to make a sudden stop. She was safer in the back.

She cocked her head inquisitively and apparently decided he wasn't going to change his mind. With a single thump of her tail, she scrambled into the back seat.

"Good girl!" He reached over to pat her head and scratch behind her ears. "Now we'll go find Jenny."

On winter nights Jennifer was never warm. From November through April, her nose, fingers and toes always felt icy. It didn't matter what the ambient temperature was. Right now she was certain the temperature in the loft was somewhere close to seventy degrees, but she still shivered beneath the down comforter and wished she had thought to bring her thermal underwear. Instead, all she had to wear to bed was a Denver Broncos T-shirt. It was Mark's, and she had started sleeping in it after his death.

Well, she told herself, thermal underwear wouldn't have made any difference. She would still be shivering and cold simply because her body seemed to go into hibernation in the winter. Instead of working harder to keep her warm, it just kind of shut down.

The comforter was thick and fluffy, and she promised herself that she would get warm shortly as her body heat elevated the temperature under all the goose down.

She had been thinking about Mark and the children ever since Rook had left. Despite hardly having slept all night, she hadn't been able to close her eyes to nap. Of course, that wasn't unusual for her. She'd never been able to nap much. Something about trying to sleep when the sun was up just didn't work. She would lie down, get all drowsy, and then suddenly get a burst of energy that drove her to get up.

Not being able to sleep this afternoon, however, had left her completely strung out. Her mind had been running around in circles, trying to deal with grief and fear and aching memories, until she had wanted to scream. Sometimes . . . sometimes when she was alone beneath the crushing weight of loss and guilt, she got angry about it. Angry that life had given her such pain, and angry with herself for using it as an instrument of self-punishment.

Because that was what she did. She nursed it and clung to it out of guilt for not having died with them. She used the grief to flog herself as if she were trying to atone for some grievous sin.

But then, when she was confined on all sides by her self-made prison of pain, she would question the justice of it. Why should she have to suffer so for the crime of living? It wasn't as if she had killed them. It wasn't as if her being on that plane could have prevented the disaster. It wasn't as if she could have done anything at all for them.

So why was it that she felt so guilty for being alive? Why did she feel she deserved to be punished? Why was she so unable to move on?

Whenever these questions occurred to her, she tried to dismiss them or ignore them. Her guilt wouldn't allow her to consider that she had any right to live at all. And when it struck her that feeling that way wasn't entirely normal, she banished that thought, too.

But sometimes, in a weak moment, she would wish it all away. She would wish that the burden of despair would lift from her shoulders and leave her fresh and able to live again. Guiltily, she would wish she could just stop hurting.

She'd done that again this afternoon, and then had fallen into an even worse pit of despair by punishing herself with the memory of her children.

And that was sick. Lying beneath the fluffy down comforter, staring into the dark after Rook's call, she realized that using the memory of her children to make herself suffer was mentally ill.

It was as if the very foundations of her existence suddenly tottered. Curling up tightly, she buried that thought, too, and fixed her attention on the night outside the window.

From where she lay, she could see over the loft railing and out through the glass doors of the living room. The moon was brilliant. Rook hadn't been wrong about that. If she'd had a pair of cross-country skis, she would have strapped them on and gone gliding over the snow in the vast emptiness of the valley where the only sound would have been the *swish* of her skis.

How long had it been since the last time she had troubled to go skiing? Especially skiing at night? Too long. Ever since her career had gotten busy. Ever since she'd had a child too young to ski. Eli would have loved it, but they'd never gotten around to taking him because Bethany was too small... and besides, she really hadn't had time.

Was that why she was feeling so guilty?

But she shied away from that question, too, and tried to imagine herself out there in the brilliant moonlight, the night almost as bright as day because of the way the snow magnified the moon's light. The air was still, and she would hear nothing at all except the sound of her own breathing, the movement of her skis through the snow and the occasional whirr as an owl swooped overhead.

Gradually she fell into the fantasy, herself alone with the night, speeding away on skis. She forgot about all the things that hurt. Forgot about all the things she feared.

Forgot about everything.

8

Moonlight turned the valley into an argent sea. The shadows beneath the evergreens became deep, mysterious pools of darkness in the gleaming expanse, wells into some netherworld. In the thin air of the high altitude, the stars were unusually bright and unblinking, coldly-watching eyes in the night.

Among the shadows something moved. Light gleamed dully off gunmetal, a darker shadow stretched and stirred.

The lights in the house below had been off when he had gotten here a few minutes ago, but signs of disturbance were evident in the snow all around. Someone had taken up residence here. He just couldn't be sure how many were in there, or if one of them was *her*.

He would have to wait and watch and see. Acting with incomplete intelligence caused serious problems, like those two cops last night. He hadn't wanted to kill them, but once they had caught him at his surveillance, he'd had no choice. No choice at all, because once she was dead they would have remembered the man who was watching her house.

So he'd told them he was a private dick hired by the husband's family, and they'd shot the breeze in the car for a few minutes before he'd made sure they would never be able to remember him.

It had been easy. So stupidly easy. But he didn't like leaving loose ends like that behind. Yes, he'd been able to make it look as if she had done it, but it had put him at far too much risk.

If he killed too many people at an isolated mountain cabin, he might become memorable. People who had seen him buying gas might remember him. People who had passed him on that nearly deserted road might remember his car. You never knew. Something might tip them off.

So he wanted to take out *only* her. And he didn't want to run the risk of being seen by someone else whom he would have to take out, too.

So he would wait. He would wait until he could see if she was alone. If she wasn't . . .

If she wasn't, he would watch and wait until she was.

And then he heard the distant sound of an approaching snowmobile, a buzzing that was a sacrilege in the silence of the night.

Moving swiftly, he shifted back deeper into the shadows and waited.

When Rook opened the back door of the A-frame, Massie was right beside him. She hesitated a moment on the threshold, sniffing the air suspiciously, but then she apparently scented Jennifer, because she was off like a shot.

Rook hoped Jenny didn't mind being wakened by two hundred pounds of cold, wet dog on her chest. A shriek thirty seconds later told him that Massie had found her target.

He flipped on the kitchen light and went back out to the sled to get the dog's supplies and the items he'd picked up at the supermarket to flesh out the staples Ira had given them.

Massie had been surprisingly good on the ride up here. Rook had had his doubts about whether the dog would stay on the sled, but she had managed beautifully. When he thought about it, he was surprised that she had come with him so willingly, given that he was a stranger taking her into strange territory.

When he had brought everything inside, he set the dog's dishes on her little table and made sure she had a big bowl of water. No food, though. The Comptons had insisted that she be fed on a strict schedule twice a day.

"Thank you."

Startled by the sound of Jennifer's husky voice, he turned quickly. Sleepy eyed, her hair tousled wildly, she stood in the kitchen doorway wearing a Broncos T-shirt and thick white socks. It was a far cry from the seductiveness of black negligees, and it turned him on as nothing in his life ever had.

In an instant he forgot all about the steak he was putting in the freezer. Forgot there was a huge and probably very protective dog standing beside her. Forgot that she was bad news because all she wanted to do was get her revenge and die. Forgot that the last thing on earth he ever wanted to do was get involved with another woman.

In two strides he was across the kitchen. The steak landed on the counter somewhere. A box skittered out of the way of his booted feet. Like some stupid Neanderthal, he wrapped his arms around Jennifer Fox and lifted her from her feet so that she was pressed hard to his chest, her face level with his.

His ski parka, still zipped, was between them. His snowmobile pants, still frigid from the night air, pressed against her bare legs. He wanted to feel her, but he couldn't. All he could do was hold her, looking into her startled green eyes and wishing they were naked on the floor in front of the fire.

And register that she didn't look frightened. That caught his attention, dragging him back from the brink of reality into the heat of a sudden fantasy. *Kiss her. Strip her. Love her.*

He was cold against her bare skin. She shivered as his icy clothes began to suck the warmth from her own scantily clad body. Her arms were pinned to her sides, and she realized she loved it. *Loved it!*

God, as long as he held her like this, as long as he imprisoned her with his strength, she wasn't responsible. She couldn't stop him. She didn't want to stop him, but she couldn't admit that.

Couldn't admit that for the first time in aeons her body was lighting with the most basic spark of life. Like a sleeper too long dormant, her womb was stirring, aching, waking. Yearning. Oh, God, she didn't want to want. She didn't want to yearn.

But she did. At her most basic level, she needed love the way a flower needed the sun. *Hold me. Kiss me. Love me. Make me live again.*

Some little part of her fiercely wanted to live again, but she couldn't acknowledge it. It made her feel guilty. She didn't deserve to live. But if he held her this way and forced her, she wouldn't be responsible. Her lips parted on words she would never speak.

Take me. Make me.

The invitation was in her eyes. Seeing it, his heart leapt. His loins leapt. Leaning forward, he claimed her mouth with his and plunged his tongue into warm, wet depths. Sweet. He felt as if he had been starving for her taste for an entire lifetime and had only just now realized it.

She shuddered as his tongue plunged deeply into her. He felt it through all the layers of clothing between them, felt the shudder turn into surrender as her head fell back and her mouth opened even wider. His entire body seemed to leap toward her, seeking to be close . . . closer. . . .

Another shudder ripped through her, and this one penetrated the fog of the fantasy that was gradually building in his mind. They weren't on the rug before the fire. She was getting cold, because they were standing in the kitchen, which had cooled down when he had the door open, and because she was wearing next to nothing. He needed to shed his outerwear, needed to get her into the warmer living room. . . .

Gently he took his mouth from hers and set her on her feet. Looking almost dazed, she gazed up at him. Disappointment speared through him as he saw the cloudy veils of passion vanish from her eyes. Suddenly she looked hurt. Lost.

"Why . . . why did you let me go?" she asked him. "Why didn't you make me?" Then she turned and fled.

Understanding crashed through him, a violent earthquake of revulsion and fury.

"Damn you!" he shouted after her. "Damn you! I'm not going to rape you just so you can feel innocent!"

Then he turned and stormed out of the house, slamming the door behind him. In the quiet night air, it sounded like a gunshot.

Jennifer huddled under the comforter, curled into a tight ball, sobbing as if every cell in her body were weeping. She felt sickened, sickened by herself, sickened over what Rook had said, sickened to realize that his accusation had been fair.

Rape was an ugly word. It didn't fit what had almost happened, did it? But what other word could you give it when you wanted someone to ride roughshod over all your objections and scruples and force you to do something you would never do on your own?

She pressed her face into the pillow, sobbing harder, feeling so painfully exposed that she might have been raped anyway. How could she have sunk so low?

Outside, Rook strode to the barn, madder than he could remember being since his life had been destroyed by the smooth lies of a smiling, spoiled scion of a West Point family. He wanted to kill someone or smash something, but he wouldn't do either. Instead, inside the barn, out of the cold and cutting wind that had suddenly kicked up, he paced in tight circles and ranted about the deceitful nature of women.

Christ! If she wanted to get laid, why couldn't she admit it? What was wrong with being *honest* about these things? He would never in a million years understand it.

But it wasn't the first time he'd run into this crap. Oh, no. It seemed to be a favorite game of women. The one time he'd been suckered into playing it, he'd wound up ankle deep in horseshit.

Jesus, he wanted a cigarette. He should have just bought a carton of the damn things at the convenience store and promised himself to quit after he sorted this mess out—if he ever did. Now he was miles from the nearest store and damned if he was going to ride the snowmobile again tonight.

The moon was setting anyway. He would just have to suck air between his lips and pretend he wasn't ready to kill for a drag of smoke.

Women! Years ago, when the double standard was strong, stuff like this might have been more understandable, but these days why couldn't they just admit they wanted it, too? Hell, he sure didn't want any woman who couldn't be honest about her desires. This wasn't supposed to be some kind of guessing game or borderline rape.

Oh, hell. There was probably more to it than that, anyway. Look at all she had been through. Maybe it was too much to expect her to know her own mind.

Well, he was going to have to be damn careful not to fall into that trap again. Whether she was just confused because of all that was going on or just congenitally incapable of being honest, he didn't need to deal with the inevitable fallout.

When he calmed down at last, he stepped back outside into the frigid night. The wind had strengthened even more, whipping up crystals of ice and stinging his face with them. He started tramping back to the house with his shoulders hunched, concentrating on only one thing: getting close to the stove and warming up. He felt as if he hadn't been warm in days.

Suddenly a new chill trickled down his spine, the unmistakable ice of knowing he was being watched.

He froze and turned slowly, straining his eyes to try to penetrate the darkness. The moon had just set, leaving only the faint gleam of starshine to illuminate the night. It was just enough to see by, if something had moved, but other than the swaying of the tall evergreens and the twisting whirlwinds of white snow, nothing appeared to stir.

He didn't like this. He had felt as if he was being watched earlier outside his lodgings, and now he felt it again. He trusted his sixth sense implicitly, but interpreting it could be a bitch. Someone might actually have been watching him then, or even now. But it was equally likely he was having a premonition of some kind, an intuitive prescience about events to come.

How could anyone have found him here? No one could possibly have thought to look for Jennifer here, could they? How would anyone make the connection?

But the feeling faded even as he stood there. Whatever the threat was, present or future, it was gone for now.

Nobody could have found Jennifer here, he told himself. No one on earth would have reason to look for her here. But just in case, he double-checked all the locks in the house and drew the curtains over the glass doors.

Then he stretched out on the couch and closed his eyes, pretending he didn't hear the faint sounds of Jennifer's weeping from upstairs.

Golden rays of sunlight were sliding beneath the curtains when Jennifer came downstairs. She had washed away the tearstains and dressed in jeans, socks and a bright green sweater. One way or another she had managed to get enough sleep, but she expected to find Rook sound asleep, since he had been up all night.

Instead, as she walked past the couch, she looked down and found him looking straight at her.

"You okay?" he asked roughly.

"Yes. Thank you." Surprise held her rooted there, even though Massie was dancing impatiently, eager to eat.

"Sorry I yelled at you." He shouldn't have done that, he had decided finally. Whatever was going on in this woman's head, he doubted she had been consciously trying to manipulate him.

"No," she said, dropping down to sit on the campaign chest coffee table and facing him. "*I'm* the one who's sorry." She closed her eyes and clenched her hands into fists in her lap. She, who had never been afraid to say what was necessary in the midst of the bitterest contract negotiation, she who had never pulled a punch, suddenly found it hard to say what needed saying. "You were right."

His tawny eyes narrowed, and he pushed himself up on one elbow. He didn't trust this. He didn't trust *any* woman.

"It's—" She broke off sharply. "I don't know if I can explain what happened."

"Don't." He didn't want to hear it. He wasn't her father confessor.

But she wasn't going to back away from it so easily. She couldn't. If nothing else she had to be honest for her own sake. "I felt so *guilty.*"

"About what, for Chrissake?"

"About cheating on Mark."

"Mark?"

"My husband."

"Are you referring to the husband who got killed in the plane crash?"

"Yes. Of course. I've never been married to anyone else."

Rook shook his head. He didn't like where this was going, but damned if he was going to pussyfoot around the truth here. "So what you're telling me is you felt like you were cheating on a dead man. Lady Fox, in *my* book, that's impossible. Correct me if I'm wrong, but the marriage vows are until *death.*" Or divorce, as the case may be, he added with silent cynicism.

"Yes, of course," she said, sitting as straight as a ramrod, her hands clenched until her knuckles were white. "You're right. I know that intellectually. But emotionally... I felt like I was cheating."

If nothing else, there was one thing he wanted to hear her admit. He needed to hear it, and she probably needed to hear it, too. "But you wanted it, didn't you? You really wanted it."

Swallowing hard, she looked away, then nodded. It was a dangerous thing to admit, she knew, because it put the power squarely in his hands. But honesty was more important. It was time, she told herself, to start being honest with herself about what was going on. She was burying herself alive, and no amount of excusing it by saying she couldn't bear the grief and loneliness changed what it was: self-immolation on the pyre of carefully nurtured sorrow. A refusal to live, even though life and fate had ruled that she should.

Mark would heartily disapprove.

But she needed to explain, needed Rook to understand, maybe because by explaining she could make herself understand. "Haven't you ever loved someone so much that losing them made life feel like a bad, meaningless joke?"

For an instant he flashed back to the court-martial, to watching his career and his future go down in flames, to the moment when his wife had looked at him and said, *You're a loser, Rook. I'm not wasting any more of my life on you.* Did he know that life was a meaningless joke?

"You just don't get it, Lady Fox. Well, here's a news flash. Life *is* a meaningless joke. You haven't lost anything that millions of people don't lose every day. You haven't even discovered anything new. Cut out the pity party and join the rest of the human race."

She jerked as if he had just struck her, giving him a wounded look, then hurried from the room without a backward glance. That was when he realized why he called her Lady Fox. There was something so damn regal about the way she held her head, the way she moved sometimes. A goddamn queen.

It was amazing how screwed up people could get. Sure, she missed her family. Sure, it hurt to lose them. Christ, there wasn't anything worse in the world. But to feel like she was cheating on a dead man? To be living for nothing but revenge? She needed a psychiatrist.

There had been a brief time when he had wanted revenge, too. But at least he'd had the sense to realize it would have cost him dearly. That was the thing that too many people failed to realize until it was too late: taking revenge meant making yourself no better than the person you wanted to get even with.

"There was a steak on the counter. It's nearly thawed. Do you want me to cook it?"

He sat up and looked at her. She was standing in the doorway to the kitchen, her hands on her hips. Behind her, he could see the dog chowing down. "I forgot to put it in the freezer. It isn't spoiled?"

"I don't think so. The center is still frozen. I wouldn't want to keep it much longer, though."

"I'll cook it. Steak and eggs for breakfast?"

She nodded. There were dark circles under her eyes, and she looked so frail he could hardly stand it. What he ought to do was bail out *now.* This damn woman was beginning to get under his skin. And now, even though she appeared to have put their discussion behind her, he felt he ought to apologize for being so brutal a few minutes ago. Brutal? Hell, he'd only been telling the truth.

While he fried the steak and eggs, she made toast and coffee. It was exactly the kind of high-octane meal he needed after the past couple of days, when he'd hardly paused to eat. As he filled his stomach, he began to feel the last of the winter chill lose its grip on him.

"Take me back to Denver."

Rook looked up from his plate. He'd been avoiding looking at Jennifer, because every time he did so, he felt an uncomfortable tug on feelings he thought he'd killed a long time ago. "That would be stupid. The police are looking for you in connection with the murder of those two cops. It was all over the news."

"Well, you can tell them I didn't do it."

"That won't keep you out of jail. They're also looking for you in connection with the deaths of your family. Unfortunately, you pulled a disappearing act, so when you show up, they're going to jail you and deny you bond—I don't care how good a lawyer you get."

She thought that over for a few moments while he devoured a hunk of steak.

"I might as well be in prison up here," she said finally. "My hands are tied just as effectively. I can't look for the murderer, and I can't defend myself against the charges."

"But there you'd be a sitting duck."

"In jail? How much safer could I be from the hit man?"

"A lot. Get real, lady. People in jail get offed all the time. Maybe the hit man couldn't get to you directly, but he could sure as hell get somebody else to run a shiv up under your ribs."

"Quit telling me to get real, Rook. My life has been about as real as it comes. Pain like this isn't a fantasy!"

"Oh, the pain is real," he agreed, stabbing another chunk of meat with his fork, "but what you're doing with it is pure crazy! Christ, a hit man to knock you off—Jesus, why didn't you do it yourself and leave the damn money to charity? There are folks out there who *want* to live who could have done a hell of a lot more with that money than the friggin' hit man!"

"I didn't want my family to know it was suicide! Do you have any idea how they would feel if they knew I'd killed myself?"

That touched a chord in him so deep and painful that he couldn't ignore it. He tossed down his fork and shoved his chair back, rising to tower over her. "Yeah," he said bitterly. "I have an idea. My daughter committed suicide."

He had to get away from her. He had to escape before he started spewing out all the anguish and anger that he kept carefully sealed in a deep crypt of his mind. Whether she meant to or not, she was digging up things he had dealt with only by putting them away for good.

Rook took the snowmobile out. The feeling of being watched that he'd had last night had refused to let go of him, and it was as good an excuse as any to get away and get a grip. At a distance of about a thousand yards, he circled the house, figuring that if anyone had come into the valley with an interest in the house, he would cross their path somewhere.

The light was blinding, sun on pristine snow, but the yellow lenses of his goggles heightened the contrast and softened the blue enough that he wasn't blinded. Unfortunately, it wasn't long before he realized that Massie had probably chased a rabbit out here. Not only did he cross his own trails from yesterday and last night, but he also crossed the trail of a rabbit, which soon converged with a much deeper and messier one that must have been made by the dog. Apparently Massie hadn't wanted to eat the rabbit—there was no sign of blood in the snow—but the chase had gone on for quite a distance, zigzagging back and forth up and down the valley.

Eventually he came across some ski tracks, but they were messed up by Massie's antics to the point where he couldn't tell much from them. Someone might have been here yesterday, but it didn't appear threatening. Whoever they were, they had moved on, and cross-country skiers crisscrossed these mountains like the warp and woof on a loom. If they had meant any harm to Jennifer, they'd had most of yesterday to do it.

Finally, reluctantly, he had to turn back to the house. He couldn't hide out here all day. He needed to call Ira and see if he had found anything. Later he would call

Tim and a couple of other people. Until he'd talked to them, there was nothing more he could do to continue the hunt.

As for who had killed Jennifer's family... He stopped the snowmobile and scanned the valley as much out of long-standing habit as a desire to check things out. As for who had killed her family, he needed to get her to write a list of all the people who might possibly have any desire to harm her or her husband. He needed to tell her to put her mind to work on the most basic questions so that they would at least have a starting point.

But he didn't want to go back into that house. It was poisoned now, full of painful memories. Looking at her, he was going to see curiosity and pity in her gaze, and he didn't want to see that. He didn't want to be reminded of his daughter every time he looked at her. Christ, he'd spent a long, long time learning not to remember her. Going back into that house and looking at Jennifer now would be tantamount to opening the door to a past he'd done his best to bury.

But he couldn't stay out here indefinitely. With heavy reluctance he completed his circumnavigation of the valley and headed back to the house.

Jennifer wanted to talk to him, but his expression absolutely forbade it. She wanted to ask him about his daughter, wanted to commiserate, but realized with a jolt that her desire was purely selfish. If *he* wanted to talk about it, he would. He didn't want to. She should just leave him alone.

A pall of silence as thick as a funeral shroud settled over the house after Rook returned. Massie went out briefly, then settled down for a nap by the wood stove.

Jennifer washed the dishes and cleaned up the kitchen, then curled up in a wingback chair with a pad of paper and a pen. Rook had asked her to make a list of anyone who might have wanted to hurt her or Mark, no matter how remote it seemed, and to list the reasons beside the names. They had to have a starting place, he said.

Then he stretched out on the couch, dozing with the cellular phone nearby, leaving her alone with her painful journey down the dusty roads of memory.

The first names that occurred to her were as obvious as they were unlikely. Big corporations didn't go around killing lawyers to solve their problems. It was too damn risky and too damn unnecessary. No, corporations and other big-money interests who wanted to silence a lawyer usually set about doing a background investigation that in most cases could come up with enough dirt to use in a complaint to the bar. The bar, as susceptible to being swayed by money and power as any other entity, would usually launch an investigation of its own, and as often as not suspend the lawyer until the matter was settled. Civil rights lawyers and lawyers for Native American interests were the usual targets of this kind of action—not contract lawyers like herself.

No, in her case the motive had to be something very personal to someone. Getting her off a particular case would have been easy. Someone had wanted her *dead*.

Well, she thought, almost anybody at the firm. Sally Carstairs had believed Jennifer was all that was standing between her and a partnership. More than one supposedly joking comment had made that apparent. Nor was Jenny the only one at the firm who had been aware of that rivalry. Felix Abernathy had mentioned it a couple of times, and so had Karl Gruber. Heck, even Karl's wife, Gretchen, had commented on it once. Sally hadn't made any secret of it, but the two women had gotten along anyway. Rivalry was part and parcel of a competitive environment, after all.

But then there was Sally's husband, Dowd. He had probably shared his wife's view, and something about him had always given Jennifer the creeps. Still, that didn't make him capable of murder.

Felix Abernathy, on the other hand, wasn't even in direct competition with her. He was already a junior partner, and he worked in the firm's criminal division, handling cases like Alan DeVries. She liked Felix a whole lot and always had. Of course, there had been that stock thing last winter, but Felix hadn't done anything wrong, and she had never for an instant believed he had. All she had been worried about was how it could look if it came to the attention of the SEC. Even the appearance of impropriety could have been devastating for both Felix and the firm.

But that had been ages ago, and Felix had been cleared. What was more, he'd even thanked her for bringing it to his attention so he could make sure that no one mistook his ignorance for involvement. As far as she was concerned, it was forgotten, and as far as Felix was concerned, it appeared to be, too—except that he felt he owed her a favor.

Chewing on the end of the pen, she looked across the room to where Rook slept on the couch, his hands clasped on his stomach, his eyes closed. This morning . . .

God, how guilty she felt about that. How guilty she felt that right now her eyes were devouring him as if she couldn't get enough of the sight of him. Her gaze trailed over him, touching his muscular thighs, his flat abdomen, the bulge between his legs, and her insides responded with a strong, clenching throb of need.

She didn't need these feelings, didn't want these feelings, but no amount of trying to banish them seemed to work. She sat there, unable to look away from Rook, her entire body coming alive to the possibilities of passion. Each time she shifted in the chair, her jeans pressed against her tender flesh, reminding her just how aroused she was. Even the slight caress of her hair against her cheek made her yearn for a lover's touch.

She tried to tell herself that this was happening only because it had been so long since she had last made love, but it was a lie, and she knew it. Never, ever, had she felt this aroused over so little.

Looking down, she tried to concentrate on the list she was making, aware that if she got out of this chair she was going to cross the room to wake Rook and let the chips fall where they may. She couldn't do that. She would hate herself if she did.

But her body wouldn't let it pass. Desperately, she was reaching for an affirmation of life in the most basic way possible. The realization unnerved her. How could she want to live and die at the same time? How could she reconcile a desire to live with her guilt over not having died?

She couldn't think about this. It wouldn't do any good, because there were no solutions for the problems in her life. The only thing she could do was concentrate on finding the person or persons who had killed her husband and children. For now she had to put aside everything else and focus on her anger. On her search for revenge. Nothing else mattered.

Oh, Mark... The yearning sigh rose in her mind and winged away on the ether. This time, though, it didn't fill her with ineffable sorrow. This time...this time she felt sad acceptance.

Shocked, guilty, she recoiled and quickly forced her attention to the list. Who might have wanted to kill her? The problem was, she couldn't seriously imagine anyone she knew as a murderer. Oh, not that there probably wasn't a sufficiency of motives. Given what she had done for a living, there were undoubtedly a number of people who wished her ill. But to imagine one of them actually killing...that was a different matter altogether.

But that wasn't the question, was it? She wasn't supposed to be sitting here figuring out who had killed her family. She was only supposed to figure out who might have had a motive, just so she would have a starting point.

Well, Felix was out of the question. He was probably the only one who was.

Scott Paxton, on the other hand, had fired her. He also had ample reason to fear a lawsuit from her, because he had violated her contract with the firm by letting her go. She hadn't sued only because she hadn't cared enough, not when her entire life was already ruined. What if he had been trying to find a way to get rid of her for a long time?

Who else? She was reluctant to write down the names of clients, because Rook would want to know what their motivations might be, and the discussion in some cases could violate confidentiality.

Besides, for all that she truly believed she was more likely to have been the target than Mark, her inability to imagine anyone she knew being capable of murder was blocking her entire thought process on the matter. She kept coming up with excuses rather than dealing with the problem: who might have had a reason to want her dead?

Well, there was Eric Billyers in the QuantumWare–Action Graphics merger. He had lied about his company's assets in a blatant attempt to make Action Graphics unappealing to QuantumWare. She had found him out and called him on it in a conference with at least twenty witnesses. He'd certainly wanted her dead at the time. It had been written all over his face.

She added him to her list.

By the time she finished she had twenty names, though she was tempted to cross off half of them. She left them anyway, figuring it couldn't hurt to check out every possibility. Dropping the pad onto the end table beside her chair, she stretched deeply, reaching to the ceiling with her hands.

Sheer curtains were drawn across the glass doors to make it difficult for anyone to look in, but she could see that the day was waning. Blue shadows dappled the snow now, highlighting every drift. What a waste of a beautiful day, she found herself thinking. She should have been out skiing in the glorious sunshine, soaking up the beauty of nature.

Her heart clenched with painful awareness that she shouldn't be thinking of enjoying anything, that she had no right to even want to enjoy things. But even as she had the thought and felt the pang, she knew she was being irrational. Life went on. Whether you wanted it to or not, it continued.

"What's wrong?"

The sound of Rook's voice startled her. She glanced his way to see he was sitting up, looking as if he had never napped at all. "Nothing, really," she answered. "I was just thinking."

"Did you finish your list?"

"Twenty names."

All of a sudden he cocked his head to one side and grinned crookedly. "You must be one hell of a bitch."

"No, I'm just one hell of a lawyer. Most of the names are people who didn't get what they wanted from my clients. The others are my co-workers."

"We'll start with the co-workers." Rising, he stretched widely.

"Why?"

"Because you were dealing with them on a daily basis. That's more likely to drive someone to murder. People who knew they were never going to have to encounter you again would probably think of other forms of revenge, such as subscribing you to every magazine in the known universe."

"Did you ever do that to someone?"

"No. Too juvenile. But I don't believe in revenge, anyway."

"Why not?"

He looked at her, wondering if she was just giving him a hard time, or if she was genuinely curious. Curious, he decided finally, although her face revealed very little. "Because taking revenge makes you no better than the person you take revenge on."

She looked down at her lap. "Are you saying I'm no better than the person who killed my family?"

"No. Not yet. But what are you going to do when you find him? Kill him? What'll you be then, Lady Fox? Hmm? Just another murderer?"

She twined her fingers together. "I wish you wouldn't call me that. My name is Jennifer."

He swore. "Listen, when are you going to start thinking about what you're doing? When are you going to wake up and deal with what's really going on here? You've lost your family, but instead of picking up and going on, you hired a hit man to kill you, and now *you're* planning to kill someone. *Think about it!*"

Stomping across the room, he halted directly in front of her and stabbed a finger at her. "Quit changing the subject, Lady Fox. Wake up and take a good long look at yourself in the mirror!"

9

Rook muttered something about stepping outside and left Jennifer alone in the darkening living room. Massie stirred, looking as if she wanted to follow Rook but didn't want to abandon Jennifer. Finally the dog chose Jennifer, coming to sit beside the chair and rest her chin on Jenny's knee.

Jennifer reached out with a trembling hand to scratch Massie. Look at herself in the mirror? Didn't he understand that she couldn't bear to do that?

Leaning forward, she pressed her face to the top of Massie's head and closed her eyes, trying to hold in the tears. Despite her efforts, they seeped between her eyelids. Massie gave a soft whimper and pressed closer, as if she understood. God, why couldn't she just stop hurting? Just for a little while?

Rook, feeling bad about his outburst, soon came back into the house and found her curled up and weeping silently into the dog's fur. He never should have yelled at her, no matter how frustrating he found her blindness. Who was he to say how long or how hard she should grieve, or in what way?

Hell, he was being a fool. She didn't need a shake, she needed a hug. She needed somebody to be patient with her and hold her close until she got through this. And she *would* get through this. Whether she knew it or not, she was reaching for life again. He could remember all too clearly how difficult that was. Every time he had started to smile, he'd felt guilty. How could you smile when someone you loved was dead?

He stood rooted to the floor for what seemed like the longest time, reluctant to get any deeper into this mire. Jennifer was an emotional black hole right now. She needed more than anyone could give, and anyone who started giving might well wind up being sucked dry. Besides, he kept his emotions out of things these days. Life was easier if you stayed on the surface as much as possible. If he tried to help this woman any more than he already was, he was going to plunge right into the depths.

Christ, he wanted a cigarette. Just one lousy cigarette.

Jennifer sniffled quietly and started to lift her head, as if she had cried enough and wanted to wipe away the scalding tears. Something about that little sniffle overrode the last of his resistance. Cursing himself for a fool, he crossed the room to her.

She looked up instantly, her cheeks wet with tears, and appeared embarrassed to have been found crying on her dog's shoulder. Massie looked up, too, her brown eyes reproaching him as if he were at fault for this. Maybe he was.

"Come here," he said roughly, and lifted Jennifer from the chair into his arms.

She gasped, stunned by the ease with which he plucked her from her chair and carried her.

"You need to eat more," he growled. "Damn it, woman, you look like hell. Just a bag of bones."

He sat down on the couch so abruptly that she gasped again, but then she was cradled on his lap, her face tucked against his warm neck, with his arms snug and powerful around her. A strong, unexpected feeling of safety suddenly swamped her, causing fresh tears to spring to her eyes.

"Probably half the reason you're so depressed is that you're starving to death," he continued in the same paradoxically gentle and rough voice. "You peck at your food like a sick bird. I don't care whether you're hungry or not, you eat more, hear? You make a point of it, or you're not going to be strong enough to wrestle all these demons."

"Demons?" The word came out on a choked whisper, little more than a hiccup of sound.

"All the demons that are driving you nuts. You sure have enough of them. But you can whip 'em, you know. You can whip every one of 'em. But you need your strength and energy to do that."

He was crazy, she thought, unconsciously snuggling closer to his warmth and strength. He was nuts to be worrying about whether she was eating enough. There were more important things to be thinking about.

"As soon as I get through hugging you, you're going to eat. Christ, woman, if you won't take care of yourself, *I* will."

It sounded like a threat, but it warmed her to her very toes. She felt herself relaxing into his embrace, and for once guilt didn't rear up to remind her that she was allowed no comfort, no joy, no rest.

His hand rubbed her arm soothingly, and from time to time reached up to comb through escaping tendrils of her hair. Not caring what she looked like, she had been pulling it back haphazardly into a clip. Letting herself go to hell. That realization whispered sadly through her mind.

"Take care of yourself," he said again. "If you really want to find the person who did this to you, you need to take care of yourself. You don't want to collapse and wind up in a hospital."

"No..." She barely sighed the word.

"And stop feeling so guilty. What happened was out of your hands. If something you did made somebody want you dead, you didn't know what it was, so you couldn't have changed it."

"What happened to your daughter?" The words tumbled out, blurted before she could stop them. His hand froze in midstroke, and his arms tightened until they felt like steel bands around her. It seemed a very long time before they relaxed. "I'm sorry," she whispered. "I shouldn't have asked."

"I've learned to live with it," he said finally. "I just don't like to rake it up."

"I can understand that."

"You need to learn to do that. Bury it. You don't have to think about it every single moment of every day."

She couldn't imagine burying it. It seemed so wrong somehow.

"There's a reason we have funerals," he said slowly. "It's not for the people who've died. It's for *us,* the living. It marks a major change in our lives and lets us know it's time to move on."

She tilted her head up and tried to see his face. "You've thought a lot about these things."

"There was a period in my life when I didn't have a lot else to do. I did a lot of thinking about death and funerals. Even did some reading. A funeral is just a ceremony in which the community recognizes a change. It's not an end for the living, Jenny, it's the *beginning* of a new stage. Somehow you've got to realize that deep inside, where it counts. The life you had with your husband and children is over, but *your* life *isn't.* Nor should it be."

She closed her eyes tightly in anticipation of the pain that reminder usually gave her, but what she felt instead was a soft ache and the lick of anger in the pit of her stomach. The despair was receding, she realized with a sense of shock. It was giving way to a quieter sorrow and anger that life had dealt her such a blow. Anger that some person had hurt...*her*. Not just Mark and the children, but *her.*

"Easy, Jenny," Rook said, as if he sensed the shock and the anger she was feeling. As if he sensed the shift within her. His arms tightened around her.

She began shaking, shaking hard, as she faced the fury she felt at the way *she* had been hurt. Yes, she missed her husband and children, still ached with loneliness for them, but for the first time she honestly faced the fact that they hadn't been the only victims. And for the first time, when she admitted her own suffering, she *didn't* feel as if she somehow deserved it. Didn't endure guilt for feeling that she had been a victim, too.

"It's okay, Jenny.... It's okay...."

She was shaking and couldn't stop. It was as if the stress on her had reached a shattering point and had set off an earthquake. She had to stop. She had to calm down.... Damn it, she had been hurt, too. She was a victim, too!

Anger bubbled up in her, thick and hot like lava spewing from the throat of a volcano, anger at the person who had condemned her to hell.

"Jenny...Jenny, you haven't been condemned." Rook's voice, deep and firm, cut into her thoughts, dragging her out of the whirlwind of anger and back into the present. She had been talking, she realized, spewing out her anger in words, breaking the barrier of silence that had locked so much inside her.

His arms were tight around her, as if he wanted to hold her together. Maybe that *was* all that was holding her together, she thought wildly. Everything else in the world seemed to be shifting like quicksand beneath her feet. Nothing was what it had seemed.

Rook would have given a year of his life to be able to do or say something that would help her through the feelings that were tearing her apart. Unfortunately, he couldn't think of a damn thing. Some things, no matter how tough, simply had to be weathered until they passed.

Finally she sagged against him, exhausted and wrung dry of tears. His hold on her gentled until it was as if he held a weary child.

But she was no child. She was a woman full-grown, and it wasn't long before his senses took complete note of that fact. She might be too thin, but her hair was as soft as silk, and her skin felt like satin. The scent of her was womanly rich and heady, and he found himself wishing he could just slip into her warm, wet depths and forget the world.

The afternoon had almost completely faded into an early-winter evening. Outside, the last of the sun's warmth had gone, and night's deep chill was replacing it. The insulated drapes needed to be drawn over the sheers before he turned on a light, so that no one in the world outside could see who was within. If anyone was out there.

But he didn't want to move. It had been a long, long time since he had held a woman on his lap. A long time since he had comforted someone who wasn't dying. It made him feel good to do even this small, positive thing.

It was dangerous, but at the moment he couldn't work up any real concern about it, not when it felt so damn good to hold her close. Closing his eyes, he just let himself feel, let his senses drink in a sensation so rare that it seemed almost alien. He hadn't let anyone this close in a long time, and while the danger worried him, it also drew him.

Bowing his head, he pressed his face to her hair and wondered when the last time was that he had been touched by something so soft. And sweet smelling. Her hair was softly perfumed with a scent like coconut.

She shifted, settling more comfortably against him, and he nearly caught his breath at the way that made him feel. It was a sign of trust, he realized. Whether or not she realized it, she had given him her trust.

And then he was feeling something he hadn't felt since his youth, a trembling anticipation and fear, as if everything depended on what happened in the next few moments. Everything else receded, even as some corner of his mind shrieked that he was taking an unconscionable risk, letting down his guard, forgetting that he needed to be on full alert because of the hit man. There were things he needed to be doing. Calls he needed to make . . .

And right now none of it mattered. Not when Jenny hesitantly turned her face up, looking at him with a question in her beautiful green eyes . . .

Jenny caught her breath as her gaze met his. He was close, so close, his tawny eyes appearing to be lit from within. When his lips parted, everything inside her seemed to go instantly soft with yearning. Her head sagged back, her own lips parting in invitation.

Why? Some sane voice deep in her mind shrieked the question. Why was she feeling this way? She hardly knew him, and he hadn't been especially nice up until now. He could be almost any kind of person. How could she be softening, opening, yielding, yearning to give herself?

Between her legs a heaviness grew, and the weight of it spread through her, holding her prisoner, making it impossible to move. Impossible to do anything except wait for him. Everything else faded away, leaving her in thrall to needs and wants older than time.

Rook took her invitation. As soon as his mouth met hers, everything else in the universe vanished. She was soft, yielding, taking him into her in a way that rocked him to his very soul. It was as if someone had lit a candle in the dark void of his life, promising warmth where before there had been only cold. And when her arms came up around his neck, that flame grew into a conflagration.

Jennifer had forgotten how much she could want to be held, kissed, touched. She melted at the touch of Rook's mouth on hers, at the heat of his tongue slipping past her lips. The conquest was symbolic, but her surrender was not. She wanted this. She wanted him. She didn't care what the consequences might be, if only she could be held and loved one more time before she died.

Every nerve in her body seemed to reach out to him, begging for a caress of any kind. Twisting, she tried to get closer, needing to be pressed to him as tightly as she could get.

He seemed to read her mind, because suddenly he lifted her and settled her again so that she straddled his lap, facing him. There was an incredible moment of awareness when her legs parted, exposing her so completely. Leaving her unprotected. And then he settled her against him snugly, giving her some of what she needed but not nearly enough.

Closer... she had to get closer.... Opening her legs even wider, she pressed herself tightly to him and nearly groaned as the much-needed pressure at once satisfied her and inflamed her even more. He whispered something she couldn't make out, but the sound of it was enough to tell her that he was feeling just what she was, needing just what she needed.

Leaning forward, she pressed her aching breasts to his chest and her face tightly to his neck. His hands slipped down her back and cupped her bottom, holding her closer still, making her feel as if the arc of a welder's torch were melding them together.

The weight in her womb was growing, becoming more demanding. His hips moved, pressing upward, bringing them closer yet. One of them groaned, neither of them knew which, nor did it matter. It was a sound born of a need so deep there were no words for it. Grasping his shoulders tightly, she tried to move even closer, pressing harder and harder....

One of his hands slipped up beneath her sweater, beneath her bra, inching up to cup her breast, pinch her nipple. A shaft of agonizing pleasure speared through her, causing her to arch backward, at once driving her hips closer and exposing her breasts for more of his exquisite torture. It seemed as if all the answers to all the impossible questions were right before her and all she had to do was reach out for them....

Suddenly there was a loud clatter from the kitchen. Both of them froze, eyes opening and staring at one another, ears straining.

"Oh, my God," Jennifer whispered as reality crashed down around her. "Oh, my God, what am I doing?"

Rook looked at her as if she had just hit him, then lifted her swiftly from his lap and dumped her unceremoniously on the couch.

"Nothing," he said roughly as he rose swiftly to his feet. "You're not doing a damn thing."

Massie was standing in the doorway of the kitchen, looking almost shamefaced. In an instant Rook realized that she must have knocked one of her stainless steel dishes off her little table. If anyone had broken in to the house, she certainly wouldn't be standing there looking at him as if she expected to be punished.

He glanced down at Jennifer and found her staring at him with wide, horrified eyes, her hand pressed to her mouth as if she thought she would vomit. Christ, he had never yet made a woman vomit. "It was the dog," he said shortly. "She must have knocked something over."

Then he strode to the kitchen, cursing himself for a fool and her for a lunatic. What a pair they made.

Massie had indeed knocked over her empty water dish. He refilled it for her and stood there watching her drink eagerly.

Women were poison, he reminded himself for the umpteenth time. Sheer poison. What the hell was he doing getting tangled up with one whose head was so messed up she didn't know if she was coming or going? Sure, he wanted to go to bed with her. For some crazy reason, she turned him on more than he'd been turned on in a hell of a long time.

But so what? She was dying of guilt and grief, and sooner or later she would crucify him, whether she intended to or not. Assuming, of course, that he let himself give a damn about her. Nope, he was going to ignore every softening tug on his emotions. He was going to stay indifferent and isolated the way he'd been since Cheryl left and his daughter died. Nothing, absolutely nothing on earth, was worth the pain of caring.

He had drawn the curtains and was stoking the fire when Jennifer at last descended from the loft. He supposed she had spent the past hour or so wallowing in guilt for no better reason than that she'd felt a very human desire to get laid. Now, it wasn't as if he didn't have some pretty high standards of his own in the areas of honor and duty, but she was carrying this well past any justifiable ethic. Her husband was dead. She deserved to live. But apparently she didn't see it that way.

Well, screw it. He had better things to do with his life than bounce off the brick wall of her problems.

When she reached the foot of the ladder staircase, she faced him with clasped hands, like a schoolgirl expecting a scolding.

"I'm sorry," she said.

Now, *that* was something he hadn't expected. "What the hell for?"

She appeared surprised. "I thought that was obvious."

"Not to me."

"But I was—I was a *tease.*"

Right then, frustrated as he was, he could have laughed. Something that had knotted tight deep inside him relaxed. "You don't know the meaning of the word. All you did was get swept away briefly by some very natural feelings. Seems like you weren't the only one getting carried away."

"Maybe so, but I know—I knew I would feel guilty. I should just have avoided the entire situation."

"That's a little like trying to fight a riptide. You'll lose every time."

He tossed another log into the firebox, adjusted the damper and closed the stove door. When he straightened and turned around, Jenny was gone. He could hear her moving around in the kitchen, along with the *tick-tick* of Massie's claws on the tile floor. Deciding to let well enough alone, at least for now, he perched on the couch and reached for the cellular phone. Time to call Ira and see if he had learned anything. And in a few hours he could call Tim.

"Hey, guy," Ira said when he answered the phone. "How are you two doing out there?"

"We're getting by. I'll probably be coming out in the morning to head back to town and check some things out. Is everything okay on your end?"

"Yup. Nary a soul has passed through here, other than a fella whose car I'm working on."

"That's good. Did you find out anything?"

"I may be a little rusty at this, ol' buddy, but my contacts are still good. Some of them, anyway. At this point, though, all I've got is rumor. Rumor says there's somebody new in the business, and he's a wild card."

"That's a lot of help," Rook said sarcastically. Shit, a wild card. Somebody so new he was unpredictable. Somebody who hadn't been at it long enough to be identified by prior acts. Somebody essentially faceless and nameless in the community. "Do you think you'll learn anything else?"

"My sources promised to keep their ears to the ground. I can't say whether they'll do any active investigating, but if they hear anything at all, they'll call me."

"Thanks, Ira. I really appreciate it."

"No prob. And, hey, I was in town the other day. I picked up some more groceries, if you need anything."

"You're a champ. What I'd like to have on hand, though, is some cross-country skis."

"For both of you? Well, hell, that's easy enough. Jeez, I must have twenty, thirty pairs you can choose from. Boots, too."

"So many?"

"I once had the stupid idea that I could rent them on the side and make some money. I never broke even."

"You aren't exactly on the beaten path."

"I realized that eventually."

Rook was still chuckling when he hung up. He'd never imagined Ira as an entrepreneur, of all things.

Jennifer was still clattering around in the kitchen, and he decided to leave her alone for a while longer yet. She was probably feeling embarrassed as well as guilty, although, as far as he could see, she didn't have any reason to feel either. Not that he was surprised. The human race seemed to have a real talent for making a hash out of a perfectly normal need.

Picking up the phone again, he dialed the number of an acquaintance in Denver, a man who was still in army intelligence.

"Hey, Rook!" Clark LaRue greeted him with surprised warmth. "Long time no see. What've you been up to?"

"A little of this and a little of that."

"Right." Clark chuckled. "I have my sources. You're keeping busy."

"Busy enough. How're Inge and the kids?"

"She took them to Germany for two months to visit relatives. Well, she hasn't been home in five years, so we kind of figured it'd be nice if she and the kids could spend Christmas with her family."

"Hell, she should have asked me to go along. *I'd* like to spend Christmas with her family." He and Clark had met while they were stationed in Germany, and both of them had been invited to spend the holidays with Inge's family after she and Clark had married. Rook cherished a lot of fond memories of the hospitality of the Wieberneit family.

"She'd probably have taken you up on it," Clark told him. "I couldn't get away for that long, and she wasn't happy about it."

"Are you going at all?"

"For a week. It's not a good time right now."

"Well, I could have gone for the whole two months."

"Then go. They'd love to see you again."

He was tempted. Sorely tempted. The Wieberneits had always offered him a home away from home. It would be nice to have a pretend family, but even nicer to get away from all this crap. This unsoluble problem. "I can't. I'm involved in a...case right now. That's actually why I called."

"What I can do, I'll do," Clark said. That was his attitude toward everything in life.

"I have a lady friend who has a hit man on her tail."

"Not good. Not good at all. But I don't swim in those waters, buddy. You know that."

"But maybe you know somebody who does and who might be able to put an ear to the ground."

Clark thought about it a moment. "Maybe," he said finally, sounding pensive. "Yeah, maybe I do. Give me whatever details you have."

Rook sketched the story quickly, including Ira's intelligence that there was a "wild card" in the area now. "Primarily I was wondering if anyone's been recently discharged locally who might have the training for this kind of thing."

"That much I'm *sure* I can check on. I'll put out some queries first thing in the morning. And when do I get to meet this lady friend?"

Rook hesitated. He'd referred to Jenny as a lady friend simply to explain his interest in this mess, but that had apparently been a mistake. He'd forgotten that Clark would naturally be interested. After all, they'd been personal friends for years. Clark and Inge had been nearly as upset by Cheryl's defection as he had. And they had been the only people who had come to visit him while he'd been in the stockade.

But now he had to explain Jenny in a way that wouldn't arouse Clark's curiosity. "She's just a friend," he said finally. "Nothing more. I don't want anything more. You know that."

"So you keep saying." But much to Rook's relief, he dropped the subject. "Just let me know when you've got a little time on your hands and we'll get together. Golf, dinner, a few drinks—whatever."

When he hung up the phone, Rook had the uneasiest feeling that he'd just failed a test of some kind, but he couldn't for the life of him explain it. He sat for a while, staring pensively into space, trying to figure out exactly what was troubling him. It was as if he was looking right past the obvious somehow.

Finally he put it on the back burner and made a couple of other calls to acquaintances who weren't as close as Clark but had lines on other information sources. If anybody in Denver knew what the hit man was up to, there was a damn good chance that his network would get wind of something.

But now there was nothing else he could do until around nine-thirty when he would call Tim.

"Rook?" Jennifer spoke quietly from behind him. "I'm making dinner. How do you like your pasta cooked?"

"Al dente. Thanks." And what the hell was he going to do about her? This whole situation stank to high heaven, and his detachment was getting scattered to the four winds. He wanted to yank her right out of all this and take her away to someplace where no one could harm her. Which was a stupid wish, and indicative of his crazy state of mind.

"You need to phone your parents tonight," he said. "I promised you would, around nine o'clock."

"What hotel are they at?"

"I have a copy of their itinerary in my jacket pocket. Let me dig it out."

"After dinner will be soon enough." She hesitated on the threshold between the kitchen and the living room. "Rook? Did you find out anything?"

"Nothing useful. It seems there's a new hit man in the area, but nobody knows anything about him. It's mostly just a rumor."

"*Somebody* has to know something about him," she argued. "Your friend put me in touch with him. *He* certainly knows."

"True." He'd already considered that, obviously. "But he won't tell me shit, because he's afraid of getting his own throat cut. Which leaves us in a real pretty position. We know one person who knows, and he ain't talking. Everything else is a stab in the dark, looking for a guy who might fit the profile."

"But hit men *have* to let *somebody* know what they do, or how will they ever get a contract?"

"Exactly, but trust me on this, Jenny, good ones don't advertise in the Yellow Pages. The people they share the information with are few and far between. And it really bugs the shit out of me that Jay was one of those people."

"Jay?"

"My friend. My *ex*-friend. This business has cast a whole new light on his character, I can tell you."

Jenny was holding a dish towel, and now she twisted it between her hands. "What do you mean?"

"I mean that when I gave you Jay's damn number, I thought he'd tell you to get lost. I never for a minute thought he'd put you in touch with a killer!" He practically shouted the words, because that was really what was eating him alive—the possibility that Jenny Fox might die because of something he had done, however indirectly. Christ, he would never sleep again if anything happened to her.

She looked at him from huge, sad eyes and whispered, "I've ruined *your* life, too, haven't I?"

"Oh, for God's sake!" This woman could make him madder faster than anyone he'd ever known. "When did you develop megalomania? What makes you think you have the *power* to ruin my life?"

Anger sparked in her eyes, and her hands clenched into fists. "It's my fault you're feeling so guilty about *me!* The whole reason you've dropped everything in your life to help me is because you inadvertently put me in touch with the hit man! Well, goddamn it, Rook, I don't need your guilt and your pity! You're not responsible for something you couldn't have known!"

He stabbed his index finger her way. "Just like you're not responsible for what happened to your family?"

"That's different! Oh, just leave and get on with your life!"

"*You* get on with *yours!*"

They stood there glaring at one another for an interminable time; then, gradually, Jennifer's expression changed to one of hurt perplexity. "It *is* the same thing, isn't it?" she asked in a small voice.

Rook hated to admit it. "Yeah," he said heavily. "We're doing the same thing."

Slowly he sat back and stared blindly at his hands. It was true; they were both taking responsibility for things that were beyond their control. It was definitely, blindingly true.

And in admitting to Jennifer that it was a case of the pot calling the kettle black, he'd lost his moral edge. How could he tell *her* not to do what *he* was doing?

He had just given up any hope of drawing her back from the precipice.

10

Dinner was a silent affair. Jennifer had managed to do something with bottled spaghetti sauce that made it taste as good as any he had ever had, and he told her so, but that was the extent of their conversation.

And that was okay, he thought. They'd both come perilously close to something neither of them was willing to face. They would be lucky if they could get through this evening without opening any other wounds.

But what sickened him was that he'd dragged out a truth that made it impossible for him to tell her to quit beating herself up over these things.

So okay, he thought. Deal with it. She's feeling responsible and guilty in the same way that you are. It was something they were both going to have to learn to live with.

After dinner, Rook offered to do the dishes while Jennifer called her parents. It was a call she didn't want to make, because she knew they were going to be full of questions she didn't want to answer.

But Rook had done his job well, she discovered. They believed she was being tracked by the same killer who had murdered her family, and that Rook was a security guard who was protecting her and trying to help her find out who was after her. They were worried about the police wanting her for the deaths of the two officers, and her father suggested it might be best if she turned herself in and straightened things out. When she explained that Rook was concerned that she might be a sitting duck in a jail cell, he changed his mind.

When she hung up, after hearing about the warm weather, sunshine and water, she found herself wishing she had just had the sense to bury her dead and go with them on this vacation. Surely baking on a beach until her skin turned brown would unknot all the terrible tangles inside her and answer all the unanswerable questions?

As he was hanging up, her father said, "I love you, Button."

Nobody had called her that since she had been ten. She'd started objecting to it because it was babyish, but now, so many years later, that simple nickname bored right through her barriers to her very heart. *I love you, Button.* All of a sudden she saw what she was doing from the perspective of her parents, who loved her just as she had loved Bethany and Eli. What was she doing to them?

For the very first time it occurred to her that she was apparently missing some kind of coping mechanism that other people had. Other people lost loved ones and found the courage to go on. Other people managed to rebuild their lives and find purpose in their days. What was wrong with *her?* Why couldn't she manage to reconcile herself to life?

"I'm going outside to check the area."

She jumped as Rook spoke from behind her. How had she forgotten she wasn't alone? It was just that she had been alone for so long now.... "Why? Do you think someone is out there?"

"I just want to be sure that no one is. I'll be gone less than an hour. In the meantime, keep the place locked and stay away from the windows."

She turned to look at him. "You think you were followed."

He expelled an impatient breath. "No, I don't. In fact, I'm damn sure I wasn't. I'm just being cautious. A number of people saw you talk to me. The cops even questioned me about you. Not very many people know I have this place, but *some* of them do. If they were questioned and mentioned it..." He shrugged, leaving the sentence incomplete. She wasn't stupid, and he didn't need to spell it out.

"We ought to go someplace else."

"I thought about that. But every place else we'd have to use credit cards. You'd be appalled how easy it is to trace a credit card transaction, and the cops are probably looking for both of us by now."

"Then we need to turn ourselves in and explain."

"No frigging way, Lady Fox. We'd be sitting ducks in a jail cell."

"Then I'm going to call an attorney. He can speak to the police for us and maybe get this straightened out."

Rook's tawny eyes bored into her. "You can't afford to trust anybody right now! We don't know who killed your family. What's more, we don't want the cops to find us."

"I can trust Felix. He's my friend, and he's a damn good lawyer. Besides, he can't reveal anything I tell him to anyone else because of attorney-client privilege. Not even to the cops."

"You'd be depending an awful lot on professional ethics."

"Felix has exceptional ethics! Just last winter, when a friend of his bought stock in a company our firm was helping with a merger, Felix reported it himself to the firm's head counsel."

Rook cocked his head. "Why? Felix didn't buy the stock."

"But he didn't want even the appearance of impropriety to damage the firm. So he reported it, and an investigation cleared him of any complicity. Not many people would be that aboveboard."

Rook shifted on his feet, uneasy, but unable to say why. "Okay, so he has great ethics. Just make sure he hasn't got a reason to be on that list of yours."

She shook her head. "I'd trust him with my life."

"That's exactly what you're doing if you pick up that phone and call him, lady."

She reached for the phone anyway.

She got Felix's service, of course. Rook wasn't happy when she left the C-phone number with them. After she hung up, he reminded her that the number could be traced back to Ira, and Ira wasn't all that far away.

"Will you relax?" she demanded. "The service won't tell anyone but Felix, and Felix is a lawyer. He'd never tell anyone the number, especially when I left a message that I want him to represent me."

"You should just have waited to call him in the morning. That way you wouldn't have had to give anyone the number."

"He'll call me back tonight. You'll see."

"What is he, a workaholic?"

"He's just a damn good lawyer."

Rook shook his head, looking vaguely disgusted, but said nothing more. Instead he picked up the phone himself, and dialed Tim.

"Well, old man," Tim told him, "I don't have any specifics for you, but I *do* have some interesting rumors. The FAA was right about deliberate sabotage to the aircraft belonging to Mark Fox. Rumor has it that Fox's wife, Jennifer, was the intended target."

"The lady kind of figured that out herself."

"Then consider this a confirmation."

"Any rumors about who or why?"

"She scared somebody bad. I don't know how or why, but the rumor is somebody is scared shitless of her."

"I'll ask her to give that angle some consideration. Maybe we can come up with something more specific."

"If you do, let me know so I can check it out. I'm kinda curious myself. Meantime, I've got my ears on. Check in again tomorrow, same time."

"Thanks, Tim."

"Who was that?" Jennifer wanted to know when he hung up. "What am I supposed to consider?"

"That was somebody I know in the government. I occasionally do him favors, so sometimes he does one for me. He says that you were the intended target of the sabotage to your husband's plane, and that it happened because you scared somebody. At least, that's the rumor."

Confirmation didn't shock her as much as it probably would have just a few weeks ago. She was becoming reconciled to events, she realized. Slowly but surely, she was learning to live with the horror. "There are rumors about things like this?"

"In certain circles, yes."

"But how? Why? Who talks about these things?"

Rook cocked his head to one side, looking at the way she sat there so tensely with the dog's massive head resting on her thigh. "People in the business. Somebody gets a job, somebody pulls a hit...people know about it. You can't very often do something like this in a vacuum."

"People in the business? What business? Killing people?"

"Sometimes."

She looked at him, afraid to ask but desperately needing to know. She couldn't remember the last time a question had seemed so important. "Are you—" Her voice cracked. "Are *you* in...that business?"

His gaze seemed to burn through her. When he didn't answer instantly, her heart began to pump in panicked thuds. This shouldn't be so important, she told herself wildly. This couldn't possibly be so important.

"No," he said finally. "Not in the way you mean. But I'm a soldier, and you'd better never forget that."

Her question had offended him. Wanting to smooth that over, she hastened to say, "I know that. That's why I came to you in the first place."

"No, you came to me because you thought I could find you a hit man. And that's the only reason I answered your question, Lady Fox—because DeVries gave you reason to think I'm in that business. But if anybody else had asked me, I would have knocked his block off."

He spoke quietly, in a tone that belied the threat of his words, and left her far more shaken than if he had blustered. Awareness made her shiver. What was she doing in the middle of nowhere with a man who made his living by violence?

He reached for the phone again and dialed a number while she watched in silence. From the outset she had been inclined to trust him, even when the cautious part of her brain was shrieking for her to be wary. Even now, when he had just reminded her of his capacity for violence, she trusted him.

"Clark. It's Rook. Did you get me anything?"

As he listened, Rook reached for the pad Jennifer had been using earlier and began to scrawl names, addresses and phone numbers on it.

"Thanks, buddy," he told Clark finally. "If you come up with any more, let me know." When he hung up, he tossed the pad to Jennifer.

She looked down at the list of six names. "What do you want me to do with this?"

"Call and ask to talk to these guys. If any of them sounds the least bit familiar, put a check by the name."

"You can't expect me to recognize the hit man's voice from one phone call."

"No. I expect you to recognize if any of these guys has a familiar voice, that's all."

"Who are they?"

"Recent dischargees and retirees from the military who've settled in the Denver area. Any one of them would have the skills to set up as a hit man."

"You mean the army teaches that?"

"The army, the navy, the marines. All of them have trained assassins. It's a fact of war, babe. Now call."

"Don't call me babe." She hated that. She had *always* hated that.

"Sorry. Call. Please."

She picked up the phone, but before she dialed the first number, she heard the drone of an approaching engine. Rook became instantly alert.

"Upstairs," he told her roughly. "Get up there and stay up there. If you hear anything that sounds like trouble, hide in the closet under the eaves."

"I'd be trapped up there."

"There's no place else to go, so hide yourself, damn it. Just go all the way to the back. You'll find a little alcove to hide in that isn't visible from the doorway. It's the best chance you'll have."

She didn't argue any further but hurried up the stairs to the loft. The closet under the eaves ran the full length of the house, and she crawled into it right away, figuring that she might not have time later.

She found the alcove he'd mentioned and crouched in it, realizing it was at the very back of the house, over the kitchen. She'd better not make any noise.

What if there were spiders in here? She shuddered and tried not to think about it.

The engine sounded closer, the familiar drone of a snowmobile. It had to be a lost vacationer, Rook told himself as he waited in the darkened kitchen. The hit man wouldn't approach them this way; it gave them too much warning.

Unless he didn't yet realize that his quarry was running from *him*. He might believe that she was running from the cops. He could come here by snowmobile, claim to be lost, get into the house and knock her off. There was no earthly reason why he needed to be surreptitious about it, unless he somehow knew that Jennifer was trying to escape *him.*

As suddenly as if he had been punched in the gut, Rook remembered the guy trying to climb into Jennifer's house by way of the tree the night the two policemen were killed. Had that been the hit man? He had believed so at the time. He'd thought the guy had been trying to sneak in because of the cops. But that didn't make any sense, because he had already killed the cops.

So why had the guy been sneaking? Did he know that Jennifer was trying to evade him? Why the hell couldn't he just ring the doorbell and shoot when she opened it? She wouldn't live long enough to identify him to anyone.

But the guy hadn't tried to get to her that way, the easy way. Why not? His gut clenched as he realized this was somehow an important clue, but damned if he could figure it out. Somehow the hit man had already figured out that Jennifer was running from him. That meant something, but what?

The snowmobile engine coughed into silence outside. Just then the cellular phone began to chirp, jarring him. He ignored it. Muffled through the curtained windows, he heard the squeaky sound of footfalls in the snow. Someone hammered at the back door. Why not the front door, the obvious way to come, where light showed in the windows?

Moving as silently as he could, Rook crossed the linoleum and peeked through a crack in the curtain.

"Damn it!" Relieved and angry all at the same time, he flung the door open and glared at Ira. "What the hell are you doing coming up here without phoning first? I could have killed you!"

"I tried to call. Maybe you ought to get off the phone sometime." Ira shook his head. "You mentioned skis. I got to thinking they might be a wise thing to have around if you have a baddie after you. You could go places he couldn't follow on a snowmobile. So I brought gear for you and Jennifer. The no-wax variety, because conditions change so fast this time of year."

Turning, he went back to his vehicle and sled. "Come help me with this stuff. I brought skis, boots, clothing...everything you should need."

Rook took a minute first to tell Jenny it was okay to come downstairs. By the time he and Ira had carried everything inside, she had joined them, looking at the equipment with a mixture of delight and confusion. "I love to ski," she said finally, "but is it safe right now?"

"This isn't for recreation," Rook answered. "But you never know when it might come in handy as a way to avoid getting killed."

"Oh." She had thought they were safe here, except that Rook kept doing things that suggested he didn't think she was all that safe after all.

Ira saw her expression. "It's just insurance," he told her. "And it was *my* idea to bring the stuff up."

"Oh." That made her feel a little better. Maybe she would even be able to sleep tonight.

Ira gratefully accepted a cup of coffee and some hot soup to warm him before he departed. Rook tried to persuade him to spend the night, but he refused. "A man is coming for his truck in the morning. Gotta open the shop early. Might as well go back tonight."

He looked at Jennifer over the rim of his coffee cup. "You're the most wanted person in Denver right now, you know."

She drew a sharp breath. "They don't really think I killed those two police officers?"

"Yeah, they do. Your picture's plastered all over the TV and on the front page of today's paper. I'd learn the art of disguise if I were you." He cocked his head to one side. "You wouldn't need a whole lot of disguising. Must be an old picture. You're a lot thinner now."

He sipped his coffee again. "You don't want to see it. They're making tabloid news out of your life story and running film clips of you at your family's funeral. They even found some tape of you at some charity thing or other. Trust me, the presentation hasn't been flattering."

Rook wanted to clobber Ira for even mentioning it. Jennifer's expression, which had been almost relaxed, had begun to darken again and grow pinched. Ira had brought it all back to her again.

"I didn't kill my family, Ira," she said in a wispy voice. "And I didn't kill those cops. I don't know how anybody could think I would do such a thing...." She clapped her hand to her mouth, stifling the words. Silencing herself.

"*I* don't believe it," Ira assured her. "Not for a minute. Problem is, cops are human, just like the rest of us. Sometimes they get blinded by what they already believe, and you're an obvious suspect. Did you really make a fifty-thousand-dollar withdrawal?"

Jennifer nodded.

"Jeez. That's a lotta money. And it's not making you look any better, I'll tell you."

Rook was staring at her as if he'd never seen her before. "Fifty thousand? You didn't pay the guy fifty thousand!"

"That's what he asked for."

Rook glared at her. "You got ripped off!"

"What guy?" Ira demanded.

Jennifer looked at Ira. "I hired a hit man to kill me."

"She hired a hit man to kill her," Ira repeated twenty minutes later as he climbed onto his snowmobile. "Damn, Rook, she's a doozy. You watch out. This one's got more than one screw loose." He'd heard the whole story from Jennifer, but he still couldn't understand it.

"She was depressed, and she did a dumb thing," Rook told him, feeling protective of Jennifer. No, he didn't need to feel that. No way. He didn't give a damn about her, right? Right.

"Depressed. Dumb. Dumb isn't the word for it." Ira made a disgusted sound and turned the key in the ignition. The roar of the engine all but killed any further conversation.

And it was more than a dumb mistake, Rook thought as he watched Ira disappear into the night until only the beam of the headlight could be seen. Much more than a dumb mistake, because she still wanted to die.

Well, it wasn't his problem what she wanted. His problem was to save her life, because he didn't want her blood on his hands. That was enough reason to keep acting like a jerk and hanging around. But once this was over, he was outta here.

"I'm going to check around outside," he called in to Jennifer. "I'll take the dog, if it's okay."

"Sure." She was still sitting at the table, staring at her hands—looking so lost, small and alone that something inside him twisted. Damn it, he *did not* care!

Tipping his head back, he looked up at the cold stars in the frigid void of the night. He'd been where she was and had come awfully close to taking his own life. He knew that kind of despair, knew it intimately. Maybe if he shared his own experiences with her, she would take some hope from it.

Yeah, right. Hope. What hope? Look at him. Look what he'd become: a mercenary living on the fringes of the civilized world, a man without a place he could call home. How was that supposed to inspire her?

Maybe everything was hopeless after all.

By the time he returned to the house, Jennifer had placed the phone calls he had asked her to make. He was surprised and not a little impressed that she had managed to pick herself up and get on it. He'd fully anticipated having to nudge her into it.

"Two of them," she told him. "Two of them sounded vaguely familiar, but I couldn't tell you if it's because I talked to them before or because they remind me of somebody I know. Another man wasn't there. The guy who answered the phone said he hadn't seen him in a few days."

"I'll check them out." He tucked the paper into his pocket. "Tomorrow I'll go into town and see what I can learn about them. I'm especially interested in the guy who hasn't been seen much."

"That's what I thought, too."

He looked at her, wishing he had some magic power to make all of this go away. She didn't deserve this. Any of this. It didn't matter what she had done to make somebody scared enough to try to kill her. It didn't matter that she had hired a hit man and gotten herself into this current mess. He just wished he could make it all magically vanish and give her back all of the life she had lost.

The phone rang, dragging him out of the dark well of his thoughts. Was depression contagious? He was beginning to wonder. He grabbed the phone before Jennifer could get to it. If someone was trying to ascertain her whereabouts, he was going to make it as difficult as possible.

"Hello?"

There was a silence from the other end, then a somewhat surprised voice said, "Do I have the right number? I'm trying to reach Jennifer Fox."

"Who are you?"

"Her friend, Felix Abernathy."

Felix. The lawyer. Rook passed the phone to her. "It's your lawyer friend." Maybe he should leave the room, but he decided against it, instead stationing himself where he could both watch her and hear her. If she started to tell Felix the wrong thing, he was by God going to stop her.

"Felix!" Jennifer sounded delighted as she spoke her friend's name and took the phone. Rook wished she would say his name that way, then crushed the thought almost before he realized it had crossed his mind. He did not care. Period.

"Oh, Felix, it's just awful! The police think I killed my family! They think I killed two police officers. Felix, I didn't kill anybody!"

"Slow down, Jenny. Slow down." His voice was warm, concerned, not entirely professional. "Are you retaining me?"

"Yes, of course!"

"All right. Then, speaking as your lawyer, you need to turn yourself in."

Jennifer felt her insides twist into a tight knot. There was only one way she was going to be able to explain this, and that was by telling the truth. Oh, God, she didn't want to have to admit to Felix that she'd hired someone to kill her. "Felix . . . Felix, I can't."

"Don't be ridiculous! You're an attorney yourself. You know the appearance that flight creates. Everyone is looking for you, and there's no way anyone will believe you aren't on the lam. *Are* you on the lam?"

"I just told you I'm not!"

"Then there's certainly no good reason not to turn yourself in."

"Yes, there is." She whispered the words hoarsely. "Oh, Felix, you don't know!"

"Then I suggest you tell me."

"You *are* my attorney?"

"I thought I said so. Yes, Jenny, I'm taking your case—although if you don't do what I say, I'll drop you."

"Just let me explain. Please...it's not safe for me to come back. Someone is...someone is trying to kill me."

A long silence greeted her words. Then Felix's voice rumbled in her ear. "What makes you think that?"

"I don't just think it. I *know* it. You see...you see, I *hired* him."

"Good God, Jennifer!" His usual professional calm had vanished.

What could she say to that? Strange how each time she admitted her act out loud, it sounded worse to her. A week ago, hiring someone to kill her had seemed to fall within the normal realm of activities. Now it struck her as insane. "I know," she said finally, her voice husky. "I think...I think I was temporarily insane."

"You must have been! And where on earth did you find someone who would agree to do it?"

"You don't need to know that."

"Yes, I by God do!" He paused a moment, gathering himself, then said calmly, "I may need to corroborate your story in order to explain your flight. Someone will have to back up your story."

"Mr. Rydell can do that."

"Someone who isn't *also* wanted by the police."

Jennifer caught her breath. She hadn't imagined this. Had never imagined that she might be dragging someone else so deeply into her personal mess. "Why is he wanted?"

"Apparently you were seen talking to him shortly after you withdrew a huge sum of money from the bank. He's a suspect in the murder of your family."

"My God. Felix, I didn't even know him back then. The first time we met was a couple of weeks ago when I asked him if he could put me in touch with a hit man!"

"Did he?"

Oh, God, Jennifer thought, no matter how she told the story, it sounded bad for Rook. She turned her head and looked across the room at him. "No," she said finally. "No. He didn't know any hit men, and he was furious with me for asking."

"I imagine so. Where is *he* now?"

"I can't answer that."

"Can't or won't? Never mind, he's not my client. My point is that I need someone besides him to verify your story. Did you talk to anyone else?"

Felix might never forgive her for this, but she could see no way around it. "I went to the prison and talked to Alan DeVries."

"You talked to *my* client?" Felix's tone had suddenly grown deadly. "Don't tell me you also looked through his file."

"Of course not! I didn't need to. For heaven's sake, Felix, it was all over the newspapers, and besides, I'd already met him, in case you'd forgotten."

"That's true. So you showed up at the prison, and he just assumed you were still associated with the firm—and possibly with me."

"I can't help what he assumed."

"Jesus, Jennifer, you took advantage of what you knew he would assume. You tried to engage a client of mine in criminal activity. If this got out—"

"But it won't. You're my attorney."

Felix swore.

"Besides, he didn't do anything wrong, just told me to talk to someone else, because he didn't personally know anyone who would do a contract hit."

Felix was silent for a long time. Finally he said, "You were really feeling that bad?"

"I was. I still do." *But not as much.* The realization terrified her. All of a sudden she couldn't imagine life without grief. It would be so empty....

"All right," Felix said presently. "You hired a hit man to terminate your life, but now you're running from him. Why?"

"Because I found out Mark and the children were murdered. I want—I *have* to find out who did it. I don't want to die before justice is done." She didn't tell him that she wanted revenge, because attorney-client privilege didn't apply to the intention to commit a new crime. If Felix understood her to mean that she was going to kill the murderer, he might well feel obliged to inform the police.

"But you still want to die."

He sounded as if he didn't quite believe it, nor did Jennifer when she heard someone else say it out loud. But she still wanted to die... didn't she? Uneasily her gaze strayed to Rook, who was listening intently and probably trying to guess Felix's side of the conversation from her responses. Why was she looking at him? He didn't have anything to do with her decision.

But she had hesitated too long. Felix spoke again.

"Of course you don't," he said firmly. "Really, Jennifer, I can understand that grief might have made you a little crazy, but you can't really mean to go ahead with this suicidal plan. Call your hit man and tell him to forget it."

She laughed. The sound burst out of her with a slightly hysterical edge. "It's not that easy, Felix. I wish it were. But I don't have his phone number, and I never did. I certainly don't have any idea who he is. There's no way I can call him off."

Again a silence. "I can get you police protection."

"Rook doesn't think it'll do any good. I'd just be a sitting duck in a jail cell. And that's where they'd put me, because I'm still a suspect. No, Felix, I don't think I'd better do that."

He sighed heavily. "Well, this is one hell of a fix."

She didn't bother to respond to that. There wasn't much she could say.

"All right. Tell me what happened the night the cops were killed."

She described that night as succinctly as she could, trying not to elaborate needlessly, but to give him enough to go on.

"So somebody was trying to get in your upstairs window?"

"That's right. We think it was the hit man, and that he must have killed the cops. While we were running up the street, a drunk skidded his car into the police car. Rook ran back to help and found the officers had been shot."

Another long silence. Then, "How do you know Rook didn't kill them himself?"

Panic washed over her for an instant as she considered the possibility. He could have. He could have shot them when he went back to help them. There was no way she could be sure, because she had been running up the street and hiding in his car. She hadn't heard anything at all but the thud and crunch of her boots in the snow.

But almost as soon as she panicked, she caught herself. Rook hadn't killed those men. No way. He didn't even have a gun. And she, too, had seen the person who was trying to get into her house.

"He didn't. He doesn't have a gun."

"Okay. I'll talk to the cops, find out what they know and what they think they know. Where can I find you?"

She hesitated. "I borrowed this phone from a friend."

"You're staying with a friend? Which friend?"

But she saw Rook stiffen and remembered his warning not to reveal their whereabouts. Besides, she reminded herself, probably too late, a cellular phone conversation wasn't secure. Anybody who happened on the frequency could listen in. "No, I'm not staying with a friend. I just borrowed a friend's phone and took it with me. I'm not sure how much longer I'll even use it. It's not very private. I'll call *you*."

"But if I need to get in touch, or find you—"

"I'll call *you,* Felix."

"This won't look very good."

"I don't care how it looks. I'm running for my *life.*"

When she hung up, she looked at Rook.

"Feel any better?" he asked.

"Yes. I do. Felix is going to find out exactly what evidence they have against me. That's the only way I can ever hope to refute it. And maybe...maybe he can convince them that I have an alibi."

"I already told them that."

Jennifer felt a trickle of shock. "You told who? When? What?"

"Back when I saw the news reports. The night after I brought you here, while I was in Denver. I called the cops and told them I was your alibi. I even told them exactly what the bullet wounds looked like so they'd know I knew what I was talking about. I told them to check for signs of that guy who tried to break in, since he'd probably been the one who killed them."

"Then why are they still looking for *me?*"

He shrugged a shoulder, but the look he gave her was dark.

"I guess," he said grimly, "they didn't believe me."

11

Jennifer awoke in the morning before the sun rose. She lay staring up into the rafters, trying to find her moorings. For some reason, the events of yesterday had left her feeling as if she had been cast adrift without even a compass to guide her.

Did she really want revenge—or did she want justice? Did she really want to die—or was she just afraid to live?

She was asking herself questions she'd never asked before, and she found nothing but confusion in answer. She didn't know anymore. She didn't know about anything anymore.

Finally, when daylight was just a faint lightening around the edges of the curtains, she went down to the kitchen. Cooking had always been a favorite escape for her, occupying her hands and organizing her thoughts in a way that precluded random anxieties.

Rook had brought up quite a bit of fresh food when he returned from Denver the other night. She found bacon, green peppers, an onion, milk . . . Without any trouble at all she could make a feast.

Humming, she bustled around, opening the curtains so she could see the dawn's arrival while she prepared an elaborate omelet. And muffins. A quick batch of cheese muffins would make a nice touch, and for some reason Rook had everything she needed. Was he a cook himself?

Twice while she was cooking, the back of her neck prickled with the feeling that she was being watched. Massie was dozing near the stove, though, and Rook appeared to be still dreaming. Just nerves, she told herself, and went back to spooning batter into a muffin tin.

Done, she carried the empty batter bowl and spoon to the sink and turned on the water. After she finished rinsing it, she dropped the wooden spoon onto the floor.

Just as she started to bend to retrieve it, the glass at the window beside her cracked with an almost dull thud, and something hot and sharp singed the side of her head.

Instinctively she flinched away from the burning pain, crouching down. A drop of blood dripped onto her hand. "Rook!" Seconds later she heard a distant *crack* echo across the valley.

Suddenly terrified, not understanding what had happened, she fell to the floor, trying to escape the threat. From the living room she heard a thud as Rook's feet hit the floor. A second later he filled the kitchen doorway, looking puffy eyed but completely alert.

"What. . . ?" His eyes took in everything in a single sweep: the hole in the cracked window glass, Jennifer huddled on the floor with blood streaking down her cheek from her hair. "Jenny! Are you all right?" He was beside her in an instant, gently probing the wound on the side of her head.

"I'm bleeding! I don't know what happened...."

He pressed a dish towel to the side of her head. "It's just a small cut. Keep the towel pressed hard against it. Stay here. Don't move a muscle. I'll be back...."

Thanking the merciful gods that he had slept with his boots on, he ran out the back door into the frigid dawn, eyes searching for the assailant. At first he could see nothing, but then a figure emerged from a stand of trees more than a thousand yards distant, skiing away up the slope of the hill toward the rim of the valley and safety.

He ran for the snowmobile, sure he could catch the guy and put an end to this for good. In fact, he almost felt exultant. Jennifer was okay except for a nasty cut, and the guy was out in the open, where he could be tracked and found. As long as he didn't make it to a road first, Rook was going to get him.

Except that the gunman had taken that into account. He'd placed a bullet right through the engine of the snowmobile.

Rook swore savagely and kicked the side of the machine. Up the western slope, the figure of the gunman grew smaller as he escaped.

Jennifer was still lying on the floor when Rook returned, but she had begun to understand what had just happened. Reaction was setting in, causing her to shake from head to foot. If not for dropping a wooden spoon, she would be dead right now, her brains splattered all over Rook's kitchen.

How had she ever thought she really wanted to die?

"Jenny." Rook was suddenly there, kneeling beside her, squeezing her shoulder tightly. "Jenny, he's gone. You're safe. Let me see that cut...."

But she couldn't stop shaking, and it was as if her muscles had frozen. She couldn't let go of the towel, couldn't make herself straighten out her arm, or her legs. "I don't want to die.... I don't want to..." She could hear herself saying that over and over in a quavery voice that she squeezed out between her clenched teeth. "I don't want to die.... Oh, God, please stop him...."

In that instant she hated herself for her weakness. *All* her weaknesses. Her weakness in wanting to die because she was lonely, and in not wanting to die now that she'd set the event in motion. What a despicable, cowardly, disgusting person she was....

Somehow Rook got the towel away from her and got her limbs straightened out. Somehow he managed to get her to hold still while he checked the wound on her head.

"It's okay," he said. "Jenny, it's okay. I don't think the bullet touched you at all. Really. I think a piece of flying glass hit you. You won't even need stitches. Honest. Just a small bandage..."

He picked her up off the floor and carried her into the living room, where he cradled her on his lap and rocked her.

"It's okay," he kept saying. "It's okay. I don't think you're despicable because you don't want to die. I don't think you're despicable because you *did* want to die.... You're just human like all the rest of us, Jenny...."

Eventually he began to get through to her. Eventually she began to realize that he wasn't running from her in disgust, that he was holding her and rocking her as if he really cared about her. Gradually her shuddering eased, and finally, utterly exhausted, she sagged against him.

"That's better," he said gently. Her wound had stopped bleeding, and he had stopped trying to kid himself that he didn't give a damn. He gave one hell of a damn what happened to this woman. If he did nothing else with his misspent life, he was going to make her safe.

"He found us," she finally said, her voice husky, barely audible.

"So it seems. I can't imagine who else would be taking potshots at you with a sniper rifle. And I don't think he was after *me.*"

"Why would anyone be after *you?*"

"No one should be, but in my business there's always a chance."

"Maybe you should change businesses."

"Believe me, I'm giving it serious thought." He looked down at her with a crooked smile. "Well, he's gone for the moment. He may think he killed you. I don't know. He *did* make sure that I couldn't follow him—he shot the snowmobile dead."

Suddenly uncomfortable about being on his lap, Jennifer slid off and sat beside him instead. She might not want to die, but she wasn't ready to be on a man's lap. Maybe she would never be ready for that again. "What do we do?"

"Get out of here. Now that he's found us, we're sitting ducks if we stay."

"But without the snowmobile..."

"Without the machine, we ski. Massie will have to walk alongside. In fact, she can pull a sled with provisions."

"I don't know...." She looked at the dog, who was looking back as serenely as always.

"Mastiffs were used in the First World War to pull caissons. Trust me, she can do it. We need to carry some stuff with us for safety, and we'll carry plenty of food for her, so the cold won't affect her. But we can't go out there without any nourishment or shelter. You know that."

She *did* know that. The weather changed fast in these mountains, often several times in the course of a single day.

He went out to the barn and came back with some rope, which he fashioned into a harness for Massie, who rather seemed to enjoy the attention.

The sled was made of aluminum tubing on steel runners and weighed almost nothing itself. They loaded it with food, candles, a small tent, sleeping bags and other things they might need if they had to be out overnight.

When they were finished, the sled wasn't overly heavy. Jennifer felt she could have pulled it herself without much difficulty, and she suggested to Rook that they take turns doing so to spell Massie. He readily agreed.

Just before they were ready to leave, Felix called.

"They still think you're guilty," he told her. "They did check out whether someone had entered the house through an upstairs window. There's evidence that someone did, but the detective argued that you could have set that up yourself. The gun that was found in your bedroom was the same one used to kill the police officers."

"I don't own a gun!"

"Neither do most criminals. They steal them. But never mind. Let me finish. The gun had been wiped clean of prints, except that one small partial was left behind. It doesn't match your prints or Rydell's, so the case against you is far from ironclad. You'd be doing yourself a favor if you turned yourself in, Jennifer."

"I can't, Felix."

"But—"

"Listen. The hit man just took a shot at me. He missed by a fraction of an inch. I've got to get out of here, and I don't know when I'll be in touch again. But I can't afford to put myself in jail, even temporarily. I'd be too easy to find."

Felix hesitated for only a moment. "You're right," he said. "Just don't quote me. I can't advise flight."

"I know. Believe me, I know. But don't bother trying to talk me into coming back. I can't, not until I get this guy off my tail for good."

"All right. Just...check in from time to time, okay?"

"When I can. Thanks, Felix."

"Just be safe, Jennifer."

Rook put the C-phone on the sled, too, but only to take it back to Ira. He didn't think the batteries would last long in this cold.

With binoculars he surveyed the surrounding area, looking for any sign that someone was watching them. He saw nothing but the faint marks of the gunman's ski tracks up the western slope. There was a road in that direction, the closest road to his cabin.

He and Jennifer headed the other way.

The skis were no-wax, a good choice, given the rapidly changing snow conditions at this time of year. They weren't quite as fast as a well-waxed ski would have been, but given that they didn't want to wear Massie out, they were traveling at a relatively slow pace, anyway. A walk, rather than a run.

Massie appeared to enjoy pulling the sled. After the first few tugs and a couple of attempts to chase it, she figured it out and pulled away, keeping close to Jennifer.

At the rim of the valley, Rook guided them under some trees and took out his binoculars again. He scanned the entire valley carefully, looking for any sign that someone might be trying to follow them. Nothing at all moved.

Their tracks through the snow left an excellent trail for anyone to follow, and he just had to hope the hit man considered the job done. Why else would he have left the area?

Except that one shot could look like a hunting accident, but he would have to kill both of them so he wouldn't leave any witnesses. Two dead people looked like a hell of a lot more than an accident. Ah, hell, none of it was adding up.

They waited in the shadows of the trees for a while, to see if anyone tried to follow them. Nothing. When Jennifer started shivering, they began to move again.

"How did he find us?" Jennifer wondered.

"I don't know. My guess would be that he saw us linked together in the press. The cops sure linked us together fast enough. There are a few people who know I have this cabin, and when I couldn't be found, this would be the next place to look for me." He shook his head, matching his strides to Jennifer's. Massie came right behind them with the sled. "Honest to God, I didn't think it would be this easy for anyone to find me." But then, he'd thought that only two or three people even knew of the existence of this place. He had no guarantees that those people hadn't talked to dozens of others, though. Now that he thought about it, he wondered if his ownership of this property wasn't common knowledge in a community that thrived on secrecy and gossiped like old women.

Christ, he was an ass. He should never have assumed that only a couple of his good friends knew about this place. He should never have assumed that his good friends wouldn't tell anyone else about it. They would have no reason to assume it was some kind of secret.

"Where are we going?" Jennifer asked him sometime later.

"Nowhere in particular." He nodded toward the darkening sky. "We're heading farther into the high country. I'm hoping those clouds'll start to drop some snow to hide our trail. Then we can head back toward civilization."

"You think we're being followed?"

"If we are, I want him to think we're heading toward Steamboat. It's just a precaution, Jen. I haven't spotted anyone behind us, but they wouldn't have to follow very closely, not with the trail we're leaving." And it would take more than a couple of inches of powder to cover it, too. The dog was acting like a snowplow.

At the top of the next valley, though, he still saw no sign that anyone was following them. Either the shooter believed he had accomplished his mission, or he felt he knew where they were heading. He hoped it was the former.

They had to stop a couple of times to get the ice out from between Massie's toes, and finally Rook had the bright idea of making mittens for her out of pieces of his T-shirt. Massie regarded them doubtfully when he tied them on her but was soon trotting happily along in them.

"That was a great idea," Jennifer told him with a wide smile.

That smile made him uneasy somehow. He shrugged. "I read about it somewhere. They do it for dogs in the Iditarod."

"Oh." But she kept right on smiling at him.

God, that woman had a beautiful smile, he thought as they poled their way up another incline. Snow was beginning to fall, tiny crystals that stung his cheeks. When he glanced back, he could hardly see the far side of the valley they had just crossed. It was disappearing into a white swirl. Good.

Another valley, another hill. The snow began to fall thickly, and the growing wind whipped it into sudden tornadoes of ice crystals that stung sharply.

They ought to stop. The dog was getting tired; they were getting tired and the conditions were becoming dangerous. But he couldn't quite shake the fear that if they stopped too soon they would be in trouble. He looked at Jennifer. She was poling along steadily, but her stride had shortened and looked less stable than it had earlier. She was growing fatigued, and behind fatigue in these conditions lay the threat of hypothermia. "We need to stop."

"Not yet." She paused, though, and looked at him. "Somebody could be right behind us."

It was possible now, in the swirling snow. They wouldn't be able to see someone who was ten feet away. "I doubt it. If anyone was following us, they were too far behind before it started snowing. The way the wind is blowing, our trail should be almost obliterated. They won't find us easily."

"I'd still like to get farther along."

He glanced down at the compass strapped to his wrist. "A little longer, then. We'll start swinging around toward Ira's place now. But, Jen, these conditions are getting dangerous."

"I know. I know. But—okay. Just a little longer."

They traveled only another ten minutes before Jennifer fell down. She picked herself up immediately, then stumbled again only two steps later. He recognized the signs. Her body was no longer able to do what she was telling it to. The earliest stages of hypothermia.

"We're stopping here," he announced. And this time she didn't argue.

He kicked off his skis and stomped down an area of snow to make a reasonably level bed for the tent in the shelter of some trees. He fumbled a little putting it up as his own body began to resist cooperating, but he managed to get it up reasonably quickly. He tossed the sleeping bags inside and told Jennifer to crawl in.

Then he turned to Massie. She, too, was getting cold and tired. When he unharnessed her, she gladly dived into the tent with Jennifer. It was going to be crowded in there, Rook thought wryly. The damn dog took up a lot of space.

He moved supplies into the tent, parked the sled alongside so it would be easy to get to, and then joined Jennifer and Massie inside.

The first thing he noticed was the comparative warmth inside. The tent was already capturing body heat from Jenny and her dog, and it blocked the chilling wind. Massie had curled up against the wall behind Jennifer, who was still struggling to untie her ski boots. She'd managed to pull off her gaiters, but the laces were defying her cold, numb fingers. Dropping to his knees beside her, Rook untied them for her.

"Pull off your jeans," he said, "and your socks. You'll warm up faster." While she complied, he unrolled the sleeping bag for her and unzipped it. She was shivering by the time she crawled into it, and he zipped it up right to her chin. "Pull your head inside. It'll help."

Massie was shivering, too. For her he had a Mylar survival blanket. He half expected her to resist it, but she lay quietly while he tucked it around her, as if she understood what he was trying to do.

Only then did he tug off his own jacket, jeans and boots and climb into the other sleeping bag.

They would warm up soon, he told himself. Out of the wind, in this nearly airtight enclosure, they would warm up rapidly from their own body heat. It wouldn't take long at all.

Before he knew it, he was sound asleep.

Jenny was too cold to sleep. The afternoon darkened with the storm, the wind howled almost savagely through the trees and snow rattled against the sides of the tent. Inside the tent it was growing warmer. She could feel it, but the heat just couldn't seem to reach past the surface.

Massie snored behind her, content. Rook lay on the other side, breathing softly through his mouth. She lay in the middle, shivering and trying to keep her teeth from chattering.

It would have been nice to just drift off to sleep, but something more than shivering was keeping her awake. Icy trickles of fear were making her feel as frozen as the snow outside had.

She didn't want to die. Not only did she not want to die, but she wanted very much to live. Nor was that realization something that had come to her simply because she had almost been killed that morning.

No, it was something she had felt from the very beginning but had been unable to face. She felt guilty because she hadn't been on the plane with her family, but she felt even more guilty because she was relieved she hadn't been. That was the truth from which she had been hiding all these months—that for all that the deaths of her husband and children had carved a bottomless chasm of grief in her heart and soul, she was still relieved to be alive.

That was why her guilt had flogged her so mercilessly all these months, why she hadn't been able to allow herself to begin moving past her loss. Because she was so ashamed of being alive, and ashamed of being relieved to have escaped the crash.

And that was why she had hired the hit man—so she would never have to face the shameful truth. To prove beyond a doubt that she really wasn't relieved to be alive.

God! Why hadn't she had the gumption to face the truth from the beginning? Her grief was both piercing and deep, an almost unbearable pain. Till the day she died she would miss Mark, Eli and Bethany. Every tear she had shed had been real, every ache of her throat, every gasping sob. Sometimes she thought she simply couldn't endure her sorrow another instant.

But she was still glad to be alive. Oh, not joyous glad, not dancing-in-the-street glad. Just quietly, sadly relieved to have breath in her body.

And that had made her feel so guilty that she had refused to acknowledge her own feelings. But she knew her feelings were normal. For God's sake, she had read enough of those coping-with-grief books in the months after the accident. Why, even knowing that her feelings were perfectly normal, had she buried them so deeply and self-destructively?

Because she felt guilty.

Shivering, she rolled onto her side and curled up into a ball, tugging the sleeping bag over her head. They didn't make the sleeping bag that would keep her warm. Nothing could keep her warm in the wintertime. Nothing could ease her fear, either. God, she had lost her mind, had been temporarily insane from guilt. There was no other explanation. Never before had she deluded herself so thoroughly.

She would give almost anything to have her family back, but that wasn't going to happen. Like it or not, she was still alive, and she ought to be looking forward rather than back. Yes, she would hurt and grieve for the rest of her days, but that didn't mean she couldn't also laugh and enjoy whatever little pleasures came her way. It didn't mean she couldn't do something useful with the rest of her life.

If she had any rest of her life. What if the gunman was even now closing in on them? Not moving like this made her feel unbearably anxious, even though she knew the blizzard must have long since buried their trail in freshly drifted snow. Even though she knew that anyone who might be tracking them would long since have been forced to find shelter.

Shivering again, she instinctively scooted closer to Rook, even though none of his warmth could reach her through the two bags. She must have nudged him, because he turned his head to look at her. In the dim tent, his golden eyes seemed to glow.

"Cold?" he asked.

"I'm never warm in the winter. Something to do with my metabolism." Another shiver ran through her.

Reaching out, he yanked down the zipper on her sleeping bag.

"What are you doing?"

"Putting the bags together."

Maybe she should have protested, but she didn't. She was cold to the bone and willing to try anything that might help. He zipped the two bags together quickly, then drew her close to his heat.

"Snuggle up, Jenny. I make enough heat for two."

There was nothing indecent about it, she told herself. They were both wearing shirts and undies, more decently dressed than they would be at the beach.

But it felt incredibly intimate when his leg covered hers, drawing her in even closer to his heat. He was so warm, almost hot against her chilled skin. When he tucked her cold hands beneath his arms, she almost felt as if she were holding them over a flame.

Warm. It was wonderful to start feeling warm again. Her hands, her legs, her torso... heat slowly started to penetrate. He warmed the air around them, too, so that even her back began to thaw.

"Does that dog always snore like that?" he asked.

"Mastiffs are great snorers. Massie's actually kind of quiet. My folks used to have one that sounded like a chain saw."

He chuckled. "Where did you get her name?"

"Eli—" Her voice trembled a little and broke. "My son was two when my folks got her, and he started calling her Massie, maybe because he couldn't say mastiff. It stuck. She has a fancy, official name on her papers, but I don't even remember what it is."

"It's funny how baby words stick, isn't it? My daughter called apples po-pos. To this day, when I see an apple I think of it as a po-po."

Had his voice grown a little husky as he spoke? Jennifer tilted her head, trying to read his face, but the day had grown too dark, and inside the tent it was almost like night. "How—how long . . . ?"

"Five years. Almost six." He closed his eyes. "She was . . . just eleven."

It seemed to Jennifer that if there was anything at all worse than losing a child, it was losing a child to suicide. Instinctively offering comfort, she slipped her arms around him and hugged him. "I'm sorry."

He could almost hear the questions she didn't ask, because he would have wanted to ask the same ones if he had been in her shoes. But he absolutely didn't want to exhume Samantha. One way or another, he'd made a kind of peace with her death, and he didn't see any reason to dig it all up and make it fresh again.

"We'll stay here for the night," he said, evading all the unspoken questions. "It's getting late, and this storm isn't likely to blow out soon."

"I don't . . . like staying in one place."

He looked down at her, wishing he could read her expression. "I don't blame you. But I honestly think we're okay here. More okay than we would be trying to get anywhere in that storm with night coming on."

And the storm would make total darkness fall even earlier. She nodded, acknowledging that they had no alternative.

"We should be out of here in the morning, though," he said by way of reassurance. "I don't see any reason we shouldn't reach Ira's place by noon."

"Then what?"

"Have you ever worn a disguise?"

He was trying to cheer her up; she could tell by the tone of his voice. She hesitated a moment, battling the inevitable guilt that always attacked her when she tried to lighten up, but she pushed it aside and joined in. "Only when I was a witch for Halloween, and I guess that wasn't really a disguise."

He chuckled. "I don't think we could hide you very well in a pointed hat."

"I guess not. So can I be a buxom blonde? In a low-cut red dress?"

He laughed again, more easily this time. "That wouldn't exactly be inconspicuous."

"I was born inconspicuous. I want to be ravishing." It was the wrong thing to say. She knew it the instant the words left her mouth. The atmosphere changed in some subtle way that left her achingly aware of the powerful leg that was thrown across hers and acutely conscious of the strong arms that surrounded her.

"You *are* ravishing." His tone was deadly serious.

She panicked. "No. I'm too thin. I don't have any breasts at all. My hair is just ordinary brown—"

He silenced her with a quick kiss. "Your hair is a gorgeous brown. Earlier, when the sun was out, it looked like it had fire in it. And your eyes . . . I don't think I've ever seen eyes as green as yours. . . ."

He sounded awkward, a little uncomfortable with offering compliments. His effort touched her all the more because it was clearly not easy for him. "Thank you."

He was glad to move back to more comfortable ground. "Trust me, you're not inconspicuous. Which is why we're going to have to make you that way. It won't take much to make you unrecognizable, but we have to take care of that PDQ. Then we can go into Denver and stash you somewhere."

"I don't want to be stashed. No, Rook, not again. Being stashed didn't make me safe. All it did was frustrate me to death. I need to be doing something to help with this mess."

Well, if she was disguised adequately . . . "All right. You can help me. The first thing I want to do is check out those guys you said sounded familiar. I'm also hoping my contact can shake something out of someone's memory at the airport. *Somebody* had to tamper with that plane."

"Who *are* these contacts of yours?"

"Just some people who have good connections."

"What exactly do you do as a mercenary?"

For some strange reason he felt she had a right to ask that question. He rarely felt a need to explain himself, but he did this time. "I consult with foreign governments, help them set up training programs for paratroops."

"Then you don't fight?"

"Not if I can help it. I've been told I'm overly picky about who I work for, but . . . I just don't want to ever have to be ashamed of what I've done."

"I can understand that." Looking back over her own professional life, she hoped she could say the same thing. She valued her own ethics highly and was glad to know Rook felt the same. Mark had once accused her of measuring everyone by her own standards, so that she just assumed everyone was as ethical and honest as she was. It was dangerous, he'd told her, warning her that someday someone was going to take serious advantage of her. So far, no one had. At least, not as far as she knew.

Massie rolled over, making a muffled sound in her sleep, then quieted. The wind still howled outside, and though the trees sheltered them from the worst of it, the sides of the tent rippled.

"I ought to break out the food and light candles," Rook said. "We all need to eat something."

She didn't want him to climb out of the sleeping bag. For some strange reason she just wanted him to stay right where he was, holding her. It was as if his arms held everything else at bay, even the grief and fear that never left her.

"I'm thirsty," he added, as if trying to motivate himself. "You must be, too." But he didn't move.

She was almost afraid to breathe for fear she would shatter the spell of whatever was happening between them. The storm faded away, the coldness of the waning afternoon outside seemed like a bad memory. Even the dog's steady snore seemed to grow fainter.

It was going to happen. Suddenly, with a certainty that reached to the depths of her very soul, she knew what was going to happen. Not even guilt reared its head to stop her. This might be her last hour on earth, and that understanding had an incredible effect on her perspective.

But she would have to take the first step. Because of what had happened between them in the kitchen yesterday, now it was up to her to make it clear that she wanted him.

Oh, it was hard! She hadn't ever made love with anyone except her husband. Not ever. Never had she been the aggressor. She had learned early in her marriage that approaching Mark usually resulted in a kindly rejection. Oh, he had never been harsh about it, but in the end she had learned to simply wait until he expressed interest.

The thought of actually making the first move... She bit her lower lip and felt herself tremble. Could she even do it?

He was looking straight down at her. It was impossible for either of them to read the other's expression, but neither was it necessary. He knew what she was thinking, and he was waiting for her to make her decision. She knew it as surely as if he had said so out loud. Against her, she felt the change in his body that signaled his interest, and he didn't try to hide it. He simply waited, leaving it up to her.

She really wished he would just take charge and take the responsibility away, but she had no right to ask that of him. To be fair, she had to make it plain to herself and to him that she wasn't going to blame him later.

She inched closer, the minutest of moves, almost undetectable. He felt it, and his body leapt in response. But still he waited. It wasn't enough. That little bit could be too easily misinterpreted.

Finally she found the courage to raise a trembling hand to his cheek. At once he turned his head and kissed her fingertips.

"Please," she said on a mere whisper of sound. "Please."

But he didn't draw her closer, didn't take the initiative. "What do you want, Jenny? Tell me. Show me. It doesn't matter. But make it clear to both of us."

She couldn't...she absolutely couldn't. There was no possible way....

But somehow she managed to slip her leg between his, bringing them closer together. And somehow she managed to draw his head down to her until their mouths met. In the end it was as hard as that, and as easy.

An instant later, nothing existed in the universe except Galen Rydell.

12

It was dark, and inside the cocoon of the sleeping bag, the temperature rose even higher. His hands were warm, and felt faintly rough with calluses when they slipped beneath her shirt and spread flat against her back. The sensation made her shiver with pure pleasure and elevated her to a state of the most exquisite awareness.

It had been so long, so very long, since the last time she had been aware of herself in the way she was now. So long since every nerve ending had sung with the sheer joy of being alive. Ordinarily she was a very cerebral person, existing in her head, hardly aware of the physical side of her nature. But now, quite suddenly, she was very much a physical being, a woman with a body that was crying out for a man's touches.

The weight of the sleeping bag on her had become a taunt, brushing lightly over nerve endings that wanted the deeper, stronger pressure of a man's weight upon them. Every movement she made seemed to cause magnified sensations on her skin, and each wave of fresh sensation caused her to press even closer to Rook.

He lifted her shirt, flinging it away into the dark. A flicker of thought warned her that it was going to be awfully cold to crawl into later, but she didn't care. She lifted her hips eagerly to help him when he reached for her panties. His clothing seemed to disappear by itself.

She was naked with him. It felt like the first time ever, a tremulous excitement mixed with fear and anticipation, a throbbing ache between her legs in a place that at once felt unprotected and yet wanted to be even more open. Had it ever before felt like this?

"Jenny..." He drew her closer, until they were pressed chest-to-chest and belly-to-belly. She felt his erection between them, and a new thrill pierced her with an almost unbearable sweetness. He wanted her. He truly wanted her. It had been so very long since she had felt wanted....

He gently pulled her over him, so that she rested on his chest with him between her legs. She felt so open, so exposed, and thought she was going to melt when his hands trailed lightly over her back and down over the curve of her rump. He could have touched her most private places, and she held her breath in expectation, but instead he slipped past them, teasing her in the most delicious way.

His hardness was between her legs, and by opening herself just a little wider she was able to press herself against him.

He murmured something, a mere breath of sound, as if the sensation delighted him as much as it did her. Encouraged, she moved closer, pressing gently in a rhythm as old as time.

The strangest thoughts flickered through her mind as her body and his hands led her through an ancient dance. It was as if by opening her body this way, she opened herself to life. A magical sense of awe at the mystery of it all, which she had thought long lost, was suddenly strong within her, making her feel all woman, warm and welcoming and yielding.

He was whispering things in her ear, broken words of pleasure, disjointed and meaningless except between lovers. All that mattered was his tone, husky with desire, encouraging her. All that mattered was his hands and their gentle exploration of her sensitive flesh. All that mattered was his body beneath hers as he opened her slowly to the wonder of love.

Her breasts were indeed small, but he seemed to like them, and when he drew one nipple into his mouth and sucked, she forgot that she had ever been self-conscious about them. Pleasure exploded through her, weakening her until she nearly collapsed, filling her with a need to make a woman's surrender.

But he wouldn't let her, not yet. He took delight in discovering her body, in learning what made her shiver and moan. He discovered that if he ran a finger lightly down her side, she undulated against him helplessly, stoking the fires even higher. He found that his tongue in her ear made her moan and press closer, and that a gentle nip on her nipple made her beg for more.

He discovered that when he slipped his hand between them and slid his finger between sensitive, moist folds of flesh, she moaned and her whole body arched, begging for more.

Slick . . . smooth . . . his finger glided slowly, learning her, learning how the least touch affected her. Damn, he'd forgotten how heady it could be to give pleasure this way. For so long now he'd avoided women except for an occasional slip in the arms of someone who invariably wanted more than he would ever give again.

This time...this time was different. Jennifer wanted nothing at all from him. In fact, he was almost positive she would scorn anything he offered. She might not be as determined to die now, but she still hadn't discovered a real desire to live. She was so imprisoned in her own past that it was a wonder she was breaking free even this much.

She was less of a threat to him than any woman he had ever been with, and it had the effect of relaxing him completely. Relaxing him enough to make love.

It had been a long time since he had felt safe enough with a woman to give completely of himself, but he gave himself completely now, trusting that she would not mistake his devotion to her pleasure as a declaration of love. She didn't want those declarations, and because she didn't, he felt safe to make them.

Ludicrous, scolded some rational corner of his mind, but he ignored it. It had been so very long since he had truly made love, and he was sinking into the experience now, a willing slave to her needs and his own. Places deep inside him, frozen for so long in the aftermath of his devastating losses, began to thaw. And because he felt safe, he didn't fight the softening that crept over him.

He held her close, treasuring the sensation of skin against skin, welcoming the warmth of another human being. He'd been so alone for so long....

But the tension was building, too, filling them both with a hunger that wouldn't be denied forever. Much as they savored each moment, much as they yearned to draw it out endlessly, culmination drew nearer and nearer.

Until passion suffused her whole body with an ache that made her press harder and harder against his answering strength. Until she felt an overwhelming emptiness inside that could be satisfied only by having him deep within her. Until her body was his and his was hers and...

He rolled them over and filled her in one easy movement. An unbearable thrill clenched her womb in a spasm of pleasure unlike any she had ever felt. Never had she wanted so much, needed so much, felt so much. The rhythmic pulsing deep within her strengthened, as if it were trying to draw him closer...deeper....

His hips thrust against hers in long, slow movements as he trailed hungry, wet kisses across her breasts. She felt surrounded by him, wanted by him.... In the act of love she had always before felt a sense of separation, as if two souls could not quite meet, the distance between them suddenly astronomical in these most intimate moments.

She didn't feel that this time. Somehow, some way, Rook made her feel as if she were truly part of him, as if he were as aware of her as he was of himself.

Whatever it was, the closeness she felt was every bit as intense as the pleasure that drove her higher... higher....

When the end came, the intensity bordered on pain, the most exquisite pain she had ever felt. Moments later, he joined her.

The next thing Jennifer was aware of was a sloppy, slurpy lick on her cheek. She giggled, recognizing that Massie was feeling ignored.

Rook eased himself off her, saying wryly, "I'm glad the dog slept through the rest of it."

"She's probably getting hungry."

"I know I am. Let me see what I can do about it." But before he climbed out of the cozy sleeping bag into the wintry world, he wanted one more kiss, one more snuggle.

Jennifer seemed to agree, turning willingly into his arms and lifting her mouth for his kiss.

"Thank you," she murmured.

He hugged her. "That was...magical." He looked down into her eyes and, even as dark as it was in the tent now, he could tell that she was smiling. His heart squeezed. "You're beautiful, you know that?"

Something sparkled on her lash—a tear?—but she kept right on smiling and pressed a quick kiss to his lips.

But then reality could be ignored no longer. His stomach was making empty noises, the dog kept nudging at the two of them with a huge, cold nose, and it sounded as if it was only getting worse outside. Reluctantly he crawled out of the sleeping bag and pulled on his clothes. "You stay right where you are," he told Jenny. "No point in both of us freezing."

The weather had made them safe. When he crawled outside, followed closely by Massie, who needed to use the outdoor facilities, he found that several more inches of snow had fallen. Beyond the edge of the trees, it looked as if the night had turned into a wild swirl of snowflakes, close to whiteout conditions. Nobody, but nobody, was going to find them in this. Which meant they could sleep easily and start out at dawn...assuming the storm had passed. The other blessing was the heavy cloud cover, which sealed in what was left of the day's warmth and was keeping the temperature from dropping as drastically as it would have on a clear night at this altitude. The fates were smiling on them tonight.

As he unstrapped the bag of dog food from the sled, along with Massie's bowls, he found himself thinking about Jennifer's husband and children. He didn't feel guilty about what had just happened but, oddly, he found himself wondering if he should.

But no. There was absolutely no reason to feel guilty. They were dead, she was alive, and, as he'd finally realized with Samantha, once someone was dead, there wasn't a whole lot you could do about anything. Even now he sometimes stewed about it, wondering what he might have done differently, knowing there wasn't a damn thing, because by then it had all been out of his control.

But earlier, before everything had blown up, perhaps there had been something he should have done. No matter how he racked his brains, however, he never came up with anything. He wondered if Jenny did the same thing, questioning how she might have prevented her family from flying off on that fateful trip. Yeah, she probably worried endlessly about what she had done that had caused all of this to happen.

But those questions didn't do any good. He'd learned that the hard way. And maybe she was learning it, too. Over the past hour or so, she seemed to have let go of the past. He paused at the door of the tent, though, afraid of what he was going to find when he went inside. He couldn't imagine that she had completely released her guilt and grief. No, they'd been her constant companions for far too long, and she wasn't going to relinquish them easily.

He just hoped she didn't rediscover them right away.

Icy air snaked under the collar of his jacket and down his spine, causing him to shiver as he squatted there at the tent flap, strangely reluctant to move.

It appalled him to realize how much it mattered to him that Jennifer not sink once again into the despair and guilt that had been swamping her.

It appalled him to realize he was beginning to care.

Christ!

Opening the tent flap, he shoved in the food, the dog's dishes, the bag of candles and matches, and a bowl of snow. "Here," he said, hardly looking at Jennifer. "I need to walk around and check things out. I'll be back shortly."

He was aware that she gave him a startled, hurt look, but he backed out and zipped up the flap, not wanting to deal with it.

He couldn't afford to care. He didn't want to care. Why had he quit smoking? He would give his left arm for a cigarette. Jesus!

He kicked at the snow, sending up a shower of ice crystals that the wind caught and threw back into his face. The icy sting focused him sharply back into the moment. No need to get so exercised about it, he told himself. No, he'd caught it early, and he would be on guard from here on out. No way was he going to let himself get in any deeper with this woman.

But the impression of satin skin against his was still fresh, the sound of her sighs and moans still echoed in his ears. He might not let himself get in any deeper, but banishing her was going to be just as hard.

Between a rock and a hard place. Hell, he'd spent his entire life that way, it sometimes seemed, caught in an untenable position between lousy choices. This was nothing new. Nothing new at all.

But he couldn't allow himself to care. He never cared.

One step took him out from beneath the sheltering trees into a clearing. A snowy night was never pitch-dark. It was as if the clouds caught the starshine and magnified it a little before passing it on, and then the snow below reflected it until there was just enough of a pale glow by which to see. The trees around the clearing were lightless shadows against snow and clouds, shadows that looked almost like doorways into a darker place beyond.

In the center of the clearing was one small fir tree, probably a blue spruce. Maybe four feet high, it looked like a lost child in a crowd of uncaring adults.

And somehow the sight of it grabbed him, filling him with yearnings he'd buried long ago. Christmas. It was almost Christmas. Since Samantha's death, Christmas had become potentially devastating, a time when, if he wasn't careful to keep overwhelmingly busy, he remembered all he had lost. Even now, on the side of a desolate mountain, he thought he could hear the faint echo of Samantha's childish glee.

The wind gusted sharply, dragging him back from the precipice where he teetered. It was all in the past now, and there was no point in reliving it—except possibly as a reminder of why he shouldn't care about anything.

But along with the ache from the past there was an ache for the future, an ache for the promises this season always seemed to make. He was human enough to be tired of being alone and of living out in the cold. He was human enough to long for companionship and a warm fire.

But those were dangerous yearnings with a price tag far too high.

Enough, he told himself sharply. He was getting as maudlin as that woman back in the tent. Obviously she was a bad influence on him. Just as soon as he got her affairs settled, he was getting the hell away before she dragged him into that pit of despair with her.

Jennifer tried to tell herself there was no reason to feel abandoned or rejected. After all, Rook had stayed with her until Massie started begging for her supper. He had even cuddled her, as if it pleased him to have her near. The only reason he had left the tent was that they needed to eat. Now he was just checking around to make sure they were safe.

But he hadn't wanted to look at her when he had shoved the supplies into the tent. Dark as it was in here, she hadn't been able to mistake the fact that he was trying to avoid her.

Well, what did she expect? She might not have wide experience of such things—in fact, Mark had been her only lover—but she had heard that men were more casual about these things and very often just wanted to get away afterward. She hadn't taken Rook to be that kind, but...

Sighing, she lit a candle and dressed, then watched Massie try to eat lying down. They hadn't brought the little stool on which Massie's dishes were usually placed, and the dog was too big to eat comfortably while standing, so she had figured out her own method, lying with her front paws on either side of the bowl. It seemed to be working just fine.

But of course it was. Sometimes Jennifer thought that dog fanciers had too low an opinion of what an animal was capable of. English mastiffs were descended from a Tibetan working breed that had most likely survived without tables to dine from.

She melted the bowl of snow over the candle until it was tepid to the touch, then drank deeply. The rest she poured in the dog's water dish.

The tent rocked a little as an errant gust of wind slipped between the guardian trees. Where was Rook? He seemed to have been gone a long time, especially if he was so sure that no one could find them in this storm. Massie finished her supper and curled up around Jennifer, sharing warmth. The dog's big head filled her lap.

What if he'd taken off, left her here to fend for herself?

The thought seemed to explode out of nowhere, without any warning. How did she know she could trust him? That question had never been satisfactorily answered, and now here she was in the middle of the woods with no idea of where she was or how to get to civilization, caught in a blizzard that would obliterate every sign of their trail. The food would run out in a day or two, and then it would only be a matter of time before she died of exposure.

She should have stayed in Denver. She should have turned herself in to the police and dealt with the consequences straightforwardly. How could she ever have thought she would be safer running?

Massie seemed to sense her distress and nuzzled her neck. The touch of the dog's cold, wet nose startled her out of her gloomy, frightened thoughts. Of course she had nothing to fear from Rook. Good heavens, if he'd wanted to kill her, he could have done so any time in the past two days. It was ridiculous to think he would bring her out here, make love to her, then abandon her.

Besides, this was just a smoke screen so she wouldn't think about the really important things... like Mark, and how she had just betrayed him. Except that she didn't feel she had. Poking at the notion mentally as if she were testing a tooth for soreness, she found none at all. Her conscience was easy on that score. At least this wasn't going to add to her overwhelming burden of guilt.

Maybe she just wasn't going to feel guilty anymore at all. But as soon as she had the thought, she knew she was wrong. The original feelings were still there and still strong, only momentarily swept aside by other things. She still felt guilty for being alive, and guilty for being glad to be alive. There was going to be no easy way to eradicate that.

Nor did she deserve to be free of guilt. After all, something she had done or said had caused the death of her family. It seemed to her that she could atone only by bringing their killer to justice.

Massie suddenly lifted her head, listening alertly. Jennifer tensed, feeling the hairs on the nape of her neck prickle. What had the dog heard?

Moments passed in silence except for the keening wind, then Massie began to growl low in her throat, her hackles rising. Jennifer's heart began to gallop wildly. What could be out there? Surely Massie wouldn't growl at Rook?

Then, just as suddenly as she had gone on the alert, Massie settled her head back onto Jennifer's lap. Whatever had disturbed her was gone. Jenny wished it was as easy for her to calm down.

Massie's head suddenly lifted again, and Jennifer wanted to yell at her to cut it out, silly as it was, but before she had time to get scared again, Rook's voice came from outside.

"Jenny? It's me."

Thank God! She didn't know how much more of this she could take. When Rook crawled through the opening into the tent, she wanted to fling herself at him and give him a great big hug of welcome.

But his expression stopped her. He was not the man who had shared a sleeping bag with her so recently. Something in his face looked closed, as if he had locked himself away.

"It's still snowing," he said as he pulled off his boots. "Nobody can find us tonight. Have you eaten?"

"I waited for you."

He nodded without looking at her and reached for a jar of peanut butter. "It's not five-star cuisine, is it?"

Using their fingers as scoops, they dined on peanut butter, water and dry cereal. Plenty of calories to keep them warm, but almost impossible to swallow.

His unexplained withdrawal wounded her almost as much as anything he might have said or done. She was a fool to have let herself care even a little bit. Damn it, how many times did she have to be kicked before she learned to stay down? If she survived all this mess, if she escaped execution and lived to be an old woman, she was never, *never* again going to let herself care enough to be hurt. It was just too damn painful, even when it was someone like Rook, for whom she had only just started to have feelings.

She was tempted to unzip the sleeping bags and make a silent statement about how she felt, but the simple truth was, it was too damn cold. She would freeze to death without Rook's body heat.

As soon as they had finished eating, they climbed back into the bags with their clothing on. For a while they lay stiffly, staring up at the roof of the tent while the candle flickered wildly in a draft. The wind outside still moaned through the treetops, and the elderly pines groaned under their burden of new snow.

"It's almost Christmas," Jennifer said.

"Mmm."

"I just suddenly realized, I've been dreading Christmas ever since...ever since the crash. It's going to seem so empty without Bethany and Eli."

"It sure will."

"Do you—do you still miss your daughter?"

"Especially at Christmas."

"How do you deal with it?"

"I pretend it isn't Christmas. If I'm lucky, I'm in some sun-drenched hell without any time to worry about it."

"Oh."

After a moment he sighed and turned his head, looking at her. "Sorry. That wasn't very helpful, and it wasn't even true. I've only been overseas once at Christmas since she died."

"So...how do you cope?"

"I usually keep busy by volunteering. If I can't make my own child smile, then I can damn well make somebody else's smile. It's purely selfish, I guess, but it works."

Selfish? Jennifer didn't consider herself to be a cynic, but she'd never known anyone who was purely altruistic. People routinely volunteered for charity because they got something out of it, even if it was only a good feeling. Rook's method for dealing with his loss spoke highly of him. If only he wasn't so distant....

"Maybe I'll try that," she said. "If I live long enough."

He swore—a short, sharp sound. "You'll live," he said flatly. "You'll live if I have to take this state apart tree limb by tree limb."

The image that sprang to her mind was so ridiculous that a laugh escaped her. The sound caused him to turn and look at her again. "There are a lot of trees in Colorado," she said by way of explanation.

A sheepish smile came to his lips. "I tend to exaggerate when I get annoyed."

"Or when you pick up your lance and get on your white charger." She laughed again. "Thanks. I needed that. So, where do you volunteer?"

"You'd be horrified how many kids spend Christmas in hospitals or hospices."

"I probably would." She thought about it for a moment, then asked, "I don't suppose you'd need the assistance of an elf?"

"How'd you know I do Santa Claus?"

"Just a good guess."

But what really struck him was that she was talking about the future, making plans to do something besides find the killer and die. Whether she knew it or not, this woman was edging steadily toward a commitment to life. There was no denying the relief he felt.

Relief and fear—fear because someone had to save her from a determined, skillful assassin. Christ, how did he get himself into these messes? Absently he touched his breast pocket, looking for the pack of cigarettes that wasn't there.

Not that he cared, of course. He never cared. It was just... *nice* in an intellectual sort of way that she no longer planned to die.

And then he wondered when he'd begun to stop believing his own lies. Hell, this was getting too damn messy.

"Sure, I can always use an elf," he said, figuring she would forget by then anyway, assuming they got all these messes straightened out and she wasn't dead, and they weren't both in jail for cop killing. When all was said and done, it seemed like a low-risk offer.

"Thanks." She gave him a smile.

"It's tough, though," he warned her. "Some of these kids are in serious trouble."

Her smile faded. "I know. There are worse things than dying in a plane crash, aren't there." It was a statement, asking for no confirmation from him.

He gave her one, anyway. "There sure are. Both for the victims and the survivors. At least you have some idea why this happened. These folks—well, they don't have any reasons. It's a thunderbolt out of nowhere."

She nodded. "At least they weren't responsible."

"They don't feel that way. I've seen mothers worrying themselves sick about whether they'd done something wrong, forgotten a vital nutrient, fed the kid some carcinogenic food additive, let him play in polluted water... the list of possible sins and omissions is endless, and the guilt is incredible. I think when it comes to children, parents just feel responsible."

"Do you?"

He'd known that was coming, and now that it had, he wondered why he hadn't evaded it. Damn it, he didn't want to rake up the past. "Yeah, I do. I always will. Damned if I know what I could have done different, but..." He let the sentence hang, incomplete.

"There's a difference between guilt and responsibility, you know," he continued when she didn't speak. He had an idea which direction her wheels were spinning. "A big difference. Responsibility entails accepting that you might have done something differently, and that it might have been critical. Guilt is just a method of beating yourself up. You might have been responsible for the deaths of your family insofar as you did something that made someone mad enough to pull that stunt, but that doesn't mean you should feel guilty."

She shook her head. "Sounds like the same thing to me."

"It's not. The question is whether you did something *wrong*. If you did nothing *wrong*, then you don't need to feel guilty about it. And given the same set of circumstances, you'd probably do the same thing now. The consequences were unforeseeable, because you didn't do anything wrong."

Jennifer saw what he was trying to get at, but at the moment it offered small comfort. "I don't know what I did, so how can I know whether I did something wrong or not?"

"I guess we'll have to find out, won't we?"

And he still hadn't told her about his daughter, she realized. He'd turned the conversation back to her and her problems, and had dragged it away from his. "What about you? Did you do something wrong?"

"Damn it, you just won't let it pass, will you?"

He was upset, she realized, and suddenly she felt guilty. He'd made peace with his demons. What was she doing trying to stir them up? "I'm sorry. It's none of my business. Honestly, it's not morbid curiosity."

No, he admitted, it wasn't. Like anyone going through a catastrophe, she wanted to know how others had dealt with it and survived. It was the only real reassurance. He closed his eyes, trying to swallow the growing lump in his throat. Thinking about Samantha always made him want to weep, and he'd already wept an ocean of tears over her. He felt as if he were about to trespass in a sacred place.

"A few years back I was involved in a covert operation in the Middle East. I can't tell you any specific details. Let's just say it went sour and lives were lost, mostly because of some orders given by the officer in charge. When we returned Stateside—those of us who were left—there was an investigation. The lieutenant who gave the orders lied, claiming those orders were mine. I'd argued against them, but all the other men saw was me arguing with the lieutenant. They didn't hear what it was about. Their version of events seemed to substantiate the lieutenant's claim that I'd overridden his authority and given my own orders."

"That's terrible!" In sympathy, she reached out for his hand, but he pulled it away, as if he couldn't bear to be touched right now.

"I was court-martialed," he said. "I was given a couple of years in prison followed by a dishonorable discharge. Mutiny isn't exactly a minor crime in the military."

"I wouldn't think so." She waited, sensing that he was about to continue.

"My wife decided to divorce me in the midst of the trial. That had been coming for a while, I guess. I was just too stupid to see it. She wasn't happy with the life-style—mostly not enough money. From what I heard later, she enjoyed the separations a whole lot. Apparently Samantha wasn't my biological daughter."

Jennifer didn't say a thing. What could she possibly say?

"That didn't matter to me," Rook continued. "Christ, I'd changed her diapers and bounced her on my knee, and taught her how to ride a bicycle. How could I possibly care where she got her genes? She was *my* daughter."

"Of course she was!"

"Cheryl didn't think so. At least, not when she decided to ditch me. The last thing she ever wanted to see again was me, and the only way she could make me gone for good was to take the kid from me. Her boyfriend had loads of money, and he used it to buy her some really good lawyers. You know what? My name wasn't even on Samantha's birth certificate."

"But that doesn't prove—"

"DNA testing proved it," he interrupted harshly. "Samantha wasn't my biological daughter. What with me going to jail, I didn't stand a chance. The judge gave Cheryl sole custody and ordered me to keep the hell away."

"Not even visitation?" Jennifer was horrified.

"Nope. Not even a letter or a phone call. You know how I heard she killed herself? She wrote me a letter right before she did it. Mailed it from a drop box. I got it three days later and—and—" He had to take a couple of deep breaths to maintain control. "She did—she did it right after the judge's order came down. That very night. Jumped out in front of a car doing sixty on the interstate—" He broke off, almost panting. "Jesus! I didn't even get to go to her funeral! Not that they would have let me..."

He rolled onto his side suddenly, clutching her to him as if she were a lifeline. His fingers dug into her shoulders.

"She said—she said she was going to make everyone sorry. For taking her daddy away."

He buried his face in Jenny's neck, as if he might actually find some solace in the warmth and fragrance of her. But there was no solace. There never would be.

13

In the morning, the blizzard had stopped. They packed up their camp quickly, after another meal of peanut butter and cereal. Jennifer felt as if a cold lump of lead were sitting in the pit of her stomach. It was a great way to start the day.

Rook refused to look at her. Whenever his gaze chanced to fall on her, it slid quickly away, as if it were somehow painful. Of course, she told herself. He was embarrassed and uncomfortable because of all he had exposed of himself last night. The poor guy was probably hoping like hell that she wouldn't mention it again. And of course she wouldn't.

But she was very glad he had shared with her last night. She felt so much closer to him now, knowing about Samantha and Cheryl and the court-martial. And she also felt oddly strengthened.

Maybe because last night she had shared something of herself, had given something of her own caring and concern to him. Proving that she had something left over, that her grief had not totally consumed her and left her an empty shell. That was heartening.

But it was also as if, in the process of reaching out to give, she had found something. Some hidden reserve, perhaps. Or possibly just a meaningful purpose. Whatever it was, she felt stronger and better this morning than she had since before the crash.

Massie frolicked briefly in the snow, but accepted the harness again readily. Jennifer got the distinct impression that the dog actually liked pulling the sled. But maybe dogs, just like people, needed to feel useful.

Last night *she* had certainly felt useful.

Muscles she hadn't used since last winter groaned a little bit as they started out, but cross-country skiing wasn't different enough from walking that she hurt all over. Just a few places, especially her arms from poling, and the ache soon worked itself out.

Clouds still hung low and heavy in the sky, but the wind had calmed considerably, and no new snow fell.

"Do you know where we are?" she asked Rook.

He pointed to the highest mountain peak to their right, glimpsed through the trees. "Close enough. We'll hit the road within a mile or so of Ira's place."

He didn't say another word. From time to time he paused to check a compass and check the position of the mountain. Several times he spelled Massie on sleigh-pulling duty. Jennifer tried to spell her, but her arms were so sore that the added weight of the sleigh proved to be a significant hindrance.

"It's all right," Rook told her when it was apparent she was slowing them down. "I'll do it. It's not a problem." He slipped the harness over his own shoulders.

"I guess I need to spend more time at the gym."

"A lot of things get overlooked when we're grieving."

It was true; she hadn't been to the gym since before the crash. She didn't even know if she still had a membership, for that matter.

Suddenly, shocking them both into utter stillness, the cellular phone rang. Even buried as it was in a knapsack to protect it, it sounded loud and unnatural in the silence of the snow-covered woods. Both Rook and Jennifer looked at the knapsack as if it were a snake poised to bite them.

It rang again.

Rook moved suddenly, as if wakened from a daze. He reached the sled in two long strides and opened the pack. Massie lay down in the snow and started nibbling at her impromptu mittens. Jennifer told her to stop. Massie looked up at her, then chuffed and put her head down on her paws.

"Hello?" The receiver was so cold that Rook didn't press it to his ear. He was amazed that the battery hadn't died in these low temperatures. The voice that came through sounded tinny and far away.

"This is Felix Abernathy. I'm calling for Jennifer Fox."

Rook turned and handed the receiver to Jenny. "Your lawyer."

She almost lost her balance as she reached for the phone. One of her skis started to slip out from beneath her, but she caught herself and planted it more firmly. Gingerly, she took the phone.

"Don't touch it to your skin," Rook warned her. "It might stick to you."

She held it an inch away. "Felix? What's up?"

"This is a terrible connection. I can hardly hear you!"

She almost told him that was hardly surprising, since she was standing on the side of a mountain holding a C-phone that should have died hours ago, but caught herself. Rook had been insistent that she not give Felix any information about where she was. "I think the battery's dying. We'd better keep this short."

"Well, I *did* manage to accomplish something for you, Jennifer. I managed to convince the judge to revoke the arrest warrant, so for the moment you're not a fugitive." He sniffed. "Nor is your friend. I figured since you're apparently in this mess together, I might as well do two for the price of one."

"Thank you, Felix! That's really great." She could hardly believe he'd pulled it off. "That's some coup!"

"It certainly wasn't easy to achieve, considering what you're wanted for. My God, girl, do you realize the cops think you're practically a mass murderer? Five bodies to your credit!"

"I didn't kill anyone!"

"*I* know that. I just hope to heaven we can persuade someone else of that little fact. The cops are still looking for evidence to hang you on, and the only reason I was able to get that warrant rescinded was because there's a paucity of proof at the moment. Basically, nobody can prove you did anything at all, but you're under suspicion because of proximity. Well, as I told the judge, proximity still isn't a crime in this country. There were at least thirty other people in their houses on that section of street that night. Any one of them is just as suspicious as you are. Except, of course, that the cops who were killed were watching you. It rather gives you a motive, but even the judge thought this was all too thin once it was laid out."

"I'm truly amazed you pulled it off, Felix."

"I am, too." He laughed shortly. "I'm a damn good lawyer, and don't you ever forget it."

"I never will." The remark seemed out of character, and she wondered if he'd been getting flak at work about something. But this didn't seem like the time to pursue it, and the cellular connection was fading.

"In other news," Felix continued, "let me add some joy to your day."

"Quickly. I'm losing the connection, Felix."

"Okay. The IRS is looking for you."

"For me? Why?" She couldn't imagine it. One thing she didn't do was cheat on her taxes.

"Well, it seems you made a large cash withdrawal from the bank. Fifty thousand, to be precise."

"I already paid taxes on that money! In June, right after the insurance paid."

"That's what Karl told them. Since he's your tax representative, he's the one who was contacted, when they couldn't get you. Anyway, long story short—and don't explain it to me, I don't want to know—if you paid that fifty thousand to someone to do something for you, then you need to file a 1099. The sum is so large, they're evidently nervous about it. They want to know what you did with it. I suggest you talk to Karl about it when you get back."

"Okay." There was a loud burst of static in her ear. "Felix, we're about to lose the connection."

"I'm through. Just remember, I want to be the first person you talk to when you get back into town."

"I promise."

She handed the receiver back to Rook, who placed it in the cradle on the battery pack and tucked it securely into the backpack.

"Everything okay?" he asked.

"Felix got the arrest warrants on both of us revoked. He managed to convince the judge that the cops didn't have enough evidence to justify them."

"Good man. Anything else?"

"Yeah." She shook her head. "I don't know whether to laugh or cry. The IRS is after me."

"What for? Did you cheat?"

"Never. Believe me, no amount of money is worth the hassle. I'm so cautious about it, I probably pay more than I have to."

"Me too." He chuckled. "I even pay on money I make overseas, and I don't have to. So what's up?"

"Well, they found out about the fifty thousand I withdrew to pay the hit man. They want to know what I did with it, because if I paid somebody to do something for me, I have to file a 1099. How can I file a 1099 when I don't know who the guy is?"

"Good question. Tell 'em you put it in a collection basket at church. The church wouldn't have to report it. Or just say it was stolen."

She was cooling down from standing there so long and was glad when he gestured for them to start moving again. Massie perked up, as if she, too, was tired of waiting.

"I hate to lie," Jenny told Rook. "Besides, they wouldn't believe it."

"So tell 'em the truth and let *them* find the hit man."

She almost laughed at that. "Think they'd have any luck?"

"Probably no more than we're having."

She skied for another few hundred feet, then remarked, "Well, I'll deal with it somehow. If worse comes to worst, I'll say I gave it away, and I'll pay the gift tax. Compared to everything else that's gone wrong in my life this year, this is nothing."

"That's a positive attitude for you."

She looked at him and burst out laughing. God, it felt so strange to laugh. To actually feel like laughing. And it felt so good. How had he done that for her?

A tendril of guilt tried to tug at her, but she brushed it impatiently away. Enough, she thought. Enough. Guilt hadn't accomplished a thing. It hadn't brought back her husband and her children. It hadn't caught the murderer or mended anything else. All it had done was lacerate her for the accident of surviving and make her totally useless to anyone else. All it had done was make her cause pain to those who cared about her. It was a useless, wasted emotion.

So she hung on to the laughter, clung to it, nurtured it. As long as she was breathing, she had a right to laugh.

Didn't she?

They reached Ira's place shortly after noon. Rook's friend was standing under a car on the pneumatic lift, looking up at the exhaust pipes as if they held the key to the universe.

"It's leaking somewhere," he said by way of greeting, "but damned if I can see where."

"I'm returning your phone, skis and sled, and picking up my car," Rook told him. "When you get the phone charges, let me know. I'll pay them."

Ira waved the offer aside. "I pay that damn company so much money every month I'll never notice a few extra calls. Now, about your car..."

Jennifer tensed, pausing doubled over as she was releasing her boots from the skis.

"Some guy was showing a whole lot of interest in it yesterday. Don't know what he was doing out back, unless it was snooping, but he claimed he was just looking because he was thinking of buying one."

"What did he look like?"

"Basically average. I couldn't see a whole lot of his face, because he was wearing those wraparound sunglasses with leather side shields—you know the ones."

"Yeah." They were popular in the mountains because they protected against both snow blindness and the wind. "Anything distinctive?"

"His voice was rough. Gravelly."

"That's him." Jennifer straightened, her heart slamming hard against the wall of her chest. "It's got to be. That's how I would have described his voice on the phone."

Rook nodded and turned back to Ira. "What was he driving?"

"A brand-new Mercedes diesel. I wrote down the tag number for you. Can you believe it? A Mercedes, and he expected me to believe he was thinking about buying an Explorer."

Ira insisted that they come inside and have a hot meal to warm them up before they continued. He and Massie hit it off immediately, and when he learned that she was pregnant, he asked for one of the pups.

"Mom will love you to death for that," Jennifer said. "The paternity is unknown, and she's wondering what she's going to do with all the puppies."

"Hell, I'll take two, then. Whoever the sire was, he was probably pretty big. He'd have to be."

"And determined," she added. "My folks have a high fence around the yard just so she can't get out when she's in heat."

Ira grinned. "I like the daddy's style. These are going to be some kickass pups."

Massie, having finished the bowl of kibble Ira had offered her, came to sit beside him and rest her head on his thigh. He was quick to oblige with a good scratch.

Inevitably, though, the conversation turned back to Jennifer's problems.

"Did you learn anything else from your sources?" Rook asked him.

"Sorry, no. They're working on it, though. I get the feeling they're just as curious about what's going on as I am. If there's anything to be found, they'll find it for sure."

"Thanks, buddy. Well, you'll be glad to know you aren't harboring fugitives. The warrants for our arrest were revoked."

Ira gave him a level look that revealed no humor. "As if I was worried about it. You ever need a place to go to ground—I don't care who's on your tail—you come *here.*" He looked at Jennifer. "You, too."

She was touched, but when she tried to thank him, he brushed it aside. "That's what friends are for."

Jennifer looked at Rook. "I like your taste in friends."

He smiled, the warmest expression she'd ever seen on his face. It reached out and touched her somewhere deep inside. "Yeah," he said. "Me too."

A half hour later, after Rook and Ira checked the car for tampering, they were on the road in the Explorer, with Massie in the back seat napping. The day was gray, and the interior of the Explorer felt cozy. It was easy to drift off into a daze and pretend that everything was all right.

But of course it wasn't, and might never be again.

* * *

The first thing Rook did as they approached the outskirts of Denver was get off the highway and onto the streets. The next thing he did was stop at an automatic teller machine and withdraw a large sum of cash. Then they left the Explorer at the airport in long-term parking and took a cab to a used car lot, where he paid cash for an old Chevy with a powerful, purring engine.

"Now," he told Jennifer as they pulled away, "we need to find a place to stay."

"Why are you doing this?" she asked him. Night was settling over the world again, and the lights of stores on either side of the street reflected off pavement wet with snowmelt.

"I figure he knows I'm with you. He certainly found you at my place and picked up on the Explorer. Damned if I'm going to give him an easy way to find us."

"I understand that, but..." She hesitated, because what she was about to say would leave her vulnerable, and she wasn't comfortable with that. She'd never been comfortable with that. Mark used to complain that she had walls higher than a fortress.

"But what?"

"Why are you doing this for *me?*"

His gloved hands tightened on the steering wheel, and he was silent for a minute or so. She had just about given up on getting an answer when he shifted in his seat and spoke.

"I don't care about much," he said slowly, sounding almost resentful. "I make it a habit not to care *at all,* as far as I can manage. Caring is a dangerous thing. Clouds your mind, helps you make foolish choices."

"And gets you hurt," she commented quietly. That was the worst of it, as she'd learned to her own sorrow.

"That too." He glanced at her, then returned his attention to the road. Ahead of them, a traffic light changed to amber. He braked, bringing them to a stop just as it turned red. "The hell of it is, I don't seem to be able to stop giving a damn about *you.*"

Her heart skipped a beat for some unknown reason, but she ignored it. "You said you felt responsible because you gave me that phone number."

"True. But that's not all of it. For some stupid reason, I don't want to see you dead."

She gave an unhappy little laugh. "I'm beginning to feel that way myself."

"Life is shit, you know?" The light turned green, and he accelerated. "I mean, when I look back at it all, I wonder why the hell I ever bothered to get out of bed. But somehow...I don't know. I guess hope springs eternal."

"Alexander Pope, *An Essay on Man.* 'Hope springs eternal in the human breast: Man never is, but always to be blest.'"

"I like the truncated version better."

Almost in spite of herself, she smiled. "Pope was also responsible for 'To err is human, to forgive divine' and 'For fools rush in where angels fear to tread.' I always thought it would be pretty neat to have your words become common sayings."

"Some of my words are common sayings—hell, damn...." He trailed off when she began to laugh.

"That isn't quite what I meant."

"I didn't think so. And I like the sound of your laugh."

Suddenly self-conscious, she fell silent.

"I just...I just want you to be able to keep on laughing."

She looked at him, touched to her very soul, but she didn't know what to say. Anything was likely to make him feel even more uncomfortable. Finally she settled on "Thank you."

He shrugged. "There." With one finger he pointed at a motel. "We should be able to stay there tonight without any trouble."

Jennifer had never stayed in this kind of place, but she suspected they wouldn't need a credit card to rent a room. Rook insisted she remain in the car while he registered, but her worst suspicions were confirmed when they entered their room and she saw the mirror tiles glued to the ceiling over the bed.

"They didn't have a room with two beds," Rook said. "They're all singles."

After what they had shared the night before, that hurt. She had the worst urge to turn on him and lash out, but she restrained herself. She was past being hurt, wasn't she? Surely, having been through the worst, she ought to be immune to such things? But she ached anyway.

"It's all right," she managed to say. "It's warm."

"Yeah. Big difference."

Massie immediately found herself a comfortable spot in a corner and went back to sleep.

A shower would be nice, too, Jennifer told herself, and was relieved when a check of the bathroom showed it to be spotless. The towels even smelled faintly of disinfectant. She'd been in nicer hotels that hadn't been this clean.

"I'll go out and get something to eat while you shower," Rook said. "We could go somewhere, but I'm not sure that's wise. Your picture's been all over the TV."

"I hope it hasn't been on that TV show where they reenact the crimes."

One corner of his mouth lifted. "I don't think you've even rated Crime Stoppers yet."

"Good. This is one area where I don't want to be famous."

"I'm sure we can find some way to disguise you, Jenny. A wig, a pair of glasses. It's usually easy enough to do. We'll check it out in the morning."

The shower was a godsend, easing her aching muscles and thawing the last of the chill from her bones. Of course, she would be cold within minutes of drying off, but she didn't worry about that. For now she was content to stand in the hot spray until her skin was reddened from the heat.

"Jenny?"

Rook's voice drew her out of some dreamy place where she had been drifting with hardly a thought in her head. A sort of stasis, as if she were in a cocoon woven of steam. She turned slowly, oddly unsurprised, and found Rook stepping into the shower behind her.

For the first time she really had a chance to see him nude, and what she saw took her breath away. Loose clothing and the bulky winter jacket hadn't given her any hint of how well muscled he was. He had broad shoulders and powerful arms, and his chest tapered down to a perfectly flat belly and narrow hips.

And he hadn't climbed in with her for the hell of it. He wanted her, wanted her enough to overcome his own barriers. Some instinct warned her that this could be a serious mistake, especially given that they were both major emotional cripples. How could either of them hope to escape being hurt when the other was emotionally unreliable?

Yet the need for closeness overrode the fear of being vulnerable and superseded the need for self-protection so swiftly that neither of them was truly aware of hesitating.

She was wrapped in heat, the prickling heat of the hot water and the silky heat of his wet skin as he stepped forward and wrapped her in his arms. She leaned into him, glorying in his strength and hardness, and tipped her head back to offer herself to him.

The taste of the water combined with theirs, flavoring their kiss. Cupping her bottom, he lifted her toward him and moaned softly into her mouth as the pressure heightened his arousal. Leaning back a little, she twisted slowly, dragging her swelling nipples across his skin.

She didn't think she'd ever felt such a sharp pang of arousal as she did then. It speared right through her and caused her womb to clench so hard it almost hurt.

"You're incredible," he mumbled roughly against her ear. "So sexy..."

No one had ever said that to her before, and it emboldened her. Her own hands started to move, exploring his contours as if she wanted to commit them to memory. He must have enjoyed it, because the rumble that rose from deep within his chest sounded exactly like the purr of a very large cat.

His own hands started roaming, one of them slipping around front to cup her breast and squeeze it. Then his fingers found her nipple and pinched it gently, causing a low moan to escape her lips. Her knees felt as if they were turning to water.

He lifted her suddenly, throwing aside the curtain and setting her gently on her feet on the bath mat.

"It's not safe in this slippery tub," he said, his voice thick with passion. "I don't want you to get hurt...."

She was past caring. Nothing at all mattered except Rook, except being as close to him as she could possibly get.

He toweled them both dry rapidly and roughly, leaving Jennifer's skin tingling pleasantly, and then he carried her toward the bed, which was already turned down.

The sheets felt cool and smooth beneath her back, not at all rough, as she had expected. The light was an added excitement, etching everything clearly in a golden glow. And then, above her, she saw herself in the mirrored tiles, saw Rook bend over her, watched his back muscles bunch as he stretched out between her legs and propped himself on his elbows over her.

The woman in the mirror looked like a stranger, her eyes heavy lidded, her lips open and eager, her arms flung out as if she couldn't manage to expose herself enough. Then she closed her eyes and forgot everything except the exquisite sensation of flesh on flesh.

For a little while she didn't have to feel cold or lonely.

Eager lips met hers, then trailed enticingly over her cheek to her ear, then down her neck to her breast. Little sparkles of excitement exploded within her, triggered by every touch of his mouth.

"Touch yourself..." he whispered roughly. "Touch yourself for me...."

The suggestion at once shocked her and excited her. Her hand trembled a little as she lifted it and brought it to her breast.

"That's it," he whispered, covering her hand with his own, encouraging her with his touch.

She could feel his growing excitement as clearly as if it were her own, and that excited her even more, making it almost easy to explore her own breast with her fingertips, discovering which touches felt best. And all the time she knew he was watching her....

Enchanting ribbons of desire seemed to draw her into a hazy mood of building passion. When he reached for her and drew her even closer, his touch was almost a part of the sensations growing deep inside her, seeming to come as much from within as from without.

She reached out, wanting to give him the same incredible feelings he was giving her, and found his shaft with her fingers. Closing her hand around him, she stroked gently and smiled when he drew a sharp, hissing breath.

Then he retaliated, slipping his own hand between her legs, opening her to deep, strong touches that were almost painful in the pleasure they caused. She trembled on that boundary, suddenly more intensely alive than she could ever remember feeling.

For an instant, just an instant, awareness struck her, warning her that Rook was in his own way as dangerous to her as the hit man. Then the thought slipped away before the rushing onslaught of his lovemaking.

She felt claimed. She felt conquered. She felt wanted in ways she had never felt before.

And she felt fulfilled in some deep place where the most basic elements of her nature hid beneath layers of civilized veneer.

She was woman, he was man, and for a little while not one other damn thing mattered.

14

"Today we're going to talk to DeVries." Rook made the announcement over eggs and Texas toast in carry-out containers. They perched on the edge of the bed to eat, since the room didn't boast anything as useful as a chair or a table.

"He's in the prison at Salida."

"I know." It would take maybe five hours to get there. Another day shot, but the more he thought about it, the more he considered it essential. DeVries had sent Jennifer to him, and maybe there was a reason for that, other than devilment. Maybe DeVries knew something and had assumed that Rook knew it, too. There was only one way to find out. "I need to stop off in the Springs, too, to talk with somebody who might have some information for me."

"Is that the man you called the other night?"

"The same. His name's Clark LaRue. He's in military intelligence. You'll like him."

Did it matter? she wondered as they finished eating. It wasn't as if she was ever going to see him again.

The drive to Colorado Springs was pleasant. The sun was shining, and the farther south they traveled, the less snow covered the ground around them. When they reached the Springs, Rook called his friend and arranged to meet him in a small diner on Tejon Street in the downtown area.

Jennifer had always loved this city and was content to look out the restaurant window at the mountains to the west while Rook and his friend talked. They reminisced in a general sort of way about their days together in the service, but finally Clark came to the point.

"I checked out these guys further, the ones you asked about? None of them could have done it, Rook. The one Mrs. Fox here thinks sounded familiar is in a wheelchair. A skiing accident last winter paralyzed him. The other two both have full-time jobs and haven't missed any work in the last couple of weeks. Not good if you're trying to stalk somebody."

"So it's a dead end."

"Looks that way."

"Well, it was worth a shot."

"Always." Clark shook his head. "I don't know what to tell you, buddy. I don't really have the kind of feelers that would get you the kind of information you need now."

"That's okay. I've got some other folks trying to help out. One of them may come up with something."

LaRue looked at Jennifer. "I can't imagine why anyone would want to put a contract on you. Whoever he is, he must be a sicko."

Jennifer felt her cheeks heat, and shame filled her. Maybe she *was* a sicko. Why had she ever thought that killing herself would fix anything? Why had she ever thought it would be a solution? If nothing else, it would cause terrible grief to her family, and she had no right to do that. Her face burning, she looked away, out toward the beautiful mountains, and was grateful when Rook didn't correct his friend's mistaken impression.

In fact, Rook was extraordinarily protective in ways that went far beyond simply trying to keep her from being executed. So far he hadn't told the truth of her sorry story to a single soul. That probably made him some kind of saint.

The last time she had been in Colorado Springs, it had been with Mark. He'd been attending a conference, and she'd tagged along for the escape. It had, in fact, been the last time they'd had something even approaching a vacation together—nearly three years ago.

But she was surprised to realize that she was remembering it nostalgically, and not as a goad to fresh pain. Even a week ago she would probably have found being here a painful reminder of happier times; now she found herself recalling those three days with a small smile, cherishing the memory rather than whipping herself with it.

Closing her eyes, she let the memories come, let them wash over her with a gentle combination of sorrow and gratitude. For all that she had clung fiercely to her anguish because it connected her with Mark and the children, she found herself feeling even closer to them now as she reclaimed her past without the distorting lens of grief.

When they departed for Salida, she was still lost in reverie, silently dragging out nuggets of memory to dust them off and reclaim them from the vault where she had locked them away. Little by little she was rebuilding her past as a good thing, not as an instrument of self-torture.

"You okay?"

Rook's voice startled her out of her thoughts, making her suddenly realize that the afternoon was half-gone and that they were almost at the prison. "I'm fine," she assured him.

"Just wondered. It's been hours since you said a word."

"I've been thinking."

He glanced at her and smiled faintly. "I kind of figured."

A mile later she spoke again. "Can you remember your daughter at all without it hurting?"

His answer was slow in coming. "Not exactly. I mean, sooner or later, any time I start remembering her, I eventually come smack up against the fact that she's gone for good. But I can still remember the good times as good times. I can remember when she started walking, or the time she hit two home runs in a softball game, and I can smile about it, Jenny. I really can. I get sad when I remember she's gone for good, but I can still...oh, hell, I don't know how to explain it. It's not the same as when I remember how she died. I try to avoid that at any cost."

"I think I understand. Since...the crash I haven't been able to remember Mark and the children at all without hurting so bad I couldn't stand it. But now...it's like I can remember all that stuff the way it really was."

"With the feelings from *then* instead of the feelings from *now.*"

She nodded slowly, thinking it over. "That's a good way of putting it. Except that I still feel sad and lonely. It's not that I don't have the feelings from now. It's just that for some reason they've stopped blocking the feelings that were part of the memory. I can feel the happiness, the laughter, the frustration...whatever. They've all come back."

And that only made her feel sadder somehow, but before she could ponder the meaning of that, they were pulling in to the visitors' parking lot at the prison.

The last time Jennifer had come here had been to speak to Alan DeVries. She was still listed on the visitors' roster as being a lawyer associated with DeVries's case, so she had only to establish her identity. Instead of being ushered to a visitor's cubicle, however, she was instead taken to the warden. Rook, who had identified himself as a friend of DeVries, was left cooling his heels in the antechamber.

The warden greeted her pleasantly enough. Unlike the characters common to cinema, Warden Paul McManus was neither a villain nor cruel. He was simply an ordinary man who was trying to hang on to his decency and optimism in an environment that could crush those qualities in the hardiest of souls. Being a jailer, he had once said in a speech to the Bar Association, was nearly as dehumanizing as being a prisoner.

"It's good to see you again, Ms. Fox," McManus said warmly. "You're here to see Alan DeVries?"

"Yes. Is there a problem?"

"Unfortunately." The warden sighed and shook his head. "We're in the midst of investigating the matter and haven't allowed the news to be released yet, or we could have saved you this trip. Mr. DeVries was murdered yesterday evening by another inmate."

Jennifer felt tendrils of ice wrap around her spine. This wasn't a coincidence, shrieked a voice in her head. No way could this be a coincidence. "H-how?" She hated the way her voice cracked, but McManus seemed not to notice.

He leaned forward, lacing his fingers together. "Old prison method—a handmade shiv under the ribs. We got him medical attention as quickly as we could, but it was too late.''

Her mind whirling, Jennifer tried to decide the best method of progressing. She really didn't have any legal right to be where she was, and certainly none to ask questions. Not since the firm had discharged her. But she had to ask anyway, and damn the consequences.

''Have you caught the perp?''

''Yes. It wasn't much of a problem, since two of the guards caught him with blood on his hands. He even admitted he'd done it because he thought DeVries was going to testify against him in another case. You might want to talk to him about it.''

''I might?''

''Oh, I suppose it would help if I told you who he is. Deland Hewitt. He's also a client of your firm, I believe.''

He was. Jennifer well remembered when Felix had taken on the case. Just before she was fired, as a matter of fact. The partners had been a little leery of taking on another drug dealer so soon after DeVries and had advised Felix to broaden his scope a little. Felix, as she recalled, had been righteously indignant.

''Yes,'' she told the warden now, ''I'd like to speak to him.'' She just hoped Felix would be able to forgive her transgression.

Ten minutes later she was facing Hewitt. He was a small, spare man with the lined, emaciated face of an addict. She wondered if he was managing to get his supplies inside, or if he just naturally looked dissipated.

''You work with Felix, huh?'' he asked flatly.

''As a matter of fact, I'm going to call him as soon as we're done talking,'' Jennifer said truthfully, allowing him to draw his own conclusions about that. "Anything you tell me will be in confidence."

He waved a hand. "I ain't worried about it. I suppose Felix is really pissed at me about this."

"I don't know. He hasn't heard about it yet. Actually, I came here to see DeVries. That's how *I* heard about it."

He nodded. "Yeah. He said he was going to talk to DeVries. He sent you to do it, huh?"

Jennifer hesitated. "No, I came on another matter. What did DeVries do to you?"

"Oh, hell, what difference does it make? They saw me do it. There's no way out of it. I'm gonna get it for murder. My own damn fault. I thought I could get away with it, but..." He shrugged. "Too late now."

"Just don't admit anything—"

"I already did," he interrupted. "What do I give a shit? The Feds are after me on drug charges, too, y'know. I'm going to spend the rest of my life in jail no matter what. I just got really pissed at DeVries, you know? But you know all about that. Hell, I didn't make no secret of it, and Felix'll figure it out the minute he hears it, anyway. DeVries was going to roll over on me in exchange for a plea bargain with the Feds."

"DeVries told you he was going to testify against you?" She couldn't believe the man had been that stupid.

"Hell, no. Felix told me. Warned me to keep my mouth shut. Too late. Al and me were partners. Al knew everything there was to know. How else was I going to shut him up? Shit, I'm a jerk. I shoulda known it wasn't going to work...."

* * *

Rook was still waiting in the antechamber when she emerged. "Did you see DeVries?" he asked. "They won't even tell me when I can visit him."

"At his funeral, most likely. Let's get the hell out of here."

Rook didn't say another word until they were on the road again, headed east toward Canon City. "What happened?"

"Another inmate killed DeVries last night. Seems his lawyer told him that DeVries was planning to testify against him."

"Stupid thing for the lawyer to do."

Jennifer suddenly had an urge to scream at him, but she restrained it, settling instead for a tone of pure ice. "Actually," she said clearly, "his lawyer had no choice but to tell him. Evidence was going to be provided to his client's detriment. What was Felix supposed to do? Hide it from the man until it came out in court?"

"Felix?" The car swerved a little as Rook jerked the wheel. "*Felix* is this guy's lawyer?"

"Yes."

"Christ! This stinks to high heaven!"

"Why? Nothing stinks. DeVries offered to roll over on Hewitt. It happens all the damn time."

"But Felix was representing both of them."

"Why not? They were partners in crime. It's not unusual for two people involved in the same crime to retain a single attorney. It's more efficient and a hell of a lot cheaper."

"Unless one of them decides to roll over on the other one. Correct me if I'm wrong, but at that point another lawyer ought to be brought in."

"I imagine Felix intended to do precisely that. It's probably one of the things he discussed with Hewitt.

Damn it, Rook, Felix is an exemplary attorney! I trust him with my life. Of course he was going to sort out this mess. But that takes time and client agreement, and from the sound of it, this all came down too fast. Hewitt's sunk anyway. He was caught in the act, and he confessed to the guards who saw him. I sure wouldn't want to be his lawyer."

"Felix probably won't, either."

"Felix has never shied away from a tough case."

Rook made an impatient sound. "Saint Felix, huh? Why don't you just canonize him?"

"What's eating you?"

"I'll tell you! Don't you find it just a little bit unsettling that the man we came here to question was killed within forty-eight hours of you telling Felix you had talked to him?"

"Rook! How can you—"

"And doesn't it just stink to high heaven that the guy was killed because of something *Felix* told another inmate?"

"Maybe it stinks, Rook, but you can't seriously be suggesting that Felix meant this to happen!" Much as events strained credulity, she simply could *not* believe that Felix had deliberately set these events in motion.

"I can't? Why not? When coincidences begin to pile up and smell like three-day-old fish, I start thinking really hard about it."

"Felix couldn't possibly be involved in anything unsavory! No way. He's one of the most decent people I've ever known!"

Rook let it drop right there, seeing no point in continuing an argument that would resolve nothing. Regardless of what she said, he was going to pay attention to his own doubts about Felix Abernathy. When things smelled funny, there was usually a reason.

The most important thing he had to do now was figure out how to keep Jenny from giving Felix any more information that he might be able to use. That would have been a whole lot easier had there been some irrefutable argument he could give her, but he didn't have one. Fact was, at this point, she might be absolutely right about Felix. There wasn't exactly any proof to the contrary. They just couldn't afford to take the risk.

"Jenny?"

"Hmm?"

She still sounded frosty. Great. "I realize you think very highly of Felix—"

"Yes, I do."

"And you know him better than me, obviously—"

"Obviously."

"So I'm not going to argue one way or another about his character."

"That's magnanimous of you."

For a few seconds he didn't respond, wrestling with a sudden awareness of how much he disliked having her angry at him. Hey, he chided himself. He was the guy who didn't care, right? "Just—could we please be cautious? That's all I'm asking. Just that we shouldn't tell *anybody* anything that could be used against us somehow. We still have to find the hit man...."

"We're never going to find him," she said, looking out the side window so he couldn't see her face. "He's going to find me first."

"Maybe not." He didn't like the note that had replaced anger in her voice. It sounded frighteningly close to resignation.

"Probably yes," she argued quietly. "It doesn't matter what either of us thinks of Felix, or whether there was any rhyme or reason to Alan DeVries's death.

All that matters is that our last hope of locating the hit man just died. So he's going to find me and blow out my brains. I might as well just make it easy for him to find me and get it over with quickly."

"Jenny—" But he was at a loss, unsure what to say.

"He'll blow out my brains, the cops can blame me for everything, and it'll be all over. You can go back to your life. My family will grieve for a while, but they're generally better at getting over these things than I am, so they'll be okay in a few months. And it'll be done."

He didn't like the sound of this at all. Not at all. "Jenny—" But he stalled again, unable to think of anything that didn't sound like a pure Pollyannaism. Finally, he said, "Don't give up." Christ, did that sound lame!

"I'm not giving up!" Surprising him, she turned and gave him a fierce look. "I'm going to keep on trying to get to the bottom of this. *All* of this. But I'm not a fool living in the land of make-believe, Rook. The chances that we're going to find the hit man now are close to nil. And maybe that's not so awful...."

She averted her face quickly, leaving him to wonder at her roller-coastering mood. Well, it was hardly surprising, he guessed. She had more on her plate than most people could handle.

Making an impulsive decision, he pulled the car into a turnout, set the brake and turned out the headlights. The early-winter night had already fallen, and the moon was rising over the narrow canyon through which the road ran. It was a beautiful, breathtaking scene, but he hardly noticed it.

All of him, every last cell of his being, was fixed on the woman beside him. She had turned to look questioningly at him, and now, when he held out his arms, she came into them willingly, heedless of the console between them.

"Jenny..." It was all he could say, a husky whisper as his throat closed up.

Her hands tightened, digging into his shoulders even through layers of winter clothing. The pain was a dull ache, a touch of reality in a night suddenly soft with wisps of fantasy and magic. No, he thought. No. But a wizard's wand had already been waved, and he was catapulted past his own defenses into a place where he had no barriers... and where he needed none.

Jenny. Just Jenny. It was a place that couldn't exist for long, a sanctuary created from dreams and hopes, so fragile that it was inevitably doomed. He clung to it anyway, damning the consequences, knowing that before long he would be required to don his carapace once more and that this taste of freedom would make it feel more confined than ever.

They didn't even kiss, they simply hung on to one another for dear life. And in those moments of closeness, he realized he had never felt this way before in his entire life. Not even with Cheryl, and he had loved her. Or believed he had. But from this new perspective he wasn't even sure about that. Maybe he had just married her because she had fitted some image he had of himself and his future.

But it had never felt like this. Not once.

What the hell was he doing?

Setting himself up for a hard fall, that was what. Getting himself tangled up in things that could come to no good. Even if this woman survived and the contract on her was put to rest, even if she got over her late husband enough to want to live and love again, she would never want a broken-down ex-soldier like him.

Well, he could handle rejection. He'd handled it before. What he didn't want was to get his whole life tied up into knots over some woman. *Any* woman. After all, they were all just selfish bitches, out for whatever they could get. But his usual litany of condemnation sounded incredibly hollow right now.

"We'll get you through this somehow," he heard himself promising. "We'll find the bad guy."

A small, despairing laugh escaped her, smothered against his jacket. "Sure."

She didn't believe it, of course, but there wasn't anything he could do about that.

Rook took Jennifer and Massie to a different motel on the far side of Denver when they got in late that evening. Jennifer flopped down on one of the beds and stared up at the ceiling, trying not to look into dark corners where things were probably crawling.

She'd been protected her whole life, she found herself thinking. First her parents, and then her relative financial comfort owing to her law career, had sheltered her from much of the seaminess of life. She'd never had to sleep in a room where the bugs were crawling, had never had to wonder if the pillow beneath her head was clean. Had never had to talk to a murderer. The ugliness she had seen had been largely limited to the scheming in corporate boardrooms.

Not that she had been unaware that ugliness existed, but it had been held safely at a distance, so that her awareness was purely intellectual.

Right now she didn't feel comfortable with that. In fact, she felt almost embarrassed at the way she had been protected, like some kind of princess in an ivory tower. Embarrassed that her response to the first real hardship she had ever known had been to fall apart and attempt suicide.

She suddenly remembered Rook's stinging remark at their first meeting about people who couldn't do their own dirty work, and she squirmed inwardly. His assessment hadn't been far from the mark. She *hadn't* wanted to do her own dirty work. Even when it came to suicide, she wanted it at a distance.

She heard him punch in a number on the phone and turned her head to look at him. He didn't resemble the people she was used to associating with, people who were privileged icons of success and socialization. No, he had the battered air of a tomcat, the look of someone who had fought hard for whatever he had. Where they looked confident, Rook looked dangerous.

It was quite a difference. If she had invited him to one of the firm's cocktail parties, she suspected he would have dealt with it well, but her associates would have been rendered uncomfortable and uneasy. Rook could handle anything. *They* wouldn't be able to handle *him*. For some reason that amused her.

"It's Rook," she heard him say. "Got anything for me?"

She was past holding her breath in anticipation. So far, hardly anything had panned out for them. Why should this phone call be any different? But her heart accelerated anyway.

"She was? How do you know that? Okay. Anything else?"

A few moments later he hung up the phone and looked straight at her. "Word is that you were at the airport the day before the crash, and that you went to the plane."

She sat up, feeling as if he had just slapped her. "What?"

"You heard me."

"But I wasn't! I *wasn't!* My God, Rook, you can't possibly believe—"

"Did I say I believed it?"

She subsided, looking at him with horror. "Somebody's lying."

He rubbed his chin, then shook his head. "Maybe. Maybe not."

"But I wasn't there!"

"I believe you. Just calm down and think. Either somebody is lying about it now, or somebody deliberately tried to make it look like you were there right before it happened. Or...maybe something else was interpreted as you being there. That's three very different possibilities, and if we can figure out any one of them, we'll be a hell of a lot closer to our perp. So use your head, okay?"

She nodded, but her mind stayed stubbornly blank, clinging to the shock of what she had just heard and the accusation inherent in it. Why would anybody want to frame her for this?

"My contact is going to try to find out what the source of the story is and what evidence there is to back it up. It might take a day or two."

She didn't want to wait that long, but what choice did she have? Her palms stung as her nails bit into them. "Okay."

"And nothing on the hit man yet." He shook his head, staring into space. "I can't figure it. How can this guy operate in a vacuum? I mean, *some*body has to know who he is if he's going to get work."

"That man you had me call knows who he is."

Rook shook his head. "I already questioned him about it. He won't tell, because if he does, he'll be the next target."

"Who's going to know it was him? Surely more than one person has to know who this guy is, Rook!"

"I know, I know, but Jay is already tied in to this because he was your contact. If you and I find this guy, Jay's head will be on the block over it."

Unfortunately, that made perfect sense, even to her.

Rook leaned back on one elbow and rubbed his eyes. "Maybe it doesn't make a damn bit of difference."

"What do you mean?"

"If Jay tells us and we find the guy, it's the same situation as if we find the guy some other way. Either way, if I fail to take him out, Jay is going to be in trouble."

Jennifer's heart stopped. He couldn't possibly mean... She waited, but he said nothing more, just stared off into space, lost in thought.

Finally she couldn't stand it anymore and said, "So I guess we just stop looking for the hit man? I mean, we wouldn't want to put your friend into danger...."

"Good God, no!" Rook looked at her, startled. "Your mind works in a really weird way sometimes, Lady Fox."

"Well, excuse me."

Anger started to burn in the pit of his stomach. "What do you think I'm going to do? Just hang you out like a target to be shot by this guy?"

"Well, you said—"

"Just exactly what do you *think* I said? Christ, I don't believe you. After all I've done, how could you possibly think I'm just going to drop you like a hot potato? Jesus, you're incredible!"

Her own temper flared. "You said that your friend would be in trouble if we find the hit man! So we can't find the hit man!"

"That isn't what I said! It wasn't even what I was thinking!"

"No? Then what the hell were you muttering about?"

"Simple. I was thinking up a way to argue Jay into telling me."

He was glaring at her, and she was glaring at him, but as his meaning penetrated, she began to feel ashamed, and she wilted.

"I'm sorry. I misunderstood."

He looked away, clearly trying to get a handle on his irritation. Nearly a minute crept by before he answered. "It's all right. Why should you trust me? You don't know me very well."

She had a very strong feeling that her suspicion had wounded him. "I know you well enough! Well enough to know that you're honest and honorable. Well enough to know that you're trustworthy."

"Hey, I was court-martialed, remember? Nobody else believed I was honest. Maybe I'm not."

"Maybe they just didn't know you."

He turned to look at her then, and something in his face softened almost undetectably. Maybe she was just imagining it.

"You don't really know me, either," he said finally. "Maybe that's a good thing to keep in mind right now."

"Maybe." But she didn't feel that way. A minute ago she had thought he might be saying there was no way they could find the hit man. Now, with absolute certainty, she knew he wouldn't abandon her. Whatever came, she could rely on him to stand fast and try to protect her. That was a rare feeling.

Picking up the phone again, Rook punched in another number. He listened for a while, then hung up. "Jay's not around."

Hardly pausing, he dialed yet another number. "Ira! What's happening?" He listened intently, his face revealing nothing. "Okay. I'll tell her." He replaced the receiver in the cradle and looked at Jennifer. "Ira says hi."

"That's nice."

"He also says the mysterious guy showed up again today."

Jennifer sat up, her heart hammering. "Did Ira find out anything?"

"The guy was still wearing those glasses, so he couldn't see his eyes at all. He said he wasn't wearing a ski cap this time, though. Dark, real curly hair. Raspy voice." He shook his head, frowning. "Sounds like a couple of people I already know."

"It's not much of a description."

"Not enough of one. As for the rest...he picked up the same story about you having been out at the airport the day before the crash. Says it comes from a mechanic at the hangar next to where your husband had his tie-down."

"But I wasn't there."

"Interesting, huh? Actually, Ira had a little more info. Basically, the mechanic says he thinks you were there, but he didn't actually see you. He's trying to remember why he has the impression that you went out there."

"Maybe somebody suggested it to him."

"Could be. Anyway, both Tim and Ira are looking into it, so if anything more turns up, we'll know about it."

He couldn't escape the feeling that with just one more piece of information the entire thing would come together, either with regard to who had killed her family or the identity of the hit man.

Not that the identity of the guy really made much difference. What they had to do was track him down. Maybe...

"Tomorrow," he said abruptly. "Tomorrow you're going to show your face. Just a little. Just briefly. We've got to draw the hit man out." He looked at her, gauging her response. "It'll be dangerous."

She nodded. "I know." Her voice cracked. "I know. Bait in a trap."

"You don't have to do it."

She looked down at her hands, then looked sadly at him. "What's the alternative? The worst that could happen is that I get exactly what I paid for."

"How *did* you pay for it?" he asked her. "That was a lot of money."

"Insurance. Mark had a lot of insurance." She shivered and shook her head, wondering if she would ever feel warm again. "I could never use that money for anything. Never."

"Well, next time you get a wild urge to get rid of money, tell me. I know a few charities that could use it a whole lot better."

A blush stained her cheeks uncomfortably, and she looked swiftly down at her hands. God! She couldn't believe how self-absorbed she had become.

"Hey." His tone was suddenly gentle. Perching beside her on the bed, he wrapped his arms around her and tugged her close. "It's okay, Lady Fox. What you've been through—well, that kind of loss would make just about anyone a little crazy."

His kindness shattered her barriers and reached within her to pluck at feelings she'd thought she would never have again. He made her feel safe, sheltered, protected. *Cared for.* It had been so long! Her throat tightened, aching painfully, and unshed tears made her eyes burn.

"It's okay," he said again, rocking her. "You're starting to come out of it. I can see it."

One scalding tear ran down her cheek to disappear into the fabric of his shirt. He was right. Deep inside her, she could feel it. Her sorrow was still there, still strong, but no longer a black malignancy that seemed to be devouring her soul. Somehow the anger she had been feeling since she had learned about the sabotage seemed to have seared away the cancer.

She still wanted to weep, still wanted to rail at the fates and demand justice from the heavens, but she was no longer afraid to accept comfort. Turning her head, she buried her face in Rook's shoulder.

"Go ahead and cry, Jenny," he said gently. "It's okay to cry. Let it go."

Wrapped in his arms, his strength and his caring, she did precisely that.

15

During the night, Jennifer awoke with a start, her heart pounding as if she had just run a race. In the next bed, Rook was breathing deeply, sound asleep. The only other sound was the lonely moan of the wind whipping around the corner of the motel.

The light seeping around the edges of the curtains seemed to have grown brighter. Uneasy from a dream she couldn't recall, she rose from her bed and padded across the thin carpet to the window. The floor felt like ice, and she shivered inside her flannel nightgown. Had it grown colder?

The heating unit beneath the window suddenly clicked on with the groaning of a reluctant fan and the popping of cold elements beginning to rapidly heat. A blast of hot, dry air hit her chin as she leaned forward and tugged the corner of the curtain aside an inch or two.

Outside, the night had turned into a wild winterland, with snow blowing crazily in every direction. The cars in the parking lot below were barely visible beneath a deepening white blanket, and the whole night seemed to be glowing pinkly in the reflected light from street lamps.

A sharp gust of wind threw icy crystals against the window with a ticking sound like a cat's claws on tile. The heater's blast was beginning to make her chin feel uncomfortably warm, while her toes still felt like icicles.

Nothing was moving out there.

Reassured, she sat in the vinyl-upholstered chair near the window and propped her feet as close to the heater as she could manage. Rook slept on, undisturbed.

Fear was stalking her, trying to spring and take her by the throat. She didn't want to die. She had faced that the morning her paid assassin had shot at her. But now, even more than not wanting to die, she was afraid she might not live. Afraid she wouldn't be around to make things right.

And she had a whole bunch of things to make right, with her family and with her past. She needed to assure the people who had been worrying about her that she was okay. She needed to apologize to Scott Paxton for the way she had treated him—after all, he'd only been doing what had been necessary for the good of the firm. And, above all, she needed time to catch the person who had killed her family. So much she needed to do, and all of it might be truncated by a hit man she had hired herself.

God, what stupidity!

A snuffling sound alerted her, and moments later Massie's massive head settled onto her knee. In the dark, Jennifer couldn't read the dog's expression, but she could still feel the animal's concern. Anybody who thought dogs were of limited intelligence had never really spent time with a dog like Massie.

Massie. She'd been a pup when Eli had named her, only a few weeks old and as big as the toddler himself. Massie's mother had tended to treat Eli as one of her litter, and the little boy and puppy had often rolled on the floor together, the boy giggling with delight, the dog wagging her entire body in pleasure.

Jenny blinked hard, fighting back the tears, and buried her fingers in Massie's coat. Massie probably missed Eli and Bethany, too. Hell, everyone who had loved them missed them. Would always miss them. But it wasn't a sin to continue living. It wasn't a crime against their memory to allow ordinary pleasures and hopes to spring to life again.

"Something wrong?" Rook spoke sleepily from his bed.

"No. I just had a bad dream."

He sat up, a dark shadow against white sheets. "Scared?"

"A little. Oh, hell, who am I kidding? I'm scared a whole lot."

"Hardly surprising." He ran his fingers through his hair and yawned. "If I were the hit man, I'd be looking for you in places where you were likely to turn up. Your house springs to mind now that the warrant has been revoked, but..." He shook his head. "Your former place of employment would be another likely place, since it's probably no secret by now that Felix is your lawyer."

"It's public record now. He had to file a notice of appearance with the court."

"So that would be another great place to watch. At this point, he's no doubt figured out that you're trying to avoid him, so if I were him, I'd be watching your lawyer's office."

Jennifer's heart slammed hard. "That easy?"

"Well, not easy, really. How many places could he be watching from? How do we draw him out where *we* can see *him* without giving him a sterling opportunity to knock you off?"

She didn't like the sound of this one bit.

"Are there any empty offices in the buildings overlooking the parking lot or front entrance of your office building?"

She shook her head. "No. It's not in the downtown business district. The firm built a three-story office building of its own in a residential area. All the suites are occupied by the firm."

"But the surrounding houses might present a view. Do you have any idea how many might be unoccupied?"

"No, I never really paid any attention."

"We need to look into that first thing." He wasn't sure if the building's location would prove to be a help or a hindrance. "Before we do anything in the morning, I want to check what's been in the papers over the last couple of days. Given the high profile of the murder case against you, he's probably been keeping up with the news. We need to know what they've printed that could be useful to him."

"Okay."

"So, first stop is the library. Second stop is the airport. I want to talk to the mechanic who thinks you were out there that day."

Jennifer felt the sudden burst of a new hope. "You do?"

"Jenny, there's no way I'm going to just sit back and wait for developments when I've got a lead like this staring me in the face. That guy thinks you were out there. There's some reason why he thinks that, and it's entirely possible that a little grease will freshen his memory."

"Grease?"

"Money. *Dinero.* In short, a bribe."

"Rook, I can't do that! And neither can you! Good Lord, that could be interpreted as tampering with a witness. Whatever you do, don't bribe him or threaten him, or you could find yourself facing a whole new raft of charges."

Rook sighed. "It's not like the movies, huh?"

"Definitely not in this case. I could certainly be charged in the crash, and you might find yourself in the same boat because of our association. It would be absolutely *stupid* to do anything that could be interpreted as tampering with a witness."

"But I *can* question him?"

"Sure."

"Okay, I'll handle him with kid gloves, trust me. But that guy remembers something, and there's a reason he's holding it back."

"Why do you say that?"

"Because he has a reason for thinking you were there, and he damn well knows what it is."

"That's circular reasoning."

"Not really. Think about it, Jenny. Something happened that day that was unusual enough for him to remember after all this time that *you* might have been out there the day before the crash. Something unusual enough that more than half a year later he can pinpoint the date."

"He might just have thought it was unusual at the time, that I was out there the day before the crash."

"Why?" Rook shook his head. "No reason why he should. You showed up the day before a big trip, maybe just to put something in the plane. No, something about it stuck in his mind as unusual, and he knows what it is. And there's a reason he's withholding that information."

"What could he possibly stand to gain?"

"Oh, I don't know. How about his fifteen minutes of celebrity?"

"But giving the complete information would make him just as famous."

"Not if it exonerates you. You need to understand, Jenny—this story is a lot more interesting to the media when *you're* the suspected murderer. The headlines are a whole lot more attention grabbing."

"That may be true, but it doesn't prove a damn thing."

"No, Counselor, it doesn't. But that's what I intend to take care of tomorrow. We're going to prove a thing or two, or I'll eat dog food for a week."

She almost laughed. Nervous and scared as she was, he was still funny. "I'll hold you to it."

"Fine. Now c'mere and give me a hug. I'm cold."

The wind gusted around the building again and whistled through some hidden opening in the window. The heater creaked and ticked and blasted a steady stream of heat that wasn't quite enough. Massie settled down beside it, as if she knew her people were about to go to sleep.

"So am I," Jennifer answered, and gladly crawled into the bed beside him. When his arms wrapped around her shoulders and his leg settled over hers, she had the most wonderful feeling that she had come home.

"Christ, we're going to need skis or a snowplow to get anywhere!"

White morning light poured through the opening where Rook had tugged the curtain aside to look out. Nothing out there was moving, and the snow was still blowing wildly and falling heavily.

"It looks like the friggin' North Pole out there."

Jennifer joined him, pulling a sweater on over her turtleneck. What she saw at once relieved her and disappointed her. On the one hand, she couldn't risk her neck today, but on the other, everything had come to a complete halt. "They'll get the roads fairly clear soon."

Already a snow blower was working in the motel parking lot, but all the cars would still have to be dug out one by one.

"Hell." He dropped the curtain and put his hands on his hips. "Okay, you and the dog stay here. I'm going next door to the restaurant to get us breakfast and the morning paper. And maybe somebody around here has the papers from the last couple of days."

"I can come with you." She hated to think of him going out into that miserable weather to get her breakfast.

"No point in all of us getting cold and wet, Jenny. Just stay here with the dog. I'll be back soon."

She watched him cross the parking lot with his shoulders hunched into the wind. When he rounded the corner of the building, she let the curtains fall closed again.

Massie had already been out, and she was still occupied with cleaning bits of snow and ice from between her toes.

"You don't like it out there any better than we do, do you, girl?" Jenny asked her.

Massie looked up, cocking her head inquisitively.

"Okay, that was a stupid question. Of course you don't. And you can't take off your boots when you come inside."

Massie resumed licking her paws. A particularly stubborn piece of ice held her attention.

With this blizzard going on, the airport was probably down to minimum operations, and that mechanic they wanted to talk to might not even be around. How were they going to find him, anyway? She had forgotten to ask Rook if he knew who the guy was.

She looked at the clock, waiting for the minutes to tick by until Felix would be in the office. He might still not know that one of his clients had been murdered by another, and she didn't want him to find out from the warden that she'd already talked to Hewitt. No, she wanted to tell him that herself before he had time to leap to a bunch of bad conclusions.

Nor did she want to leave a message with his service. That would mean leaving her number here, and that number could be traced. Rook was adamant that she not give anyone any means of finding them, and given that they were paralyzed by the storm, she kind of agreed with him. Once somebody else had their phone number, things could go awry.

But nine o'clock was still a long way away, and Felix might already be in court for all she knew. Damn, she hated waiting. There had been a time when she had prided herself on her patience, but not anymore. Not since this mess had begun to unfold. Now she didn't have the patience to wait even an hour.

Rook seemed to be gone forever, although the clock assured her it was just thirty-five minutes. He showed up with a stack of food containers and a pile of newspapers.

He flashed her a grin as he kicked the door closed behind him. "We're in luck. The cashier at the restaurant is a recycler. He had a whole bunch of newspapers he kindly shared with me."

Jenny looked at the pile of papers with a sinking stomach. "Maybe I'm weird, but I don't think it's lucky that I get to read all about my life of crime."

He wagged a finger at her. "Now, now, you want to keep a positive attitude." But the teasing was thin, and when they sat down to eat at the small table by the window, he pulled the papers toward himself. "I'll do the reading," he told her. "I have a better idea what would be significant, anyway, and there's no point in ruining your digestion."

But it was already too late. The scrambled eggs tasted like cardboard, the bacon tasted burned and the pancakes had about as much flavor as rainwater. She barely nibbled at the food, and when Rook turned one of the papers over and she saw her official portrait from the firm, she completely gave up.

Her picture was on the front page of the paper, but not because she had done something wonderful. The caption over the two-column-wide story beside it was legible even from where she sat: Police Seek Lawyer In Multiple Slayings.

Her stomach turned over with a sickening lurch, and she turned her gaze quickly away... not that anything would ever erase that shrieking headline from her memory. The feeling of being trapped in a nightmare was washing over her again, making her feel dislocated.

Rook caught her look of horror. "Not exactly the stuff dreams are made of, huh?"

"I don't have any dreams," she said quickly. Lying. No dreams? Of course she had dreams. Dreams of vengeance. Dreams of... Rook. Her stomach rolled again as she admitted to herself that there were still things she wanted out of life, and some of them were things that would require a commitment to living. How much easier it would be, she thought almost bitterly, to want nothing at all.

"Like hell you don't." He scowled at her and snapped the newspaper open. "Anybody who *breathes* has dreams. You aren't indifferent enough yet to be dead."

"Yeah? Well, what are *your* dreams?" She felt her chin thrust forward the way it did when she was being deliberately argumentative. It was a surprisingly good feeling after being little more than a whipped dog for so long.

"My dreams?" His scowl deepened. "We're not talking about me here."

"Why not? You're always so full of two-bit advice about what I should be doing and cheap comments about what I am or am not. Why can't we point the cannon your way for once? If everybody who breathes has dreams, according to you, then you have dreams. What are they?"

Christ, he'd sure gotten under *her* skin. She was spoiling for a fight now; he could see it in the set of her chin and the fire in her eyes.

But then, she'd gotten under his skin by turning his comments back on him. He didn't want to consider his dreams any more than she wanted to consider hers. It had, in fact, been one hell of a long time since he'd allowed any such thoughts to cross his mind. He didn't care about such things.

Or rather, he tried to *avoid* caring about such things, and one of the best ways to avoid caring was simply to ignore them.

But now that Jenny forced him to think about it, he didn't like what he saw. Yeah, he had dreams. He'd shoved them into a dark closet and nailed the door shut on them, but they were still there, peeking out through cracks in the boards.

What did he want? God, it hurt to even think about it. Normalcy. He wanted real normalcy, the kind of life most people seemed to have, with friends and backed-up plumbing, and kids, and cars that needed to go to the shop, and a wife who would think he was wonderful but would tell him to take his feet off the table.... Normalcy.

No more sudden trips to the ends of the earth to teach people murderous skills that might well get them killed. No more tightrope walking around political sensitivities he couldn't begin to understand. No more living for months where he couldn't even speak his native tongue, couldn't eat hamburgers and hot dogs or watch a football game or use a flush toilet. No more eating rations out of a can and drinking water out of a canteen. No more wondering if that prickling heat he felt all over was some new tropical fever taking hold, or whether a bout of loose bowels signaled another round of debilitating dysentery.

No more. Give him the picket fence, the minivan, the 2.4 kids and all the attendant headaches. They sounded damn good, actually.

But he didn't want to admit that. Least of all did he want to admit that to the woman who was beginning to invade his dreams at night, a woman who wasn't ready to bury her dead husband and start all over again. Jesus, talk about setting himself up for a fall!

"Never mind," he growled, lifting the paper higher so he couldn't see her. "Maybe you don't have any dreams. So what?"

He heard her draw a shaky breath, then she spoke in a voice so sad it made him ache.

"I had dreams," she said. "I had lots of dreams, some of them downright silly. I dreamed of having a couple more children. Ridiculous, right? Anybody with half a brain knows that's too much to handle, especially when you're working eighty-hour weeks like I was sometimes. But I wanted a large family. I wanted to get to a point where I didn't have to work so hard, so I could spend a lot more time with them."

"Why'd you have to work so hard?"

"To fulfill another dream. I wanted to be a partner in the firm." She drew another shaky breath. "It seems stupid now. What I should have done was hang out my own shingle and practice law for people who really needed me, not waste all my time on the stupid wheeling and dealing."

"You enjoyed it, didn't you?" He lowered the paper reluctantly, involved in spite of himself.

"Yeah, I did," she admitted. "I've been thinking a lot about that. I enjoyed it because it was a power trip. It went straight to my head. I was *important*. I should have realized there were only three people I needed to be important to, but..." She shrugged, looking out the window at the blizzard, carefully avoiding his gaze.

He hesitated a moment, then spoke gently. "What you're saying is, you haven't been feeling guilty just because you survived."

She turned, looking at him with tear-filled eyes. "Oh, no. Not just because I survived. I think I can deal with that. What I can't deal with is remembering all the hours I wasted. All the time I *didn't* spend with them. All the weekends I worked, all the nights I didn't get home until after the children were in bed. And I wonder—" Her voice broke, then steadied. "I wonder how I could have gone so far astray. All I wanted... really, all I wanted was to have a beautiful family...." Her voice broke again, and her chin quivered. She looked quickly away, blinking like mad to hold back the tears.

He lowered the paper to his lap. "Yeah," he said quietly. His throat was so tight now that he felt as if he were being garroted. "Yeah. I know. Me too."

"We're a couple of screwups."

"It feels that way."

Jennifer raised her hand and dashed her tears away impatiently. "So what were your dreams?"

"Pretty much the same as yours. Only I was gone too much, and Cheryl didn't want any more kids after Sam was born."

"Why not?"

"She just—I don't know. I really don't know. She was just completely dead set against it."

"Maybe she was worried that you might get killed at any instant, because of your job."

He thought about it, then shrugged. "I don't know. Trouble is, I can't remember if she ever even loved me. I'm not sure she did. Even when things weren't too bad, I figured she'd married me to get away from her dad. He was an alcoholic and cuffed her around quite a bit. Always trying to be the boss, especially when he was falling down drunk."

"How awful."

"Yeah." He gave a disgusted laugh and shook his head. "What's really stupid is that I thought I could rescue her. Y'know, for every woman who tries to rescue some 'bad boy' kind of guy, there's a stupid guy who tries to rescue some woman from whatever mess she happens to be in. Problem is, rescue doesn't make a good basis for a relationship."

Jennifer's heart lurched uncomfortably as she recognized the justice of his words—and recognized that he was rescuing her. Oh, God, how was she going to bear this?

Rook shrugged and reached for another paper. "It's okay to rescue a damsel in distress, but you shouldn't confuse rescue with love. And you shouldn't think marriage is going to rescue anyone. Near as I can tell, it just becomes another trap."

Jennifer compressed her lips and looked down, feeling a fresh prickle in her eyes. Damn, she was so tired of crying. So tired of hurting.

Rook read through the rest of the papers swiftly, then tossed them aside. "Nothing in there that we wouldn't expect. What the hell. Let's get out of here."

He pulled the curtain aside and looked out at the snowy day. "It's slowing down. If we're careful, we can get to the airport. I wanna talk to that damn mechanic."

"I need to call Felix." It was after nine, and all this talk had driven the call from her mind. "I need to tell him about DeVries."

"Won't he find out from the warden?"

"I need to talk to him first." She leaned forward urgently. "Rook, I talked to his client without his permission. I could get into serious trouble for that."

He studied her briefly, then shook his head. "You lawyers are hemmed in with all kinds of rules, aren't you?"

"They're called professional ethics. And lately I've been treading a little too close to the line."

Felix was at his desk and took her call immediately. "Jennifer, where are you? Damn it, you can't expect me to handle your case if I can't get in touch with you!"

"Has something happened?"

"I think you know damn well something has happened, and if you weren't a dear friend of mine I'd—" He broke off sharply, as if catching himself. "What the hell were you doing at the prison yesterday?"

"That's what I'm calling about. Felix—"

"Damn it, Jennifer, you know you have no business talking to my clients! You're not even a member of this firm anymore!"

"I know. I know. But I couldn't ask you to get involved. Felix, you know how sticky things get for an attorney if he gets information involving a crime that has not yet been committed. I couldn't possibly drag you into this mess!"

"But—"

"Felix, I just wanted to ask DeVries about the hit man. I thought maybe since he referred me to someone else he might have some idea who contacted me and took the contract. That's all, I swear."

"How could you even think—Jen, you weren't covered by attorney-client privilege because you weren't his attorney! Anything DeVries told you could have been dragged out of you in court! And now you've talked to Hewitt, and anything he told you—"

"He didn't tell me anything he hadn't already told the guards. And if you say I spoke to him on your behalf, nothing he said can be dragged out of me."

"You misrepresented yourself to the warden—"

"Which is exactly why no one will question me about it. Felix, I swear, I didn't ask for anything from Hewitt that he hadn't already admitted to. I swear I'll never repeat a word of it in or out of court, okay?"

To Jenny it seemed that Felix was silent for a long time. Finally he sighed heavily. "Okay. Forget that for now. But, Christ, Jennifer, what's come over you? You're not yourself!"

She answered levelly, without embroidery or evasion. "My family was murdered."

Felix drew a sharp breath. Then he said, "Yes. Of course. And that's something else we need to discuss. You're still the primary suspect in two different murder investigations, and I'm not sure how long I can keep the judge from reissuing the warrant. So maybe you'd better tell me what you've got to offer in your own defense. In fact, maybe you'd better come in to the office so we can hash this whole thing out and start building your case."

Jennifer started to mention the mechanic at the airport, but something held her back. It shocked her to realize that for some reason she no longer felt she could confide in Felix. But perhaps that was just because she was in such a dangerous situation that she had begun to be far more cautious about everything.

"Felix? Why did you tell Hewitt about DeVries?" The question was out before she knew it was coming, and it astonished her even as she asked it. Why was she questioning him?

"Jennifer, I'm shocked. How can you possibly think I could have withheld that information from Hewitt? I would have been failing my duty as his attorney."

"You weren't going to continue representing both of them, were you?"

"Of course not! How can you even suspect such a thing? Jennifer, are you losing your mind?"

"I—I guess maybe I am. There's been so much strain lately...." She trailed off, well aware that she was lying but suddenly afraid of provoking him any further.

"Yes, there has," he said sternly. "And while we're on the subject of your strange behavior, maybe you should consider the person you're hanging around with. Don't forget, this Rook Rydell was a friend of

Alan DeVries, and you know the kind of man DeVries was. Good heavens, Jennifer, you're associating with a common thug! Perhaps it was *he* who killed those policemen. Can you be sure it wasn't? Now, when are you going to come in to see me?"

Her lips felt stiff, and her mind was strangely numb. "Um, tomorrow, Felix. I'll come in tomorrow."

"At one, then. Be sure that you're here." With that he disconnected.

Rook was watching her from tawny, narrowed eyes. "Well?"

"He... wants to see me."

"Tomorrow. I heard. What else?"

"He...asked me how I could be sure *you* weren't the person who killed those cops."

His gaze never wavered, and his face remained as rigid as stone. "How can you?"

"I just am. I am absolutely sure you didn't kill those men, Rook."

He started to say something, then shook his head. "I ought to tell you not to be so trusting, but this time you're right. I didn't do it. Did he say anything else?"

She looked at him, trying to come to grips with an uneasy, ugly suspicion. "He... he seems to know an awful lot about you, Rook."

He shrugged. "There's been a lot about me in the papers. I'm wanted, too, remember?"

"But did any of those stories say you were a friend of Alan DeVries? Or that he directed me to you?"

Rook suddenly stiffened. "No. How would anyone even know that?"

Jennifer's mouth was almost too dry to speak. "You know, that's exactly the question I'm asking myself. How would anyone know DeVries sent me to you?"

"Unless DeVries told him."

She nodded slowly. "Exactly. But why would he do that?"

None of the answers that occurred to her were even remotely acceptable. Felix was her friend.

Wasn't he?

Driving slowly over slick, snow-covered streets, Rook got them to the airport. The plows there had been working even faster, and near-normal operations had been restored even before watery sunlight managed to peek through the clouds.

Walking over wet pavement and snow, they went to the hangar where the mechanic worked. Mal Stevens was his name, and he was the only person there when they arrived.

He was working on a small single-engine Ercoupe, an older plane so tiny it almost looked like a toy.

"A real classic," Stevens said fondly, patting a wing gently. "What can I do for you?"

He looked straight at Jennifer and didn't recognize her. Relief began to seep through her.

"My name's Galen Rydell, Mr. Stevens." Rook offered his hand. "I'm investigating the crash of Mark Fox's plane, and I understand you say his wife was out here the day before the crash. Would you mind answering a few questions?"

Stevens hesitated, then shrugged. "I guess. No one told me I couldn't. And I actually didn't see Mrs. Fox, which is probably why nobody really cares what I have to say."

"What do you mean?"

Stevens waved the wrench he was holding. "What I saw was a chauffeured car."

"A lot of chauffeured cars come out this way."

The mechanic grinned at Rook. "They sure do. Not much to talk about. Thing was, it was here a while, and I got to talking to the driver, who told me he worked for Paxton, Wilcox and Moore, Mrs. Fox's company. I asked him what the heck he was doing here. I mean, I never saw Mrs. Fox out here, and I kinda gathered the plane didn't much interest her. Mark was out here a lot working on it, but he usually came alone. Anyway, the chauffeur said the Foxes was taking a big trip the next day, and Mrs. Fox wanted some things put on the plane for her husband."

"But you never actually saw Mrs. Fox?"

Stevens sucked his teeth. "Nope. Never saw anyone go near the plane, neither, but I was too busy talking to the chauffeur. Could be the chauffeur put the stuff on the plane. Not my place to be guarding them planes, anyway." Reaching into the back pocket of his overalls, he pulled out a tin of chewing tobacco. He took a few moments to tuck a wad into his cheek, then carefully closed the tin. "Didn't know lawyers rode around in chauffeured cars. Must be nice."

"We don't," Jennifer told Rook a short time later as they drove away from the airport. "We drive ourselves."

"Does Paxton, Wilcox and Moore own a chauffeured limo?"

"Actually, yes. It's reserved for clients and the partners, usually, although associates are occasionally allowed to use it."

"Then I guess we need to find out who was using the limo the day before your family was killed."

"That means going to the office." She felt her heart accelerate, and her mouth suddenly tasted metallic.

"Yeah. I guess it does. Who at the firm would want you dead, Jenny?"

Then, for the first time, she forced herself to face the truth—the truth about herself. "I wasn't an especially nice person, Rook. I was...driven. Ethical, but... driven."

He glanced her way, then astonished her by reaching out to take one of her hands and squeeze it. "So it could have been almost anyone?"

"I'm afraid so." She shook her head and gave a shaky laugh. "What a hell of a commentary."

Anyone at the firm. And for that she had no one but herself to blame.

16

"A wig and sunglasses," Rook said as they stood in a park and watched Massie frolic in the snow. "That ought to be enough to keep you from being ID'd when you go into the office building."

She could have used the sunglasses right now. Despite the cloud cover, the day was bright enough that the glare off the snow was painful to her eyes. "Will it?" She didn't like the whole idea of walking into the law offices in broad daylight. Not when she would have willingly bet her last dollar that Rook was right and that was where the hit man would be looking for her.

"Our advantage," he said, "is that your appointment with Felix is for tomorrow."

She looked up at him. "Why should that make any difference? There's no reason why anyone outside the firm would even know about it."

"If I were hunting you, and I knew that Felix Abernathy was your lawyer, I'd find someone in that damn firm to let me know when you were scheduled to come in. Tell me that would be impossible."

A chill was snaking along her spine, and she didn't think it was the cold of the day. "I can't tell you that."

"Of course you can't. How many employees does that place have? A hundred? Any one of them could probably get a good look at the appointment books without a whole lot of trouble."

The firm treated even that simple kind of information as confidential, but it wasn't hard to imagine that someone could be bribed into providing it.

Rook suddenly spoke in a low voice. "Don't look now, but that cop over there is showing an awful lot of interest in us."

"So? There's no warrant." But her heart skipped into high gear anyway.

"That's what *Felix* said."

Jennifer looked up at him, ready to argue in Felix's defense, but somehow the words wouldn't come.

"Call Massie *now,*" Rook ordered quietly. "The cop's coming this way, and I don't like the way he's resting his hand on his gun butt."

She just had time to give a soft whistle for the dog when Rook grabbed her arm and starting moving her swiftly to the car.

"Don't look back," he said. "Don't look as if you're aware of him, but move fast, damn it."

It was hard to hurry in the snow, but she managed to keep up with Rook's long strides without running. Massie thought it was some kind of game and barked excitedly as she ran rings around them.

The dog, Jennifer realized, made them appear normal. Made their hurry acceptable by making it look like a game. She wondered if the cop was chasing them.

Apparently not. They reached the car and got swiftly into it, the dog climbing over the seat into the back, and drove away. When Jennifer glanced back, she saw the cop staring after them.

"He made the car," Rook said. "Damn it, we've got to get a new set of wheels."

"But there isn't any warrant!"

He barely spared her a glance. "I think I'm going to check that out right now."

He drove them through a maze of city streets before at last stopping at a convenience store. The same convenience store, Jennifer realized with a lurch of her stomach, where she'd left the money for the hit man.

She'd gone white as a sheet, Rook noticed just as he was about to get out of the car. "What's wrong? Did something happen?"

"This is where I left the money for the hit man. In the trash bin out back."

"Jesus." He sat back in the seat and looked around. "I come here all the time."

Icy fingers scraped along her spine. "You do?"

"Yeah. I live not too far from here. Well, actually, I have a furnished room of sorts. It's convenient for when I'm between jobs. Damn it, I come here all the time!" He couldn't believe this.

"Does it mean anything?"

"I don't know. It must mean something, but I'm damned if I know what."

"Maybe..." She hesitated, not sure exactly what she was trying to get at. "Maybe someone knows you come here a lot."

He turned to look at her. "You mean *I'm* being set up?"

"Maybe." She swallowed hard. "I mean... maybe when I'm dead it's supposed to look like you did it."

"Shit." He barely breathed the word. An instant later he threw the car into gear and they roared out of the lot and back onto the street. They had driven halfway across the city before he spoke again.

"I'm going to paint the car."

"Why?"

"So it's not what the cops are looking for. Just some spray paint." Even as he spoke he wheeled into the back lot of an auto supply store. It hadn't been plowed, and they skidded a little, but no one else was parked there.

"You stay here with the dog and keep down," Rook said. "I'll be right back."

Her mind still awhirl with horrifying possibilities, Jennifer didn't argue. Hunkering down in the seat, she listened to Massie snore and tried to convince herself that the ideas that had occurred to her were all impossible.

Rook wasn't gone long. He returned with half a dozen cans of rust-covering paint and proceeded to spray the car without regard to water, mud or anything else. "It'll flake off, some of it really fast, but it'll just make the car harder to identify," he explained.

When he finished, what had been a reasonably well-kept older car looked like a rust bucket on its last legs. Then he shamelessly splashed mud on the license plates until both of them were difficult to read at any real distance.

"It'll just wash off on these wet streets," Jennifer said.

"Maybe. But I can't paint 'em. That'd be too obvious."

The paint dried fast in the cold air, and it wasn't long before they were on the move again, this time heading for a place that carried ready-to-wear wigs. A half hour later Jennifer had long, curly, light brown hair and a pair of wraparound sunglasses that made her look like just another serious skier while effectively concealing her identity. In Colorado at this season it was one disguise guaranteed not to look out of place.

Rook reversed his jacket so that it was burgundy instead of black, then donned a ski cap and a pair of yellow shooter's glasses that made his tawny eyes look browner.

Satisfied they had done as much as necessary to make themselves less obvious, he then stopped at a gas station to use the pay phone.

Jenny watched him from the car, her heart beating uncomfortably as she wondered what he was going to learn. That the policeman at the park hadn't exactly acted as if he had a warrant to serve was no reassurance. He had still showed a great deal of interest in them, and there could have been any number of reasons why he hadn't moved to arrest them. Like, for example, she was believed to be a cop killer, armed and dangerous. Or maybe he just hadn't been sure it was them.

Rook was taking longer than she had expected, and she watched him stab his finger into the air as if forcefully making a point. Finally he slammed the receiver down, then picked it up again and punched in another number.

This discussion was different in tenor, quieter and more restrained but suggestive of even greater urgency. After a couple of minutes he hung up and came back to the car.

When he slid in, he paused for a moment to pat Massie, then turned the car back onto the street.

"Well?" Jennifer asked finally.

"The warrant was never rescinded."

She gasped, and her heart slammed against her chest wall. "What? That's not possible!"

"It's not only possible, but it's true. The cops show that the warrant for you is still outstanding and the clerk of the court shows it's still outstanding. You're a wanted woman, Lady Fox."

"But . . . Felix said . . ." Her mind was whirling, unable to assimilate this contradiction. Felix was her friend . . . wasn't he?

"I know what Felix said. What's the likelihood the judge just hasn't signed the order rescinding the warrant?"

"Not very likely." The words came out reluctantly. "Felix would have prepared a copy of the order and taken it to court with him. He would ask the judge to sign it on the spot, not just wait for him to get to it—not on something like this. That's not how Felix works."

"Then something sure as hell is fishy. So ask yourself, my dear, just what is the likelihood that Felix didn't do a damn thing about the warrant at all?"

"But why would he say he had?" That was the question that kept tripping her up, begging for an answer she didn't want to give.

"Oh, I don't know," Rook said sarcastically. "How about that he'd feel a whole lot more comfortable if you were behind bars?"

"But why?"

"That's an interesting question, isn't it? How many answers can *you* come up with?"

"But I'll just make bail! There's no point—" She broke off sharply, realizing she was thinking emotionally, not logically. "No, I won't get bail. I'm a flight risk. That's already been proven."

"Exactly. Plus, you're a suspected cop killer. So you can expect to stay behind bars until you're acquitted or convicted, either one of which gets you out of somebody's hair for a long, long time. Permanently, if the hit man has his way. So that leaves a couple of questions. Who would want you out of the way for a long time? *Why* does he or she want you out of the way? And does he or she know about the hit man—which would make this an even more interesting situation?"

There was something almost frantic in the way her thoughts were racing, looking for answers to unanswerable questions. "There's also the question of whether the hit man is somehow trying to link you to my death. Whether all of this is related somehow."

"No. No, that's too farfetched. It wouldn't surprise me if whoever wants you arrested is opportunistic enough to hope the hit man will take you out and end the entire problem, whatever it is, but I don't think they were linked up to begin with. And as to whether there's some attempt to link me to your death..." He shrugged. "That convenience store is in a bad part of town. A lot of people who don't use their real names hang out there. It's probably just a coincidence."

She turned on the seat, looking straight at him. "Would anyone want *you* out of the way, Rook?"

It was something he hadn't really been giving any thought to because he hadn't considered himself to be anything but a target of opportunity. After all, the cops had seen him talking to Jennifer right about the time they began to suspect her, and then he had disappeared at the same time. Naturally he had become a suspect. But as for anyone else...

"You gave me the impression DeVries might have something against you."

"Maybe he did." He didn't especially want to discuss it. "It's not related."

If there was one thing lawyering had taught her, it was that things that appeared to be unrelated could often turn out to be very important. "What happened? Why did he send me to you?"

"Probably to embroil me in the mess that was bound to follow. But he's dead, Jenny."

"That doesn't mean someone isn't going to embroil you anyway."

He had been planning to head for the offices of Paxton, Wilcox and Moore, but now he turned instead toward another section of town, where they could grab a late lunch and be completely ignored. He knew too many of those places, he decided abruptly. Far too much of his life had been spent trying to be inconspicuous. Maybe it was time for a change of life-style.

No one even glanced up when they entered the diner. In tacit agreement they took a booth in a corner away from everyone else. The waitress was a redhead wearing a ratty blue sweater under a stained white apron. She had a friendly smile, though, and took their orders efficiently.

When she strolled away, Rook leaned forward toward Jenny, as if he would have preferred to whisper what he was about to stay. Responding to his posture, she leaned forward, too.

"It was a long time ago. Around four years, just after I got out of jail and started working as a mercenary. We were . . . well, I don't want to tell you exactly where we were. Let me just fill in what's important. I was working for revolutionary forces there, training their troops in demolitions. One of the other mercs was a new guy, green behind the ears, hardly any experience to speak of. Name was Jay. We kinda became friends. Anyway, Jay was captured by the government forces and I . . . called on some friends to help me get him out. Made it just in time, too. They'd just put a noose around Jay's neck and were stringing him up when I got to him. His voice has never been the same."

"DeVries was one of the friends who helped you?"

"You could say that. He got me the information about where Jay was being held, and he did it because we were friends." He shrugged. "One of the ironies of a merc's life. Sometimes you find yourself on opposite sides from a friend."

Jenny couldn't imagine how that must feel, or even want to. Why would anyone put up with such things? "So why did he want to get you?"

"Well..." He trailed off as the waitress approached with their burgers and drinks, and waited until she was gone. "DeVries was playing a dangerous game, working both ends against the middle."

Jennifer cocked her head, not sure what he meant. "You mean he was working for both sides at once?"

"Pretty much. He was actually spying for both sides. When I found out, I got pretty disgusted with him. You could say it ruined our friendship, but, hell, even mercs ought to have some sense of honor. Anyway, somebody spilled the beans and DeVries got his ass in a serious crack for a while there. It wasn't me that squealed, and I always thought he knew that, but now I'm beginning to wonder."

He shook his head and took a bite of his burger, chewing while he thought about it. "Nah. It doesn't add up. He knew damn well I don't know any hit men. It's not my style. He must have just wanted a chance to make me squirm without getting himself into any more trouble. After all, he was already sitting in prison. He could hardly want to set up a hit and find himself in trouble all over again."

"It was just an easy way to get rid of me and make you uncomfortable?"

He nodded. "That would be my guess."

"But it didn't work that way."

"No, and that's my fault. Too damn much tequila that night. If I hadn't been half-looped, I'd never have given you Jay's number. I mean, Christ, Jenny, Jay's a friend. Why would I want to drag him into anything like this? I just didn't want you to start asking all the other men in the room. Something bad would have happened."

She looked down at her plate, then gave him a crooked smile. "I never would have asked anyone else, you know. I'm not that gutsy. Or that crazy."

"How was I to know?" He shook his head disgustedly. "Look what a frigging mess I got us all into."

"Rook, not even by the longest stretch of the imagination do I think you can hold yourself responsible for this mess. I pretty much did it all on my own. And if you hadn't directed me to Jay, I'd have found someone, somewhere. I was absolutely determined to end my life, and I didn't want my family to know it was suicide. What could you have done?"

Nothing at all, he admitted to himself, although he hated to.

Massie ate three hamburgers in the parking lot while Rook tried again to get hold of Jay. For the past couple of days all he had gotten was the man's answering machine, and now he got it once again. After slamming the receiver down in disgust, he climbed back into the car with Massie and Jenny. The dog had cleaned up the burgers in a couple of huge mouthfuls and now was blowing onion breath over the back of the seat.

"Jay must have gotten a job," Rook said. "I keep getting his machine. Okay, why don't we go scout Paxton, Wilcox and Moore? Maybe we can even find out who took the limo to the airport that day."

"I doubt they'll give me access to the log. I don't work there anymore."

Rook glanced her way. "Try the sympathy thing. For God's sake, Jenny, somebody at that place must feel sympathy for your plight. But if you really don't think they'll talk to you, then I'll go in and claim to be a private investigator."

Jenny shook her head. "That would be guaranteed to shut all their mouths. No, I'll give it a shot. Heck, if worse comes to worst, I can always threaten to subpoena the damn thing."

"Maybe that'll persuade 'em."

She gave him a tired, tense smile. "Sure. Philipina Marlowe, here I come."

The law offices of Paxton, Wilcox and Moore occupied an entire residential block. A three-story redbrick building in a neo-Georgian style, it blended well enough with the surrounding large homes—some brick, most clapboard, with black or green shutters.

It was a neighborhood in transition, the old grace of an earlier age gradually eroding and being replaced by businesses. Some of the residences had been made over into doctors' offices, and a discreet sign in front of one announced an insurance agency and a real estate brokerage.

It was worse than he thought. Rook drove slowly, but he didn't stop anywhere. "I don't know about this," he said finally.

"Why?"

"Because when you said the law offices were in a residential area, I imagined family homes. Not houses stuffed with little businesses where strangers aren't remarkable. My God, you could be watched from almost any doctor's waiting room on the street!"

Jenny felt the back of her neck prickle uneasily. She hadn't really thought of that, but Rook was right. A waiting room would be a good place to hang out and watch the front doors of Paxton, Wilcox and Moore.

"He couldn't stay there all day," she argued, not sure she believed it. "Sooner or later someone would ask what he was doing."

"There are a million easy explanations for that one, sweetheart."

The back of her neck prickled even more strongly, and Massie seemed to pick up on it. The dog sat up and leaned forward, licking her cheek.

"He won't recognize me," Jennifer said finally. "That was the point of the wig, wasn't it?"

"Right. *Maybe* he won't recognize you."

"He's probably not watching, anyway. I'm not supposed to see Felix until tomorrow."

That was true. Hell, that was part of what he'd been hinging this visit on. The hit man wouldn't look for her until tomorrow, and the disguise would probably protect her at any other time. But now that they were actually facing doing it, he was scared to death that all his calculations were wrong, and that something terrible was going to happen to Jenny.

"Really, Rook. He's not looking for me today."

He could tell she was scared. There was a tremor around her mouth that he wasn't used to seeing, and her hands were clenched so tightly in her lap that her knuckles were white. He kept driving.

"No. No, I'm not going to let you do it. I'd never forgive myself if something happened to you."

"You don't have to forgive yourself. I'm the one who hired that hit man." She spoke bravely enough, but fear had turned her mouth as dry as cotton, and her heart was hammering so loudly that she could hardly hear her own voice. No, she didn't want to die. Not now. Not when Rook had made her want to live again.

"And Felix," Rook continued almost savagely, taking them around another block. "Damn it, I don't trust him. That guy is sure as hell up to something. I just wish I could figure out what it is."

"It doesn't make any sense, Rook. Felix has always been my friend! He's probably the only person in the firm that I honestly think has no reason to want to hurt me!"

"Then what about that warrant?"

The sticking point. Again. It didn't add up. Her heart didn't want to believe Felix had any reason to hurt her, but her mind couldn't accept any other possibility. For whatever unimaginable reason, Felix apparently wanted her in jail. "I'll call him. I'll ask him what's going on."

Rook braked and turned toward her, his expression and voice almost savage. "Don't you dare! Christ, woman, don't let him know we're on to him! We need every damn advantage we can get!"

"What advantage? Damn it, Rook, only two weeks ago Felix was telling me how grateful he was to me for allowing him to report something that could have affected his career instead of going ahead and reporting it myself. He even offered to help me find a job! Does that sound like someone who would want to hurt me?"

But even as she argued, she found herself pulling back from her unquestioning belief in Felix. She was arguing with herself, she realized, because her faith was waning. Why had he lied about the warrant?

"What little thing did you let him report?"

"Oh, it's complicated."

He released the brake and started them moving forward again. "The stock thing, right? I'm all ears."

"Well, I don't know if you're aware of securities regulations, but basically, if someone has inside information on events that could affect the price of a publicly traded stock, he has to keep that completely secret, and he can't buy any stock himself."

"I know about that."

"Well, that rule extends even further than you would think. Say I had inside information, and say you, without even knowing what that information was, went ahead and purchased some stock in the involved company. I could find myself under serious investigation for securities fraud."

"That's ridiculous."

"That's the way it is. If my next door neighbor, whom I don't even know, bought that stock, I'd have some explaining to do. Well, someone that Felix knows only vaguely made a killing on some stock in a company I was negotiating a merger for. I didn't for a minute think Felix had anything to do with it, but it needed to be reported just so it wouldn't look bad. Just a little thing, no big deal, but it would keep both Felix and me out of trouble."

"I follow."

"Anyway, as a courtesy, I told Felix first, before I went up to speak to the corporate counsel. Felix was as eager to report it as I was, and we went up together... but at the last minute I decided to let him go ahead and report it himself. I didn't want it to look like I'd forced him to do it."

"And Felix is still grateful for that."

"Yes."

"Lying about that warrant seems a strange way to show that."

"Maybe he didn't lie. Maybe he honestly thought it had been revoked. Oh, hell, I just don't know, but it doesn't seem like Felix at all!"

"I'd be willing to bet that most people who know you would say hiring a hit man doesn't sound like *you* at all."

Point taken. She shook her head finally and looked away. "All right. It's possible Felix has something against me. I'd more willingly believe that about almost anyone else, though."

"I can understand that. But you can't afford to trust anyone right now."

"You're right." Snow was beginning to fall again, and the afternoon was waning. Staring out the car window as they drove slowly down a street full of stately homes, she gathered her courage with both hands. She'd gotten herself into this mess, and now she needed to get herself out of it. Dillydallying wasn't going to solve a damn thing. "And we still need to find out who used the limo that day at the airport, so just drop me off right in front of the door."

"Can I get that close?"

"Within six feet. There's a driveway there. You just can't see it from the street under all the snow."

"Are you sure, Jenny?" He didn't like this. He didn't like this at all. For some reason, last night it had seemed reasonable that she should walk into the office herself. Now it seemed like utter lunacy. He would much rather take the risks himself.

"I'm sure." She managed a smile for him. "Time to put my money where my mouth is, I guess. If I really want to get to the bottom of this, then it's time to start digging."

"All right. But if anything makes you uneasy, you get the hell out of there, you hear me?"

She nodded. The thought of spending any time at all in jail made her insides curdle. She had to get to the bottom of this before someone put her behind bars, and if it seemed likely that someone at the firm was calling the police on her—but no. No one would do that. Their entire criminal law practice would evaporate if anyone at Paxton, Wilcox and Moore called the police on a client.

Rook drove right up to the front door and was relieved when a group of people came out of the building just as Jennifer climbed out of the car. It was about the best protection she could get from a sniper's bullet during those few seconds it took her to get inside.

Then he parked the car where he could see the door and settled down with the dog to wait.

Jennifer stepped through the door into the familiar lobby and felt as if she had been gut-punched. Not so very long ago she had walked in here feeling that this was *her* place. Her world. Now she was just an interloper. It felt so strange to stand here in a jacket and jeans where once she had worn only expensive suits, nylons and pumps.

The receptionist, a new employee, greeted her with a practiced smile. "May I help you?"

"I just need to see Gina French for a minute to ask a question. I'll be right back."

Leaving the woman staring after her, Jenny barreled down the hall toward Gina's office as if she owned the place.

The firm had several bookkeepers working for it under the supervision of the comptroller, but Gina was the only one Jennifer had actually gotten to know. Gina handled the expense accounts for the staff lawyers, and the two women had become friendly when

Jennifer returned from an overseas trip and needed help to straighten out her expenses, owing to all the complicated currency exchanges.

Gina's office was a windowed cubicle in the accounting department, preventing anyone from overhearing their conversation but making Jenny glad she'd worn a disguise. The other bookkeepers, all visible from Gina's cubicle, were busy at their computers.

"Jennifer?" Gina looked astonished. "Is it really you? You look so different. Girl, you're wasting away!"

Before Jenny could answer, the black woman had rounded her desk and swept her into a bear hug. Tears prickled in Jenny's eyes and she had to blink them back.

"It's so good to see you again," Gina said fiercely. "And I don't believe a word of it. Not a word of it! I just want you to know that. Nobody who knows you could believe you're capable of killing your family."

Jenny's throat tightened painfully. "Thanks, Gina."

The older woman rewarded her with a huge smile. "Now, sit and tell me what's going on with you. And what can I do to help?"

Jennifer was glad to obey. While she was sitting she could no longer be seen outside the cubicle. The phone rang and Gina reached for it, giving her an apologetic smile.

"No," she said into the receiver. "It's all right, Ruth, really. She's an old friend of mine. No, don't worry about it, okay?" She hung up and looked apologetically at Jennifer. "New receptionist. Sorry about that."

"It's okay. I did kind of sweep by her, but I didn't want to be seen by a whole bunch of people."

"I can't believe there's a warrant out on you! That's just beyond imagining. Girl, you need to get yourself a good lawyer."

"I did. Felix Abernathy."

"Well, I hear tell he's better than most. But can you afford him?" Gina waggled her eyebrows meaningfully.

Jenny nearly laughed. "I can afford him for a couple of weeks. I'm hoping to get rid of this mess a lot sooner. And that's what I'm here about, Gina. Part of the reason I'm in trouble is that somebody said I was out at the airport the day before the crash to put something in my husband's plane."

"Were you?"

"No. I didn't go anywhere near the place. That was always Mark's thing. But the mechanic who works where Mark used to keep the plane said he talked to the firm's chauffeur. So I need to know who was using the car that day."

Gina nodded slowly. "You know that's all supposed to be confidential."

"I know." Her hands tightened into fists on her lap, and for the first time since Gina had greeted her so warmly, she realized she might still fail to get the information. "But I need to know. It could be very important in exonerating me."

The bookkeeper hesitated visibly, plainly torn between helping a friend and protecting corporate confidentiality. Jennifer bit her lower lip, reluctant to try forcing the issue, wanting Gina to agree on her own.

"Oh, I guess it won't hurt," Gina said finally. "You were a member of the firm back then, anyway, and besides—" she flashed a quick grin "—you lawyers can always find a way to get what you want. You'd probably have me slapped with a subpoena before closing time."

Jennifer laughed, not wanting to admit how close she had come to saying exactly that.

"I'll be right back," Gina said, rising. "I need to get the log book. That was late last spring, right?"

"May 10."

"Okey-doke."

For a variety of reasons ranging from taxes to client billing, the chauffeur was required to keep a detailed log of times, places, passengers and mileage. The log was turned in to bookkeeping once a month.

Gina was away only a few minutes. When she returned, she sat behind her desk and began to flip through the pages. "Prentiss is meticulous, but his handwriting is *terrible.* I've spent years learning to decipher... ah, here it is. Thursday, May 10th. The car was signed out to... hmm." She pulled open a drawer and pulled out a magnifying glass. "It's not a problem when he uses a lawyer's name—I recognize his scribble for all of those—but when he's using a client's name..."

She peered through the glass at the log for a full half minute before saying finally, "Oh! Of course. A.D.V. Just initials." She looked up, frowning. "I'm really sorry, Jenny. I don't know who that is, and I can't breach confidentiality by telling you a client's name, anyway. If it were a lawyer..."

"Is there any way to find out which lawyer ordered the limo for his client?" But she already had a very sick feeling about that. A.D.V. could mean only one thing, as far as she knew: Alan DeVries.

"Well, let's see...." Gina flipped to another page in the log and nodded. "Yes, here it is. Felix ordered it."

Jennifer's stomach sank to her feet. She could think of no honest reason on earth why Alan DeVries should have been hanging around her husband's plane while telling the chauffeur he was putting something in it for "Mrs. Fox."

"Thanks, Gina. I appreciate the info."

She had to get out of here now. *Now!* The walls seemed to be closing in on her. She hardly heard what Gina said in parting, was hardly aware of her feet carrying her down the hall and out into the parking lot.

She felt as if her world had just come to an end...all over again.

17

It was just past five o'clock when Jennifer emerged from the building into the deepening winter night. Along with her streamed a crowd of laughing and talking employees.

Rook's first thought was that she would be safe in the crowd, but that didn't prevent him from scanning the surrounding area, looking for potential threats. Damn it, why hadn't she followed instructions and waited for him just inside the door?

The people pouring out of the building prevented him from driving over to intercept her, so he climbed out of the car, looking rapidly around for anything that seemed out of place.

Workers were emerging from offices all along the street, turning the quiet neighborhood into a bustling city street. Turning it into a potentially deadly trap.

The assassin could be anywhere among the crowd, and there would be no way to pick him out.

Christ. The skin on the back of his neck was crawling with a warning he knew better than to ignore. The killer was out there. Somewhere among the moving, shifting crowds of people, he lurked. Maybe he'd identified Jenny, maybe he hadn't, but he was out there watching.

The streetlights were bright, but they also created dark shadows where anything might hide. The yellow lenses of his shooters weren't helping now, and he ripped them off impatiently. Letting his eyes go slightly out of focus the way he had learned to do so long ago in his army training, he let his brain search for identifiable shapes among the crowd—a gun, a knife, anything dangerously out of place.

Nothing.

Frustrated, his nerves stretched nearly to snapping, he pivoted, surveying the entire area as groups of departing workers surged and broke around him like waves against a pillar of rock.

Jennifer was halfway across the lot now, walking as if in a daze. Whatever she had learned in there must have really shaken her. He wanted to run toward her, to try to shield her, but knew that would single her out in a way that might prove deadly.

Instead he cursed himself for a fool, for ever having convinced himself that the assassin would wait to show up tomorrow when Jenny had her appointment with Felix. Only a fool would question employees of the firm about Jennifer. One of them might well remember him and his interest after she was dead, and mention it to the police. No, the guy was probably watching the place and waiting, knowing that sooner or later Jennifer would show up to see her lawyer.

Rook turned again, viewing the streets from another angle. The crowds seemed to be thinning just a little, although there was a traffic jam at the southwest corner as people bottlenecked at the four-way stop.

All of a sudden Rook's gaze snapped into sharp focus as he registered a familiar face. *Jay Miller.* What the hell was Jay doing here? Seeing a lawyer?

But no, he was scanning the crowd as if he was looking for someone. Looking for...

"Jennifer!" The word ripped out of Rook's mouth almost before his mind finished making connections. "Jennifer! Down! Get down!"

He glanced in her direction just long enough to see her startled expression, to see that she dropped immediately to the ground, then turned his attention back to Jay. Their eyes connected, just long enough to bring recognition to Jay's eyes, just long enough for Rook to see that his friend was holding a gun. Then the younger man turned and scrambled into a waiting car. Before Rook had taken two steps in his direction, Jay was speeding away, driving ruthlessly over snow-covered lawns to bypass the traffic.

"Shit!" Swearing savagely, Rook slammed his hand down on the hood of a car. People all around had frozen when he had shouted, and now they turned to look curiously at him. Ignoring them, he went to help Jennifer to her feet. The fronts of her jacket and jeans were soaking wet.

"Let's get the hell out of here," he said roughly. "Now!"

He half dragged her to the car and helped her in. She fumbled the seat belt so badly that he finally reached out in impatience and fastened it for her. Not until they were several blocks away did he speak again.

"I know who your assassin is," he said flatly.

"And I know who killed my family," she replied in a voice that sounded almost mechanical.

"Great. Wonderful. God, can you believe our frigging luck? Now, what the hell are we going to do about it, Lady Fox?"

It was a good question, but neither of them seemed to have an answer.

They stayed in a different motel that night. Massie seemed to catch their mood and retreated to a corner, resting her chin on her paws and watching them from sorrowful brown eyes.

It was Jennifer who finally broke their silence, saying abruptly, "I can't prove it."

"Can't prove what?"

"That Felix was behind the murder of my family."

It was a strange day, Rook found himself thinking. Things he had half expected were shocking him by turning out to be true. And now that he was faced with it, he didn't want to believe that Jenny's friend had tried to kill her. "What exactly did you find out?"

"The car was ordered by Felix and used by someone with the initials A.D.V."

Rook straightened in his chair. "Alan DeVries."

"Inescapable, isn't it?" She gave him a humorless half smile. "But Alan DeVries didn't have any reason at all to want me or any member of my family dead. Hell, he didn't even know me until a few weeks ago. That leaves only one conclusion."

"That you weren't the first person to approach DeVries for a hit." It was as clear as handwriting on the wall, Rook thought. Right down to the story that had been fed to the chauffeur, designed no doubt to make the crash look like a murder-suicide, if its cause was ever uncovered.

"Evidently not." Her half smile became infinitely sad. "Felix was my friend, Rook. I believed he really cared about me. How could he do such a thing?"

"Maybe the insider trading thing was bigger than a single incident. Maybe you put a serious crimp on a big money-making scheme."

Jennifer caught her breath, aghast. "I didn't even think of that!"

"It's the only thing that occurs to me. I mean, a single incident is nothing to worry about. The two of you straightened it out between yourselves, and that was the end of it as far as you were concerned. But if he really *was* involved in insider trading, and if he was doing it on a regular basis, you were a threat simply because you'd already made the connection once. If you made it again, he'd be up to his ass in crocodiles."

"But he already makes so much money! Why would he do something illegal to get more?"

"I never yet met a man who didn't think he could use more money. It's a character flaw, Jenny. Just that simple. He thought he could make easy money and not get caught. Someone tries that every so often."

"I know, I know, but Felix . . ." She trailed off miserably and shook her head. "God, I can't believe he killed my family! I thought he was a friend. . . ." She fell silent, staring blankly at the wall behind him.

"Yeah. Friends can be really shitty at times."

Something in his tone snagged her attention, drawing her back from her sorrowful preoccupation. "What happened? What did you find out?"

"Just that your executioner is none other than my buddy Jay Miller."

Jennifer had thought herself unable to reel anymore after the shock of learning about Felix, but she felt another sharp pang of shock, this one in sympathy for Rook. "You're sure?"

"Yeah. I'm sure. Jesus!" He shook his head as if he wanted to shake free of something awful. "Can you believe that bastard sat there and listened to me tell him you had changed your mind, but he still came after you?"

It was like Cheryl all over again, he found himself thinking. The same kind of sneaking, stinking betrayal. If he ever again was stupid enough to trust anyone, he was going to turn himself in to a mental hospital.

"You saw him?" Jennifer asked.

"Oh, yeah. Plain as day. With a gun in his hand. The hell of it is, now that he knows I've spotted him, he's going to be harder than the devil to find. It just gets worse and worse! Shit. Now, what about Felix? What did you mean you couldn't prove anything?"

"I can't." She spread her hands hopelessly. "What can I demonstrate? That Felix loaned the company car and chauffeur to a client? How could I prove that Felix was behind it—or even that DeVries was the one who tampered with the plane? Remember, the mechanic only saw Prentiss."

"Prentiss?"

"The chauffeur."

"Well, it looks as plain as day to me."

"To me, too." Jenny smothered a miserable sigh. "The standard of proof is a little different in the courtroom, though. I'll need quite a few more dots if I'm going to connect them in front of a judge or jury. Heck, I don't even have enough to convince the police to arrest him. It's way too circumstantial."

Rook had seen people hanged on a great deal less, but not in this country. At least, not that he knew of. "What we need to do is get him to confess, then."

"Right." Jenny spoke with dry sarcasm. "May I remind you that Felix is a criminal defense attorney? He knows better than that."

"Maybe not if he thinks no one will ever hear what he has to say. But it would be hearsay, wouldn't it?"

"No. It's an admission by the accused, and it's perfectly admissible. If I tell you I killed someone, you can testify to that in court. It's evidentiary. It would be hearsay only if someone else told you that I'd said I'd killed someone."

He nodded understanding, a line appearing between his brows as he thought. "So we've got to get him to tell us, but he won't do that unless he thinks we'll never testify against him."

"That's about it. Pretty hard to do."

"At this point I'd be willing to bet you he told Hewitt that DeVries was going to testify against him precisely so that Hewitt would kill DeVries."

"Oh . . . I don't think—"

"Think about it, anyway. Don't forget, this is the guy who ordered the execution of your family. What makes you think he'd stick at killing an accomplice? Which leads to some interesting methods for getting Felix to talk. . . ."

"What? What are you thinking of?"

But he shook his head. "Let me chew it over for a little while. The details need some hammering out first."

Later she stirred herself to call her parents. They were still on vacation, soaking up sun, sea and sand.

They were even gladder when they heard about the abominable weather they were missing.

"How's Massie?" Lenore wanted to know. "Is she doing well?"

"She's doing just fine."

"And what about you? Have you managed to clear up the mess?"

The mess. What a description for all the threats she was facing. That word *mess* relegated murder to a class along with coffee spills and clutter. "Not quite, Mother, but we're getting there. I don't think it will be much longer."

"I hope not! You poor dear, what you've been through! I just wish there was something I could do to help."

"There isn't anything at all, Mother. Really. It's a great help just to know you're all safely out of it."

There was a pause, long enough that Jennifer detected her mother's hesitation. "Mom? What's wrong?"

"Oh, nothing, really. It's just that the police called us here to see if we knew where you were. And then a man—a lawyer, he said—wanted to know the same thing. He said it was urgent. I told him that if he was your lawyer you'd certainly know how to reach him and would call him yourself."

Jennifer's heart was pounding. "When was that, Mother?"

"Oh, yesterday, I believe. Frankly, I didn't think it would be so easy to track us down."

"Neither did I. Maybe . . . maybe you should move to another hotel until I get this sorted out."

"We've already made arrangements, dear. Let me tell you, it wasn't easy! But we're moving tomorrow.

I'll call and let you know the number when we get settled. Where can I reach you?"

Jennifer opened her mouth to answer, then caught herself. Someone had managed to find out where her parents were. Information was evidently getting around somehow. Rook was right; it was safest not to tell anyone. "It's better if I don't tell you that, Mother. Besides, we'll be staying somewhere different tomorrow night, anyway."

"I don't like not being able to get in touch with you! I worry myself sick."

"I don't see any way around it right now. And really, Rook is taking good care of me. I'll be just fine."

She had basically the same conversation with her father, then spent a few minutes talking to her sister and her niece and nephew. When she hung up, she felt emotionally wrung out.

Rook astonished her by taking her into his arms and holding her close and tight.

"It'll be okay," he said. "Really. I've got it figured out."

She tilted her head to look up at him, opening her mouth to ask what he was planning. But before a sound escaped her, he had covered her mouth with his and plunged his tongue deeply into her. A shockingly swift spear of arousal ripped through her straight to her core.

"I'll get him for you, honey," Rook murmured roughly as he trailed his mouth hungrily over her cheek toward her ear. "I'll get him...."

Her legs gave way before the onslaught of need that was sweeping her away. So hot, so swift, so fast...never had she imagined it could be possible....

"I need you... oh, God, Jenny... I need you...." His whisper was ragged, rough, filling her with even greater excitement.

"Yes... yes..."

The room whirled wildly as he swung her onto the bed. She watched from half-closed eyes as he tugged impatiently at her clothing. A shudder of absolute delight passed through her as he yanked open the zipper on her jeans and his hot fingers touched her cool, soft, sensitive skin. Her hips began to move, a gentle rocking she was helpless to prevent, a blatant signal that she needed him, too....

Her sweater vanished over her head, and the cool air met her skin, causing her to shiver, but then Rook was over her, his body covering hers, keeping her warm with his own heat, teasing her even higher with his mouth and hands.

Oh, it felt so good! So good to have Rook's impatient hands on her soft flesh. So good to feel his eagerness and hear his rough murmurs. So good...

So good to be alive.

The understanding shocked her into tears. Rook lifted his head, looking down at her with consternation, wondering what the hell he had done wrong. He couldn't have mistaken her eagerness....

But it didn't matter, did it? She was crying. Huge tears and gasping sobs poured from her. Moving to lie beside her, he tucked her head into his shoulder and wrapped her tightly in his arms. "It's okay," he whispered. "It's okay. Sweetheart, we'll get through this somehow. I swear it."

Christ, he felt like a fraud, making promises he wasn't sure he could keep. He was damn well going to *try* to keep them, was even willing to put his neck on the line to do it, but, by God, he shouldn't be promising what he wasn't sure he could deliver.

She shook her head against his shoulder, made a muffled sound and burst into renewed tears. He patted her shoulder gently, wishing there was something he could do to make her feel better.

"I'm sorry," he said helplessly, not sure exactly what he was apologizing for. That life could be a bitch sometimes? Hell, it wasn't his place to apologize for that.

"It's . . . okay," she said brokenly, her voice muffled against his shoulder. "It's . . . I'm not upset. Really."

Startled, he tried to look down at her but could only see the soft shell of her ear. "What?"

She sniffled, sounding just like a little kid, and turned her head so that their eyes could meet. "It's dumb, but . . . I'm crying because I'm hap-happy!"

Happy? "Well, that's okay. What are you happy about?"

Her arms crept up around his neck and pulled him even closer. "I'm just happy to be alive. I never thought I'd feel that way again, but I'm so happy just to be alive!"

She burst into fresh tears, and he held her for a long, long time, wondering at the incredible irony of life.

Eventually she softened and grew quiet, then lifted her leg so that it lay over his. Moments later he was deep inside her, home at last.

They made love then, slowly, gently, as if they had all the time in the world. As if their souls needed to express themselves.

As if terrible things weren't waiting just ahead.

"Tell Mr. Abernathy that I'm calling on behalf of Jennifer Fox," Rook said into the telephone. He sat on the edge of the bed, wearing nothing at all. Jennifer lay beside him, blanket drawn up to her chin, watching and listening. Beyond the window the morning was gray, calm and cold.

This was it, Jennifer thought, holding the blanket tightly with cold hands. Rook was setting events into motion that, one way or another, were going to precipitate further events. She just hoped this didn't make anything worse.

"Mr. Abernathy, my name is Galen Rydell. I'm sure you know who I am. Yes. But what you may not know is that Alan DeVries introduced Ms. Fox and myself."

Rook listened for a few moments, then smiled in a way that sent chills down Jennifer's spine.

"Alan told me an interesting story, Mr. Abernathy," he said into the phone. "It would be to your advantage to meet with me and hear about it. No, not at your office. There's a warehouse at the south end of town. Can you meet me there in an hour?"

Apparently Felix agreed, because Rook gave him directions, and repeated, "One hour. If you're not there, I'll assume you don't care who hears my story."

Then he hung up the phone and turned to Jennifer. "Bingo. Now you stay here while I take care of this bozo."

"No!" Jennifer sat up, heedless that the blanket fell to her waist. "No, I need to be there!"

"It'll be dangerous. I'd really prefer it if you'd stay here where you're safe. Where I don't have to worry about protecting *you.*"

She shook her head vehemently. "I can't, Rook. Don't you see? I have to hear him admit it. I'll never be able to get past this if I don't hear it from his own lips!"

He understood. Kind of. But he didn't like it. "You can hear it from the tape."

"It won't be the same, Rook. Honestly. I need . . . I need to watch him sweat while he admits it. I need to take that memory out every time I think of how he hurt my family. Don't you see? That's the only revenge I'll ever truly have. The only peace I can get, knowing that he admitted it. That he convicted himself."

He sighed. "Okay. But you stay the hell out of the way. I don't want him to even know you're there."

18

Rook stopped to purchase a gun and a microcassette recorder at a pawn shop where he was greeted by name. When he said he was in a hurry, the owner hustled, completing the transaction in just under ten minutes.

"I had occasion to buy some stuff there a few months ago," Rook explained when they returned to the car. "A friend of mine was robbed, and I found some of the items there. I didn't see why the pawn shop owner should have to pay for the theft."

"No, it doesn't seem right, does it? But that's a risk of his trade."

"Of course it is. That doesn't make it right."

Not for the first time, Jenny was impressed by Rook's sense of honor and fair play. Well, why wouldn't she be? He'd taken on her problems out of a sense of honor, after all.

They arrived at the warehouse about fifteen minutes before Felix was due, which gave them time to scout a place for Jenny to hide.

A car cruised past as they pulled in to the fenced lot, but the driver never looked their way. Rook waited for a few minutes to see if the car returned, disturbed by the feeling that they were being watched. When the car didn't return, he climbed out and looked around for some vantage from which someone could be watching them. Nothing.

Christ, he was getting jumpy in his old age.

The best place to hide Jenny proved to be a gallery that ran along the length of the building on one side, and that was accessible both by stairs outside the building and by stairs inside. Some small rooms indicated that once there had been offices up here, overlooking the warehouse floor. Debris still littered the place, creating ample hiding places.

"You stay up here," Rook told her. "Just hunker down and be quiet as a mouse."

She nodded, looking at him with wide, worried eyes. "Be careful."

"Of course." He flashed her a smile and then zoomed in for the kiss he'd been wanting to give her ever since they'd left the motel. For an instant she seemed to forget what they were here for, growing soft and welcoming against him. It was only with the greatest reluctance that he let go of her.

"Lie down and be quiet," he told her one last time, then turned to hurry down the stairs to the warehouse floor.

Obediently, she lay facedown in the dust, peering around the edge of a rotting cardboard box.

The place was cold, musty, smelling of mildew and decay. Here and there on the floor below were wet black lumps that looked like decaying animal carcasses. Something had killed, then left its prey to rot.

Rook stationed himself carefully behind a stack of wooden pallets once used by forklifts. Between the pallets he could see the entire warehouse with almost no obstruction. If Felix Abernathy didn't come alone, Rook wasn't going to be taken by surprise.

He wished they hadn't had to leave Massie in the car. He would have felt a lot better if the dog had been here to protect Jennifer, but there was no way they could ensure the mastiff's silence. If she got restless and gave one of those groany yawns of hers, or if she was startled by something into barking, it would give away Jenny's presence and probably cause Felix to clam up.

Still . . .

A clank warned him that someone was opening the small door at the far end of the warehouse. A moment later a diminutive man wearing a gray business suit and overcoat stepped inside. The door thudded closed behind him.

It must be Felix, Rook decided. The man matched Jenny's description of him: small, dapper, almost feminine in his build. A man who would have looked equally good had he been born female.

The new arrival stepped cautiously forward a few paces, looking around. "Hello? Mr. Rydell? Mr. Rydell, I'm Felix Abernathy."

Rook remained where he was, wanting his opponent to grow more unnerved. Wanting Felix to step closer and closer so that he could better gauge whether the man was armed—as he probably was.

"Hello?" Felix called again. When no one answered him, he was apparently emboldened. His posture straightened, and he walked forward with more confidence.

And he was heading straight for the stack of pallets where Rook hid, probably intending to hide himself and await the other man's arrival. Rook smiled to himself. In a few seconds he was going to give Felix Abernathy the biggest scare of his life.

Felix rounded the edge of the pallets like a man who believed he must be alone. Not too smart for a lawyer,

Rook thought, and nearly laughed when the other man saw him and jumped.

But he stopped laughing when Felix's hand dived beneath his coat. Before the lawyer's hand even started to reemerge with whatever he'd been reaching for, Rook was on him, knocking him to the floor. An instant later he had wrenched a pistol from Abernathy's hand.

"Not the best way to negotiate," Rook told the man beneath him. Abernathy made a small sound like a whimper and looked up at him with abject terror as Rook pointed the lawyer's gun right at his head.

"Always stupid to bring a gun to a fight if you don't know how to handle it," Rook continued conversationally. "An awful lot of upstanding citizens get killed with their own guns when a criminal takes it from them. More of them than the criminals, actually. That's why I could never understand the universal desire in this country to carry weapons."

Felix looked as if he thought he had fallen into the hands of a madman. But that was exactly what Rook was trying to do: keep him off balance so he would start talking.

Reaching with his free hand into his jacket pocket, Rook turned on the tape recorder. The microphone was clipped under his lapel.

"Now, we can stay like this, Felix ol' buddy, me on top of you, you on the hard cement, or we can get up and talk like civilized people. But we're only going to get up if you promise to behave. I don't want to shoot you unnecessarily. You wouldn't be worth anything to me dead."

Felix's eyes lit up, as if he understood. "You want money. I can pay you. What do you want? Ten thousand?"

"Get up." Rook levered himself easily to his feet. Felix, out of condition because of a life spent behind a desk, got up awkwardly, pausing often to look at the gun Rook still leveled at him.

When he was standing, Felix nervously adjusted his tie and brushed at his gray overcoat. "Twenty thousand," he offered. "I can give you twenty."

"You paid more than that for the hit man."

The lawyer blanched. "I didn't—"

"You did. You want Jennifer Fox dead, and you paid some hit man who messed up and who's still stalking her."

Felix seemed to grow even paler. "No...no..."

"Look, I know all about it. Remember Alan DeVries? He was an old friend of mine. A real old friend. He told me everything. Just who the hell do you think you're kidding?"

"Alan was lying!"

"Really? Alan wanted me to know everything. Said he might need some protection from you. Only it didn't work, did it? Alan's dead, isn't he? You wouldn't happen to know anything about that, of course."

Felix shuddered, looking around wildly. Taking advantage of the man's fear, Rook stepped closer and pointed the muzzle of the .45 right at the lawyer's head, so that the man was looking down the barrel. Felix's eyes grew so big they would have been comical under other circumstances.

"Tell me just what you *do* know, Felix, or so help me, I'm going to blow your brains out right this minute."

"I don't know anything!" He almost shrieked the words, holding his hands out imploringly. "I don't. I swear!"

"Right." Rook cocked the pistol.

"No! No, please. I'll tell you what I do know! I asked Alan to kill her last winter, but he messed up and killed her family instead. God! I never thought...I swear I didn't know how he intended to do it. I thought he'd just get somebody to knock her off. I never imagined he'd take out her whole family! And then she wasn't even on the plane...." He started to blubber. "It was awful! I could see how hurt she was, how wrecked.... I would have given anything to undo it! Really, I would have!"

"Yeah, right," Rook said sarcastically. "Why did you want her dead in the first place?"

"Because she found out I was involved in insider trading! Good God, do you know what that could have done to my career? My life?"

"But you convinced her you weren't involved and she dropped it."

"I didn't dare do any more of it, anyway. Not when someone knew. But I needed the money!"

Rook looked down at him, feeling a roiling disgust such as he had seldom felt. "You worm. Money was more important than the lives of two innocent children?"

"I didn't mean for them to die! I swear it! Just Jennifer. I didn't want to have her killed, believe me. I *like* her! I like her a lot! We were really good friends until the stock thing. Christ, I even figured after she left the firm that I didn't need to worry about her anymore, so why would I have her killed *now?*"

Rook shrugged, waving the gun a little to remind the man that it was still there, still pointing at him. "You don't get it, do you? Why am I supposed to believe you wouldn't hurt her now after what you did before? I'm supposed to believe you don't need any more money?"

"No! No! Don't you see? I had to get rid of her or I was going to be killed!"

Something cold and slimy seemed to slither along Rook's spine. Christ, this was a filthy business, and it just kept getting filthier. "Who the hell was going to kill you?"

"My supplier. Jesus. My supplier." Crumbling, Felix covered his face with his hands, whimpering like a baby.

"You do drugs?"

Felix sniffled but didn't answer. Rook tapped him with the gun, causing the man to look up in terror.

"Answer me," Rook growled. "What supplier, and why was he going to kill you?"

"Cocaine. It's cocaine. I... I can't live without it. I've tried. Honestly, I've tried to get off it! A few years ago I put myself in a treatment program, but after I got out, I only managed to stay clean for a couple of weeks. You don't understand. Only an addict can understand...."

Rook squatted, looking the man straight in the eye, never allowing the gun to waver from its target. "Oh, I understand. I understand that you're a weak, disgusting excuse for a man. Why was your supplier going to kill you?"

"Money. I owe him a lot of money. That's why I needed to make a killing in stocks. That's why I got so scared when I couldn't do it anymore because I was afraid Jennifer would find out. I owed the guy so much money...."

"Who? Who was it?"

"Alan DeVries."

"DeVries!" Rook had known, of course, that Alan had gone to prison for dealing drugs, but he'd never imagined this kind of connection between the attorney and his former friend. "Is that why you had him killed? But what could he do to you from prison?"

"Plenty! You don't think he worked alone, do you? Hewitt was just one of his partners in crime. Besides, when I heard Jennifer knew DeVries, I figured she'd go back to question him. DeVries wasn't too fond of me, since I couldn't keep him from getting convicted, and I was afraid he'd get even by spilling the beans on me...which I guess he did." For a moment, resentment replaced fear in his eyes. Rook restored the balance by waving the gun a little.

"So you persuaded Hewitt to kill him."

"It didn't take much. Hewitt is a despicable character. I think he kills for the joy of it. It was easy enough."

"You know what I think, slime ball? I think *you're* the despicable character. You have other people doing your dirty work."

"Of course!" Felix looked surprised. "Good heavens, I'm not a *murderer!*"

From above, Jenny could see everything, and it was all she could do to keep still and quiet. She wanted to hurt Felix, wanted to hurt him badly for what he had done to her family. Most especially for what he had done to her children.

I'm not a murderer. He spoke the words with such passion that she could tell he honestly believed them. How could he be so deluded? Had cocaine made him this way? What had happened to the man she had once believed him to be? When had he become this despicable slug?

Shivering—the warehouse was cold, and having to hold still like this was preventing her from keeping herself warm—she tried to remain as silent as a mouse.

They had enough now to nail Felix in a court of law. By his own admission he had hired someone to kill her. By his own admission this person had killed her husband and children. By his own admission he was involved in insider trading. Felix Abernathy was going up the river for a long, long time.

But Rook apparently wanted to find out something more, so she waited patiently, trying not to shiver so hard that she made noise.

"Don't make a sound, or I'll kill you right here."

She froze, terror turning her to ice. She recognized that whisper. Even though he didn't speak out loud, there was something about the way he enunciated . . .

"Get up quietly. Don't make a sound, or I'll put a bullet through your kneecap."

Slowly, slowly, hardly able to breathe as her heart raced in panic, Jennifer got to her hands and knees, then to her feet. Below her, Rook and Felix were still talking, now about Hewitt and DeVries.

Please look up, she prayed silently. *Please, Rook!* But he didn't hear anything, didn't glance up, just continued questioning Felix.

With a gun in her back, the man forced her to walk to the door and descend the steel stairs outside the building. Surely Rook had heard something, she told herself. He must have. Even with a gun in her back reminding her to be silent, she knew she had made some small noises.

But nothing happened. No one seemed to hear. And little by little she was moving toward her own execution.

Rook thought he heard a small sound from above, but didn't dare look. Felix was pouring out in excruciating detail the way he had manipulated Hewitt into killing DeVries. Rook didn't want to stem the flow if he didn't have to, not while the lawyer was cooperating so eagerly.

Then, suddenly, he heard the dog barking from outside. Muffled through the closed door, it still reached him, sounding frantic. He hesitated, wondering what could be wrong. Then, horrifying him, a gunshot. At once he switched off the tape recorder.

"Stay here," he told Felix. "Stay here, or I'll kill you."

Felix sagged onto the concrete, still sniveling. Without another glance at him, Rook turned and ran for the door. Jenny was going to kill him if anything happened to that damn dog....

He burst through the steel door into the lot outside and froze at what he saw.

Massie was going berserk, throwing herself against the partially open side window of the car, trying desperately to get out. Even from here, he could see both the glass and the door bow outward before the dog's weight. And in the door was a bullet hole.

There, to the left, was Jay Miller, holding Jennifer in front of him with one arm around her throat and a gun to her head.

"Don't move, Rook," Jay said sharply. "I'll kill her here and now."

"Why do you have to kill her at all? For God's sake, Jay, you've already got the money! What more could you want?"

Jay shook his head. "It doesn't matter whether you understand or not."

Rook was feeling almost as frantic as the dog, but he couldn't figure out what to do. He didn't have a clear shot, and he knew Jay was too well trained to be easily disarmed or distracted. He had to keep him talking until some kind of opportunity appeared....

"Sure it matters," he heard himself say hoarsely. "We're friends, Jay. We've been friends for a long time. I even saved your life."

"That's the only reason you're not dead already, man. You keep getting in the fucking way!"

"Well, now you're going to have to kill me. Don't you think I have a right to know why my *friend* is killing me? Come on, Jay. What'll it cost you? A couple of minutes of your time? At least let me know why you won't just let her go. Christ, you've got the money! All you had to do was drop it when you found out she'd changed her mind."

"It doesn't work that way, Rook. It doesn't work that way at all. I got a reputation to protect. If I don't follow through on a job, how many more jobs do you think I'll get?"

"But the person who hired you changed her mind!"

"Doesn't matter. If she ever tells anybody, I'm ruined. No, I finish my jobs no matter what."

A cold gust of wind blew through the snow-covered lot, tossing Jenny's hair, causing her to shiver so hard that Rook could see it from twenty feet away. God, let me help her, he found himself praying. Please God, don't let her die. But he couldn't afford to give in to feelings. He had to keep a cold, clear head until he could find a way to help her.

"Christ, somebody shut that damn dog up," Jay said.

Massie ignored him, throwing herself once again at the window. This time a webwork of cracks spread through it.

But Jay didn't notice. A movement behind Rook had caught his attention. Rook instinctively turned, too and saw Felix coming out of the warehouse. "Felix, no!"

But the man had a gun, and he wasn't thinking too clearly. He pointed it, but he was unsteady on his feet and his hands were shaking like leaves in a hurricane. Rook felt a wave of cold fury at himself for not having searched the lawyer thoroughly. Before Felix could aim, Jay shot him. One neat bullet to the brain put Felix Abernathy to rest forever.

And now, Rook thought with a sinking of his stomach, there was absolutely no hope on earth that Jay would let Jennifer go. They had witnessed him killing someone, and they knew who he was.

"Just tell me why, Jay," Rook said hoarsely. "Just tell me why you're doing this. Why you kill people."

Jay gave a short bark of laughter even as Massie lunged at the window once again, shattering it even more.

"Why? Why? What difference does it make? It's no different than being in an army, Rook. Why is there some bloody big difference between killing people for a thousand bucks a month or killing them at fifty thousand a head? One way just pays better!"

"But—"

"Oh, hell, don't argue with me. That's why you don't fight anymore. That's why you're just an adviser. One step removed, but that's all, Rook, my man. One step removed. Me, I got tired of taking orders from tin gods with an extra stripe or a piece of brass. I got tired of doing it all and barely making enough to get by. So I went into business for myself. Before you know it, I'll be able to retire permanently."

"Why not retire right now?"

Jay laughed. "Because I need more money. Because I kinda like what I do. Haven't you felt it, man? The power when you hold somebody's life in your hands? When you know it's up to you whether they live or die?''

"I can't say—"

Just then Massie broke free, showering pebbles of safety glass in every direction as she lunged through at last.

Immediately Jay swore and pointed his gun at the dog, but Jenny became suddenly galvanized, grabbing at his gun arm and fighting him.

"No, damn you!" she shrieked. "You're not going to kill my dog...."

His shot went wild, and just then Massie reached them. Jay's instinctive reaction was to let Jenny go in order to protect himself from the dog's attack. As he flung her aside, Rook lifted his own .45 and plugged Jay right in the middle of his chest.

Looking surprised, Jay crumbled to the ground. Massie halted, momentarily confused, then raced to Jenny's side.

It was over.

19

The interrogation room at the police department was small, windowless and cold. Jenny had to keep rubbing her hands for warmth. Massie sat beside her, looking at once interested and exhausted. She flinched a little when Jenny touched her shoulder, suggesting she had been bruised.

Rook slouched in a plastic chair nearby, answering the same set of questions for the umpteenth time. The police seemed very reluctant to believe he had shot Jay Miller to protect Jennifer. They kept hinting around that he had somehow been involved, despite Jennifer's insistence that Jay had been holding a gun to her head.

Nor did they seem entirely happy with the notion that Felix had hired the hit man.

"It's obvious, isn't it?" Rook asked the cop. "He must have hired Jay Miller to kill her. After all, he hired DeVries to kill her before."

"But he says on your damn tape that he didn't do it."

"If he'd admitted he had, admitted that he knew who the guy was, his days would have been numbered for sure. Miller would have come looking for him. You know that, Detective. You don't need me to tell you."

The detective, Hodgekiss, looked at his partner, Garcia. "It's too neat."

"Yeah," Garcia said. "Maybe. But it's all you're gonna get, Hank. Besides, if Abernathy didn't hire the hit, then who did? You wanna start digging into that?" He looked straight at Jennifer, as if he knew the truth. "What good'll that do? Sometimes it's best to let sleeping dogs lie."

Hodgekiss hesitated. "I don't know. Let's go talk to the lieutenant."

"About what?" Garcia asked as he followed his partner out of the room. "You don't have a damn thing to go on other than a feeling."

The door closed behind them, and Jennifer looked at Rook. "They know," she murmured.

"Shh." He put his fingers to his lips and pointed toward the mirror on the wall. Someone might be watching and listening.

Massie whimpered, and Jennifer looked down at the dog. It was over, but it wasn't over. By hiring the hit man, she had committed a crime, and she knew it as well as anyone. She ought to have the guts to stand up and confess to it, but what possible good would that do? If Jay hadn't come after her, he would have gone after someone else...and someone else would be dead. As for her part, if she was even charged, a jury would very likely acquit her on grounds of temporary insanity.

And she *had* been insane. Looking back over the past six months, she was appalled by the black shroud that seemed to have been suffocating her, appalled at the way she had often behaved. Despair had turned her into a person she could hardly recognize. And now that she had somehow burst free of that enveloping depression, she wanted only to be allowed to pick up the pieces of her life. To try to build something worth living for.

Garcia returned alone. "You both can go now. If we need anything else, we'll give you a call."

Rook looked him straight in the eye. "Am I going to be charged?"

The cop suddenly grinned. "Nah. It wouldn't look good for us to charge a guy who was rescuing a woman from the man who had recently killed her family...especially when we've already got egg on our face over charging the two of you in the first place. Now get out of here and have a merry Christmas."

Outside, night held icy sway. It was nearly two in the morning, and the world seemed to have gone to sleep. Only a few cars moved on the glistening roads, and the stars above shone with cold brilliance in a moonless sky.

Earlier they had been transported to the police station in official vehicles, but a police officer had driven their car to a lot near the station. With directions from an officer, they set out on a frigid hike.

"Well, Lady Fox," Rook remarked, "you can go home now."

She thought about that and wondered why it didn't sound wonderful. "What about you?"

"Oh, I'll start looking for work again. There's always a war somewhere."

"I suppose." She trudged alongside him, her head scrunched turtlelike into her shoulders to reduce her exposure to the cold wind. Massie seemed glad to be out of the police station and pranced a short distance ahead of them. "Do you like being a mercenary?"

They reached the car before Rook answered. "No," he said. "I hate it."

"Then why don't you do something else?"

"Because soldiering is all I know."

The car started instantly, despite the cold.

"It's a good car," Rook said, patting the dash before driving them out of the lot. "What should we do with this rust bucket, do you think?"

"It's your car," she reminded him. "You paid for it."

"Maybe I'll keep it. It has a kind of charm, y'know?"

She smiled; she couldn't help it. Inside her, funny things were happening, feelings as if something in her heart was about to rupture painfully—but that was ridiculous, wasn't it? She'd already lost all she could lose. There wasn't another thing anyone could take from her.

She looked at Rook and wondered if there was some way they could remain friends. Somehow—somehow she just couldn't imagine never seeing him again.

"Speaking of money," he said, "what are you going to tell the IRS?"

"That's easy. I have until February 29 of next year to file a 1099, and I *will* file it."

"File it on who?"

"Jay Miller, of course. I paid the man fifty thousand dollars. If anyone wants to know what for, I'll say I hired him to investigate the crash. Let the IRS figure out where he stashed it so they can take their cut."

A snort escaped Rook and then was followed by a roaring laugh of pure delight. "God, you're wonderful!"

A warm feeling trickled through her, making her want to hug herself in delight. Nobody, but nobody, had ever said that to her before, and it was especially nice to hear it from Rook.

He headed straight for her home. When she offered to help him get his Explorer from the airport—he would need two drivers, after all—he told her he would handle it himself, not to worry.

And that was when she suddenly realized exactly how much she didn't want him to go away. How much she wanted them to be together every minute. How much she wanted to invite him to spend the night.

She tried to tell herself she'd just gotten used to having him around over the past few terrible days, that her attachment was psychological and nothing else.

But she didn't believe it. Rook was going to leave her, and she was going to have another gaping hole in her heart. She wondered if she had learned anything at all about surviving these losses, or if she was going to go into another terrible funk. And she wondered why she should even have to find out.

But there didn't seem to be any way to ask him to stay. He was a mercenary, a wanderer, and he wasn't going to give that up, no matter how much he said he hated it. Besides, when he'd spoken of his marriage, she'd heard something in his voice that had said Rook Rydell was never going to care again.

Of course he wasn't. And she was a damn fool for caring at all. Hadn't she learned the price already? Why was she doing this to herself?

When they reached her house, he escorted her to the door and insisted on coming inside to check things out. Except for a layer of dust and fingerprint powder on nearly every flat surface, and a broken latch on the window through which Jay had broken in to the house, everything seemed to be as she had left it.

"I guess I'm going to need a cleaning crew first thing," Jennifer remarked as they went downstairs.

"Funny, I would've thought you already had one."

"I did... before. When I was working full-time. I couldn't keep up with it. But since..." She trailed off and shrugged. "I need to get this place ready to sell."

"Sell? It's a nice house."

"It's also a mausoleum. I need to start out fresh, without so many reminders."

"I can understand that."

At the door they faced each other. Rook looked down at her with a crooked smile. "You've come a long way, Lady Fox. It's hard to believe you're the same woman I met a few weeks ago."

"I'm *not* the same woman." She looked up at him with her heart in her throat and every nerve ending in her body straining toward him. Those tawny eyes of his were the most beautiful eyes she had ever seen. That crooked little smile, with one corner of his mouth lifted, was an image she was going to tuck away in her heart and cherish forever.

Bending, he brushed a kiss on her cheek. Before she could react, he had opened the door.

"I'll call you," he said, and walked away.

Her barely born hopes shriveled to dust and blew away on the icy night wind.

A week later, after a teary three-day reunion with her family, she bought some boxes and began to pack up the children's rooms. It was time. Last night she had dreamed of them, dreamed that Mark and Bethany and Eli had come to her and hugged her, and told her to let them go. And for some reason she had awakened this morning feeling as if her soul had been healed.

She still missed them. She would always miss them, but her sorrow had become a wistful and gentle thing, no longer the ravening beast that had once mercilessly tormented her.

They had gone to a better place. Never for a moment had she doubted that, but now, finally, the belief comforted her.

She had finished Bethany's room and was halfway through Eli's when a sound behind her caused her to scream and whirl around. Even now, she couldn't quite believe in her safety. She hoped her nerves would calm down eventually.

Rook stood there, dressed in a suit and overcoat, looking a little sheepish. "Sorry. You didn't answer my knock, and the door was unlocked. I guess I should have hollered."

"It's okay. It's okay." Her knees were suddenly rubbery, and she sat abruptly on the edge of Eli's bed.

He looked around the half-bare room, at the packing boxes. "I see you were serious about moving on."

"It's time. I have to let them go."

He nodded. "After...after Sam died I—" He broke off. "You're going to think I'm crazy."

"So what?"

He smiled at that. "Yeah. So what. After she died I saw her. It was...I can't explain it. I was in my cell late one night, trying to figure out how to get even with the whole damn world, and suddenly she was there. And it didn't seem odd that she was." He shrugged. "Crazy, like I said but... She smiled at me and said, 'Daddy, it's time for me to go. Please, just let me go.'"

He looked away for a moment, then sort of shrugged and gave her an embarrassed smile. "You're the only person I ever told about that."

"Did you feel better?"

"Yeah. It was weird but . . . I still believe Sam came to see me and make me feel better."

Jennifer nodded. "Me too. I dreamed of them last night, and it's as if . . ."

"As if the hard ache is gone."

"As if I'm healed."

They looked at each other for a minute or so in wondering silence.

Finally Rook stirred, breaking the spell of wonderment. "Can I help?"

Jenny looked around the room. "It's almost done. Anyway, you're all dressed up. Why are you dressed up?"

He glanced down at himself. "Had a job interview."

Her heart felt as if a huge fist had squeezed it, and suddenly she couldn't breathe. Oh, God, he'd come to tell her he was going away.

"They hired me," he said. "And I kind of got to wondering if you'd go out to dinner with me to celebrate."

Celebrate? Did he really expect her to celebrate his going away? "Where . . . where are you going to?"

"Going? I'm not going anywhere. I'm staying right here in Denver. The Philpott Agency hired me."

The biggest private investigation firm in Denver. "What are you going to do for them?"

"Surveillance. It's one of my specialties." He shrugged. "I figure I'll learn enough that in a few years I can open my own place. Maybe." He shrugged again. "If not, I'll find something else. But it's time to get out of the soldiering business."

She nodded, feeling so relieved she hardly trusted herself to speak.

"What about you?" he asked. "What are you going to do?"

"Open my own practice. I think enough people will remember my name to get me started."

"I don't doubt it."

Awkwardness settled over them, causing them to look nervously away from one another. Finally Rook said, "How about that dinner?"

"Yes. I'd love to."

Feeling as if her world were upside down, as if she could no longer tell where true north was, Jennifer rose and walked toward the bedroom door. Rook didn't move out of her way as she expected, merely looked at her with a curious smile in the crinkled corners of his eyes.

When she tried to edge past him, he leaned toward her, catching her in a gentle trap against his body.

"I swore," he said softly, "that I'd never give a damn about anyone or anything again. Caring hurts. Sooner or later it hurts, and I told myself it's not worth it."

His eyes held hers. "I...can understand that." Here it was, she thought. He was going to tell her that she could toss away any little hopes she might have harbored for a relationship with him. He was going to tell her that he was never going to get involved again.

"Well," he said in that same quiet tone, "I blew it. I got involved. I got in head over heels."

With whom? she wondered wildly. She had this awful feeling that he was about to tell her he was in love with someone else....

"But I figured," he continued, "that it wouldn't be fair to say anything when I was still working as a mercenary. I mean...well, anyway, I decided to go away and think about it a bit. I mean, it seemed impossible...."

Her heart was slamming so hard that she thought it was going to burst from her chest. Please, she prayed. Oh, please...

"Nobody in her right mind would want to marry someone who's going to be gone for long stretches and maybe get himself killed. So I figured there wasn't a chance."

"Rook..." What was she going to say? That she would love him even if he'd volunteered for a mission to Mars?

"Shh." He laid a tender finger over her lips. "Let me finish. I went away, right? I didn't see you for a week, right? And you know what, Lady Fox? I found out it was going to hurt anyway, so it might as well hurt later. No point doing it to myself."

She was beginning to understand, and hope locked her breath in her throat. She made not a sound, not a whisper. Not a movement that might cause him to stop. She had to hear it. She *had* to.

"In fact," he told her almost wryly, "I discovered that it would probably have been easier to cut off my own arm than to live without you. So I decided I better get a regular day job so I could be around to court you."

"Rook!" The joy that was blossoming in her was almost too much to comprehend.

"I know, I know. It's too soon for you to even think about such a thing. But the last day or so we were together, I got the feeling you were starting to want to live again and...well, will you give me a chance to become part of your future?"

"Why?" Say it, Rook. Oh, please say it....

"I guess I forgot to say, I'm crazy in love with you, Jenny Fox."

For an instant she was locked in a joy too exquisite for words; then she threw her arms around his neck and hugged him as tightly as she could.

"I love you, too, Galen Rydell. I love you so much I'd die if you went away...."

He moved suddenly, lifting her, carrying her into the hall, so he could step back a little and look down into her shining face. "Really?" His voice cracked, so he said it again. "Really?"

"Really, truly, honestly. I love you, love you, love you...."

Laughing, he picked her up and swung her in circles until she was laughing with him.

And there, amidst the relics of the past, they laid the foundation for their future.